PENDANT of FORTUNE

by Kyell Gold

PENDANT OF FORTUNE

Copyright 2006 by Kyell Gold

Published by Sofawolf Press
St. Paul, Minnesota
http://www.sofawolf.com

ISBN 978-0-9769212-3-3

Printed in the United States of America
First trade paperback edition: January 2006
Fourth Printing: June 2019

Cover and interior art by Sara Palmer

For my own white wolf,
who inspired, loved, supported, and never stopped believing in
both this book
and myself.

If I have not been able to convey love and romance in these pages,
the fault lies only with my skill in writing,
not with any lack of experience.

This book,
my heart,
and all my love go out to you,
my dear.

Thank you.

Contents

What Has Gone Before ix

Chapter 1 1

"Sorry to disturb you, sir, but I require your valuables." 11

Chapter 2 14

The weasel was wearing a loose cotton shirt, short leather pants, and a broad smile. 22

Chapter 3 32

Chapter 4 46

"May I present my mate, Streak." 49

Chapter 5 79

"What if he did do it?" 87

Chapter 6 91

Chapter 7 117

His fingers closed around a warm, solid paw. 124

Chapter 8 151

Chapter 9 170

He swore that he would get even with the rat for this. 177

Chapter 10 182

Chapter 11 221

"It's not a pleasant business." 233

Chapter 12 240

Chapter 13 256

"Esteemed fox, there has been an inordinate amount of buzzing around you ever since you arrived at the palace." 270

Chapter 14 275

"I think we can say that you've learned from this experience." 282

Chapter 15 290

Epilogue 293

"Things aren't always what they seem." 298

What Has Gone Before

A summary of the events chronicled in the novel "Volle" and the novella "The Prisoner's Release"

For much of their history, relations between the countries of Tephos and Ferrenis have not been good. A mountain range separates the two countries, save for a fertile river plain in the very center of the range: the Reysfields. These fields have been the object of several wars, and currently belong to Ferrenis, though by treaty neither side can station armies within fifty miles.

Ferrenis is ruled by a royal family of cougars. Tephos's kings are appointed according to a Circle dictated by the Panbestian Church, and the current ruler is from the Ursid house. Both countries maintain active espionage programs, and that is where our hero enters the story.

Volle is a fox from the streets of Ferrenis's capital city, Caril, who was admitted to the prestigious Royal Academy and enrolled as a spy-in-training. He has been somewhat of a disappointment to his instructors, doing just enough to get by in his classes and using the rest of his free time to get acquainted with the young males of Caril.

Rumors have reached the Ferrenians of a plot against their country within the Tephossian nobility. When word comes from a contact in Tephos that there is an opportunity for a Ferrenian spy to infiltrate the nobility there, Volle's superiors are thrilled—until they hear that the spy must be a red fox. With no other foxes even close to ready, Volle is pressed into service. He becomes part of a small team sent to Divalia, the capital city of Tephos, where he presents himself as the heir to the Vinton estates, in the far southern reaches of the country. The rest of his team consists of his roommate and best friend, Reese (a hare), and their mentor, Seir (a mouse). Reese poses as a merchant, and he and Seir join a Ferrenian team already in place in Divalia, while Volle goes on to the castle alone.

The Vinton nobility are foxes, but the last one died many years ago. Volle claims to have been the bastard son of the last Lord Vinton, conceived after a minor border skirmish in which the Lord led his forces into Ferrenis. Thanks to a recommendation from an old black wolf, Lord Tistunish, he gains the confidence of the palace's nobility and assumes the role of Lord Vinton.

Lord Tistunish, who goes by "Tish" to his friends, becomes Volle's friend and confidant. Volle quickly makes another friend, a young weasel noble by the name of Helfer, whose title is Lord Ikling of Vellenland. "Hef" disdains politics, but is only too happy to show Volle the nightlife of Divalia, introducing him to an all-male brothel of a much higher class than the fox was previously used to.

Volle meets another gay resident of the castle, Dereath Talison, a rat who is an assistant to Lord Fardew, the Minister of Defense. Dereath already seems to know a lot about him and wants to get to know him better. Volle, in resisting his advances, offends the rat, who is quick to turn on him.

Apart from avoiding Dereath, he finds life at the castle pleasurable. He does not find any evidence of a plot against Ferrenis, so he relaxes and settles into life. Tish and his wife, Tika, arrange for him to meet and become engaged to a young vulpine noble lady, Ilyana Rodion, and when Volle isn't helping plan her cotillion, he is finding romance in the unlikeliest places in the castle. His romance with a cougar soldier named Xiller is short and passionate, and exacerbates his situation with Dereath, who is jealous of them both.

Things seem to be going well, until Prince Gennic of Ferrenis is assassinated—by Xiller, who is executed almost immediately for the crime. Volle is shattered, not just at the dual loss, but also because he holds himself responsible for not uncovering the plot. He applies himself to making up for his mistake, and discovers the mastermind, allowing his colleagues to exact a measure of revenge. Dereath appears to have uncovered his secret, having sniffed out something odd about Volle's past, but Volle's superiors have covered his tracks well enough to dismiss the rat's accusations, though the rat refuses to be convinced of Volle's innocence.

In the process, Volle discovers that his friend Tish is more involved with Ferrenian intelligence than he had thought, and the shared secret cements their friendship further. Ilyana bears him a son and takes the cub down to the Vinton estates to be raised, allowing her to live in the Vinton palace and be seen by the people, and allowing Volle the freedom to continue his espionage.

Five years after these events, Volle gets wind of a covert scheme to deploy troops to the Reysfields and take them back in a single bold stroke. Because of the covert nature, only one set of plans has been drawn up. In an attempt to delay the deployment, Volle steals them from the office of Lord Fardew, hoping that if the King thinks the plans have been taken to Ferrenis, he will delay or abandon the attack. Before he can take two steps outside the Minister's office, however, he hears pursuit. He barely has time to stash the plans in a secret hiding place before he is captured by Dereath, now the top assistant to Lord Fardew, and thrown in jail for espionage.

Although the plans were not discovered on him, Dereath keeps him prisoner in secret, while everyone else assumes he has run away or been killed. After five months, Dereath sends a young white wolf to torture Volle, intending that the two should fall in love so that he can use the wolf to get Volle's secret. The wolf, whom Volle nicknames "Streak," falls in love with him and helps him escape instead.

Volle manages to retrieve the plans and contact his associates, and when it comes time for him to flee the city and return to Ferrenis, he invites

Streak to come with him. In recognition of his service, he is granted a small estate in Ferrenis, where he and Streak live happily for the better part of a year. And then, a letter arrives written in a familiar paw …

Chapter 1

"You're not going."

Volle looked at the white wolf's blue eyes and set jaw. "I have to."

"Then I'm going with you."

"You can't. It's too dangerous."

"It's dangerous for you, too."

He waved the letter from Tish. "I'll be protected. They don't have any witnesses to testify against me. The worst that will happen is that I'll be found guilty of impersonating a noble, and I can claim it was all a mistake. You're a deserter from the palace guard."

The white wolf waved a paw. "Deserters leave all the time. We never had any in the jails when I was there."

"But Dereath knows you're important to me, and he'll take any excuse to put you away or hurt you."

"Let him try."

Volle sighed at the wolf's defiant pose. "Streak, you're not going."

"Then you're not going."

And so the whole conversation came around in a circle again. "I know you think you need to protect me, but you don't. I'll be fine, and I'll be back here in a month."

"Why do you need to be there at all?"

"I have to defend myself. If it were just me, I wouldn't care. But Ilyana…she's still my wife, and if I'm stripped of my honor, then so is she. If there's a chance I can save her status, I have to take it. Fox tells us to look to our pack."

Streak looked at him and then sat down on the bed. He was naked, but the tail that curled over his waist covered his sheath and the black streak on his hip that was the only mark on his white-furred body. One paw twisted the tip of his tail as he kept his eyes on Volle. "I know you've been bored," he said in a low voice.

Volle's ears twitched. He put the letter down and walked over to the bed, trying to find the right words. "It's been a difficult adjustment," he admitted, "but not boring." His slender muzzle touched Streak's broader one, and he smiled at the wolf.

Streak smiled back weakly. "It's okay," he said. "I know you're used to the excitement of the castle, and the farm is quieter. And I'm not as clever as your other friends."

"Hush," Volle silenced him with a soft kiss. "I love you, okay?"

"I know. I love you, too. But I don't think you're happy here."

There was more than a little truth to that. Volle *had* been bored over the last year, ever since he'd finished debriefing with Seir and Duke Avery at the palace in Caril. The farm had been nice and restful at first, and he enjoyed having the minor title of Count of Farrian, but he missed the palace at Divalia in Tephos, the intrigue layered upon intrigue, spying for the Ferrenians on the Tephossians, for one faction of the Tephossians on another faction, and the intricate workings of the political machinery that six years had brought him only a few steps of the way to figuring out. And he missed his friends.

Seir had been recalled at the same time he had come home, and she visited him from time to time, but the visits were always brief. She was engaged to a tradesmouse and expecting a family, and so her visits were less and less frequent.

"It's a relief to be free of all that, isn't it?" he'd asked her once, hoping she would contradict him.

"It really is," she said thoughtfully. "I thought I would miss it, but I don't. Jordan is wonderful, and we're planning a family. I spent ten years in the service of the King, and I'm glad it's over." She smiled. "You got off easy with only six."

"You really don't miss it?" he pressed.

She shook her head. "Life goes in stages, Volle, and you can't keep looking back at the previous stage or you'll never enjoy the present." She patted his paw with her tiny fingers. "You're lucky. You've got a farm and a mate, and I'm sure if you petitioned the King, he'd grant you a child to adopt. If you wanted one. Do you?"

He shook his head, then shrugged. "Not now. Maybe. We haven't really talked about it." He changed the subject then, feeling more and more uneasy with his desire for the life he'd led when he'd been pretending to be Lord Vinton. It wasn't just the perks of lordship that he missed, though Fox knew he could use a personal servant again some days; it was the game that called at him, woke him in the middle of the night at least once a week wondering what the conspirators over in Tephos were hatching since he'd ruined their latest scheme to foment war between the countries, wondering whether they'd decided he was a traitor or not, wondering whether Tish's peace-loving group had gained any ground, and wondering what his old nemesis Dereath Talison, the rat who was the assistant to the Minister of Defense and in charge of all the Tephossian intelligence now, was doing.

All of this rushed through his head as he knelt beside the bed, one black paw on Streak's knee, trying to express the conflict that made him want to be both in the arms of the young white wolf and far away in a cold room in the palace of a foreign country. The desire frustrated him because it was so obviously impossible, yet he couldn't dismiss it from his mind, and the fact that Streak had noticed it meant he was worse at hiding it than he'd thought.

And the harder he tried to forget it, the more forcefully it would return.

"I am happy," he insisted.

"Then why are you trying to run away from me?"

Volle looked into the wolf's clear blue eyes. He couldn't lie to him, so he avoided the truth. "I said I'll be back, and I will. I don't need to be there for more than a week."

Streak met his gaze, then lowered his head. "All right," he conceded, and tugged Volle's paw toward him, rolling back onto the bed and smiling up at the fox.

Volle smiled back, aware that the argument hadn't been resolved, just postponed. He slid his pants off, enjoying showing off for the wolf, and stretched his arms up. He'd gained a few pounds in his year on the farm, but he still felt he was in good shape. Streak wasn't looking at his stomach, of course; his eyes were fixed a few inches lower, and Volle shook his sheath gently from side to side, grinning. Slowly, he slid the golden pendant he wore off his neck and placed it on the side table, then climbed onto the bed and over the wolf. On all fours astride the prone white body, Volle lowered his muzzle and met Streak's in a gentle kiss, feeling the wolf's paw rise up to cup and rub his sheath as they kissed.

Really, he thought, *why am I so anxious to leave this behind?* He grinned at his own pun and rubbed into the paw more forcefully, arousal growing as he did so.

After a few more panting minutes of snuggling, he slid his hips back and lowered the tip of his erect member to rest below Streak's sac. The wolf responded by lifting his hips eagerly, and after a quick application of scented oil, Volle slipped familiarly into the warm tightness there. He closed his oily paw around Streak's own erection and stroked gently as he pushed his hips forward and back, rocking in a gentle rhythm and letting the sensations wash through him.

Streak wriggled a bit around him, and he lifted the wolf's member further from his chest as he stroked. He knew Streak liked that tension at the base of his sheath, knew just how tightly he liked to be stroked, and how fast. Sometimes he teased the wolf, bringing him close and then stopping, bringing him close and stopping again, until Streak whimpered mock-piteously at him and he relented. Tonight, he preferred a slow, leisurely lovemaking, setting his own pace and bringing his lover along to match.

He felt his knot swell as the blood surged through him, but restrained his desire to thrust more quickly. His legs trembled at the effort of maintaining control, just as he saw Streak's paws were trembling and clawing at the sheets. Each stage of the wolf's arousal was familiar to him, and he did enjoy being able to move him from one to the other, to the final one, which was not too far now, judging from his panting growls and the size of his knot.

Volle, panting quite a bit himself, thrust into Streak only up to his knot, letting it swell a bit more (and giving himself some relief from the shivering pleasure of pressing it through the wolf's tail hole), and then, when he felt about to burst, pressed hard forward. A moment of resistance, then a soft pop that he barely heard because his ears were suddenly alight with the rush of blood through him, and he was locked inside the wolf, his body singing for a release that could no longer be postponed. His paw moved swiftly, but his timing was a bit off; Streak howled softly and came onto his paw, his last spurt trickling out a moment before Volle moaned and filled him.

They writhed together, sharing the physical pleasure and emotional joy, and when the peak had passed and they were basking in the warm ebb of the sensations, Volle leaned forward to kiss the wolf, paw still tight around his warm and sticky hardness. Their muzzles touched, merged, and slowly drew apart, tongues brushing. Eyes met and warm smiles were exchanged as Streak slid his arms around the fox and pulled him close.

Volle rubbed the fingers of his spare paw up and down Streak's side, eyes half-closed as the wolf rubbed down his back with both paws, fingers pushing through the fur and then smoothing it down. To have this, to know this wolf so well, to have this bed to come to every night—that couldn't be bad. And yet, something in his heart missed the joy of discovery, of that first time with a new partner, the hesitant exploration of new territory, the delight that came with the formation of new bonds, and the pleasure in bringing a gasp of excitement to a new muzzle. That part of him, quietest at times like this, still looked critically at all the aspects of sex that were the same and thought, *for ever and ever, just this. Is that enough?*

It could be, Volle argued to himself. But he knew he missed that as much as the palace, and that even if everything else were exciting, there would still be that voice inside him that spurred him to new conquests and new experiences. It would remind him of the way that wolf's tongue had caressed him under the table of the bar, of the softness of Richy's paws, the force of Xiller's embrace (and that was always a dangerous place to look, though time had hardened the wound somewhat). And mostly, he could keep that voice quiet. Mostly, it didn't bother him.

Mostly.

They were curled up together, still sticky, as the moon shone down through the windows of the small house. Volle had slid out of Streak and now held the wolf in his arms, half-dozing to the slow rhythm of his breathing. He couldn't fall asleep, though, and after an indeterminate time, he found the moon in his eyes. He extricated himself carefully from the embrace, wincing at the tug of sticky fur, and slid from the bed. The room was chilly with the approaching winter, but Volle was quite comfortable in his fur. Naked, he padded over to the desk and found Tish's letter.

His eyes could see the words clearly in the moonlight that suffused the room.

My dear Lord Vinton, Tish began, as though he really were still taking on that role or had some legitimate claim to it.

I hope this finds you in good health. Tika and I are still well despite our advancing years. The company of our son and his mate is at once a blessing and a trial.

Volle shook his head. The old wolf might be aged in body, but in spirit he was still a bright-eyed pup. He was sure he had no trouble keeping up with his son.

As you know, it is the King's custom to spend two weeks a year relaxing at the estate of one of his lords. Some of the kings choose only their favored nobles; others choose the estates with the best climates. Our King Barris, as befits his species, is more equitable, and this year the lot has fallen to your friend Lord Ikling to host the royal retreat…

Volle smiled at Tish's didacticism, creeping into even a brief letter, and then his thoughts turned to Helfer, the weasel who ruled the Ikling lands, and his best friend in Tephos. He remembered Helfer agonizing about the royal retreat when Vellenland was chosen for it, and that had been three years ago. He smiled at the memory of the weasel's frenetic paw-waving as he protested his unsuitability for hosting the King, while Volle knew the weasel was just annoyed at the trouble he would have to go to.

…(though I am not sure that climate did not play a part, given that for the last two years the royal retreat has been in northern climes). The King often takes advantage of this vacation to address pressing or sensitive matters, ones that either require more than the usual attention or which would be better handled outside the rather porous walls of the palace. This year, it seems you have provided him with an issue that meets both criteria.

I admit, it took a little persuading to convince him to hold your hearing at Vellenland. I used both the above arguments, and still he hesitated. Your friendship with Lord Ikling is well known, and I believe he feared some partisan influence might be brought to bear. I reminded him, however, of Lord Ikling's equally well-known aversion to politics, and pointed out that only in such a friendly environment might we have any hope of producing you in your own defense.

This was the part that Volle read over and over again. Tish was unmistakably saying that Volle's presence was desirable, but he backed off from explicitly telling him to attend.

The royal retreat this year will be over the midwinter holiday, a week on either side. I expect your hearing will take place after the holiday itself, as the King has a few other matters to attend to. I will be in attendance, of course, as will Tika. I do not believe that your wife has plans to leave Vinton, perhaps for fear of what will happen to her should the hearing be decided against you. Lord Fardew will be in attendance, but none of his assistants are scheduled to make the trip.

That was a relief, at least. Dereath had worked his way up to being first assistant to the old wolf in charge of defense, and Volle had been sure he'd have to contend with the rat again if he returned to Tephos. In fact, he thought for the first time, since Dereath had all the evidence against him, it was odd indeed that the rat wouldn't be making the trip to the hearing where he would have the chance to use it. Maybe he'd given it all to Lord Fardew to present. That didn't seem like his style, but Tish had made a point of saying that Dereath wouldn't be in attendance. Volle felt he was missing something, and that worried him, because Tish's information was always layered, and to read simply the surface was to miss some of the more important points.

By the beginning of Ursal Days, we should know definitely what your status in the kingdom is. I still hold out hope that the hearing will turn out favorably, especially as there are no direct witnesses to be presented against you. It seems to be an even chance at this point, but the outcome can be affected by so many variables that I don't dare predict any further than that.

There, again. He seemed to be hinting that Volle himself could affect the outcome of the hearing by appearing in person. Certainly such a move would argue his innocence, making it seem as if he had nothing to fear; but then again, such boldness might be construed as desperation as well. Volle tapped the paper thoughtfully.

Give my best to your companion, and may Canis guide your path,
Tish

Volle set the letter down and gazed over at the window, at the bed where the moon cast Streak's profile into bright relief. His fur, already stark white, seemed brighter still in the moonlight, and Volle felt a surge of love for the young wolf. Streak had trusted him, had allowed Volle to take him away from everything he'd ever known. What would it do to him to be left behind, alone?

He was adapting to farm life better than Volle, at least. He'd grown up on a farm and he knew what had to be done. He even helped the servants around the farm, although the five of them were more than adequate for the chores, especially now that harvest was over. Streak just enjoyed the work, and the servants enjoyed his help and company. Volle suspected that Kaylei, one of a pair of otters they employed, was slacking off because of Streak's help, but Kaylei's brother, Kayman, was a good worker, and Volle didn't want to lose Kayman by dismissing Kaylei.

With a shake of the head, he returned to his current problem. The other variable in the letter was Tish's discussion of his son. He'd mentioned two letters ago that his son and daughter-in-law had come to stay at the palace, and that his son was learning about palace life. The implication was that Tish was planning to retire soon. He'd wanted Volle to take his place as the main Ferrenian contact inside the palace, and either he had another plan or he thought that goal was still attainable. Certainly, if the King decided that Volle was innocent of spying charges and was still worthy of the Vinton peerage, Volle could return to the palace as Lord Vinton. He rather doubted that Dereath would allow that to happen, though, and if it did, what would become of Streak?

He looked at the wolf again and his ears twitched when he saw that one eye was open, dark in the shadow cast by the moon, watching him.

"Hi," he said softly.

"You're going, aren't you?"

He sighed, put the letter down, and padded back to the bed. Streak shifted over, letting him slip under the covers. "I have to go."

The wolf's paw rested on his side. "Let me go with you."

He wavered. He would be going to Helfer's estate, not the palace, and

Dereath wouldn't be there. "I don't know if I'd be able to protect you."

"Let me worry about that. I'm supposed to protect you, remember?" Streak sensed his advantage and pressed, verbally and physically.

Volle resisted, trying to seem light-hearted about it. "Who'll look after the farm?"

"What's to look after? It's winter. Kayman can manage the chores." Streak's muzzle pushed against Volle's, licking at his whiskers and neck. "You'll miss me."

"I will?"

"Yeah." The playful eyes sobered. "And I'll miss you."

Volle looked back for a long moment. Love and concern and frustration warred in him, and at the end of it, he didn't know what to do, so he said, "All right," more because it would end the discussion than because he could see a good reason to give in. The problem was, he couldn't see a good reason not to give in, either.

Streak sighed happily and snuggled into him, and Volle ran his paws through the wolf's soft white fur. He hoped he wasn't making a big mistake.

In the morning, they sat down with Kayman and told him they would be gone for a month, and discussed the things that needed to be done. Volle let Streak handle most of the conversation; although he was getting a feel for farm life, he didn't have the years of experience that Streak did. The young wolf was used to a farm in a slightly colder climate, but his knowledge was thorough and he'd only made a couple mistakes.

When they were done, Kayman nodded, and Volle felt the farm would be left in good paws. Streak apparently agreed, because he patted the otter on the shoulder and smiled. The otter, older than Volle and much older than Streak, returned the smile tolerantly and bowed his head before returning to the cottage where all five servants lived, behind the main house.

"We'll leave in a week," Volle said when they were alone. Streak munched on a bit of root left over from the previous night's dinner, and perked his ears to listen. "We'll need to check in with the Duke in Caril, and I'll need to get appropriate clothes. I left all my clothes at the palace when we escaped. And we'll have to get clothes for you, too."

"All right," Streak said, in the same attentive tone that Volle often used when Streak was teaching him about farm chores.

Volle smiled. "After that, we'll book a carriage to Vellenland." His eyes drifted past the white wolf, looking out the window to where the haze of morning was just lifting over the hills. "And then...we'll see."

The Duke of Westermarch was visibly older than when he had sent Volle to Tephos for the first time. His muzzle had greyed, and he no longer had the timbre to his voice that had once made Volle tremble—though Volle was older, too, no longer a young fox going on his first assignment, cocksure and scared all at the same time.

Duke Avery's eyes, though, still glowed with the same fire they always had. "You're very lucky," he told Volle. "I'm not at all sure we should be pressing your luck, despite what Duke Geris says."

"The Foreign Minister? Why is he involved?"

"Tephos has initiated a dialogue that he thinks may lead to an exchange of ambassadors. You were right about them abandoning their plans, but we didn't expect things to go so far in the other direction."

"I didn't know there was a dialogue." He bit his lip. "When did this start?"

"A month after you returned. Only a few people know. It is very preliminary and is intentionally being kept very private." The wolf stared fixedly at him. "So. Do you think you'll be declared innocent?"

Despite the fact that he had more confidence and more success to his name, Volle still found himself squirming under the Duke's scrutiny. "Tish thinks the chances are good. He says there are two arguments we can make: first, that I didn't steal the plans at all. There are no witnesses to the theft; even Dereath only saw me come out of the office. If that fails, then I can claim I was just trying to delay an aggressive movement I'd learned of, because I wanted peace between the countries. If I were a spy, I could've just looked at the plans and reported their contents."

"Not a good defense. Stealing the plans sends a message, which was in fact your intent, that their element of surprise was gone."

"That's what we discussed beforehand."

"So that could also be a motive for a spy." Avery tapped the papers on his desk. Volle recognized the report they were talking about, the one that had started all this trouble. "Doesn't the argument that you didn't steal the plans at all rather preclude you using the other argument?"

"Not the way Tish sees it. He says that we can maintain my innocence of taking the document, even if the King doesn't believe it, but justify the taking of the document without admitting my part in it."

Avery stroked his muzzle. "It still sounds risky. On the other paw, you're not doing anything for us now but sitting on your tail at a farm. So if you want to go ahead with it," he shrugged, "go ahead. We'll support you."

"Thank you," Volle said. "Nice to know I'm cared about."

"You did a lot for your country. You've earned retirement if you want it. If you don't, then it's your tail. Frankly, I thought you'd be dead or captured long before this anyway."

"I remember," Volle said. "You actually threatened to castrate me, if I recall."

"Yes." The wolf showed a gleaming row of teeth. "But not this time. The worst that can happen, from my perspective, is exactly the current situation, except we have to find another Count Farrian."

"Count of Farrian," Volle corrected him.

"Yes, whatever. You've proven remarkably resistant to torture, and I trust you won't let yourself be taken into custody again anyway. So tell me, what will you need?"

"Clothes. Transportation. And a contact in Vellenland in case I need help or a courier."

"We're working on the last one already. He'll contact you when you arrive."

"I really find all this secrecy very annoying. Who is it?"

The Duke smiled again. "We are spies, Volle. Secrecy is what we do best. Don't worry, it's someone reliable." He handed a stack of gold coins over. "Here. That should outfit you down on Raisle Lane. As for transportation, come back here on Feliday. Is that when you wanted to leave?"

Volle nodded, gathering the coins into his leather purse. "Assuming it's going to be about a week long trip."

"That sounds right. Well, good luck. Let my assistant know if you need anything. Otherwise we probably won't speak again." They both stood, and the Duke extended a paw. When Volle grasped it, the Duke pulled him close and showed his teeth again. "Oh, one thing. Make sure that wolf you're with now isn't a security risk. They could torture *him*, you know, and he knows things about you."

"I know." Volle sighed. "I didn't want to bring him, but he insisted."

The Duke's eyes narrowed, and he squeezed Volle's paw a bit harder. "You shouldn't be letting him tell you what to do."

"It's more complicated than that." Volle tried not to tug on his paw, because he knew the Duke wanted to make him uncomfortable.

"No, it's very simple. You're safer—and we're safer—if he doesn't go."

Volle wrested his paw free. "I've already told him he can go."

Avery looked at his paw with the hint of a smile, then looked up at his muzzle. "He can be left behind. Kept here. There are a number of ways to handle it."

"I'll handle it my way," Volle said bravely, though his heart was beating fast. "I think I've earned it."

The wolf's eyes searched his for several long seconds, and Volle forced himself not to look away. Finally, the Duke turned away. "Maybe you have, at that. Go ahead, make your own decision. Just remember what I said."

"I will." Volle bowed his head respectfully, then stepped out the door.

The Duke called to him from inside the room, stopping his paws. "Volle." He turned and saw the fiery eyes muted, and the grey muzzle creased in concern. "Be careful. And good luck."

He bowed again. "Thank you, Duke Avery."

Just as he had seven years ago, Volle watched the city of Caril disappear behind a hill. This might be the last time he ever saw it, he thought, and then remembered the young fox seven years ago thinking the same thing.

He looked across the carriage at the empty seat, then out the other side. They were going to circle the mountains a bit more than usual, avoiding the treacherous passes and seeking a quiet road that would bring them up into the south of Vellenland. He didn't think they had to avoid attention while crossing this time, as they had last time, but it would be simpler if he could sustain the illusion that he'd been in Vinton or in southern Ferrenis, which is what Tish said most of the palace believed. Anywhere but the capital city.

The driver he'd been assigned was a talkative marmot who'd been driving merchants back and forth between Ferrenis and Tephos for years, and who had so far guided the carriage and the horses with a deft surety that relaxed Volle. He was not part of Duke Avery's network; what he'd been told was that Volle was a wealthy Tephossian returning to his home country.

Volle almost felt the part. His year on the farm had been nice, but more like a vacation than settling into a home. On his first trip to Tephos, he'd been seized with melancholy at leaving the only home he'd ever known. Now he felt a strange stirring of excitement and nostalgia, as if he were returning home, not leaving it again. It can't and won't be the same, he told himself, but all the same, he found his gaze more drawn to the mountains on his right than to the hill behind which Caril had disappeared on the other side.

There was a scuffling outside, barely noticeable over the noise of the road. He turned back to his left in time to see a cloaked figure swing the door open and step into the carriage, pulling the door closed after him.

The tall white wolf in the red mask held up a short sword and advanced on Volle, sweeping his cloak around behind him. "Sorry to disturb you, sir, but I require your valuables."

Volle unfastened the pouch from his waist and dropped it on the seat, making the coins inside clink. The highway-wolf spared it barely a look. "I know that the most valuable things are kept on your person." The sword's tip nicked the strings that fastened the top of his shirt. "Take your shirt off."

Slowly, Volle unfastened his shirt, letting the fabric hang open to reveal his white-furred chest. He slid his arms out of the sleeves and handed the shirt to the wolf, who searched it cursorily and then tossed it onto the seat. The sword brushed his pendant. "What's that?"

"Just an heirloom. A gift from my father."

"Take it off." Volle obeyed, and the wolf took it from him, but gave it barely more attention than the shirt. The sword dropped lower. "Now the pants."

Volle felt his heart beat faster as he reached down to unfasten his pants. As he slid the soft fabric down, he intentionally brushed his sheath, which was already swollen with excitement. His pink tip slipped into view as he pulled his feet out of the pants and handed them to the wolf.

The wolf cast them aside without even looking, his eyes fixed on Volle's sheath. "So the greatest treasure of all was kept under your very fur."

Volle looked up at him with a wide grin.

Afterwards, they lay back on the seats, panting hard. The wolf took off the mask, the last piece of clothing he was wearing, and grinned. "Wow. I did like that. Was I a good Red Menace?"

"Sorry to disturb you, sir, but I require your valuables."

Volle nodded happily. "Very good. It was just as I'd imagined it."

"Mmm." Streak's tail wagged as well. He swung his legs up onto the seat and patted his lap. "Come sit here?"

Volle nodded, and scrambled to his feet. In a few moments he'd settled into Streak's lap, tail pressing back against the wolf's still-hard member. Streak's arms held him tightly and brushed through his chest and stomach-fur, and wandered down to tease his sheath before coming back up.

"How long before we stop?" Volle murmured, contented and sleepy.

"A few hours. I told the driver not to disturb us."

"Good." He leaned his head against Streak's shoulder, and in a few minutes both were fast asleep.

For much of the trip, Streak talked about the people he'd known at the guard house and on his farm, speculating about how they were doing and what they were doing, though in most cases he didn't care. Volle stayed quieter, watching the mountains on their right and thinking about going home again. At the border post, Volle let the driver do the talking, and the bored guards waved them through without a question. They had been a bit more cautious six years ago, he reflected, and wondered if the change were a reflection of general attitudes, or just due to the different personalities of different guards.

During his time in Tephos, he'd stayed at the palace most of the time and hadn't seen much of the countryside. Compared to Ferrenis, the terrain was similar, if greener. Tephos boasted more riverine valleys than Ferrenis did, but had nothing to match the Crystal Lake and Red Mountains for spectacular glory. The people, too, were very similar, more so than any of the neighboring countries, and that was partly the reason for the countries' long history of belligerence. Lately Tephos had been the aggressor, but Volle knew that over the past few hundred years, both sides had shed their share of blood in an attempt to unite the two countries—and by 'unite,' of course, each side meant 'unite under our King.'

The excitement in his chest kept growing, day by day. On the morning of what should be their last day of travel, he was so lost in thoughts of Helfer, Tish, and his other friends that he barely noticed when Streak stopped talking. He wouldn't see all of his friends, of course, but he suspected Lord Dewanne, the only other fox in the nobility, would be in attendance. Lady Dewanne demanded long and frequent vacations to warm spots for her health, and Lord Dewanne was therefore not at the palace as often as he would like. Vellenland was warm and welcoming, and Volle was sure that Dewanne would take the opportunity to mingle his wife's demands with his own desire to be near the seat of government.

Volle was just wondering whether Lord Ullik, the grey squirrel who served as the King's Exchequer, would be there when he felt a tug at his pants and looked down to see Streak with a paw on his sheath, rubbing. Volle grinned. "Frisky?"

"Well, you didn't answer when I talked to you, and I couldn't think of any other way to get your attention."

He caressed Streak's ears gently, smiling. "I'm sorry. I'm just…"

"Excited?" The wolf sounded a bit wistful.

"Well…"

Streak nodded. "I can tell. Are you worried at all?"

Volle thought about that, his fingers brushing the thin furred triangles of Streak's ears. "Maybe a little. But I feel pretty safe. I think that if the hearing doesn't go well, I'll still be able to get away before I'm arrested again. I'll have friends there, and I trust…" he paused, "them." He was remembering Duke Avery's words. He'd never told Streak or anyone else about Tish, mostly because he hadn't talked about his life at the castle in the past year. Now that he was going back to Tephos, he would have to be very careful about what he said.

"Is there anything I can do to help while we're there?"

Volle looked down at the paw on his pants, and grinned. "Besides that, you mean?"

Streak grinned back. "Yes."

"I don't think so. It's probably safest for you to stay out of everything."

The ears folded down over Volle's fingers. "I'd like to help."

"I know. But…" But there are a lot of things going on, and you're not equipped to handle them. "It's just safer if you don't." He felt guilty saying it, because he knew the young wolf wanted badly to help him. He just couldn't imagine Streak playing the political game. He didn't have the background or the experience to do it well, and he could easily be manipulated or exploited.

"Maybe I shouldn't have come along at all."

"Oh, don't talk like that." Volle rubbed the base of Streak's ears. "I'm glad you're here. I really am. I'd be missing you if you hadn't come along."

"Really?"

"Really. And I'll be more attentive, I promise. You won't have to grope me to get a response."

Streak smiled and lifted his paw from Volle's pants. "All right. Thanks, fox."

Volle smiled back. "I didn't say stop."

Chapter 2

Volle could tell when they entered Vellenland. To his right as they drove north, vineyards terraced the hills, and between the hills and the roads, rows of trees clung to their last leaves, a tapestry of yellow and brown. It would have been beautiful a month ago, he thought, and then chuckled as he made the connection between that and the timing of Helfer's annual trips home.

Patches of green persisted here and there, citrus groves that remained green year round. As they drove through one, Volle could see the lemons hanging from the trees. Streak was fascinated.

"I've never seen lemon trees before." He opened the door and poked his muzzle out, breathing in deeply. The air was chilly, but warmer than it had been in Caril. Volle could smell the rich, moist smell of the ground and the tartness of the lemons. He smiled, watching Streak's ears flick back and forth and his nose search out smells on the air rushing past the carriage. The wolf's cub-like excitement at new things was one of the things that so endeared him to Volle.

"Can you smell that?" Streak turned and moved aside, leaving room for Volle to poke his muzzle out of the door. "Fresh lemons!"

Volle nodded and grinned, taking the proffered space and inhaling. The air currents brought smells similar to those he'd grown used to on the farm, but these were deeper and richer. He could tell with his eyes closed that the soil was more fertile here. "Smells a bit better than our farm, doesn't it?"

"Our farm smells fine," Streak said. "This is better land, that's all." He breathed in again. "They take good care of it."

"That's all I meant." Volle nuzzled the wolf. "We take good care of our farm, too."

"Thanks to Kayman."

"And to you."

Streak smiled, and drew his muzzle back into the carriage, closing the door when Volle followed suit. "I did the best I could. But the climate's a little different than I'm used to. Without Kayman, I think our fields would have flooded."

"We're learning." Volle put an arm around the wolf, but his thoughts of the future weren't of the farm.

"Oh, look!" The carriage was rounding a curve, and coming into view atop a large hill in the distance was what Volle assumed was Helfer's palace. It looked from this distance to be built of the same grey stone that was ubiquitous in Tephos, and it followed the model of the King's palace in Divalia: a low, walled structure with narrowed slits for windows. The Vellenland model, in contrast to its urban cousin, had three tall towers, which Volle thought defined the shape of the palace, though it was a bit far to tell for sure. Atop each tower a fluttering pennant flew, and again, it was too far to tell for sure what the designs on the pennants were.

This palace resembled the Divalia palace, albeit smaller, but it was much more elegantly presented. Volle could understand why Streak was still staring at it. Its perch atop the hill and the graceful curve of the wall between the towers gave it an elegant, haughty air, and because it wasn't surrounded with similarly grey buildings, it stood out from the rest of the landscape.

"What a view they must have," Streak murmured.

"It looks old. Probably dates to before Vellenland was part of Tephos."

"When was that?"

"Few hundred years ago. King...now I've forgotten his name. Anyway. He was King of Tephos province, and he united the other five provinces under his rule. We can ask Tish more about him. I'm sure he knows."

"Tish?"

Volle froze for a moment, then realized that in that context, there was nothing to worry about. "Lord Tistunish. He's a wolf, friend of mine. He's helping in the hearing and he'll be there. He knows all the history I do, and much more."

"Is he pretty old?"

"In his sixties, I think. Old enough."

"Wow." Streak nodded.

The carriage turned again, and the castle moved out of their view. Out of the other side, they could see the road that led up the hill. Before they reached it, they would pass through the town at the base of the hill. The cluster of buildings, at this distance, looked like it lay under a brick-red blanket. As they approached, the individual roofs became visible, and soon they could see the white brick walls and the red tiles on the roofs.

As they passed the first buildings, the dusty, crowded smell made its way into the carriage. It had a distinctly musteline air to it, rich and musky. Volle didn't bother to try to sort out the scents, just let them drift past his nose, all the inhabitants of Ikling, their houses and food and clothing, and the plants and animals that lived in the town with them.

"Public house okay?" the driver called down cheerfully. "There's one up ahead for out-of-towners."

"For now, yes," Volle called back. He wondered briefly why this pub was particularly for foreigners, but didn't ask. "We'll probably be going up the mountain later today, though."

"Oh, staying with the governor?" The driver whistled. "Very nice."

He pulled around back of a public house called the "Cup and Barrel," and tended to the horses while Volle and Streak made their way to the front. Like most of the other buildings in the town, the pub was made of a soft white brick and the roof was flat red tile, though this building was taller than its neighbors. The streets were white with dust, so that their paws kicked up clouds with every step and were soon frosted with white as well. The change wasn't noticeable on Streak's paws, which were already white, but the white dusting on Volle's black paws made him look old. He scuffled his paws against the backs of his legs to clean them before they walked into the building.

The pub was moderately crowded, which struck Volle as odd for the middle of the day. Looking around the clientele, he noticed that many of them were young, and many bore crests that were familiar to him from his days at the palace. Squires, pages, personal servants maybe. He led Streak up to the bar and waited several moments for the bartender to notice him.

The harried-looking weasel, Volle noticed, was at his eye level. Glancing behind the bar, he saw that the floor there was raised about three feet, probably to enable the weasel to look his taller customers in the eye. The barmaids were all weasels, with the exception of one vixen, but they had no trouble reaching the tables. He did notice that when they went to pick up drinks, they walked around to the side of the bar where there was a step.

"Just a moment, sahr," the weasel said as he scooted past Volle for the fourth time. "Be right with you."

Volle nodded, his gaze wandering around trying to identify crests. He pointed them out to Streak. "Over there, that's Lord Villutian's crest. He's a bear. I met him a few times." He scanned a few other crests. "Don't know those...that's Lord Alister's crest there." He indicated a mouse, ears drooping, eyes half-lidded. "He's the Steward and probably very busy. Surprised Jerish was able to slip away."

"You know him?" Streak said in an undertone.

"Jerish? Yes, but not that well." His eyes drifted downwards as he thought of Alister's former assistant, a fox named Arrin who had been interested in him when he first arrived at the palace. Arrin had left the year before Volle's capture, taking a position as a clerk with a lawyer in the city.

"Will he recognize you?"

Volle looked up from his reverie. "He looks wiped out. I don't think he'd recognize Alister if he were sitting right across from him."

The bartender had come up behind them. "Yes, sahr?" He looked a bit suspicious, and Volle wondered how much he'd heard.

"Two ales, please, and can you tell us how to get up to the governor's residence?"

The weasel filled two mugs and brought them over. "Governor's residence is up the mountain. Follow the main road out of town, it don't go nowhere else." His eyes measured them. "But you'll likely be staying at the old palace with the King and the Lords from the city. That's further up the mountain, end of the road."

"Thanks." Volle left a gold piece on the counter. "Keep the change."

The bartender's expression didn't change, but his tone was much more polite as he said, "Thank you, M'Lord. May your stay in Ikling be pleasant."

Volle lifted his tankard. "It's beginning wonderfully."

The weasel flashed a quick smile before scooting away to deal with another customer. Streak lapped at his ale while Volle kept sipping his, examining the room over the lip of the tankard.

"See someone else you recognize?" Streak asked softly.

Volle shook his head. "No. Sorry, force of habit. Checking out a crowded room." He didn't mention the rabbit in the corner, the one who seemed to be looking away whenever Volle was looking at him, but who looked back when he thought Volle had looked away. Just because Dereath wasn't here didn't mean they didn't have to be careful, but he didn't want to worry Streak. It was possible the rabbit was just curious and shy. And well-dressed. Volle tried to see if his clothing sported a crest, but he couldn't make any out.

"This ale is pretty good. I guess everything I heard about Vellenland is true."

Volle nodded. "The meads are better, but I didn't want to get too tipsy before going up to the mansion."

"I never liked mead anyway."

"You'll have to try the apricot. It's wonderful."

Streak grinned. "Maybe tonight."

Volle smiled back distractedly. The rabbit was getting up and about to leave, but Volle still couldn't see any mark on his clothes. He committed as much of his appearance to memory as he could: small for a rabbit, about the height of the weasels, and wearing a plain linen shirt and leather trousers. There was a cloak folded over his arm that was plain dark blue, and if there was a mark on that, it was hidden by the folds.

When the rabbit had left, Volle downed the rest of his ale. "We should get out of here."

Streak finished his ale in two more swallows, and nodded. He followed Volle out of the crowded pub and around back to the stables, where they found their driver talking to a short weasel wearing Ikling's colors. When he saw them coming, the weasel smiled and saluted cheerfully. He was about three and a half feet tall, half a foot short of Helfer's height (as Volle remembered) and a good two feet shorter than Volle himself. His leather trousers were dyed a rich forest green, as was the vest he wore over a ruffled white shirt. His ears were upright, matching the good humor of his smile.

"Lord Vinton?" Volle nodded. The weasel stuck out a paw. "I'm Huster, Governor Burren's steward. Lord Ikling sent me down to wait for you."

"Pleased to meet you. This is Streak." He'd acquired the habit of introducing the wolf by the nickname Volle had given him, as Streak never offered his real name. He hadn't even told Volle, who suspected that it had to do with the life he'd given up. He didn't press. He was happy enough to have the wolf at his side, under whatever name he preferred.

Huster shook his paw, then Streak's, and motioned to the carriage. "May I ride back up with you?"

"Certainly. After you."

Huster insisted that Volle and Streak precede him, and after an exchange of courtesies they were all seated inside the carriage. As the driver maneuvered through the narrow streets, Huster settled back in the carriage seat and smiled at Volle, beside him, and then across at Streak.

"We have about half an hour, and Lord Ikling thought you might be interested in some of the history of the area. Do you have any questions I can answer?"

Volle nodded. "I'm a bit surprised you were free. Aren't you rather busy?"

Huster chuckled and crossed his legs, clasping his paws behind his head. "Lord Alister was kind enough to take over most of the scheduling duties for the King's visit. Some folk might be miffed that he'd taken it away, but not me. I can use the vacation. So I'm just responsible for the governor, as usual, and he's mostly attending the royal functions anyway."

Volle grinned. "Are all the Ikling natives weasels?"

"Mustelids, yes."

"And why are we staying at the old palace, and not the governor's residence?"

"Ah." Huster tapped his nose and grinned widely. "*You* are not. Lord Ikling felt that you would be better accommodated by quarters close to his, away from the rest of the royal party. He did not disclose to me the reasons, and I didn't ask."

"All right. So why is the King staying in the old palace? Not enough room in the governor's mansion?"

Huster grinned even wider. "You might say that. It all ties in with the history of Vellenland, and of Ikling."

Volle leaned back against the carriage wall. "All right, all right. Tell us the history."

The weasel's short tail wagged quickly. "Vellenland has always been a richly gifted land. Its name comes from an ancient Felid word *vellis*, meaning sweet. The Felids were the first rulers here, before the Panbestian Church, and Vellenland was actually one of the last to accept the Church, even though the prophet Gaïs was said to have stopped here in person." He paused. "If you're interested in that sort of thing, the place where he delivered the "bounty of the earth" sermon is about fifty miles south of here."

"Not familiar with that one," Volle said, and Streak shook his head too.

"Well, it's not one of the better known ones. It's in the book of Felis."

"So what happened to the cats who ruled here?"

"They built that big castle up on the hill, and ruled for several hundred years. There were good and bad rulers, but the last one was the worst of all. He was a bobcat, name of Xiffle, and he is, ironically, the most celebrated of the rulers. We still celebrate Ziff Day here in his honor. Well, in the honor of the victorious weasel army that stormed the castle and installed Alfer in his place."

"Why isn't it called Alfer Day?"

Huster nodded to Streak. "Alfer insisted that the entire army should be honored. They spent years organizing and training, and he was just the noble they chose to install in power. Weasels, otters, and minks were the majority of the serfs under the bobcat's rule at the time and they worked together for the first time to expel the felids from Vellenland. Alfer was proud of the heart his people had shown, and so they decided to name the day for the enemy who had brought their ranks together, so they might always remember the fortitude and unity they had felt; "the entire shaft of the arrow, not just the stone placed at its tip, for without a dependable body and well-placed feathers, and a paw to aim it, the point of the arrow could never find its mark.""

"I've heard that before," Volle said.

"It gets repeated a lot. Alfer was a good ruler, and his family has been in power ever since then. They've had good and bad rulers, too, but the people are much more tolerant because they're weasels, like most of us are."

"Weren't there ever any canids or rodents or anything but weasels here?"

"Weasels settled Vellenland and shared it with the felids from the north until one of the northern clan of pumas took over the country and established felid rule. They're the ones who built the castle atop the mountain."

"Ah," Volle said. "So Alfer built a new mansion, without all the history of the old."

"That's right. And one more tailored for the rightful lords of Vellenland."

"Tailored?" The weasel was grinning back at Volle. "Oh, I think I see."

Huster nodded. "The buildings are scaled to the proportions of weasels and otters. Don't worry, a hundred years ago a small suite of guest rooms was added for taller guests, but it's not nearly enough for the King and all his retinue. Plenty of room for a wolf and fox, though."

Streak smiled. "I'm sure it'll be fine."

The weasel peered out the window. "Those are the governor's orchards, by the way." He pointed at a grove of trees by the roadside. "Private stock is brewed from that. The river's just over on the other side of the fields. These are some of the best orchards in the country." He said it with personal pride, as if he tended the fields himself.

"Helfer always had the best brews," Volle said.

"Still does." Huster waved past the fields. "On the other side of the river are the vineyards. These are very good. The ones down south of Ikling are even better." He looked the other way. "You can see the governor's mansion now. We'll be there in a few minutes."

Volle couldn't keep his tail still. It had been so long since he'd seen Helfer, and he'd thought he never might again. He'd had no closer friend during his six years as a spy—even the people who knew his mission had only talked to him once every two weeks. He'd seen Helfer every day for a morning run through the palace gardens. They'd shared meals, some secrets, and even (occasionally) lovers.

He watched the main gate go by and turned to Huster. The weasel anticipated his question. "The guest suite has its own side entrance. Although the main gate looks pretty big, the main entrance is our size. I was told to bring you around to the side."

Two foot-servants were there to meet them when the carriage stopped. The first, a pine marten, held the door open while the second, an otter, helped Volle and Streak down. Huster addressed them both by name.

"Hi, Jereamy, thanks. Roferro, could you get the luggage and bring the guests to the guest suite?" The pine marten nodded. "Lord Vinton, Mister Streak, it's been a pleasure to meet you. If you need anything while staying here, please let me know."

"Thank you for the escort and the history lesson." Volle smiled and shook Huster's paw, and Streak did likewise. Volle watched Huster as the weasel strolled into the mansion, then examined the mansion itself while Roferro and their driver pulled the luggage down.

It was a curious structure. He could tell that the guest suite had been added on later. Not only did it look newer than the rest of the building, it was on a slightly different scale. Its roof came up to the middle of the second floor of the surrounding building, which was two stories tall all around and had a small third story in the center. Like the other buildings Volle had seen in the town, the mansion was built of white brick, with a roof of reddish clay tiles and broad, unshuttered windows. A small weasel was shaking sheets out of one of the windows; she spotted Volle and waved cheerfully to him. He raised a paw and waved back.

Roferro hefted Volle's case onto his back. He stopped in front of the fox and said, "If sahr will follow me."

Volle nodded and followed the otter along a path of crushed white brick up to a simple staircase, at the head of which the pine marten was holding open a wooden door. The door was strengthened with two crossbars, but it was plain and undecorated. A relief in the keystone of the doorway showed the Vellenland crest, but that was the only marking Volle could see.

Inside, the house was nearly the same temperature as the outside air. It was a little warm for Volle's taste, but not as warm as the palace in Divalia got in the summer months, he recalled. The floor's brown and red ceramic tiles were cool to his paws, and the wide hallways allowed him to walk at Streak's side, while Roferro walked ahead with his case and their driver followed with Streak's. The hallway grew dimmer as the pine marten closed the doors, but he must have remained on the outside, because when Volle turned his head to look, the hallway was empty.

The faint musteline smell Volle had noticed outside was stronger inside. He thought he detected Helfer's scent, but there were so many and they were all part of such a strong background that he gave up trying to sort them out. He was even having difficulty finding the scents of the marmot and otter who were walking down the hall with them. Of course he could smell Streak, but the wolf's scent was so familiar that he couldn't imagine not being able to detect it if even a trace of it were around.

Frescoes adorned the walls, which were bare of the portraits Volle remembered from the stone walls of the palace in Divalia. They depicted peaceful orchard scenes with weasels working the fields, festive banquets, and a large outdoor festival with all six Houses of the Orthodox Church represented: Mustelids, Canids, Felids, Rodents, Herbivores, and Ursids. Volle had seen the representations in any number of religious portraits, so he recognized them immediately, but in this mural they were not separate. The fox was seated next to the bear and they were playing a game of chess; the bobcat and weasel were sampling a pie, and the mouse and rabbit were preparing to run a race. He admired the detail in the mural, pausing to inspect it several times as they walked down the hall.

Roferro had stopped before the door at the other end of the hallway and was gesturing that they should precede him inside. Streak had gotten a few steps ahead of Volle as the fox perused the frescoes, so he entered first, and Volle stepped quickly in after him.

The spacious room they entered had a soft carpet on the floor, a set of large windows at the far end, and several couches around the walls. A cabinet to Volle's left was slightly open, and he could see the outlines of bottles inside. Next to that, a windowed cabinet showed off a variety of glassware, neatly arranged in rows so that it was easy to tell that one was missing. And on the right hand side of the room, sitting on a couch, was the reason for both the missing glass and the open cabinet.

"Hef!"

The weasel was wearing a loose cotton shirt, short leather pants, and a broad smile. He put down the drink he was holding and stood up, walking toward Volle as the fox walked to meet him. They embraced in the middle of the room and nuzzled affectionately.

"Glad you made it," Helfer said when they stood apart. "I thought maybe you might not come. Lord Tistunish said he thought you would."

"Tish knew what to say to get me here," Volle said.

Helfer looked at the otter and marmot. "Roferro, why don't you show this young gentleman where the stables and servants' quarters are? He looks like he won't be too uncomfortable in them."

Roferro, who was the same height as the driver at about four and a half feet, bowed. "Yes, my Lord." He led the young marmot into the hall and closed the door on his way out.

"So this building is built for mustelids," Volle said, still smiling.

Helfer nodded. "Weasels, mostly. We didn't want to use the big palace because it didn't reflect who we are. So we built this house, on the hill amidst all the orchards. It's smaller, more open, and just nicer to be in. To tell you the truth, though, I usually stay in the guest suite when I'm home. I got used to the big rooms at the palace in Divalia, and the smaller rooms feel

The weasel was wearing a loose cotton shirt, short leather pants, and a broad smile.

cramped now."

"Sorry to be taking your place," Streak said.

"Don't worry about it. I thought you would be better off here. What did Lord Tistunish say to you?" He looked back at Volle.

"He said he thought there was a good chance we could win the hearing, and that Lord Fardew came on his own, so Dereath wouldn't be here."

Helfer's ears folded back. "He said that?"

Volle nodded. "Why?"

"Did he tell you who Lord Fardew is?" Volle's fur prickled and his own ears flattened. Helfer nodded. "Rallish left a couple months ago. Dereath was appointed to his place."

"So that's what he meant," Volle hissed. "He knew I'd be much more reluctant to come if Dereath were here."

"Probably. That's one reason I thought you'd be safer here. Dereath's up at the castle with the King's party. The only nobles not there are you, and me. I pleaded local responsibilities. Though you know how much I would love to be up there."

Helfer was trying to cheer him up, Volle knew, but he was still upset at Tish's deceit. He made an effort to smile. "Yes, I can imagine how it wounds you to be this far from where all that politicking is going on." Streak was looking puzzled, so he said to the wolf, "Hef hates politics. I'm sure he'd be even happier if he could have figured a way to stay in Divalia for these two weeks."

"Ah." Streak turned to a doorway. "Is this where our bedroom is?"

"Two rooms in," Helfer said. "You have a private bathroom and a parlor." He winked at Volle. "And a closet full of, um, supplies." As Volle's ears came up, he grinned. "I told you, I usually stay here. My staff knows what to stock."

Volle felt his annoyance subside, and he put it aside. He would deal with Tish later. "I would expect they do," he said. "Do you have a Jackal's Staff type of place around here too?"

"Nothing exclusively male, but the Pink Flower in town has some nice males who occasionally get invited up to the palace."

"When you're through with your duty to the lineage?"

Helfer clasped his paws to his chest. "Thank Weasel, I am done with that duty."

"Really?"

The weasel nodded. "Burren finally found another female who was ready, and I have a third son now."

Volle slapped him on the back. "Congratulations! Maybe now your trips home will be more pleasant."

"Or at least easier to remember." They shared a grin. "I'll introduce you to the cub and proud mother tonight, if you can stay for dinner. I'd introduce you to the other two, but they're too old to stay quiet and so they've been banished to the town for the King's visit. You can stay for dinner?"

"We'd love to. I think I need to go up to the castle and have a few words with Tish, but that shouldn't take more than an hour."

"And it's half an hour up there and back," Helfer said. "I'll have them prepare dinner in about three hours. Do you want a carriage up to the castle or can you ride?"

"I'd better not ride, if you have a carriage to spare."

"We have some one-horse buggies besides my personal one. I'll put one at your disposal."

"Thanks, Hef."

Helfer patted his shoulder. "I've missed you, Volle. Doing my morning runs all by myself, it's lonely, you know?"

"I know. I'm sorry."

"Someday you'll have to sit down and explain it all to me. Or you could just invite me to the hearing."

"Really, Hef? I'd have thought you'd want to stay far away from that. Of course you can come."

"Thanks." He fingered the gold chain on Volle's neck. "What's this? Something you got in your year away?"

Volle shook his head. "It's been in my family for a while, but ..." But Seir had told him not to wear it to Tephos, and Duke Avery himself had told him to go ahead and wear it on this journey. "I didn't think it would fit my image as a noble. You know, it's just a Ferrenian family's heirloom."

Helfer nodded and let the pendant drop. "Not so worried about that anymore?"

"Not really. They know me now. Who I am doesn't depend on what I wear or what I look like."

"Good philosophy. I look forward to catching up with you. And to getting to know this wolf of yours." He flashed Streak a grin, and the wolf returned his smile.

"You could stay here while I go up to the castle."

"I thought I was going." Streak's ears fell.

Volle lowered his ears, too. "I'm sorry. I kind of think...this first time I should go alone. I'll take you up there tomorrow, I promise." He wanted to be able to talk to Tish openly without having to shoo Streak out of the room.

Streak sighed. "Okay."

Helfer walked over and patted the wolf's side. "I'll stay with you for an hour, then I'll have to go look after dinner and take care of some affairs. But welcome to Vellenland, both of you."

Volle smiled. "It's a lovely country. You don't have the accent, I noticed."

Helfer shook his head. "Born and raised in Divalia, and so were my parents." He grinned. "I get teased about that."

"I'm sure. Well, let us get settled, and I'll call for the buggy in a bit when I'm ready to go up."

"Get 'settled.' All right." Helfer laughed, then walked over to Volle. His soft brown paws clasped Volle's larger black one. "It's good to see you again, Volle. I'm glad you're okay. Be careful, all right?"

Volle nodded. "I will. And thanks for all your help."

"Oh." Helfer dug into a pocket and produced a sheet of paper with the King's seal. "Alister asked me to give this to you until you get to the castle."

Volle took it. "Thanks, again." He put it down on the side table.

Helfer glanced at Streak. "Take good care of this fox, okay?"

"I'm doing my best," the wolf replied with a grin. "When he lets me."

"Help yourself to any supplies you need to 'get settled'," Helfer winked as he slipped out through the door. "See you in a bit."

"Let's see the bedroom," Streak said as soon as the door closed.

Volle grinned. "I know what's on your mind."

"His, too, or didn't you hear him?" The wolf wagged his tail as he entered the next room. "This is great!"

The parlor was large, with a frescoed ceiling whose four support beams were gilded, reaching to the corners of the room. The four panels of the ceiling created by those separators were each decorated with a scene featuring different Mustelids: in one, a village of weasels worked industriously under the benevolent gaze of their lord; in the next, an army of minks fought valiantly against savage-looking bobcats; in the third, a family of otters played by a stream; and in the last, a group of heavyset martens built a palace that was probably intended for the weasel lord depicted in the first.

The walls of the parlor were adorned only with a simple pattern, cunningly worked into the wood panels. The furniture was similar to the furniture in the outer room: simple varnished oak, sturdily constructed. There was a table against the wall of windows with eight chairs around it and a centerpiece of flowers; on the opposite wall, a sideboard with a chest of drawers stood. The small silver weasel statues on the sideboard proved to be candleholders, and Volle suspected that the drawers held the place settings for the table, but he didn't inspect further.

A smaller room with three desks and two simple benches lay beyond the parlor. It had only two windows, one above each of the two larger desks, and the third desk seemed to be mostly used for storage. Between the desks was a large table that Volle paused at for a moment. He ran his paws along the surface, lost in thought.

Streak came up behind him and put an arm around his waist. "Something wrong, fox?"

The table had a raised edge, which Volle ran his finger pads along. "This table. It just reminds me of the one in the office beside Lord Fardew's. The one their war plans were on. They had a map…" He drew his claws along the finished surface. "It was older than this one, scarred. And bigger. But it was this height, had this edge." He ran his claws along the inside of the edge. "To keep papers on the table. They had paperweights too. I took the papers and…and ended up in prison."

Streak hugged him. "I got you out."

Volle nuzzled his cheek ruff. "So you did. I wouldn't be here now if not for you."

"Did someone see you take it?" The wolf's voice was soft and hesitant. They'd never spoken of Volle's crime, nor of the prison, since the escape.

Volle shook his head. "I don't think so. Dereath noticed the papers were gone, and saw me running away from him, but I'd already hidden them. He was convinced I was guilty anyway."

"He locked you up for five months without proof?" Streak was horrified. "I assumed they'd seen you take it..."

"No. From what Tish told me, the King didn't know much about it except what Dereath told him. That's why they never took me to a trial, and that's why Tish thinks we can beat the hearing. No evidence."

"That's good."

"I hope so. Sorry, just..." He traced his paw along the table again and then gave Streak's muzzle a lick. "One more room to see."

"Yeah." The wolf's tail wagged as they walked into the bedroom. Volle closed the door behind them.

The bedroom was narrow, but long. Three windows let fresh air into the room, and on the opposite wall was a large bed. A cushion had been added to the foot of the bed, extending it another two feet, and it had been made with fresh linen that spanned both the original bed and the addition. The extra two feet made it long enough for Volle and Streak, and Volle sprawled out on it immediately, stretching his arms over his head.

Streak licked his nose and then went to investigate the closet, in the far corner opposite the window. Volle saw the door open and then saw the wolf's tail start to wag. "Wow," Streak said. "He's prepared for just about anything." He sniffed up and down and then took a few things out. He padded back to the bed, holding them behind his back with a smile.

"What?" Volle looked up into the grinning muzzle.

The white wolf reached down to one of Volle's outstretched wrists and looped a leather strap around it. "I thought maybe we could relive our first meeting."

Startled, Volle pulled hard against the strap reflexively, panting, "No!" as he struggled. His tail bristled out and he drew his body up. The leather around his wrist changed in his mind to metal, and the room seemed to grow colder. His chest tightened, and a small moan escaped him.

Streak dropped the strap, surprised, and Volle yanked his wrist out of it and threw it across the room. He sat up, still panting, ears back, and tried to smooth out his tail. For a moment, ashamed, he didn't look at Streak, but the wolf sat beside him and he couldn't help meeting the soft blue eyes. "Sorry," he said. "I was in there for five months. I just..."

The wolf hugged him tightly across his shoulders. "No, no, I'm sorry. I shouldn't have surprised you. You reminded me of that time and I saw the straps there, and I thought...I'm sorry, fox."

Volle nuzzled him. "I know you didn't mean it. We haven't really talked about it. We just tried to start a new life at the farm and that's what I wanted."

"Is it?" Streak licked his nose gently. "You seem really happy to be here."

"It's good to see Helfer again." Volle closed his eyes as the wolf's tongue moved up his muzzle. The cold memory was already fading beneath that warmth. "I missed him a lot." And he was glad to be back in politicking, he had to admit. The news that Dereath was here had angered him, but also excited him. He couldn't wait to go see Tish and discuss what had been happening. His blood was racing and the scent of the wolf's fur as he pushed his muzzle down inside Streak's shirt just intoxicated him further.

"Mmm, you must have." The wolf giggled and nipped Volle's ears. "Didn't you tell me you and he weren't lovers? You're getting very frisky."

"We weren't," Volle said muffledly, nibbling Streak's chest-fur and undoing his shirt with his paw. "It's all you, sweet wolf."

Streak giggled, trying to undo Volle's shirt at the same time. Volle withdrew his muzzle and lifted Streak's shirt, licking around the line defined by the wolf's ribcage and down his stomach, which the wolf tensed and tightened as Volle's muzzle brushed along it. Volle grinned and poked at the hard-furred surface with his nose, and enjoyed the wolf's squirming as he did.

He untied the leather lace at Streak's waist as the wolf was pulling off first his own shirt, then Volle's. They lay back on the bed together and Volle began nosing down inside the wolf's pants, inhaling the rich musk. His nose found the tip of the wolf's sheath and the warm pink shaft already out of it. He exhaled across it and then pressed forward with the cold tip of his nose, flicking his ears when he heard Streak's exaggerated yelp.

Using his warm tongue instead, he teased the ridged pink surface, tasting the small drop of pre that had already formed at the tip. The wolf's paws stroked his tail as he licked, and the wolf's member grew firmer and longer under his tongue. The musky smell, so familiar, intoxicated him; he couldn't inhale enough of it, couldn't lick fast or hard enough to satisfy himself.

Judging from the way Streak's paws were stroking his tail, almost clutching it, he couldn't lick fast or hard enough for the wolf, either. He wagged his tail's tip and kept licking, and his licks became broader and wider until he found that the wolf's maleness was entirely inside his muzzle. He closed it then and let his tongue wash up and down, curling around the now-rigid member and slowly unwinding.

A white paw strayed down to Volle's pants, undoing them and sliding inside to cup the fullness of his sheath. The other kept stroking his tail, claws digging down to the skin as they moved through the thick tail fur. Volle pressed his hips into the wolf's paw, starting to work back and forth while his muzzle held still. His tongue kept flickering until the wolf's squirms became more pronounced and Volle's own member was hard and full against the wolf's paw pads.

Streak stroked back and forth, but distractedly, obviously more focused on Volle's muzzle, which the fox had started to move up and down
along the slick pink length. He teased the tip with his canines, pressing his
tongue against the member as it slid back and forth, taking his time because
he wanted the wolf to feel he was loved and valued, and he knew Streak
wouldn't want him to leave when they were done. He had plenty of time,
and he was enjoying the feel and smell in his muzzle almost as much as the
wolf's softly stroking paw.

For several minutes, they made love gently, shifting weights slightly
but keeping the same motions. Volle let his mind wander to Tish and what
he would say when he saw him, and what Tish might reply, but he stopped
thinking about the old wolf when he felt Streak's paw quicken and realized
his erection was subsiding. It only took a few seconds of focusing on the
feel of the pawpads moving over his skin for him to restore it, and then he
started moving his muzzle more quickly.

Streak thrust up into his muzzle, panting harder, and his strokes became less regular as Volle's tongue brought shivers to his fur. Volle heard the
low moans and felt the tremors against his tongue, and he wagged his tail as
he started up the path he'd climbed so often with the white wolf.

Streak's paw dug into the fur of his tail as the wolf moaned more
loudly and his thrusts slid along Volle's tongue. Volle felt the wolf's paw
tighten around his member, squeezing up and down erratically as his muscles tensed. He knew when the wolf was close, and knew when he was very
close, and knew just when to stop moving his muzzle and wait for the warm
rush of wolf musk to splash onto his tongue.

He wasn't disappointed; the musk filled his muzzle as Streak's howling moans filled his ears. He licked harder, cleaning off the seed as fast as
it spurted out, smiling and wagging his tail harder. A few moments later,
Streak lay back, panting. "Oh. Fox."

Volle grinned and lifted his muzzle off the dripping member. He gave
it a lick. "Nice?"

"Very."

He rested his head against the wolf's stomach, feeling the quickness of
his panting through the white coat of fur. "Mmm. Good."

"It's always good, fox."

Volle turned his head to look up into Streak's eyes. He smiled. "I know.
For me, too."

The wolf's paw trailed along his member. "Give me a minute."

"As long as you keep doing that."

Streak grinned, brushing the soft white fur on back of his paw over
Volle's sensitive length. After a moment of silence, he said, "Can you stay
tonight?" Volle sighed, and immediately Streak said, "I'm sorry. I know you
have to go."

"I won't be gone long, I promise. There's just some stuff I have to talk
about."

"I know, I know. Aw, I'm sorry. Look what I did." He started rubbing a bit more vigorously.

Volle smiled and tried to relax, letting his arousal come back. He pressed his head against Streak's fur and closed his eyes, letting everything fade away except for the paw at his sheath. He wondered if Streak would try to take him in his muzzle, but the wolf seemed content to hold him and use his paw. A year of experience showed in subtle things like the placement of his fingers, the firmness of his strokes, and the angle of his paw, and Volle luxuriated in the erotic touch that was, if not just right, at least the closest he'd felt from another's paw. His fur tingled and his body shivered as he pressed his nose into the soft white fur and inhaled again.

Streak was stroking gently, and Volle thought fleetingly that in order to keep him here, the wolf might be prepared to do this all evening. But as his arousal grew, he began to push his hips against the gentle strokes, and Streak obligingly stroked a little harder, a little faster. Volle's tail curled up behind him despite the paw pressing down on it, and soon he was shuddering with familiar delight, moaning in time with each wonderful stroke, tensing his body in preparation, the pressure building and building, and then the convulsions of pleasure, the rasping low moans as Streak's loving paw coaxed his trembling shaft to spend itself on his stomach-fur, white on white. His musk filled the air, mixing with the wolf musk thick in his nose, a warm, comfortable, and erotic scent that sustained his climax for a moment before dropping him, panting, back into the wolf's lap where he lay limply for a moment.

Streak kept one paw on his sheath, the other on his tail, and leaned down to lick at one of Volle's ears. Volle smiled and turned his muzzle to nuzzle the wolf; their tongues met as they washed each other's muzzles tenderly.

The physical sensations had quieted Volle's impatience to see Tish again, but after a few minutes of blissful dozing against his white wolf, he found the old black wolf returning to his thoughts. He would have to clean up quickly if he wanted to get up there and back by dinner. Sighing, he reached down to push his pants down his legs, careful not to get anything sticky on his leg-fur.

Streak paused in his caresses, then helped without a word. When the pants lay in a heap on the floor, he ran his paw down the reddish fur from Volle's side to his ankle, smoothing it down and leaving tracks in it with his claws. Volle smiled and licked the wolf one more time, then slowly got up.

Streak leaned back against the window, fastening his pants over his sheath and drawing up his knees to rest his muzzle on them. Volle saw him watching as the fox stood, stretched, and then headed for the door that he guessed was the private bathroom. As he opened it, he gave Streak a smile and a wag of his tail, and the wolf grinned at him.

"I like watching you walk around."

"Still?" Volle angled his hip, posing.

Streak nodded and his tail thumped the bed. Volle smiled and blew him a kiss before slipping into the bathroom.

As at the palace, Helfer kept his bathroom well stocked. Volle pored through the seven different scented powders, bringing each ceramic pot down from the shelf. His sensitive nose could identify the scents without removing the lid, and he didn't even need to remove the pots from the shelf. He just liked the smooth feel of the glazed ceramic and the raised patterns around the sides. The colors and designs were simple combinations of yellow, white, and blue shapes, but he enjoyed their unassuming repetitive march around the circumference of the pot.

This one was lavender, similar to the lavender scent they kept stocked on the farm. This was a brassy cinnamon scent that he knew Helfer favored, though Volle found it a bit sharp to wear on his own fur. This one was vanilla, and that brought back memories of the palace. It hadn't been Volle's favorite scent, but it was one that Tephos got in trade with one of the southern nations, and he hadn't been able to get it back on his farm. He opened the pot, selected one of the brushes that looked less used, and sprinkled the powder on the sticky patch of his fur, brushing it through to dry and clean his fur.

Usually, this grooming was relaxing, and often Streak helped him with it, but today Volle found himself hurrying the brush and snagging it on knots in his fur. He growled softly at himself and slowed down, forcing himself to work the powder into his fur with slow, even strokes until the smell of his musk was well hidden. After half an hour's ride up to the castle, he judged, it wouldn't be detectable even by another canid, like Tish.

For good measure, he brushed some powder along his sheath and then rubbed some under his tail, where his scent was strongest. He'd gotten out of the habit during his year on the farm, but he remembered that foxes and mustelids, with their stronger scents, were often expected to mask them at least slightly. Too late he thought that here in musteline Vellenland, he probably didn't have to worry about it as much. Old habits are easy to fall back into, he told himself ruefully, and took the brush to his tail, though it was already well groomed by Streak.

When he emerged from the bathroom, Streak was gazing out of one of the windows. He turned, nose flaring to Volle's scent, and tilted his head curiously.

"I don't recognize that one. It smells nice, though."

"Vanilla. It's sort of exotic."

"Mmm." He didn't say anything else, just watched as Volle opened their luggage and started moving clothes into the wardrobe, setting aside pants and a shirt as he found an outfit that he liked. He'd just put the shirt on, nothing else, and was posing for a giggling Streak when a few sharp knocks came at the door.

Quickly, Volle slipped on a pair of dyed yellow cotton pants and called, "Come in."

Helfer slipped through the door and closed it again, grinning from the wolf to the fox. "Shucks," he said. "Just missed."

Volle grinned back. "Just getting ready to go."

"I sent the buggy around to the side to wait for you."

"Thanks."

Helfer stepped closer to Volle and sniffed the air. "Got into my scents already, did you? You canids."

Volle chuckled. "As much as I appreciate the constant odor in the air here, I am going up to the palace. Er, the castle."

"Yeah, I know." He turned to Streak. "Lucky you don't have a fox's or weasel's scent. We have to bathe every day. I know some of the bears didn't bathe more than once or twice a week."

Streak smiled. "I usually bathe whenever Volle does. It's more fun."

"I bet." Helfer grinned and sat on the bed next to the wolf. "So tell me, what have you been up to since we last met?"

Volle fastened the doublet over his shirt, smiling as Streak started talking about life on the farm, hesitantly at first, then with more enthusiasm. Helfer listened and chipped in with comments of his own, and Volle was surprised to find that his friend knew a good deal about farming as well.

"Comes from listening to Burren go on two weeks a year," Helfer replied when Volle said as much. "You can't help but pick some of it up."

"You know more than Volle did when he started," Streak said, grinning.

"Weren't you on the Agriculture committee for a while?" Helfer looked slyly at Volle.

Volle coughed. "I'd better get going." He shook his head. "Though now I'm not sure I should leave the two of you together."

"Oh, go ahead," Helfer said. "We'll just compare embarrassing things we know about you."

Volle grinned. "Wonderful." He padded to the bedroom door and opened it. "See you for dinner."

"Uh-huh." Helfer turned to Streak. "So has he told you about the time he got drunk in the pub and tried to take all his clothes off?"

Volle snorted. "If you're going to make up stories, why not tell him it was a royal banquet?"

Both Helfer and Streak laughed at that, and Helfer said, "Oh, I forgot about that time!" Their renewed laughter followed Volle out the door.

Chapter 3

As the buggy approached the castle, Volle admired the architecture, though at the same time he could understand why the victorious weasel army had decided to build a new seat of government. The three towers did indeed define the shape of the castle, as he'd guessed. Each one anchored a section of the wall and rose above it, and now that he was closer, Volle thought he saw the remains of bridges going from one tower to another. The pennants that flew at the top of them were clearer now: one was the royal flag of Tephos, one was the crest of Vellenland, and the third one Volle finally recognized as the King's personal crest. He wondered what would fly there when the King wasn't visiting.

The castle was beautiful in its own way, but it was also very stark, and the wind whipped against the buggy as it roared around the mountain. Volle had thought his doublet would be a little warm, given the weather, but now the wind sliced through his clothes and chilled his fur. He rubbed his arms and curled his tail around himself, watching the castle change perspective as the road wound around it.

The walls were mossy but seemed well tended. The castle was obviously maintained well, or had been cleaned up for the King's visit. Now that he was closer, he could see crumbling stone at the top of the walls and cracks around the window slits, but it was obviously still livable. A column of smoke that he hadn't noticed before emerged from behind one of the towers, and then he noticed another, and another. He was amused that in this warm climate, anyone would build a residence on the frigid top of the mountain so as to require fireplaces. It might have suited a race of haughty felines, but he couldn't see Helfer and his ancestors being comfortable here.

The buggy pulled up in front of the main gate, where a guard opened the door and waited for Volle to step down. He was a large mountain goat who was bundled up against the wind in a thick overcoat that bore the King's crest.

"I see the King brought his security from Divalia," Volle remarked, rubbing his arms as the wind bit at them.

The guard nodded politely. "Papers, my Lord?"

Volle handed over the paper Helfer had given him. The guard scanned it and then returned it to him. "Thank you, my Lord. Go ahead in."

"Thank you. Say, do you know where Lord Tistunish is staying?"

"I do not, my Lord, but the footservant would know. You can find him at the main door."

"Thank you again."

The goat nodded. "You're welcome, my Lord." He pulled the gate shut behind Volle, then retreated quickly into his alcove.

Volle hurried up the long path to the door, anxious to reach shelter. Ancient sculptures lined either side of the path, some looking newly cleaned. Beyond them was what looked like a rock garden, but he didn't linger to admire it.

The main door of the castle was large and ancient. The wood was pitted and scarred so that the designs on it were hardly recognizable. Volle pounded on it with his fist and had enough time to decipher the outline of a feline warrior before the door creaked open.

A slender pine marten stood there, and Volle recognized his scent. "Renaldo?"

The marten smiled. "Lord Vinton! Come in, come in, get out of the wind." Volle slipped in, and the marten closed the door behind him. "We haven't seen you in about a year."

"No, I've been away."

Renaldo bowed his head, and Volle was sure he'd heard all the stories. The marten was a model of tact. He changed the subject. "I'm here to see Lord Tistunish. Where's he staying?"

The marten drew himself up and stood against the wall. "The castle is built on a triangular pattern. The great hall—that's where dinner will be tomorrow night—is against the northeastern wall." He pointed to his left, and looked sideways at Volle. "Just so you can get your bearings, my Lord."

Volle grinned and nodded. "Understood."

"There's a central staircase where this hallway meets the one that leads to the great hall. All the lords are staying on the second floor. Go up the stairs and toward the great hall, and you should be able to find Lord Tistunish's apartments on the left hand side."

"Thank you, Renaldo. I'm sure I can sniff him out if I'm in the right area."

"I'm sure you can, my Lord. You're not staying in the castle?"

"No. I'm staying with Lord Ikling, down the mountain."

"Very good. Oh, Lord Vinton," Renaldo said as Volle turned to walk down the hallway. He turned his head to look back at the marten.

"A third hallway joins the other two at the staircase. That leads to the throne room." Volle nodded. "That's where your hearing will be."

Volle flicked his ear. "Thanks."

"You'll be cleared, my Lord." The marten smiled encouragingly.

"I hope the King shares your conviction." He gave Renaldo a wave, and started down the hallway.

Some tapestries had been laid over the floor, probably to insulate the nobles' paws from the chilly stone. They smelled a little musty, and the designs on them were old and uninspiring, mostly faded portraits of weasels. He glanced down every now and then, but looked up when the hallway opened up into the central chamber.

It must have been very grand once, a receiving chamber that extended up through all three stories of the castle, and Volle thought he could make out the remains of a fresco on the bits of plaster that still clung to the ceiling. At each story, the round chamber was dotted with sconces that could have all held lamps, though now only every third one did. As a result, the room was light enough to see, but was criss-crossed with shadows. A few bears strolled through the room, glancing at him before starting up the stair.

The grand stair stood across from him, between two other archways. Parallel staircases to the left and right led up to a large landing, from which more hallways spread out. A deer and a raccoon in formal clothes, both female, looked at him from over the balustrade, and there was a shadowy figure that he thought might be the rabbit from the pub. He looked closer, but the figure stepped back into a hallway and disappeared.

Volle considered pursuing him, but decided against it, especially with everyone watching. He raised a paw to the ladies and mounted the stairs slowly, looking up to the landing and then down at the stairs. He could see the worn spots where countless paws had walked up and down, hundreds of years ago.

On the second floor, he sniffed the air until he recognized Tish's scent. The door was on the left hand side and looked somewhat newer, or at least more well-preserved, than the main door. He gave it a sharp knock, and stood back.

The door opened, and Volle looked into the black mask of a formally dressed raccoon. "Hello, Alcis," he said.

"Lord Vinton. His lordship is expecting you." The raccoon stood aside and let Volle enter the chambers. He closed the door and then left the room via another door, in the left hand wall.

The room was large, but not nearly as cozy or as well-decorated as Volle's chambers in Helfer's mansion. There had obviously not been enough tapestries to go around, because the walls and floor were bare cold stone. A thick curtain hung on the wall over what Volle assumed was a window; he could hear the wind through it and caught a scent of fresh air in the room that hadn't been present in the hallway. A few wooden pieces of furniture stood around the room, and on one, a large chair, sat a portly black wolf. A smile creased the graying fur of his muzzle as Volle entered.

"Hello, Lord Vinton," he said in a familiar deep voice.

"Hi, Tish." Volle smiled broadly at the wagging of the wolf's tail, matching his own. He held out a paw, but a moment later the wolf was up from the chair and embracing Volle tightly. Volle returned the embrace, touching his muzzle to the wolf's and breathing his scent as Tish breathed in his. Then he remembered that he was angry at the wolf, and stepped back.

Tish saw the glint in his eyes. "What's the matter?"

"You lied to me. About Dereath."

The wolf sighed. "Not technically."

"You misled me."

"Would you have come if you knew that he was not only going to be here, but was the new Minister of Defense?"

Volle paused. "Maybe. But I would not have brought Streak."

Tish's eyes widened slightly. "Your companion? You brought him?"

"Yes. He wanted to come."

The wolf rubbed his muzzle. "And did you want him to come?"

Volle sighed. "No. But I'd have made sure he didn't, if I'd known."

Tish nodded. "We'll take care of it. Don't worry. I wouldn't have tried to get you here if I didn't feel confident, Dereath or no."

"I still would rather have known. You haven't played those information games with me in a while."

"I only stopped, dear boy, because you were getting as much information as I was."

Volle had to grin, then. "So what's your great plan?"

Tish reached out and fingered the chain around Volle's neck. "Is this...?" He lifted the pendant out and examined it. "Ah."

"What?"

The wolf chuckled. "I feel silly doing this after you just scolded me for it, but I'm not sure I should tell you yet." He turned and sat down in his chair.

Volle followed him. "Tish!" He stood next to the adjacent chair, then sat down when Tish waved him into it.

"All right, all right. I think that pendant may be useful in proving your heritage."

Volle blinked at him. "What? How?"

"Dereath isn't aware of it, but I think I can use the pendant to convince the King that you are who you say you are. Or at least, who we say you are."

"How?"

Tish raised a paw. "Now, that I will keep to myself. You just need to wear that pendant to your hearing."

Volle glowered at him, but tucked the pendant back into his shirt. "Is that your whole strategy?"

"No, no. As you know, Dereath has no direct witnesses other than himself. You didn't give up any names under torture—which, by the way, we are all very grateful for." His eyes were sober. "I know what you went through there, now."

Volle nodded. "I did what I had to. It helped that I...I didn't think I was going to get out of there."

"I didn't know until it was too late. If I had..."

"I know. It's okay."

"Your only hope was that Dereath would over-reach himself. And he did. I hope he will again, because really, he has very little case. In his favor is that you escaped and fled rather than defend yourself, but I think you can explain that as a natural reaction. He doesn't have very much credibility with the King where you're concerned. He still remembers the whole debacle of..." Tish trailed off, sympathy in his eyes.

"Xiller." Volle said it evenly. "I know."

Tish nodded. "The King seems to believe that Dereath is intelligent and capable...except where you are concerned. That will work in our favor, actually. If Rallish had been presenting the evidence, I'd actually be more worried."

"All right. Is there anything I need to do?"

"Just watch yourself and that wolf of yours."

"I will."

Tish examined him closely, and smiled. "If we do win, you'll have to return to the palace. Will you bring him with you?"

"I don't think I'll be able to leave him behind."

"But do you want to bring him?"

"Yes. I mean, I want him with me."

"In your bed, or in your life?"

"Well...both?"

Tish looked at him steadily. "It's not fair to him if you're unsure. Do you want to share your life at the palace with him? I don't know how you've gotten on this year, and maybe it's none of my business, but you brought him here, so he must be very attached to you, and either you are attached to him, or you aren't but don't mind having him along. In the former case, by all means bring him to the palace. If it's the second case, then maybe you should think about it."

Volle sat back in the chair and rubbed his muzzle. "I never really looked at it that way before." He smiled. "So now you're giving out romantic advice?"

"Tika told me to ask you about it. She wanted to ask you herself, but I told her that would have to wait."

"Is she here?"

"Yes. She's out with Lady Villutian and Lady Barclaw now. They're probably making up gossip, since there isn't enough here to keep going on. Though you're helping."

"I'm sure." Volle rubbed his muzzle. "I feel responsible for Streak. He left his home, his job, and his country for me. And he saved my life. I guess I feel more worried about him than anything else. I don't know how much he'll enjoy being in the palace."

"Probably more if you want him there."

"I do. At least, I think I do," honesty made him add. "Well, I'll bring him up here tomorrow for the banquet. Maybe we should be staying up here."

"No, I'm sure you're better off down there. But I do think it's a good idea to bring him up here. I know at least Tika would like to meet him."

"We'll sit near you at the banquet." Volle grinned.

"Of course you will. I've already arranged it with Alister. I'll have to tell him to add an extra seat, but we can do that."

"I feel almost proud that I managed to do something you didn't expect.

And somehow worried."

Tish smiled and flicked his ears. "Just be careful. Someone you love is leverage, and if Dereath can find a way to use him against you, he will."

"Do you think I haven't thought of that? I'm surprised I haven't seen Dereath by now. Speaking of which…you said none of his assistants came along, right?"

"As far as I know."

"There's a rabbit who's been looking at me suspiciously. I saw him down in the pub and up here in the castle just now, I think. Sound familiar?"

Tish stroked his whiskers. "I don't know everyone who came with us from Divalia. I do know that none of the Defense assistants came along, but as I think of it, I wonder if Dereath inherited Lord Fardew's personal servant. Alcis!"

The raccoon opened the door he'd left through and stepped into the room. "Yes, sir?"

"Do you know Lord Fardew's personal servant?"

"Only slightly, sir. He brought a new servant in when he assumed the post."

"Is he a rabbit?"

"Indeed, sir."

"Thank you, Alcis." After the raccoon had left, Tish turned back to Volle. "There you go. It appears you were right."

"Maybe he's just keeping an eye on me, waiting. Usually he likes to appear when I'm not expecting him. Catch me off guard."

"Maybe. Speaking of guards…I know you were worried about your wolf being arrested as a deserter. Those laws haven't been enforced since the last war, but," Tish held up a paw, "knowing how you worry, I checked some months ago, and there is a provision for desertion under extraordinary circumstances to save the life of a noble. It's a provision instituted during the reign of King Oric, a squirrel, when Lord Creane…" He saw Volle's expression and harrumphed. "Yes, well, it's fascinating if you care about history. The gist of it is, if you win your case and are reinstated, your rescuer has nothing to fear. Is he safe now?"

"Helfer's with him. And he can take care of himself." Volle felt a twinge of worry, but suppressed it.

"All right." Tish looked at him closely. "I look forward to meeting him tomorrow."

"I look forward to introducing you to him," Volle said, and as he smiled he found that he really was.

Tish nodded. "We'll have about a week until your hearing. During that time you should be up here most days. Don't be obtrusive, but don't act like you're hiding out, either. This is a vacation time, so on days when it's not quite as windy as today, there will be outdoor games." His ear swiveled back to where the wind whistled against the window, and his nose wrinkled. "Today I believe they are playing chess in some of the rooms downstairs, and some people are playing with cards. Can't see what they see in those things."

Volle grinned. "They can be fun. So I don't need to do anything in particular?"

"I don't think so. Just be careful. Things may be a little less safe than I'd thought. Still, you have Lord Ikling looking out for you."

"He'll do what he can. I don't know how much that is if I'm up here, though."

"Every little bit helps. I'm doing what I can, too, though I can't be too direct to the King."

"I know. You're amazing, Tish."

The black wolf grinned. "You've been talking to Tika."

Volle laughed. "Not recently, but I'm looking forward to seeing her again."

"She's looking forward to seeing you as well, of course." He smiled. "Be prepared for a long line of questions about your love life. I've told her not to talk about anything concerning the hearing, and she complained that all that left her was your social life."

Volle flicked his ears. "Wonderful. Well, I'll be prepared. Is there anything else I should know? In general?"

"I don't think there's anything else I wanted to tell you. Except: welcome back. It's been very dull at the palace without you." He grinned as the fox stretched out in his chair. "Now, maybe you can tell me what happened while you were imprisoned and how you escaped? I know that Dereath tried to get you to talk by sending that wolf to fall in love with you. Apparently it worked too well."

"Much too well." Volle chuckled softly and then launched into the story of his capture and imprisonment. In the palace, you could always be sure of someone listening behind a door, but here, with fewer people and fewer servants, they could speak more freely. Still, he kept his voice down. Tish interrupted him occasionally, to ask for clarification or more detail, but mostly stayed silent as he told his story.

When Volle had finished, he nodded, stroking his whiskers thoughtfully. "I always thought that the mobilization plans were very odd. They'd been drawn up very quickly, and not only that, but the—" here he dropped his voice to a whisper, "plans themselves displayed a speed uncharacteristic of the King. So many troop movements, so complicated. But of course, we didn't know that until afterwards."

"I remember you mentioning something about that, just that it was odd they'd come about so quickly. We figured it was the influence of Lord Fardew. They definitely had the King's blessing."

Tish nodded. "And they are plausible, if slightly extreme. It looked like the beginning of an aggressive campaign."

"Or a trap, you said."

"Yes." The wolf looked past Volle, his gaze losing focus. "We couldn't take the chance then, and now it's irrelevant."

Volle smiled. "So that's my story. Tell me about your son and his mate."

Tish leaned back. "Oh, what's to tell? He was brought up by my wife's brother because he didn't like the palace. We should have forced him to live there, but he didn't want to leave our house. Never had any ambition. Never wanted to be Lord after me. Unfortunately, he doesn't get a choice in that. And since I would like to retire to that same house while I still have enough years left to enjoy my life, he has rather resentfully moved to the palace with his mate."

"But he didn't come up here?"

"He wasn't invited."

Tish could have arranged an invitation, Volle knew. He suspected one had been proffered and rejected. "I see."

"His mate is expecting." Tish traced a pattern on the arm of the chair. "They didn't want to bear the cub and then move to the palace, so it'll be born in the palace."

"He wasn't happy about that," Volle said softly.

Tish shook his head. "No. Nor was she."

"I'm sorry." Volle followed his train of thought away from the prickly subject. "How is…Ilyana? And Volyan?"

"They're fine and safe in Vinton, last I heard. Ilyana wasn't happy, but Dereath hasn't made any move and so she's just waiting to see how the hearing comes out." He paused. "Volyan is a fine cub. She always speaks of him as bright and playful."

Volle nodded. "I should have gone to visit him more often. I thought I'd have time."

"You may yet, my boy. We'll do our best to see that you get that chance."

"I could have gone this past year."

"It was best that you not leave Ferrenis." Again Tish lowered his voice to a whisper. "You were safest where you were."

"I know."

They sat in silence for a few moments after that. Volle noticed that the window closest to him had a lovely view of the valley. He watched the last vestiges of the sunset, noticing the subtle changes in color as his eyes adjusted to the darkening room.

"I'd better get back," he said finally. "Helfer's planning a dinner."

"You should. We'll see you tomorrow." Tish stood at the same time Volle did, and they embraced again, nuzzling. "Have a safe trip back."

"Tell Tika I'll see her soon."

Tish smiled. "I will."

Volle found his way back to the main gate without incident. He passed several lords and ladies, and to the few who recognized him and waved, he waved back with a smile. The ones who recognized him but did not greet him, he smiled to anyway. At the main door, Renaldo bowed to him, and he said a quick goodbye to the servant before climbing in the waiting buggy and huddling against the wind, which was even sharper now that the sun had set.

In the darkness, the trip back down the mountain seemed much less scenic and much more treacherous. Even his night-adjusted eyes couldn't pierce some of the pools of darkness, and the monochromatic landscape defined by the soft moonlight seemed angular and forbidding. He supposed the driver could see the road, but there was no telling what might be lurking by the side, or around the next corner. He forced himself to settle back and relax.

You've walked around the farm any number of nights, he told himself, and answered immediately. Yes, but that was familiar, especially after a month. I knew each hillock, each trench, and there were no surprises.

And Streak was there.

He sighed, thinking of the comforting arm of the white wolf around his shoulder or waist, and was glad that he was heading toward him. As he thought this, he heard a clatter and saw another horse to his left, then the buggy it was pulling. The shape inside was shrouded in darkness, and though he tried hard to see who was hidden there, the buggy had whisked past before he could make out even a silhouette.

Who would be visiting the castle at this late hour? Or returning? His fur prickled with a twinge of anxiety, then again, he forced himself to relax. Everything isn't a threat, he told himself.

Nevertheless, he was glad to see the silvery shape of Helfer's mansion growing larger, and gladder still when the buggy stopped outside the main gate. He disembarked carefully, helped by Roferro, who opened the gate for him and escorted him inside.

Streak was sitting on the bed, paws folded into his lap. He looked up as Volle came in and smiled, but the smile seemed forced.

"Hi," Volle said, and crossed the room to him. "Thanks for waiting. I promise I'll take you up—we'll go up together tomorrow."

Streak nodded, and hugged Volle. "It's okay. I had a nice talk with Helfer before he left to prepare dinner. He's a nice guy."

"He really is. I'm glad you think so too. You'll enjoy meeting Tish and Tika." He smiled and nuzzled the wolf, trying to cheer him up.

"I can't wait." Streak smiled back and kissed his nose.

"How much time do we have until dinner?"

"He said to go into the dining room as soon as you got back. He told me how to get there. He did warn me that the ceilings are low."

Volle grinned. "No dining room for us big people, eh?"

"I don't know about that, but he said the corridors on the way there were low."

The dining hall had relatively high ceilings, as it happened, and Volle and Streak were able to walk in without ducking their heads. They both looked up, massaging their necks as they entered the large hall. The arched ceiling had the most elaborate frescoes Volle had yet seen in the mansion, all depicting religious scenes. Volle glanced at them, taking in the six Houses and the central mandala, then walked to the seats next to Helfer, where the valet was leading them.

The weasel greeted Volle with a smile. "Nice visit up at the castle?"

"Very. We're both going up tomorrow. Will you be there?"

"Of course. I have to be there pretty much every day. Today is my only day free. Why don't you ride up with me, then?"

"That would be fine." Volle turned to Streak, who nodded without saying anything. "So what did you guys talk about?"

Helfer chuckled. "You, for a bit. Then I told him something about Vellenland and he told me about his farm. And—ah, here's someone I wanted you to meet." He stood up as a small female weasel in elegant robes approached the table, led by another female in servant's clothes. She smiled at Helfer as he helped ease her into the chair, and only then did Volle see that she was carrying an infant.

"Volle, this is Laya. Laya, this is Lord Vinton, and his companion Streak."

Volle stood and bowed. "Pleased to meet you." He smiled at the tiny cub. "And who is this?"

"This is Lyfar," she said, looking tenderly at the cub's sleeping form. Her voice was strong and sure, and he could see the happiness in her eyes when she looked back at him. "He's four months old and healthy."

"That's wonderful," Streak said, straightening up from his bow. "He looks beautiful."

"He is," she said.

Helfer was beaming as he sat back down. "So that's my latest heir, and his mother," he said.

"You're truly blessed," Volle said out of courtesy.

"It was bound to happen," Helfer said as another weasel sat on the other side of Laya. "Isn't that right, Burren?"

"Indeed, Lord Ikling," the governor said as he sat. "I appreciate your cooperation. I know how hard it was for you." His dry tone and Helfer's answering smile told Volle that it was a long-standing joke between them.

"It wasn't hard," Helfer muttered to Volle under his breath. "That was the problem."

Volle grinned. "You got the job done."

"Somehow." He leaned back and sighed, just as the servants brought in the first course, a light soup that smelled mostly of onions, with traces of fruit and herbs below the acrid scent. Once Helfer had given the nod for everyone to start, Volle sampled his and found it quite good. He wasn't surprised; in a rich land governed by a weasel with refined tastes, he would have been surprised if the food were plain.

Streak seemed to enjoy the soup, too. Conversation died as they all bent to it, and when it was finished, Helfer gave them an inquiring look. Volle smiled in reply. "It's good," he said, and Helfer's grin broadened.

"Glad we can satisfy your discriminating palate." He gestured to a servant, and the fine ceramic bowls were taken away almost instantly. He saw Volle's glance at him. "What?"

Volle shook his head. "It's just interesting to see you in your own place. In the palace, you always keep to yourself. Here, people look up to you and you seem to like it. You're really in charge."

"Shh!" Helfer gestured at him in mock dismay. "You'll ruin my reputation here. They only see me once a year!"

Volle chuckled, as Laya certainly didn't seem to think Helfer had much reputation to ruin. Paying only casual attention to their words, she had handed the infant to her servant, and now was smiling at Streak across the table. "How did you come to be with Lord Vinton?" she asked.

"We met in Divalia," he said softly, glancing at Volle. "And then when he left, I left with him."

"I see. How long ago was that?"

"About a year." He was more confident in that response. She still looked curious, so he added, "We've been spending some time on his...family's farm. Just relaxing."

"Ah. It is nice to get away once in a while."

Streak nodded. "We enjoyed it there. It's nice to be near the land again."

"Again?"

"Oh. I grew up on a farm."

"And you did, too, right?" Helfer chimed in, looking at Volle.

He had grown up on the streets of Caril in Ferrenis, but his identity as Lord Vinton included a childhood on a farm. For six years he had inhabited that identity, and he found himself falling back into it. "Yes, I did too."

Streak was looking at him strangely; of course, he'd told the wolf that he'd never lived on a farm, and even if he hadn't, it would have been obvious. He gave Streak a quick look back, and the wolf looked down. He should have prepared him better, he knew, but he hadn't thought about the conflicts that might arise.

"Nice to have that in common," Laya was saying. "Helfer grew up in Divalia, of course, and I grew up on an orchard in Vellenland, so we don't have much in common."

"I still spend most of the year in Divalia, though, so we don't really have to." Helfer grinned at Volle.

Laya glanced at him, managed a small smile, and then turned to check on the servant, who showed her the cub.

The second course arrived then, a tray of roasted vegetables with spices that were familiar to Volle from the palace dinners. He mentioned this to Helfer as they ate, and the weasel nodded. "These don't grow around here, but we get them in trade like the palace does."

"Do you mostly trade ale and mead?" Streak was picking at his vegetables, and looked up from them to Helfer.

"Mostly. But also dried fruit and some other goods."

Streak nodded and turned back to his plate. Volle gave him a smile that he wasn't sure the wolf saw, then kept talking to Helfer. "So what else is going on at the palace?"

The weasel grinned. "You know I don't have access to all the best gossip." He proceeded to tell Volle all the gossip he had heard, a recitation that lasted until midway through the dessert course.

"…and Lord and Lady Oncit are back together; you remember he'd sent her away."

Volle nodded and said around a mouthful of rich cake, "We thought she was going to have a cub and he didn't want it to be at the palace."

"Supposedly she actually didn't. They seem really happy together now. It's charming. And a bit sickening." He speared the remaining berries from atop his cake and slid them into his muzzle, then pushed the plate aside. "And that's all I know."

Volle chuckled, working on his dessert. He looked back at Streak and smiled. "The palace is a very interesting place."

"Sounds like it. I'm not sure I could remember all those names."

"Oh, you'd learn them."

"I guess so. This cake is terrific," he said, looking at Helfer.

"Thanks." The weasel smiled more broadly.

"We're very proud of the cook and the kitchen staff." Laya leaned over and chimed in. "My brother works in the kitchen."

The servants cleared the dessert plates and poured a small glass of brandy for everyone. Streak downed half of his in one swallow, while the others sipped politely. "Very nice," Volle said. "I don't recognize it."

"Private stock," Helfer said. He sipped again, then swirled it in his glass, eyes lost in the golden liquid. "Pear brandy, aged fifteen years. My father liked it particularly."

Volle just nodded. Laya dropped her eyes sympathetically, but Volle thought he saw or smelled a bit of curiosity from her. Streak had finished his and held the empty glass out to a servant, who refilled it quickly.

It took only a moment for Helfer's cheerful personality to resurface. "And it's not hard to tell why, eh?" He smiled at Streak. "You seem to share his taste for it."

"It's very good." The wolf smiled, working his way through the second glass. In the ensuing silence, he said, "So you had no brothers or sisters?"

Helfer shook his head. "One sister, who died when I was seven."

"Me too. I had a brother who died when I was six."

Laya looked quickly at her infant cub and took him back from the servant, rocking him gently. "Lyfar's fine," Helfer said with a smile. "My sister was never healthy, at least that's what my mother used to tell me. I remember they told me not to pick her up."

"My brother got kicked by a horse," Streak said. He downed the rest of his pear brandy, but didn't hold out the glass for a refill this time. "I ran to town to get the surgeon, but we didn't get back in time."

The conversation slowed after this morbid turn, though the rest of the table was still chattering away. Volle finished his pear brandy and set it down. It glowed nicely in his stomach, and he could feel his eyelids drooping. "Maybe we should get some rest." He tried to cover his yawn. "We have a big day tomorrow."

Helfer grinned. "I'll let you two get to bed, then." He rose from the table, and at that, many of the other guests rose as well.

Volle stood, as did Streak, though the wolf had a bit of trouble with his chair. Volle smiled at the clatter and took the nearest white paw. "It'll be good to rest. It's been a long trip."

Helfer walked them to the door, passing under the low archway with ease. Volle ducked his head, but a thump from behind him told him that Streak had forgotten to.

"Ow." The wolf leaned against the wall, hunched over, one paw pressed to his forehead.

"Are you okay?" Volle put an arm around him.

"Yeah, just...wasn't watching where I was going."

"Too much brandy." Helfer grinned, but was looking a bit abashed. "Sorry about the ceilings."

"Not your fault," Streak muttered. "Should've been looking where I was going." He straightened up as much as he could. "I'll be okay."

Volle insisted on walking behind him as they made their way back to the guest wing, where they could stand at their full height again. Helfer left them at the entrance to their rooms, clasping paws with both of them. He held Volle's and smiled. "See you in the morning. I'll send someone to wake you when we're near ready."

"We won't need much time." Volle grinned. "Even though I lived in the palace for six years, I can still dress myself."

"Good. I was going to ask." Helfer released his paw and clapped him on the shoulder. "Hopefully you'll be in the palace again soon."

"He will," said Streak unexpectedly.

"I sure hope so." Volle grinned. "Sleep well, Hef."

"You too." The weasel closed the door behind him as he left their suite.

Streak was already making his way to the bedroom, only lurching once. Volle hurried after him. "Are you feeling okay? You never drink that much."

"We n-never have pear brandy like that." He went into the bedroom and tugged at his shirt, pulling it off and dropping it to the floor.

Volle sat on the bed, undoing his own clothes. "You were also acting strange. Are you mad at me for going up to the castle?"

"No!" The wolf turned quickly to look at him, then lowered his head. "No, I'm just a bit...overwhelmed. It's all so much."

"It'll be okay tomorrow." Volle slid his pants down and sat on the bed, curling his tail around his ankles. "You never told me about your brother."

"I don't think of him very much."

"How old was he? When it happened?"

"Three." He'd stepped out of his pants and was rubbing his head again. Volle just looked up at his muzzle, silvery in the moonlight from the window. His eyes were closed and one arm hung at his side while the other was pressed to his head. "We'd put him in the stable and somehow he let one of the horses out. I found him. There was so much blood, I thought he was already dead. But mother said he wasn't, that I should run for the doctor. She trusted me, and I didn't get back in time."

Volle reached out for the paw hanging at the wolf's side and squeezed it. After a moment, Streak squeezed back. "Come to bed," Volle said softly, and Streak climbed in with him.

He protested when Volle put an arm around him. "My head still hurts."

Volle nuzzled him gently. "I just want to hold you, silly. We had our fun this afternoon."

"We've done twice a day before. A lot." But he didn't object as Volle pulled him against his chest. Volle felt the wolf relax, slowly, and the white tail curled back around his waist.

"Not today." Volle licked the edge of his ear, and felt it quiver, then flick. He smiled. "You were, what, seven? There's no way you could be expected to save his life. I don't see how it could have mattered."

The wolf tensed, then relaxed again. "I was six. I know. I told you, I don't think about it much."

"Okay. I just want to make sure." He rubbed his paw up and down Streak's chest.

Streak turned and kissed him on the nose. "Thanks, fox," he said, and smiled. "Let's get some rest. Tomorrow's a big day."

Volle nodded and tightened his embrace. Streak snuggled back against him and clasped his paw tightly, and Volle remembered no more until the morning.

Chapter 4

*H*elfer had brought breakfast rolls in the buggy, and they ate them on the trip up. The sun shone brightly on the hills and fields, and in through the window onto their knees. "Sorry we didn't get to do our run this morning," he said with a smile at Volle. "Maybe tomorrow, when I don't have to go up quite this early."

"I was amazed to see you awake," Volle said around bites of his roll. "They must really have threatened you."

The weasel chuckled, and handed another roll to Streak. "Alister wants to be at my side every hour of the day. With services tomorrow and all, he's getting frantic. I had to promise I'd be there early today when I told him I wasn't going to be around at all tomorrow." He sighed, and shook his head. "It wouldn't be so bad if he were a rabbit."

"I think it'd be worse. You wouldn't be able to concentrate on anything."

"Ah, you're probably right." He grinned across the coach at the two of them. "I don't know how you manage to concentrate on anything with him around."

Volle flicked his ears. "Cause I know I can concentrate on him at the end of the day."

"Or sometimes in the middle," Streak added with a smile.

"Mmm. Or sometimes both." Volle nuzzled the wolf and smiled back.

"Oh, you two are as bad as Lord Black and his paramour. No, you're worse."

Volle chuckled. "Tish didn't know much about Blackie and Ashtora. How are they doing?"

"She's still living in the palace. Black wants to marry her but there are a couple questions about her lineage that she's trying to clear up. I don't think it'll stop him, but it'll smooth things over a lot if she does get them clear."

"He should hold onto her. I don't remember many noble raccoon families around."

Helfer shook his head. "There aren't. They're mainly concentrated up in the northwest. That's where Black, Creane, and Ryngs are all from."

"Are we going to meet any of these lords?" Streak interrupted.

Volle looked at Helfer, who shook his head. "Creane is the only one senior enough to be invited and he didn't want to travel."

"Lord Black is a friend of mine and Hef's, though we stopped seeing him as much when Ashtora showed up. And Ryngs is a friend of Tish's."

Streak nodded and finished off his roll. He waved off the offer of another one from Helfer. "So I'm just meeting Lord Tistunish and his wife?"

"As far as I know."

"They're wolves, right?"

Volle patted his knee. "Don't be nervous. Yes, they're wolves. In fact, Tish is a black wolf. You and he will set each other off well."

"Better if they weren't wearing clothes," Helfer offered.

"Tish isn't into that, and anyway, he's mine." Volle clasped Streak's paw, and the wolf squeezed back with a smile.

"You'd still love me even if…" Streak trailed off.

"If you slept with Tish?" Volle laughed. "I don't really see that happening, but of course I would, dear. I hope you get along well with Tish. If things go well, you'll be seeing a lot more of him. Until he retires."

Streak smiled, and said unexpectedly, "I hope to."

Volle looked at him curiously but decided not to ask why the wolf was suddenly eager to move to the palace. He felt a lot better after a long night of sleep, and maybe Streak did, too; he'd been very affectionate that morning. He looked past the wolf's white muzzle, edged by the morning light, and watched the increasingly barren hills and rocks roll past.

When they arrived at the ancient castle, a mouse scurried up to the carriage as Renaldo opened the door for them. "Lord Ikling!" he squeaked.

Helfer rolled his eyes at Volle, and sighed. "Hello, Jerish," he said.

"Lord Ikling, Lord Alister respectfully requests your presence as he is desperately trying to determine the schedules for the next few days and especially the way the services are going to be held and what facilities you have to accommodate the King's party and what arrangements are going to be made to accommodate your own people at the same time—" He paused as Helfer held up a paw.

"Take a breath, Jerish. I'm coming. Volle, Streak, have fun. I'll likely not see you until dinner." He sighed and followed Jerish as the mouse scampered into the castle.

"Dinner?"

Renaldo closed the buggy door. "Dinner tonight is served just after sundown in the banquet hall.You will both have places there."

Volle smiled. "I believe Lord Tistunish is expecting us. I know the way."

Renaldo bowed. "I am at your disposal should you need assistance, my Lord."

"Thank you." Streak followed him to the front door, and inside the palace.

When the door had closed behind them, the wolf looked at him. "I can see why you want to get back to the palace. It's just like having a whole house full of servants, except they're polite."

"And you have to share them with the rest of the palace. All except your personal servant."

"Would—would that be me?"

Volle laughed and slipped an arm around the wolf's waist. "No, silly. I was attended by a skunk named Welcis when I was at the palace. He didn't leave with us, obviously. No, you would be Lady Vinton."

"Lady?!" Streak yelped, loudly enough to make a pair of ladies further down the hall turn around. He glanced down his front, then back at Volle. "I think I'd rather be a servant."

"It's the palace custom," Volle said. "I'm sure we could find some nice dresses that would set off your fur. White goes with anything."

"Oh, dresses! I see. I thought I'd have to make some adjustments to my, er, privates."

"No, no. I wouldn't let anyone touch those. Except me, of course."

"Of course." Streak licked his nose, then lifted his head to look around as they reached the central chamber. "Wow. This must have been really beautiful once."

Volle nodded. "They didn't really keep it up over the years. But it looks like they did a nice job restoring it for the King's visit."

Streak traced a paw along the railing as they walked up the stairs. He nodded to a bear who was lumbering down the stairs, then glanced back after they'd passed him. "Do you know him?" he whispered.

"Villutian," Volle whispered back. "Not well. He's high ranking, or was when I was there."

"He didn't seem to recognize you."

"I'm sure he did." They'd reached the top of the stairs, and Lord Villutian had disappeared into one of the side hallways, so Volle spoke normally. "We never spoke much, and maybe he's worrying about associating with me until the hearing's over."

Streak just patted his shoulder, looking at the doors as they passed them. Volle stopped in front of Tish's door and knocked. Alcis opened the door a moment later. "You are expected, sir," he said, and stepped aside to let them enter.

Tish and Tika were seated in the parlor, but got up as Volle entered. Tika was smiling, but Tish looked apprehensive; his ears were halfway back and he kept glancing at the door leading further into their suite. He clasped Volle's paw, touched muzzles with him, and then turned to Streak.

"May I present my mate, Streak." Volle stepped back.

Streak held out his paw for Tish to clasp and leaned forward. The two touched muzzles for several seconds, getting to know each other's scents, then stepped back. "My mate, Tika," Tish said, and stepped back as the gray wolf stepped forward. Streak clasped her paw and touched his muzzle to hers as well.

Tika curtsied when she'd stepped back. "A pleasure to meet you, finally. I've heard so much about you."

Streak smiled. "Volle has talked about you, too."

The door Tish had been glancing at opened, and a short vixen walked out. She strode to the space between Tish and Volle, and folded her arms, eyes fixed on Volle.

"May I present my mate, Streak."

He let his tail droop as he met her flashing eyes. "Oh," he said. "Hello, Ilyana."

"Hello, *Volle*." Behind her, Tish was lowering his ears and shrugging minutely.

"When did you get here? I didn't know you were coming."

"Last night, late. I didn't plan to come until I knew you were going to be here."

"I'm...flattered."

"You shouldn't be. I just wanted to see you nose to nose."

"Did you leave Volyan in Vinton?"

"No, he's here. He's playing with his nurse in our chambers. Why, do you actually care about him?"

"Why don't we retire to the dining room?" Tika offered Streak her arm. "These two can join us when they've had a chance to talk."

Volle wanted to protest, but after another look at Ilyana, he couldn't bring himself to avoid her. He knew what was coming and he might as well get it over with. He nodded to Streak, who was looking at him with ears perked questioningly. "Go ahead. I'll be in in a minute."

Streak nodded and took Tika's arm. Tish followed them into the dining room, and closed the door behind them.

"So how was the trip?"

Volle's attempt to stay friendly was cut short with an angry bark. "All I wanted from you was a noble lineage. Not fidelity, not much in the way of support, not a social calendar—just a noble son to take care of and a secure family. You couldn't even tell the truth about that." She lifted a paw and cuffed him across the muzzle. "Bastard."

"Listen," he sighed, rubbing his muzzle, "I couldn't tell you anything. I didn't know this was going to happen."

"But you knew there'd be a chance."

"You're automatically assuming I'm guilty."

"Well? Aren't you? In my experience, when someone's arrested and flees the country, they'd have no reason to do so if they weren't guilty. If you weren't guilty, why not stay?"

"Because they were making up a case against me. Dereath thought I was a spy and was doing his best to make up enough evidence to prove it." So far, he hadn't lied to her.

"How on earth would he get that idea? Why would they make up a case if there wasn't enough evidence to prove it?"

"He hates me." He tried to figure out how to summarize his relationship with the rat. "When I first got to the palace, he came on to me and I turned him down. So he was mad, and then because Hef and I got to be such good friends, he was jealous of us. And so he kept trying more and more things, and getting madder and madder when they didn't work. And then..." He fixed his eyes on a distant point. "There was someone he was very interested in, involved in some nasty business, and he and I got involved."

"You stole his boyfriend."

"They weren't boyfriends." He tried not to snap. "They weren't even dating. But Dereath doesn't have any concept of how these things are supposed to work. In his mind, he 'owned' him. And he was furious when his 'pet' chose to come stay with me."

"I still don't understand how he got the idea that you're a spy."

"Oh, because the nasty business he was involved in was political, he got the idea that I was deliberately interfering with it. So he traveled down to Vinton and tried to piece together how I got into the country from Ferrenis. I didn't travel with any fanfare, so he got some of the pieces wrong and it made him suspicious. He figured I was covering up the pieces he couldn't find, so he made them up."

Her ears were coming back up, and he thought that maybe she was softening a bit. She'd obviously been working herself up. "What was the nasty business?"

He sidestepped the question. "How did you know I left the country? Nobody knew where I went except for Tish."

"And Tika, who wrote me." Her amber eyes were flashing again. "You didn't even think to do that."

"We never wrote each other. I knew you'd be safe in Vinton. I thought about you and Volyan, but I thought if I wrote it might make you look bad. If Dereath succeeded in his plan. Otherwise you could just claim you didn't know anything."

That prompted the first significant change in her expression. "Oh, Volle. I hadn't thought about that. You're right."

He shook his head. "I'm really sorry all this happened. If I'm cleared at the hearing, things will be okay."

"Won't this rat keep after you?"

"Maybe. But after that first time, he was reprimanded pretty severely. If he doesn't succeed this time, I don't think he'll dare try again." He tried not to think about what Dereath would resort to in that case. "And he's the Minister of Defense now, so he has a lot of other things on his mind. Hopefully he'll just let it go."

"Do you really think so?"

No. "I hope so."

She sighed. "Does it help for me to be here?"

"I'm glad you came," he said, and though it wasn't a lie, it wasn't totally honest, either. "But are you sure you want to stand by me? If the hearing goes badly, you could be getting yourself into a lot of trouble."

"If you are innocent, then Canis says loyalty to the pack is our duty. And you're my husband. We can't be much more of a pack than that." She glanced at the dining room. "Though it seems you've added another member since I've been gone. How long have you been with him?"

"Just over a year. He's the one who helped me get out of prison."

Her ears flicked, and perked up. "Did he know you before that, or was that your introduction?"

He chuckled softly and gave her the condensed story of how he and Streak had met, fallen in love, and escaped to Ferrenis. When he was done, she shook her head. "All I made you do was go to a cotillion and wedding. This poor wolf had to break you out of prison."

"I wouldn't have been much of a partner if he hadn't."

"Nor much of a husband. I suppose I should thank him." She looked down, and when she looked back up, her ears stayed down slightly. "I don't want to annul our marriage."

He shook his head. "I wouldn't expect you to."

"So you'd be willing to remain my husband and live with him at the palace?"

"I don't know if he wants to live at the palace."

She tilted her head slightly. "Don't you want to go back?"

"Of course I do. But we've been living alone on a farm, and I don't know if he'll want to be thrust into the insanity at the palace. He seems to be doing okay so far." He smiled. "I guess we'll see how he gets along with Tika and Tish."

"Tika can talk him into anything."

"I hope so…" He smiled. "I'd forgotten how easy it is to talk to you."

She flicked an ear and gave him a half-smile. "It has been almost four years, dear husband."

"Yes." He thought of two things at the same time, and brought a paw up to rub his whiskers. "Do you have a lover?"

"I've had a few. No foxes. And none right now. Volyan keeps me busy."

"Yes, I expect so." He looked away. "I was thinking that when I get back to the palace…it might be time to bring him to Divalia and let him start learning about court life. He will be the next Lord Vinton, after all."

Her ears and expression fell. "Yes," she said softly, "it is past the time. I haven't wanted to let him go. But for his sake, I have to. That's partly why I brought him."

"I'm sorry," he said, but she waved his apology away.

"I knew it would have to happen sooner or later. When you were arrested, that was my second thought: who will bring him up at the palace? I could have asked Tika, but they're going to retire, and she's always complaining about her son, how he doesn't have any of the instincts necessary to survive at the court. And I didn't want Volyan to end up like that. That's partly why I was mad at you too."

"Tish would have arranged something."

"Then," she continued as if he hadn't spoken, "I realized that he wouldn't be going to the palace if you were arrested."

"Oh. Right." He shifted his paws uncomfortably.

She looked straight at him, amber eyes meeting his. "You'll win the hearing. With Canis on your side, you will."

"More importantly," he said, "Tish is on my side."

She grinned at that and then leaned forward to touch her nose to his. Impulsively, he slid his arms around her and turned the greeting into a kiss. She pressed against him, tail brushing his paw, and leaned into the kiss.

It was a friendly kiss, not a lovers' kiss, for all that they held the embrace longer than might have been proper for friends. She was beautiful and her scent was subtle and pleasing, but not alluring. Volle smiled at her as they stepped apart, and saw a hint of sadness in her answering smile.

"It's been a while since a nice fox kissed me," she said. "Such a shame."

He flicked his ears and smiled apologetically. "Fox—Canis made me this way."

"Oh, I know. No doubt He had His reasons." She chuckled. "I see you've been attending Ferrenian services again."

"Very few Orthodox churches over there."

"I suppose. You'll attend tomorrow?"

He nodded. "Of course."

"All right. I'll bring Volyan. You can see him then." She smiled. "He's dying to meet his father."

Volle felt a soft pang. "I can't wait to see how he's grown."

"You'll be proud. Oh, come in, Tika, we're done." The grey wolf's nose had poked out of the dining room.

Tika swung the door open and walked in, relaxing when she saw their smiles. "Everything okay, then?" They nodded. "You see, Ilyana, I told you it would be."

"I know." She looked at Volle. "I guess I just needed to let him know how I felt."

Volle rubbed his muzzle where she'd cuffed it. "You did that." He wondered why it was that he'd been able to reassure Ilyana when Tika hadn't. Maybe it was just that Tika didn't have all the information, or had been holding back some because she wasn't sure what was appropriate to tell.

"Sorry." She clasped her paws together.

"Don't be. You had a right to be angry." The dining room door remained ajar, he could see out of the corner of his eye, but neither Streak nor Tish emerged. He guessed that Tish was giving the younger wolf one of his talks, or maybe a history lesson.

"It's not constructive, though. There's nothing you can do about it. I'm more useful helping you regain your position at the palace than being mad at you for the position you put me in." The glint in her eyes told him that she wasn't entirely rid of the anger.

"I'm not sure what you can do to help. But thank you."

"If you're all seen together at services, that will be a good image," Tika said. "My dears, you look so lovely together that nobody would deny that you are nobility."

Volle smiled, and saw Ilyana's muzzle crack a smile as well. "I appreciate that, Tika."

"And with an adorable cub? Oh, they won't be able to resist."

"I hope it's that easy."

"Haven't I taught you yet about appearances? Tch." She turned to Ilyana. "You'd think after six years…but no. He is smart, but very thick-headed. As are you, young vixen, so don't laugh too hard."

"All right, all right." Ilyana's tail swished as she smoothed down her dress. "Well, I should get back to Volyan and his nurse. I'll leave you here."

"I am sorry about dinner. We will have some food sent to you."

"That's all right. I wouldn't have expected to be invited to the palace dinner anyway. I certainly wasn't invited here."

"Where are you staying?" Volle asked.

"At an inn down in Ikling. Tika could get me into the castle here, but not to stay. I can come to services, though."

"They're being held down in the town, because the church there is in better shape," Tika interjected.

"Okay." Volle leaned forward. "I'll see you there, then."

Ilyana nodded and touched her muzzle to his. "Goodbye, Volle. Goodbye, Tika, and thank you." She saw herself out without waiting for Alcis to emerge from the dining room.

"She was an excellent choice," Tika mused after the door had closed.

"You were the one who chose her," Volle pointed out.

Tika smiled sweetly at him. "I know, dear. Come, sit down and tell me about Streak. He's really quite charming, if a little quiet."

"I don't know how you can tell when someone's quiet," Volle said, following her to one of the chairs by the window. "Between you and Tish, I'm lucky if I can get in three words."

"Don't be rude. You contribute to your share of the conversation. Your white wolf listens a lot. And when he does talk, it's measured and considered." She paused, and looked at him. "You could learn from him."

Volle rolled his eyes, but smiled. "He grew up on a farm and I don't think he had many people to talk to there. You two were probably very intimidating."

"We didn't gang up on him. Honestly, Volle, what do you take us for? Tish asked him about how he's been this past year, and I just told him a little bit about what life is like at the palace. Oh, don't give me that look. I didn't go into lots of details. I talked about the big gala a couple years ago. You remember, the one Ilyana wanted to come back for? She got sick, or was it Volyan? Yes, it was Volyan." Volle remembered that; he'd almost traveled down to Vinton, but had been stopped by Tish. "I told him about the candles, and the performers—especially that ermine who kept doing the flips with the lighted torch—and the dancing, until all hours of the night."

Volle just grinned. "And what did he say?"

"I think he said, 'That sounds very nice,' or something like that. So what do you two do, there on the farm?"

Volle considered the question, then leaned back. "Chores. Cooking.

Reading over the latest letter from Tish."

"For fun?" She waggled a finger at him. "Besides the obvious."

He smiled. "We go for walks. Sit in bed and watch the sun rise. I have a chess set, but he's not really interested in playing."

"It sounds divine."

"What do you and Tish plan to do when he retires?"

Her ears flicked, but she countered that sign of worry with a smile. "Canis only knows. I think he'll go crazy without all the Tistunish affairs to manage. I'll have to take some ideas from you to keep him occupied."

"Get him something to work on, like a farm or painting or something. Make him write his memoirs."

"Now there's an idea. I just might do that." She rubbed her muzzle thoughtfully. "He's had a very interesting life."

"As opposed to me." Volle grinned. "I thought about taking up painting, but I couldn't get the materials. It was challenging enough getting the farm running. I don't know if I could have done it without his help."

"I don't think Tish knows much about farming."

"Then make sure you get good help. We have two good people who are running the farm now. They keep the others in line."

"Oh, I know the importance of good help. Why do you think we kept Alcis so long?" The raccoon had returned from the dining room and was standing discreetly at attention near the main door.

"I know. I miss Welcis sometimes."

"We see him occasionally, and he sometimes asks about you. He knows we keep in touch. We told him you're doing fine, but not much more. It wouldn't do to have the servants gossiping."

Volle nodded, thinking privately that Welcis probably knew more than Tika gave him credit for. Most servants did. Helfer's servant had seen him with Streak and had actually helped him get the documents out of the palace. He was grateful that Caresh was down at Helfer's mansion and not up at the castle. He did trust Caresh; being a fox, he shared a species bond, and being Helfer's servant, he was very well disposed toward Volle. Still, it was best to have him and the little knowledge he had out of the way of Dereath and the hearing.

"Alcis excepted, of course," Tika continued, looking at the raccoon, who gave no indication he could hear them. "He is the soul of discretion."

Volle grinned. "Everyone's servant is the soul of discretion. Welcis knows some things I think he's never told. But then, I did take pains to keep some things from him."

"Ah, and if you kept them from him, I don't suppose you would tell me."

He smiled and shook his head. "I might not even remember now. But they were important at the time, to me."

"Oh, that kind of secret. Those are the best kind."

Volle thought he heard movement in the other room, and he saw Tika's ears swivel too. "Anything else you wanted to ask me about Streak?" he said in a low tone.

Tika shook her head and smiled. "Later. I've already seen the answer to my most important question."

Volle flicked his ears and smiled self-consciously. He looked up in time to see Streak walk through the dining room door, Tish behind him. They paused just inside the room, looking around to take in the situation, and Volle was struck by the similarities, and also the contrasts of white and black fur. They seemed at ease together, relaxed, and for a moment he envied them the bond of their species, which he would never share.

The white wolf smiled at him and came over to stand near him. Tish stood on the other side of Tika until Alcis brought two more chairs over.

As they sat down, Volle reached out and put a paw on Streak's shoulder. "They weren't too hard on you, were they?"

Streak shook his head and smiled ruefully. "I'm okay. Tish knows a lot."

Volle laughed, and Tish and Tika joined in. "I didn't tell you the *entire* history of my family. Just the relevant parts."

"So only the last two hundred years?" Volle said.

Streak patted his paw. "It was very educational."

"Tish always is," Volle replied, and smiled.

"I try to be." The wolf was caressing his wife's ears gently.

"So what can we do around here other than sit around and discuss family history?" Volle asked.

"You make it sound so distasteful." Tish grinned at him.

Tika, leaning back into the caresses, spoke up. "There are some games planned downstairs. We were going to do outdoor games, but it turns out the weather up here isn't quite as nice as in the lower regions of Vellenland."

"They didn't know that?"

"I believe Lord Ikling assumed the King knew the castle was on the top of a mountain, and Alister assumed Lord Ikling would have told them if the castle weren't as warm as the rest of Vellenland. It was a slight embarrassment, but that rolls off your friend's back rather like water does." Tish had an amused smile as he spoke. "For some, the weather isn't a hardship, but there are one or two lords who would gladly pack Lord Ikling in ice for the journey back to Divalia."

Volle grinned. "As you said, I doubt he worries about that too much. So how has this retreat been?"

Tika shook her head. "Not too bad, but not too good. These are supposed to be relaxing breaks from palace life, but a lot of people are annoyed at the weather, and I hear the King has been kept busy with court issues. Not yours, dear. That comes later, and I doubt he's even thinking about that now."

"Where do you usually go on these retreats?" Streak asked.

Tish rubbed his wife's ears a bit more firmly. "We've gone on the last ten or so, and a few before that, and they were all different. Some of them were to warm climates, but the last few were colder. Some were to senior lords, some to junior. The most fun, I think, was when we went to Villutian, because it was beautiful there and Lord Villutian had a circus in town for the entire time that performed a different show every day. Lord Ikling doesn't seem to have realized that he needs to entertain his guests."

"It doesn't help that his mansion is mostly built for weasels." Streak chimed in.

"That's hardly his fault," Volle said.

"No, but it is a good point," Tish replied.

"They did a good job fixing up this place. I can't imagine what it used to be like."

Streak patted Volle's ears. "I'm sure he's trying his best. I just meant it was more difficult because he couldn't host the whole royal party himself. I think we're lucky to be staying down there."

"Undoubtedly you are." Tish smiled. "I think it's a good idea for a number of reasons."

Volle nodded. "More private, for one thing." He turned to smile at Streak, and though the wolf returned his smile, he did it with lowered ears, which Volle found a little odd.

He filed it away to ask about later, because Tish had started talking again. "That, and it keeps you away from the King and politics until your hearing."

"We are spending the day up here."

"Yes, but the perception is that you are staying somewhat removed."

Volle leaned back toward the black wolf. "Are people actually paying that much attention?"

He shrugged. "Some may be."

"Who?" Tish just gave him a stern look in reply. "Well, okay. Alacris. Villutian. Barclaw? Is he here?"

"Yes. But I don't know if he's involved in the hearing. You should look him up, though."

"I will. He's a good bear. Maybe tomorrow." Volle turned to smile at Streak. "They're a gay couple, very nice."

"So his mate is Lady Barclaw?"

"Of course," Tika said. "What did you expect?"

Streak smiled and scratched Volle behind the ear. "I never know how much you're teasing me."

"Lady Barclaw doesn't wear a dress," Volle admitted with a grin.

"He doesn't really have the figure for it." Tika smiled.

"Lady Villutian manages," Volle murmured.

"Now, now." Tika wagged a finger at him. "She's not the only lady at court with large hips."

"Tika, you are just about the slenderest lady at court. Except for Lady Dewanne, perhaps, but even that would be close."

The plump wolf smiled and shook her head. "Poor Dewanne. She made him take her down to the village where there's a hot springs, you know. He hasn't been to most of the meals here."

"I know. Tish told me last night."

"But he didn't tell Streak, did he?" Tika looked at the white wolf, who seemed confused. "Dewanne is the other fox in the peerage."

"Ah, okay." He rubbed Volle's ears and then idly ruffled the fur on the back of his neck. "It must be difficult for you without many other foxes there."

"I got used to it."

"There were other foxes, as I recall, just not in the peerage." Tish grinned at Volle.

"Yes, true." He chuckled. "I should look up Dewanne. Maybe we'll go down to Ikling one day."

Streak nodded. "I'd like that."

They chatted easily for a little while longer, until Alcis reminded them that lunch would be served soon. Tish and Tika retreated to their bedroom to get ready, leaving Volle and Streak in the parlor. Alcis bowed to them and followed the wolves, closing the door behind him.

"They're nice," Streak said before Volle could ask.

"You seem to get along well with them."

"Well, they're wolves, for one thing. That helps." He smiled. "They're also friends of yours, so I don't feel I have to be on my guard all the time."

"Just don't say anything to Tika that you wouldn't want to hear all the servants discussing the next day."

Streak chuckled. "I gathered that." He pulled his chair around to be closer to Volle, so their knees touched. "How much do they know about you?" he asked quietly.

Volle shook his head and put a finger to the front of his muzzle, and Streak nodded. "Sorry."

The fox brushed his knee with a soft black paw. "I just don't want to discuss that here."

"All right." Streak glanced at Volle's pants, then up at the fox's muzzle. "How long will they be?" His tail thumped against the arm of the chair.

Volle grinned, matching the movement with his own tail. "Probably not long enough. They're just getting dressed." But he felt himself respond to the thought. "When we get back tonight, we'll have plenty of time."

Streak nodded, and sat back in his chair. Alcis returned to the room a few minutes later and informed them that Lord and Lady Tistunish would be back in just a moment, then busied himself about the room, wiping down some of the goblets and straightening the furniture. Volle watched him for a moment, looking at some of the small items he picked up and carefully dusted. There was a small wooden box that looked very old, a lacquered wooden jewelry box, and a small mirror, slightly tarnished, surrounded by a decorative floral border in silver. For a moment, Volle regretted the loss of his own possessions, abandoned in his chambers back at the palace. Tish had written to say that he was holding some of the more valuable ones, but the others had been lost.

Alcis finished his dusting, and set about polishing the silver mirror. Volle thought the raccoon was watching them in the reflection, so he whispered half-jokingly to Streak, "I wonder if they sent him back out to watch us in case we did something."

The wolf looked surprised. "How would they have known?"

"They probably wouldn't. I just think it's a funny idea. I did things like that sometimes."

"Back at the palace?"

"Yeah."

"You told me about that one time. Did you do it a lot?"

"What? No, no, just…there were a couple times…but it hadn't been for years." Volle stumbled over the words. "I mean, life at the palace wasn't all about that."

Tish reappeared at the door. "Tika will be joining us in a moment. Are you ready for lunch?"

The dining hall was smaller than the one Volle remembered at the palace, but it was still impressive. The vaulted ceiling rose so high he could barely see the cracks and patches. The walls had been freshly plastered, giving the room a warm feel, and the carpets on the floor were soft under their bare paws. The table was not covered with a cloth, and when he sat down, Volle thought he could tell why. It was a finely crafted table, clearly much newer than the palace, with reliefs around the border and in the center, leaving the serving area flat and polished. From the dark hue of the serving area, he suspected it was mahogany, but the reliefs were lighter, probably of cherry wood. It was an exquisite piece of craftsmanship.

Tish noticed him running his paws over the reliefs. "Beautiful, eh?" Volle and Streak both nodded. "I've been trying to find out who worked on it, but I haven't succeeded yet. Maybe you can ask Lord Ikling. I understand this is to be made a gift to the King when he leaves."

"I'll ask him," Volle promised.

Lunch was a short but filling meal of vegetable soup, honey bread, and some roasted fowl done in a tangy, sweet sauce. A tray of small iced cakes made the rounds for dessert, which Volle noted were slightly stale. "Brought from the palace," Tish said. "There's no working oven to bake in here, apparently. At least they knew that. I shudder to think of what these cakes will be like in a week." He really did shudder, then. "But for now they still taste all right."

"You're doing your best to make sure there won't be any left in a week," Volle observed, which brought a laugh from Tika and a crumb-filled protest from Tish.

Streak grinned, looking around the table at the collection of overweight nobles. He hadn't eaten much of the lunch and had refused the cakes altogether. "They're really okay," Volle said, munching on his second.

"I know."

"Are you feeling okay?"

"Yes." He answered quickly, and loudly enough that the stag and doe to his left turned to look at them. "I'm fine," he said in a lower voice.

The stag caught Volle's eye as he turned to his mate. "Careful," he said, deliberately pitching his voice so Volle could hear. "Don't say anything you wouldn't want repeated to the Ferrenians."

Volle lowered his ears. "Nice to see you, too, Lord Wallen."

"One is tempted to wonder why your *wife* isn't at your side. But then, it seems loyalty isn't your strong suit."

Streak started to growl, but Volle put a paw on his arm. "Maybe you should inform the King that you've already made a decision. You know, spare him the trouble of actually listening to the trumped-up evidence against me."

"Don't think I haven't suggested it," the stag said. He lifted his head, grizzled and noble despite the short growth of antlers atop it. "You may have tricked all your fellow carnivores, but I can see you clearly."

"Good to know your vision isn't failing yet," Volle said affably. "May you continue to enjoy good health."

The stag grunted something, snorted, and turned back to his meal. "Hear that, Tish?" Volle said softly. "You've been tricked."

"Don't pick fights," the wolf replied tersely.

"He didn't," Streak protested.

Tish looked at them and nodded. "Just be as polite as you can," he said softly.

"He started it," Streak said under his breath to Volle as they left the dining hall a few minutes later, Tish and Tika behind them.

"I know. He's always touchy around a lot of carnivores. Feels threatened. Did you deal with many herbivores in the guards?" Streak shook his head. "Them and the rodents...they still get a bit twitchy if there's a confrontation with a carnivore. Wallen's worse around me, because his grandfather, or great-grandfather, was executed by King Bucher. So he has a thing about foxes." He shrugged. "I shouldn't have baited him."

"Did you have to deal with him a lot?"

"Before? No. But there's always someone like him. Always watching what you say..."

Tish put a paw on his shoulder. "You were good at that. It'll come back to you."

Volle smiled. "I don't want it to have to come back. I'm disappointed that it ever left."

"You shouldn't worry," Streak said. "You picked up the farming really quickly. I'm sure you'll get back into the flow of things here in a day or so."

"Thanks." Volle nuzzled him and brushed the wolf's tail with his own.

"You two are so cute." Tika giggled behind them.

They headed for the smaller of the two common rooms, where Tish and Volle set up a chess board and played a relaxed game, watched by Tika, Streak, and Lady Alacris. There were a few other bears in the room socializing or playing games, as well as a beaver couple and another wolf couple. Lady Alacris, a rotund bear, told them that the outdoor games that morning had gone over moderately well, but the wind had picked up as a threatening-looking bank of clouds moved in. "I didn't mind, but some of the others wanted to come inside."

Tish won the first game, Volle the second, but they never finished the third. They had paused to discuss Lady Oncit, because Lady Alacris thought she was perhaps not as happy as Tish and Tika did. She and Tika were arguing when Lord Alacris lumbered into the room. He was portly rather than overweight, but still easily outweighed any of the canids at the small table.

"Hello, dear," he said to his wife as he walked up, then turned to Tish. "Tish, the King wants you in on this next meeting. Probably go all the way to dinner."

Tish got up and nodded. "Excuse me, all. I'll catch up with you at dinner." He started toward the door, but Alacris remained at the table.

"Vinton," he rumbled. "Good to see you here. Best of luck." He extended a paw.

"Thanks." Volle stood, grasped the immense paw, and bowed.

Alacris nodded curtly and then strode out of the room, Tish close behind him. Volle sat down again, feeling a little better. "Good to know he's on my side."

"We never doubted your innocence," Lady Alacris said. "Merro argued against promoting that rat to Lord Fardew, but it didn't do any good."

"Really?" Volle rubbed his muzzle. If Lord Alacris couldn't stop an appointment, maybe he wasn't the closest advisor to the King any more.

"There were few other options. Rallish had disgraced himself—you heard about that, right?"

Volle shook his head. "Hef just said he retired."

"Well, yes. But it wasn't entirely his choice. You didn't know about this, Tika? I'm surprised. I know it was kept quiet, but I didn't think you'd have missed it. He liked rodents, I guess. And one day this mouse, a, er, lady for hire, shows up at the palace asking to see him. She doesn't have papers, so the guards bring Secretary Marsten down to see her, and she tells him she has these papers Lord Fardew left in her room last night and are they important?"

"Oh, no." Tika's paw flew to her muzzle, and Volle winced. He had visited pleasure houses, of course, but he always was very careful to empty his purse of any palace business.

Lady Alacris nodded. "They weren't terribly important, but still. Poor Rallish had to resign. The King needed a replacement quickly, and that rat was the only one with enough experience to fill the post."

"What about the other assistant? What was his name?"

The bear nodded to Volle. "Hialis. He had been there for a couple years and might have been good enough, but he'd just left the previous month on an envoy to the north."

"What happened to the mouse?" Volle thought the whole thing sounded a bit too neat.

"I don't know. I expect she went back to the house."

"That's not all that interesting," Tika said, sounding disappointed. "You did a good job keeping it quiet, though."

Lady Alacris smiled apologetically. "If I'd known you didn't know, dear, I would have told you weeks ago."

A few more people were filing into the game room, some brushing water from their fur. Lady Alacris looked up and waved to one of them, another female bear. "Shira! Bored of the games already?"

"Starting to drizzle," grumbled the bear in reply. "We're going to read some poetry over here. Want to come?"

"As long as you don't read any Dowinna."

Shira shook her head. "It's only...Jellia really likes him."

"All right, then. I'll be there in a minute." Shira wandered off, and Alacris turned to the rest of them. "Tika, will you join us?"

The wolf looked at Volle and Streak. Streak put a paw on Volle's and said hastily, "We were going to take a walk. Go ahead."

"I'll see you at dinner, then." Tika got up as Lady Alacris did. The two males got up and bowed, watching the ladies join a small cluster in another corner of the room.

"A walk?" Volle tilted his muzzle.

Streak nodded. "Come on." He took Volle's paw and tugged on it. When Volle gave him another inquiring look, ears flicking down, Streak smiled briefly in reply. "Come on?" he repeated.

"All right, all right." Volle's tail twitched as they walked out of the game room and along a dark stone corridor. "How do you know where you're going?"

"Following my nose," the wolf said.

"All I smell is wet fur."

"Exactly." He paused at an intersection. "This way."

They came to a wooden door, attended by a foot-servant beaver, who filled out the blue and green uniform rather more than Renaldo the marten did. He was peering out the door, but snapped to attention when he heard them come up behind him. "My Lords!"

"Just wanted to take a walk outside," Streak said. "Is that okay?"

"Of course, my Lord. But...it's raining."

"I know. We have thick fur. Not as thick as yours, but it'll do."

"Yes, my Lord." The beaver opened the door and stood smartly at attention as they walked by him.

The fine drizzle hung in the air, almost an extension of the clouds above rather than a product of them. Volle and Streak looked around the deserted courtyard, and then Streak began to stroll across it.

Volle walked beside him. "Did you just want to walk in the rain?" The courtyard was sheltered from most of the wind, but he could still feel the chilly breeze ruffling his fur. He folded his ears back.

"Not really." The wolf was alternately looking up at the walls surrounding the courtyard and down at the path they were walking along. The courtyard was paved with chilly stone, but a path of soft grass had been laid down—recently, Volle surmised from the freshness of the grass. He looked up at the walls and saw that they were in slightly better shape than the outside walls, probably because they were protected from at least some of the weathering the outer walls had gone through. Though cracked in spots, the stone appeared to be solid, and that was more than a simple restoration could have done. Ancient windows dotted the walls at irregular intervals, and obviously the task of fitting glass to them had been too much to ask. Through the two that were not completely dark, Volle saw the folds of curtains and recalled the thick curtains on the windows in Tish's chambers.

"Helfer said something about the walls, about fixing up this courtyard. I just wanted to see if…" He paused, nose lifted, then padded quickly off the path, toward a corner of the courtyard where the paving was less even. The stones there were cracked, some tilted at noticeable angles, and Volle wanted to call out to Streak to watch his step on the slippery stones, but the wolf was sure-footed and reached the outer wall without stumbling. He beckoned to Volle, then got down on his paws and knees and disappeared into the wall.

Volle hurried to the spot in the wall, slipping once on the wet stone, and dropped to his knees. Ah, there it was—a small break in the wall hidden from the path. He could see through to the other side, where Streak's tail was just disappearing from view as the wolf stood. It would be a tight fit, though not as tight as it had undoubtedly been for the poor wolf. He lowered his head and crawled forward into the space.

Wind battered his ears and eyes as he poked his head out on the other side. He ducked away from it instinctively, only registering that he was looking out over a rocky plateau that ended about fifty feet from where they were. The light mist was blown into his fur and clothes as he crawled all the way through. When he turned his back to it, he found a white paw held down at his muzzle level. He grasped it and used it to pull himself up.

Streak didn't let go, but pulled him into a tight hug. The warmth of the embrace took a moment to sink through the rain-chilled clothes and his fur. Volle rested his head against the wolf's shoulder, and smiled. "You could have hugged me inside," he said, though he suspected Streak had more in mind than just a hug.

The wolf's muzzle touched the inside of his ear, the breath warm on the cold skin. "I know," he said softly, and in a fluid motion sank to his knees. His paws slid down Volle's sides and around to the front of his pants, undoing the lacing and pulling them down. Cold air caressed Volle's sheath as Streak's paws brushed down either side of it, cupping his sac and smiling up at the fox.

Volle curled his tail around his leg, no longer caring quite so much about the rain and chilling mist. He said, without much conviction, "We could wait until tonight, when it's warm."

"Mm." Streak lowered his head to Volle's sheath, which was swelling somewhat, and licked at the end of it. Volle watched the pink tongue slide across his fur, feeling the swath of warmth against his rapidly cooling fur. After a couple licks, Streak murmured loudly enough for Volle to hear, "Where is he hiding?" and slid his tongue into the opening at the tip of the fox's sheath.

Volle gasped and braced himself against the wall. His erection grew quickly, pushing out against the wolf's questing tongue. His knees trembled and he let out a moan. "You never did that before."

"Never had the chance. You were always out of your sheath before I got there." Streak sat back and watched as Volle's erection grew, pushing out of the top of his sheath. He leaned forward again and covered the tip with his muzzle before the cold could register on it.

As his arousal grew, Volle could feel the cold on his bare skin when the wolf's muzzle lifted from it. He barely had time to shiver before it was enveloped in warmth again. The warm tongue and muzzle felt even better on the cold skin; in fact, Streak's muzzle seemed to linger at his tip, letting the air chill the rest of his length before the wolf's lips slid easily down the slick skin.

Volle let his gaze wander to the rocks on the plateau, the cold and misty sky beyond, and back to the pitted and cracked castle walls. He looked up, wondering if anyone could see them, noticing that there were no windows in the outside wall. The wall's stone was cold against his paw, but he didn't dare move it for fear he would fall, as his legs shivered with each slow lick.

Another moan escaped his slightly parted muzzle. The wolf knew just the right places to touch and caress with his tongue. Volle looked down at the white ears, the long, thick muzzle, and the soft paw that alternately cupped his sac and held the base of his shaft. He hoped Streak was warming to the idea of palace life, because Volle wouldn't want to have to choose between the wolf and the palace.

His tail was twitching as his body shivered, the fire within fighting the cold without, and winning. He closed his eyes, letting the wolf's tongue battle the chill and rain. Slowly, the world outside lost focus, his blood raced faster, and when he finally moaned in release, his hips thrust forward, and all he could feel was the warmth of the muzzle around his shuddering length.

He opened his eyes to the cold rocks and the warm smile in the white-furred muzzle below him. "Mmm." Streak was licking his lips, and Volle felt the cold air on his wet erection. He panted, still moaning slightly, and let his tail uncurl from the back of his leg, which felt very warm compared to the rest of him—all except the warm spot at the base of his shaft, resisting the cold still.

Streak washed his length with one more lick, then stood and touched Volle's nose with his own. Volle licked the white muzzle as he pulled his pants up. "What brought that on?"

He couldn't read Streak's eyes, slitted against the wind. The wolf was quiet for a moment, then said, "I always wanted to take you outside on the farm, but I was worried one of the servants would see it."

"Oh?" For the moment, that would do. He rubbed his paw against the bulge in Streak's pants, warm despite the chill of the cloth. "And did you want me to take you outside, too?"

The grin was answer enough. Volle turned the wolf so the wind was at his back and used his body as shelter. He knelt, adjusting his position to find something comfortable on the uneven ground, and wrestled with the wet lacings of Streak's pants, picking at them with his claws until they fell apart. When he pulled them down, he saw that he would have no chance to explore the inside of the wolf's white sheath: his erection was already showing, dangling invitingly in front of his white shirt. Volle grinned, letting the cold air and mist brush over it, then teased with his tongue, applying warmth here and there in places he knew were sensitive. He had to fold his ears back against the mist, but he wasn't listening anyway. He was smelling the wolf's musk, stronger in the damp air; he was feeling the familiar warm length with paws and tongue; he was seeing the bright pink against white and the small beads of moisture that formed on it when he let the mist collect.

Just as he had tuned out the world when the wolf's muzzle was on him, so he focused his awareness on the pleasurable task before him. He left the wolf's erection out in the cold until he heard a soft whimper; then he relented and lowered his warm muzzle over it. Even though the air was cold and his knees were starting to hurt, even though he was outside in an unfamiliar place, the feeling of the slick hardness against his tongue was reassuring, and the warm scent that made its way to his nostrils was a good one. He slid back and forth along the wolf, just playing with his arousal and feeling it grow. A paw gripped his shoulder; he brought up his own paw to circle the furry sheath and pull it down, giving his long muzzle more room to play along it.

His wet tail wagged against his legs after several long, pleasurable minutes of this. Streak was starting to pant, and Volle was ready. He adjusted his licking, curling his tongue around certain spots and pressing up as his muzzle withdrew, speeding up the strokes and squeezing slightly with his paw. The wolf responded with a harsh gasp and more pressure on his shoulder.

Volle savored every inch of the hard, musky length in his muzzle. The voices in the back of his head returned, asking whether he could remember what others had felt like and tasted like. He remembered some, had forgotten others, couldn't even remember whether he'd tasted some others. He recalled a pub in Caril, the dark warm space under a table, a wolf whose name he didn't even know sitting with an ale in one paw while Volle's muzzle worked on his member, out of sight of the other patrons. Funny that he should remember that one, but Streak reminded him of that wolf, or at least his memory of that wolf, though he never had before. Maybe it was the exposure, being outside where anyone could potentially discover them.

Would he ever taste anyone else again? Did he ever want to? The questions fled from his mind as the hot shaft thrust harder into his muzzle, back and forth. He held the wolf's tight rump in his other paw, feeling the movement of the tail as the hips pushed through his lips, the long maleness rubbing against his tongue and palate, moans and scent and the fingers on his shoulder all becoming sharper. The musky scent of sex filled his nostrils and muzzle, and moments later he heard a raspy howl and tasted the salty sweetness on his tongue as Streak shuddered and came.

Warm liquid on his tongue, warm hardness between his lips, warm body beneath his paws. The cold outside battered at him but could not get in. He swallowed, with difficulty, around the hard shaft, not wanting to let it go, and coaxed the last drops out of it with his tongue, while over his head ragged pants mixed with the wind's gusts.

His black fingers drifted over the now-wet fur on the wolf's sheath and sac, tracing furrows with his claws that the water held apart. Letting the spent member slide out from between his lips, over his tongue, he nuzzled the wet fur and licked it, tasting Streak, tasting the rain, and tasting the slowly fading arousal. The musk was still strong on his tongue as he sat back and then stood, smiling up at the wolf. Streak's tongue still hung from his muzzle, but he drew it back in and gave Volle a warm kiss, pulling him tightly against him.

The embrace lasted for the space of several heartbeats. Finally, Volle drew his muzzle back and licked the water from Streak's whiskers. "We should get back in," he said. "We're going to have to clean up for dinner."

"Or we could stay out here," Streak said. "Just leave our clothes behind, live naked like animals in the mountains."

Volle tilted his muzzle, flicking his ears to rid them of water. "But animals don't get to eat roasted fowl and little cakes. And they don't get to screw on perfumed sheets."

"Mmm. I guess we should go back, then."

"You should pull your pants up first. Otherwise the ladies will be all over you."

Streak grinned at him, pulling his pants up over Volle's paw and threatening to lace them up before the fox could get his paw off of the wolf's sheath. Volle managed to extricate his paw, and crawled back through the hole, Streak batting at his tail as he did.

They found Tika still in the game room, reading over poetry with several other ladies. She gasped at their wet and scuffed clothes and fur. "You're soaked!"

"We went for a walk, and sort of lost track of time." Volle lowered his ears and grinned sheepishly.

"I'll bet." She eyed them. "You'll have to use our bathroom to clean up. Tell Alcis to find you some new clothes somewhere, too."

"We can send down to Helfer's place for them," Volle said. "If someone goes on horseback, they can get there and back in time. I'll do that on the way up. Thanks, Tika. We were hoping you'd offer."

"All right, all right, but hurry. Dinner's in an hour."

They stopped at the front gate to leave their request with Renaldo, telling him that they would be in Lord Tistunish's chambers. Then they ran upstairs, ignoring the looks they got from the noble lords and ladies they passed.

Alcis's frown was harder to ignore, but Volle tried anyway, winded and half-giggling. "Tika said we could use the bath. And we've sent for replacement clothes."

"Yes, sir." The raccoon's ears were half-lowered in frosty disapproval, but he led them to the bathroom anyway. "Please leave your clothes here, near the door. I will have them attended to."

"Thank you, Alcis." Volle closed the door and grinned at Streak, who was already starting to strip. The bathroom was small and was powder-only, but that was okay; they had enough water in their fur. Beside the main basin of soft talcum was a shelf of three small bottles, fragrances to be added to the powder. The shelf above that one held two brushes, both wood, one with a mother-of-pearl inlay. They had been carefully cleaned of all residual fur, but Volle guessed the fancier one was Tika's.

While he looked around, Streak had shed all his clothes. He grinned at Volle and wagged his tail, getting his hips into the motion. The black streak gleamed darkly against his wet white fur. "I guess I get to go first."

"Go ahead," Volle laughed, struggling with the soaked laces of his pants. Streak climbed into the basin and lay on his stomach, rolling back and forth and watching Volle undress. Volle made a show of sliding out of his pants once he finally got them undone, turning and letting his shirt dangle over his sheath. Slowly, he unfastened his shirt, pulled it over his head, then dropped it by the door and clambered into the small basin on top of the wolf.

Streak giggled and struggled, easily overturning the lighter fox and rolling him in the powder. "Look at how dirty your fur is," he said, rubbing powder all over Volle's stomach while the fox squirmed and giggled. "Especially here." His paw lingered around Volle's groin, rubbing more gently there.

"You're filthy there," Volle countered, bringing his own paw up into the wolf's crotch and rubbing up and under his tail. "Got to get you all clean for dinner."

"Mmm," Streak grinned, and leaned in close for a kiss, and they held that position for a nice long moment. Volle pressed his hips up against the wolf's, feeling the stirrings of arousal again, though he knew they didn't have enough time to do anything here. He wasn't sure he had the energy anyway.

Afterwards, they took turns brushing each other off on the cloth in the corner, getting all the powder out of their now-dry fur. Streak was just working on Volle's bushy tail when Alcis opened the door.

"Your clothes have arrived," he announced, setting them on the small stand next to the door and picking up the wet clothes from the floor.

"Thank you." Volle covered himself, but Alcis wasn't looking.

"Lord Tistunish requests a word with you before dinner, Lord Vinton."

"All right. I'll be out in ten minutes."

They dressed quickly and hugged before leaving the bathroom. Tika slipped in to freshen up before dinner, and Streak waited out in the parlor.

"What did you want to talk about?" Volle eyed Tish warily. The wolf's ears were down and his scent carried overtones of concern.

"Did anyone see you?" He shot the question at Volle quietly.

At first, Volle thought he meant that afternoon with Streak. Before he could even wonder how Tish would know, he realized the wolf meant during his theft of the documents. "I'm pretty sure they didn't. Why?"

Tish paced the room. "Dereath has a witness."

"What?"

"A witness. He submitted a brief for the hearing today and it includes a witness. We asked around and he did bring a guest up from the castle. Another rat or something. We thought it was just his prostitute. Could it have been one of the servants from the palace? We tend not to notice them."

"Tish, I notice everyone. You know that."

The wolf sighed. "I know." His ears flicked back. "What could this person have seen?"

Volle shook his head. "I've no idea. I could swear there was nobody in the office. I mean, I would have smelled him. Or her."

"All right. Well, let's not worry about it." He rested a paw on Volle's shoulder. "Just enjoy your dinner. I hate not knowing, though. Ah, ready to go down, dear?"

Tika had emerged from the bathroom and was gathering a few things from the bedroom. She had tied a pink silk ribbon over one ear to match the pink gown she wore. "You men are done talking?"

"Yes, we're ready." Tish smiled and extended a paw through the doorway.

Tika took it. "Then I'm ready too. Let's go down."

They collected Streak in the parlor and proceeded down to the banquet hall, where nobles were already gathered. The two servants standing in front of the doors scanned the crowd, and a few minutes later, one raised his horn and blew a short call to attention. The other spoke loudly once the crowd had quieted down.

"Lords and Ladies! His Majesty King Barris and her Majesty Queen

Murinne welcome you officially to the King's Annual Retreat. Their Royal Majesties hope that everyone will enjoy this time away from the palace, and return refreshed and relaxed."

"I'll certainly be glad to get back," a bear with her back to Volle muttered.

"Lord Vinton and…guest." The badger announcing the names paused before the last word as if unsure what it meant.

"Just me?" Volle hissed to Tish as he started to walk forward. Usually the younger nobles were announced in groups.

"Smaller crowd." Tish grinned at him and shoved him forward.

"I thought I got to be Lady Vinton," Streak said as they walked toward the doors. His ears were partway down, and Volle thought, *he can't be that upset about it.*

"That's if we're officially mated."

"Oh."

They passed through the doors as the servants bowed to them, and entered the small dining hall. The table had been cleared and re-set, and at the head of it sat the King and Queen.

Streak fell a step behind Volle as they walked up the table. Volle was afraid the wolf was going to hang back, but he kept pace. The royal couple looked up as they approached, and their expressions betrayed no emotion when they glimpsed the fox and wolf. Volle looked behind them, where the King's personal servant and the head dining steward, a hare and badger respectively, stood, but their expressions were carefully neutral as well. There was no indication of the prevailing attitudes toward him.

"Lord Vinton." The King was wearing casual robes, still fancier than most things Volle owned. They were dark blue with white trim, velvet and lace, hanging elegantly off his frame. He also wore a simple silver coronet that offset the graying fur on his muzzle. His eyes were sharp and clear, betraying no emotion as they searched Volle's.

Volle bowed deeply. "Your Majesty." Behind him, Streak also bowed; he could feel the wolf's muzzle brush his tail.

"We are pleased that you chose to attend, Lord Vinton. We hope the outcome of your hearing will prove your loyalty." If he believed the words he spoke, Volle couldn't tell. The inflections were carefully neutral.

"I have every hope that any doubts his Majesty has about my loyalty will be dispelled soon," Volle said. "I have never wished any harm to his Majesty."

Barris smiled then. "Enjoy the dinner, Lord Vinton."

"Thank you, your Majesty." Alioran, the badger, stepped in front of him and guided him and Streak to a place on the table while the servant outside announced, "Lord Ikling and guest."

Volle and Streak took their seats as Helfer and Laya were shown into the hall. The weasel gave Volle a harried-looking smile as he walked up to greet the King and Queen. Volle caught only a few words: "grateful for your hospitality" and Helfer's reponse, "my pleasure to serve." When they were done, Alioran led them to the seats on Volle's right. Laya was about to sit next to him, but Helfer waved her to the other seat and slipped into the one next to Volle.

"I hope I never see that Canis-cursed coyote again," he grumbled. "Nine hours. *Nine* hours!"

Volle had been about to ask where Lyfar was, but it was obvious Helfer didn't want to talk about it. "You spent the whole day with him?"

"Not just with him: with him *and* his assistant going over every detail of the next eleven days." He growled. "As if I'm supposed to know where to get a hundred fresh green plums this time of year. And when I tell them that, they act like I'm holding out or hoarding them for myself or something. You should have heard Jerish trying to catch me out."

"Catch you out?"

"He'd wait until we were talking about something else and then casually say 'So what about those plums, Lord Ikling?' Like I'd suddenly forget and say 'Oh, the ones in my bedroom?' Gah!" He suddenly looked up and gave a friendly wave, and Volle saw Lord Alister and his assistant walking down the other side of the table. The coyote raised a paw in acknowledgement, but the mouse ignored him, more intent on the royal figures.

"I don't like that Jerish," Helfer said. "Far too intent on meeting the King and proving himself. Alister's good enough, if always overwhelmed. But that mouse…" He glared at the mouse's back and then sighed. "I'm glad you're here, Volle. If something like this happened and I didn't have anyone to talk to, I'd have to go run around the palace five or six times to get it out of my system. Speaking of which, feel like going for a run tomorrow morning?"

"Absolutely. Can we bring Streak?"

"If he wants to come, sure."

Volle turned to ask Streak if he'd be interested, and the wolf nodded, already listening with a cocked ear. He nodded to Helfer. "I think we'll both join you."

"Good. Can't wait. I haven't had a proper run since this retreat started. My legs are getting all weak."

"I doubt that," Volle said, and just then Tish and Tika sat down on the other side of Streak.

Tish, seated closer to the white wolf, said to him and Volle, "Welcome to the first official banquet, m'boys. Should be a good one. Hello, Lord Ikling. We all appreciate your hospitality, and especially you taking in these two troublemakers."

"Oh, they're no trouble, sir," Helfer said with a grin. "Not too much, anyway. And Weasel knows we could use a bit more trouble around here, eh?"

"I'm sure Weasel thinks so," Tish retorted, "but I'm not sure His brothers would agree."

"Well, then let them host this damn retreat." Helfer was grinning, but there was a ferocity to his words that spoke to the underlying truth.

"Well spoken." Tish grinned and turned to Streak to ask him a question. Volle listened to the first part of it, then was caught up in more complaints from Helfer.

The weasel talked about Alister through the appetizer course, even with his mouth full of the fruit-and-quail egg mixture that he told Volle was a specialty of his land. He ran out of steam at about the same time he ran out of appetizers, though, and his usual good humor took over. "You know," he said as the servants were clearing the plates and setting down salads with tangerine slices arrayed at their sides, "at least it's over now. I'll probably have to see him every day, but hopefully not all day any more. So maybe I can relax and enjoy myself."

"I hope so," Volle said with a grin. "Isn't that the point of this retreat?"

"Maybe for them. I've never been on one, and likely won't be on another. You have to be important."

"The whole year is a kind of retreat for you."

Helfer gave him a wink. "You could look at it that way. I guess this isn't too bad a tradeoff, then."

The salads were delicious, seasoned with a blackberry vinegar that Volle remembered from palace meals. He crunched lettuce and carrots between his teeth and looked around the table for the first time. He recognized most of the lords and ladies, and from the looks of it, most of them recognized him. A few met his eyes, and others turned quickly away when they caught him looking at them. Easy to pick me out with Lord Dewanne still gone, he thought, and it was as he was looking around Laya to see if Dewanne really was gone that he caught his first glimpse of Dereath.

The rat was eating quietly, and as far as Volle could see, he was alone. He looked well-groomed, and Volle could just see the shoulder of the blue vest he wore over his white shirt. That was a bit of a shock in itself; as long as Volle had known him, Dereath had always worn black. For a moment, he wondered if he were mistaken, if perhaps Lord Asith had been moved up in the peerage. But no, the rat turned his head, saw Volle, and there was no mistaking the dark eyes and crooked smile.

"Don't worry," Streak said behind him. "He won't hurt you."

Volle turned, slightly surprised. "What?"

"He won't hurt you," Streak repeated. "He'll lose the hearing."

Tish was listening now, too. Volle said gently, "I appreciate that. But I'm not convinced it'll be easy."

"He doesn't have any witnesses, does he?"

Volle and Tish exchanged a look. Tish said, "Apparently he does. We're not sure exactly what the witness knows."

Streak looked down and mumbled something. Volle didn't catch it, but thought it sounded like *won't be a problem*. He put a paw on the wolf's shoulder. "Hey, don't worry. We'll win." He had to stop talking as the servants chose that moment to clear his plate and bring the main course out to the table.

The spices on the roasted pig made Volle's nose twitch. They were also familiar from his time at the palace, not as different as the meal he'd had at Helfer's the previous night. The vegetable dishes were very small, he noticed, probably because most of the important lords were carnivores. He noticed only a scattering of herbivores around the table, Lord and Lady Wallen among them.

Before anyone could begin eating, Lord Alister stood up. "Welcome to their Majesties' Annual Retreat, hosted this year in Vellenland. It is perhaps a trifle colder and wetter than we had anticipated, but I'm sure we will be able to make it a relaxing time for all."

He was met with a little grumbling, but most of the table clapped politely.

"And now," Alister continued, "let us drink to the health of their majesties."

"To their health," the crowd called as one, raising glasses and drinking.

"Thank you," King Barris said, nodding to Alister and rising as the coyote sat down. "My friends, I would like to propose another toast, to Lord Ikling and Governor Burren for their hospitality. Your health." He raised his goblet, looking down at Helfer.

Volle realized that Governor Burren was on the other side of Laya. He hadn't noticed him before. He raised his glass with the rest, grinning at Helfer. The weasel, aware of the King's eyes on him, just looked modestly down at his plate, but he kicked Volle under the table. The toast was somewhat less enthusiastic than the previous one, but nobody refused to drink, at least.

And then they were allowed to eat. Of course, the food was delicious. Helfer chewed a mouthful of roast pig and sighed happily. "You know, I like my local cooking, but I'm used to this."

Volle nodded. "It's good to taste the palace food again. But I liked your cook's food too."

"She's good, but this...ooh." Volle could see Helfer's little tail wagging against the chair.

He grinned and turned to Streak, but the wolf had only taken a couple bites of his food and was staring at his plate. "Are you feeling okay?"

Streak nodded. "Just ate too much earlier. Not really hungry."

Volle wrinkled his muzzle, concerned, but just then Helfer tugged on his sleeve. "So, Volle, listen, I suggested to Alister that maybe one of the days the lords could travel down to the orchards. Nice weather, we can get them freshly picked fruit, and hopefully it'll make them feel better about the retreat. What do you think?"

"Oh. Sounds like a good idea." Out of the corner of his eye, he noticed that Tish was talking to Streak, so he focused on Helfer. "Say, shouldn't your steward be planning this sort of thing?"

"Don't worry, I'm going to go back to Huster with a long list tonight and he'll be up here tomorrow. But it looked better for me to be here today."

"Looked better? Since when do you care about that?"

"I don't. But I have to stay on at least a neutral footing or I might get kicked out of the palace. Or at least lose my quarters. I wouldn't want that."

"No, I guess not. Say, do you know who's in my old quarters now?"

"Nobody. Nobody new has come to the palace, so yours are still empty. They did take most of the stuff out of them, looking for…you know. But I guess they didn't find anything."

"Nothing to find," Volle said simply and truthfully. There were things he prized, a couple of them, but he kept nothing around that would incriminate him.

Helfer looked at him and grinned. "Oh, yes there was."

Volle blinked, about to take a drink of wine. "What?"

"You still had two of my P. Zinsky books."

Volle choked on the wine and laughed. "I'm sorry!"

"Somehow," Helfer said, "they knew to bring them back to me."

"I don't suppose anyone else reads gay romance novels."

"Some of the ladies do." Helfer was grinning. "You'd be surprised at the number of requests I got after they were returned to me. I'm a regular library."

"Like who?" Volle lowered his voice.

Helfer tapped his muzzle with a finger, signifying quiet, and indicated a few of the ladies around the table by pointing his muzzle. Volle chuckled. "My, my."

"Interesting, eh?"

"Just wondering if it means they're unhappy."

"I don't think so. I just think they're curious about two males getting frisky."

"You could ask. Maybe you could invite them along to the Staff and sell tickets."

"If I needed the money." Helfer grinned.

They were finishing up the main course by that time, and only a few minutes later the servants reappeared to clear the table and bring out a cheese course. Volle turned to Streak, but the wolf's attention was elsewhere as Tish explained the different kinds of cheeses to him. He turned back to Helfer and kept talking to him through the cheese course and dessert, turning every so often to smile at Streak and ask if he was enjoying the meal.

As the servants were clearing away the remains of the rich berry-topped butter cake with cream, Lord Alister stood up again and cleared his throat. He was near the head of the table, and the King and Queen turned to look at him, as did the rest of the nobles.

"Lords and ladies, I hope you have enjoyed this meal. There is a group of merchants currently waiting in the reception area, to the right as you exit the banquet hall. They were chosen by the King's staff, and without their help, we could not have prepared this banquet for you. If you would like to pass by and express your appreciation in person, I'm sure they would be grateful." They would also love the chance to acquire more noble patrons, Volle knew. Abandoning their shops in the city for two weeks or more cost them, and most merchants did so with the hope of gaining new clients from the peerage.

"We will announce tomorrow's activities and have the information distributed to your servants. Until then, have a good night." He was cheered again as he sat down. A moment later, the King and Queen rose and lumbered toward the exit, pausing occasionally to talk to people along the table as they passed. When they reached the doors and passed through them, the crowd began to rise themselves.

"We're going back to the mansion very soon," Helfer said. "If you're leaving soon, I'll go back with you. Otherwise I'll have to go with these two." He tilted his head toward Laya and the governor.

"I think we're leaving pretty soon," Volle said. Streak raised a paw, but Tish cut in before he could say anything.

"I think you should come with us to see the merchants, Volle."

"I'm not sure…all right." Volle changed his answer when he saw the look in Tish's eyes. "Can you wait that long, Hef?"

"I think so. I'll just send these two on their way." He turned back to Laya and Burren to do that.

"Shall we?" Volle gestured to the three wolves on his left.

"Certainly." Tish downed the last of his sweet wine and rose, then helped Tika to her feet. They followed the three weasels out of the dining room and gathered in the entrance, where Volle could see the crowd of merchants off to the right. Glimpsing a familiar pair of ear tips, he suddenly knew why Tish had wanted him to see the merchants.

"Hef, you coming?"

"Sure, why not."

Streak spoke up unexpectedly. "You know, I'll just…meet you here afterwards. Okay?"

"That's fine. You'll be here?" Volle looked at him curiously.

The wolf seemed to be looking at part of the crowd of nobles, or trying to avoid looking at part of the crowd. "Yeah. I should be. I might wander a bit."

"We won't be long." He was starting to feel a little concerned, but didn't want to make a scene in front of the others. He touched his nose to Streak's and smiled to let him know he trusted him, and got a weak smile back. "See you back here, then."

Streak nodded, and raised a paw. "Back here."

As they walked away, Volle looked back to see the wolf, but he had already disappeared into the crowd. He thought he saw a white head walking quickly away from the banquet hall, but then he bumped into Helfer, and by the time he could look back around, the head was gone.

He recognized a few of the merchants, but one in particular was a welcome sight. Volle approached the table, glancing only briefly at the samples of finely crafted glassware on it. He smiled as he extended his paw to the tall rabbit behind the table. "Mister…Marik, isn't it?"

Reese smiled. "It is indeed. I am flattered that you remember me, Lord Vinton."

"How could I forget such a worthy merchant, whose wares have been invaluable?"

"You flatter me further."

"I would be most interested in seeing what new wares you have. I have been out of the city for quite some time."

Reese held up a goblet. "This is one of our newest creations. We have a very talented glass-shaper now, and he only sells his wares to us. Nowhere else in Divalia will you find workmanship like this."

"It looks exquisite," Volle said without taking his eyes from the rabbit's face. "I'd be delighted to own a set."

"We can discuss it later," Reese said. "You will be here for the whole retreat?"

"That is still my intention, yes."

"Excellent." Helfer had moved on to the next merchant, and Tish was deliberately stalling behind him. Reese leaned a little closer and whispered, "Good to see you again. You doing okay?"

"Same here," Volle whispered back. "Avery didn't tell me you'd be here. Yes, fine. Dereath has a witness. We don't know more than that."

"I almost wasn't here. Invitation came at the last minute. Would've had to send Sherr." Sherr, the porcupine, didn't have cover as a merchant to get him into the castle.

"That would've been tough. Glad it's you." Volle leaned back and smiled, raising his voice. "I'm staying down at Lord Ikling's mansion. Perhaps you could bring some of the samples by and we could discuss my purchase?"

"Delighted, my Lord." Reese didn't say it with the mockery he usually did when he had to address Volle with that title. "Day after tomorrow? We will be busy with services tomorrow, of course."

"That would be fine." Volle extended a paw, and Reese shook it, returning Volle's smile. "Until then."

He hadn't seen Reese in over a year; before that, he'd met with him every other week to pass along information from the palace. And before that, they'd been roommates at the Caril Academy. Volle found it hard to remember those days now, but Reese's bucktoothed smile was like a shock of memory, bringing back the meetings in Divalia as well as the late nights in their tiny room at the Academy.

Lingering would probably be suspicious, so he moved on just as Tish, no doubt thinking the same thing, joined him at the table. "Merchant Marik," he said, extending a paw. "You have some new wares."

"Indeed," Reese said smoothly. "We have been waiting for a month to show these new goblets off."

Volle raised a paw and moved on, his tail arched jauntily as he rejoined Helfer at a silver merchant's table. "Good evening, my Lord," said the goat, nostrils flaring.

"Lovely silver," Volle said absently, picking up a sugar bowl that was identical to one he'd seen at lunch. "I loved the settings at dinner." The merchant smiled and bowed.

"That rabbit interested in you?" Helfer asked with a nudge. "Maybe he wants company? He's pretty cute. Looks a bit familiar."

"Oh, all rabbits look familiar to you," Volle said lightly, putting the bowl down and smiling at the merchant. "I don't think there's one in Divalia you haven't ogled."

"Probably right," the weasel said cheerfully as they moved on.

In twenty minutes, they'd seen all the tables. Volle examined the merchants' wares with only half-feigned interest. So much finery, so many niceties; though he didn't really own many things of value, he did admire craftsmanship and enjoyed seeing it, a taste that six years in the palace had cultivated in him. Cloth especially, because of its texture and variety of scents, held interest for him, and he stopped with Tish and Tika in front of a fabric merchant examining scraps of fabric with different colors and scents for several minutes. The wolves were similarly entranced by fabric; their sense of smell was as keen or keener than Volle's.

The foyer outside the dining hall was mostly empty when they returned; specifically, it was empty of white wolves. Volle glanced around, checking down the corridors. "Where could he have gone? Who else does he know at the castle here?"

"We were going to retire. If he's in our chambers, I'll send him down," Tish said. "I wouldn't worry too much. He's probably just lost. He'll find his way back here eventually."

"I hope so." Volle leaned against a wall, ears flicking around to catch any sound.

Tish rested a paw on his shoulder. "You're best just staying here and waiting for him. He knows you're waiting here."

"Yeah."

The black wolf smiled. "He's fine, Volle. Really."

"I know." But he couldn't stop his tail from twitching.

"I'll stay with you," Helfer volunteered. "Got to wait anyway."

"Don't you two get into any trouble," Tish said with a grin.

Tika took Volle's paws and rubbed muzzles lightly. "Good night, dear. Lovely to see you back again. Don't worry about your wolf. He's still trying to get used to all this palace life. He'll be fine."

"Thanks, Tika." Volle nuzzled her back and smiled.

Once the wolves had left, Helfer asked one of the servants to fetch two chairs from the dining room. The badger brought them out immediately, and the weasel sank into one. Volle took the other, ears still swiveling around.

"Maybe he found a bit of action," Helfer grinned.

"I doubt it." Volle lowered his voice as a pair of lords walked by from the merchant room. "We had a bit before dinner."

"Really? Here in the castle? Where?"

"One of the holes in the wall you mentioned to him. We snuck through and had some private time outside."

Helfer grinned, wagging his tail. "In the wind and rain?"

"Yes, wind and rain. We had to clean up for quite a while afterwards."

"I bet." Helfer chuckled. "You did a better job of it than I did at the summer festival a few years ago. Remember?"

Volle laughed. "How could I forget? None of the canids wanted to sit near you."

Helfer patted his knee. "But you did."

"I held my breath the entire time."

Remembering the past distracted Volle from the worries of the present. He tried to keep from worrying, but he couldn't keep himself from glancing at the corridors every few seconds. The last of the nobles left the merchants' area, and the merchants packed up and left, and still Streak didn't appear. Volle tried to maintain his good humor, but as the minutes wore into what he was sure was over an hour, his tail twitched more and more impatiently. He got up and paced, despite Helfer's plea for him to sit down.

"He wouldn't do this, Helfer. Something's happened to him."

"What could happen?"

"Dereath could happen." He remembered the rat's smirk at dinner. What if he'd found Streak wandering the corridors alone? The wolf could defend himself, but not if he were jumped from behind. He suppressed the macabre scenarios whirling through his mind. "I'm going to go look for him."

"Volle…"

"Stay here, and if he shows up, tell him to wait. I'll be back."

"Why don't I go, and you wait here?" Helfer got up from his chair.

"Because I have better hearing and smell than you do."

"Fine. Rub it in."

"Sorry, Hef. But…" His ears perked. "There's something going on outside. Hear it?"

"How could I, with my small ears?"

"Stop pouting and come on." He waved Helfer forward and the weasel joined him, straining to hear. As they moved down the corridor, the sounds became louder: many people talking, different species. Volle couldn't make out any words.

They got most of the way to the large junction, coming up to a large stag in guard's uniform standing about twenty feet down the corridor. He raised his lance sideways as they approached. "Please don't go any further, my Lords."

"What? What's going on?"

"I've been ordered to let nobody pass, in either direction."

"Why?" Volle strained to hear what was going on ahead. He could make out several bears and wolves moving back and forth, but nothing else.

He shook his head. "King's orders, my Lord."

Helfer suddenly jumped up and waved. "Archie! Hey!"

A weasel, walking through the open area, turned and started walking toward them. "Evening, Lord Ikling."

"Archie, what's going on?"

The weasel looked tired and harried. He had light brown fur, but his dark eyes were dull and sad. The Vellenland arms adorned the shoulder of his jerkin, which looked like it had been thrown on hastily over his wrinkled shirt. He was a little taller than Helfer, meaning he was still two feet shorter than Volle or the deer. When he reached them, he looked up at them, then at Helfer. "Sorry, Lord Ikling. Captain Nero's ordered everyone to stay where they are for the moment until we can get this sorted out."

"Get what sorted out? What *happened*?"

Archie sighed and ran his claws through his already disheveled head fur. "There's been a murder."

"*What?*" Helfer's voice was so high it was almost a squeak. Volle just stared dumbly at the weasel, heart racing.

"A murder. I know. Listen, my Lords, do either of you know a female mouse?" They shook their heads.

"No," Helfer said softly, and Volle relaxed.

But Archie didn't move on. He looked at them both, and said, "How about a male white wolf?"

Chapter 5

*V*olle dropped to his knees, his tail curled tightly around one thigh. Helfer put an arm around his shoulder. "Yes, Archie," he said quietly. "We know a white wolf."

"All right. I'll have Captain Nero come over as soon as he's free." He turned and started to walk away.

"Wait," Volle croaked. Archie turned around. "Was he...who was murdered?"

"Don't know. I just got here. Cap'n just told me to ask everyone if they know a male white wolf or a female mouse."

"Send him quick, would you, Archie?" Helfer squeezed Volle.

Archie just nodded, and walked away.

"Not again," Volle whispered.

"Maybe it's not him," Helfer whispered unconvincingly.

"Hef, I can't go through that again. I..."

"Come on, let's go back." Helfer looked at the guard as he helped Volle to his feet. They walked back toward the chairs.

"If it's Dereath," Volle said, abruptly, "I don't care what happens to me. I will find him and I will tear his throat out with my teeth."

"If it's him, I'll guard the door while you do it. But let's just wait for Nero. Did you know he was here?"

Volle shook his head. "No idea. Does he always come along on the retreats?"

"I don't know. I've never been on one either."

The pictures were returning to Volle's head, more disturbing than ever. His memory dredged up another weasel, Tella, sitting in a carriage and saying, ferociously, "He's *dead*." It had taken him years to get over that death — those deaths — and another one now would be more than he could take.

"Who's Archie?" He had to keep his mind away from the pictures it was insisting on flashing at him.

"My 'Captain Nero.' He heads up all the detective-work and investigations in Ikling. Usually he doesn't have to go out himself, but for something big..." Helfer trailed off.

"So you trust him?"

"'Course I trust him. He caught the fellow who was killing all the mice here six or seven years ago. I never told you about that? It was bad. But he found the guy."

"Think he's better than Nero?"

Helfer laughed, a short nervous squeak. "Well, no. I'd have to be a fool to say that. But the two of them working together should be impressive.

They'll catch..."

Volle covered his muzzle with his paws again and folded his ears back. He had enough time to imagine the worst over and over again, torturing himself and trying to build up enough resistance to be able to deal with the confirmation, when he finally heard it. And desperately, passionately, hoping he wouldn't need it. *Please, Fox, please, Wolf,* he prayed silently, *don't let it be him.*

Footsteps echoed down the corridor. He smelled a large wolf and Archie the weasel, and lifted his head.

Captain Nero was an imposing wolf. Large and round, with a shaggy mane of brown fur jumbled around his pointed ears, he presented the appearance of a hedonist who had enjoyed too many dinners and disdained the trouble of presenting himself neatly. His dark green eyes were the only part of him that did not fit that picture. They scanned every person and thing in the room he stood in constantly, never missing a detail. His attire was much as Volle had remembered it: royal blue vest stretched over his rotund frame, shirt tucked carelessly into his overstretched pants. He would almost be comical, except for those piercing, deadly serious eyes.

They examined Volle now, then slid over to Helfer. "So you two know the wolf."

Volle nodded. "What's...is he...?"

"What's his name?"

"Streak," Volle whispered numbly. They didn't know his name. So he was a corpse. He felt his fingers twitch.

"What kind of name is that, Archie?" The weasel shrugged. "That's all he told us, too. Well, if that's his name, then that's his name."

Volle felt his heart unclench, and he made a small sound that brought curious looks from both wolf and weasel. "He's alive."

"Of course he's alive. He's the suspect, not the victim. Archie, didn't you tell them that?"

"I didn't know until five minutes ago," the weasel said defensively.

"Observe the emotional strain Lord Vinton is under, Archie. Lord Vinton, we must apologize. Though I am afraid the truth is not much better."

The words seemed to be oozing into Volle's consciousness with the speed of honey. "Suspect?"

"How long have you known him?"

"For a year. A bit longer than a year. What do you mean, he's a suspect?"

"In a moment." Nero held up a large paw. "Did he seem at all preoccupied or distressed tonight? When was the last time you saw him, and where?"

"Here, right after dinner. We went to see the merchants, and he said he'd wait here. He said he might wander off, but that he'd be back."

"Did he seem distressed?"

"He was quiet," Helfer put in. "But I think he was disoriented. It was his first time at a royal banquet."

Archie seemed surprised. "How long have you known him, Lord Ikling?"

"Only a couple days." Helfer glanced at Volle. "I talked to him extensively yesterday. I must say I can't believe he would do anything like that."

"Belief, sadly, is a luxury I do not have," Nero said pompously. "I deal only in facts."

"What does he say about it?" Volle asked through gritted teeth.

"He claims innocence. But he was found with the body, and his scent is all over the weapon that killed her. Nobody else was in the whole suite of rooms."

"Whose rooms?"

"Mine." Dereath strolled down the corridor, smirking at Volle. He was wearing the same outfit he'd worn at dinner—no, the vest was green instead of blue. But the white shirt, the leather pants, and the smug expression were all the same. He walked up beside Archie and stood there, arms folded. "I was looking for you, Captain, and what do I find? The motive." His high, nasal voice grated on Volle as it always had.

"Pay attention, Archie," said Nero. "It sounds as though Lord Fardew is going to educate us."

Volle saw Dereath's whiskers twitch, but the rat didn't react otherwise. "Lord Vinton is on trial later in this retreat," he snapped. "I had concealed a witness to his crime without which his chances of escaping justice would be vastly improved. Today I was forced to reveal the witness to the court, and tonight, the fox's lover kills the witness. Coincidence? You tell me, Captain."

"It would be extraordinary if it were. Don't you think, Archie?"

"I would think so." The weasel was looking only at Dereath.

"Lord Ikling." Dereath looked across Volle at Helfer. "I am glad to see you here as well. I am taking the suspect into royal custody, since the victim was part of a royal proceeding. Your local authority is superseded."

"Fine," Helfer snapped back at him. "Just make sure nothing happens to him, so when he's proven innocent, he can be released."

"Oh, he won't be proven innocent." Dereath wore a nasty smile as he turned back to Volle. "The pendant of fortune swings back and forth, *Lord Vinton*, and though you have benefited from it in the past, it is swinging back my way. Deny it if you wish, but you cannot avoid it."

"What business did you have with me, Lord Fardew?" Nero had waited patiently through this outburst.

"I wanted to tell you that the prisoner has been moved to the north tower. It's the most sound, and we have a lock on the door and a guard. When you need to interrogate him further, go there. The guard is instructed to let you in as he concluded, "and *only* you."

"What about me?" Archie folded his arms.

"Yes, yes, I'll tell him to let you in too." Dereath looked up at Nero. "Please finish your report as soon as possible. I'd like to have the execution as soon as you've established his guilt."

Archie and Helfer both straightened indignantly at that, and Volle stood from his chair, but Nero quieted them with a paw. "I hardly think that the King would appreciate an execution during his retreat. I'm sure the sentence can wait until we return to Divalia."

"It's been quite the retreat so far, hasn't it?" Dereath said with a sneer at Helfer. "Rain, cold, and murder. I'm surprised the food wasn't spoiled." He turned on his heel and walked quickly down the corridor.

Silence remained in the small room, until Helfer spoke. "I shouldn't have had them fix all the holes in the floor. It would be nice to think he could drop into one."

"He's not guilty." Volle remained standing, looking at Nero, but as he said the words he was starting to wonder, really wonder. Streak wouldn't kill anyone, but what if he thought he would be saving Volle? What if he felt the need to protect him?

"That remains to be seen," Nero replied. "I have not looked at all the facts yet, and I hate to form an opinion without all the facts. Make a note of that, Archie."

"Yes, sir. I never would have thought of that one." The weasel didn't make a move.

"Might I trouble you for one of those chairs, my Lords? I am quite tired of standing. Ah, thank you." He settled himself into Volle's chair. "Now, Lord Vinton. Can you recall anything else that might have a bearing on the events of tonight? Any response to Lord Fardew's allegations?"

Volle paced back and forth, tail lashing. "He only found out about the witness at dinner. He couldn't have found out where she was and killed her in that time. Could he?"

The large wolf stroked his whiskers. "If you are asking whether that is possible, then I would have to answer yes. Wouldn't you think so, Archie? But if you are asking whether it is probable, that I will reserve judgment on. Though the fact that he was found with the body certainly increases the chances." He resettled his bulk. "Now, if you don't mind, my Lord, I would like to continue asking questions. Is it true you and he were lovers."

"Yes." Volle stared defiantly at Nero, then at Archie, who appeared completely unfazed by this. "I brought him here because once I win the hearing, I intend to bring him to the palace."

"So what Lord Fardew said was true?"

"Which part?"

"Any of it."

Volle shrugged. "I already told you we're lovers. And I know he did have a witness. We found out about it this afternoon."

"I thought you said 'Streak' found out about it at dinner."

"Lord Tistunish told me this afternoon. He heard it from Lord Alacris. But Streak wasn't there. He didn't find out until we were discussing it at dinner."

"How did it come up at dinner?"

Volle thought back. "I spotted Dereath—Lord Fardew. And that reminded Streak of the hearing, and he asked if Dereath had any witnesses."

"That's an odd thing to ask."

"Well, he didn't say it like that." Volle looked away from the wolf's penetrating eyes. "He said…Hef, do you remember what he said?" The weasel shook his head. "He said something like 'Well, he doesn't have any witnesses, does he?' Like that."

"And you said…"

"We told him we'd just found out about one."

"What did he say then?"

"I don't know. Nothing." Volle remembered the desperate mutter (*won't be a problem*), but he couldn't bring himself to mention it to the detectives. He hadn't heard it clearly. What if he were making it sound sinister to himself in retrospect? Or—worse—what if he weren't?

"I see."

There was a long pause, during which Volle felt his heart constrict again. "Can I see him?" He tried to keep the desperation out of his voice, but he couldn't keep his tail or ears up. He needed to see Streak again, to look into his eyes and see the truth there.

Nero shook his head slowly. "You heard Lord Fardew."

"But if I were with you…he said the guards would let you pass."

The wolf turned to the weasel. "What do you think, Archie? Are you moved by the pleas of young love?"

"I don't see that it could do any harm, sir."

"Perhaps not." Nero looked at Volle, stroking his muzzle. "A short visit, under my supervision. Perhaps he will be more forthcoming to you than he was to us." He sighed and pushed himself out of the chair.

"What did he say to you?" Volle asked as he followed the wolf along the corridor. Behind them, Helfer and Archie hurried to keep up.

"Nothing, really. He says he didn't kill her, that he was in those rooms for a meeting, but he won't say with whom or about what."

"Maybe he just wanted to look around to see if there were anything that would help me. And he stumbled on the body."

Volle was surprised at how quickly the old wolf could move. He brushed them past the deer guard, pausing only to ask him directions to the north tower. Then he was off again through the central room and down the indicated corridor. He waited until they were past the small crowd of guards and nobles before replying. "The body was discovered by a chambermaid who heard a scream. She rushed into the parlor and saw the white wolf standing just inside the bedroom."

"What does he say happened?"

"He says the bedroom door was closed. He heard the scream and didn't know if he should investigate it right away, but decided to go in case someone was in trouble. He opened the door, looked in, and saw the body and blood. While he was waiting to decide what to do, the servant found him there." When Volle didn't reply to that, Nero glanced at him. "You must admit, Lord Vinton, it does not sound very likely."

It didn't, but Volle didn't want to think about that. "Did he notice any other scents in the room?"

"I will ask him."

They walked the rest of the way in silence. At the north tower, a burly cougar stopped them. "Sorry, my Lords. I'm under orders to let only the Captain through."

"They're with me, Arnut."

The cougar shook his head. "Nevertheless, sir. Lord Fardew's orders."

Nero turned to Volle, and for the first time his eyes did not appear to be searching for information. "I'm sorry, Lord Vinton," he said. "I would like to speak to him for a few minutes. If there is a message you would like to convey, I will deliver it."

Volle looked at the steps leading up into the tower, then at the cougar guard. He imagined Streak sitting alone at the top of the tower, confused and scared, and part of him wanted to dash up the stairs past the guard. "Tell him…" He paused to steady his voice. "Tell him I love him. Tell him I believe him."

"All right." Nero turned to the guard, who produced a large black key from his belt and handed it to him. The wolf turned to Volle as he mounted the stairs. "I'll be right back."

There was nowhere comfortable to sit. Volle leaned against the wall opposite the guard, while Helfer and Archie stood near him. "It's Dereath," Volle said to nobody in particular. "He wants to isolate us."

"Why?" Helfer asked. Archie followed the discussion but remained silent.

"I don't know. Maybe just because he can. Out of spite."

Helfer nodded. At Archie's questioning glance, he explained, "Dereath's had it in for Volle for years. For both of us, kind of. More for him, though."

"He doesn't waste any time, does he, Hef?" Volle stared at the floor. "Barely two days, and already he's found a way to make me miserable."

"Listen." They both turned to Archie. "If he really is innocent, Captain Nero will figure it out. He's the best detective Tephos has ever seen, despite his quirks. He's booked hundreds of criminals. Only one unsolved murder in his twelve years there."

"Secretary Prewitt." Volle said the name almost without realizing it.

Archie folded his ears back and narrowed his eyes. "Yes, that was the one. Still, I'm just glad at the chance to work with him on this one case. It will be educational and, my Lord, will help me enforce your laws better here in Vellenland."

"I'm all for that." Helfer nodded. "But first get to the bottom of this one."

They heard the grunting and heavy footfalls as the detective descended the stairs. He nodded to the guard, then joined the three of them and addressed Volle. "He is still in good health. He told me to tell you that he loves you too." He stroked his whiskers. "I am going to ask Lord Fardew to allow you to visit with me. I think there are things he might tell you that he would not tell me."

Volle sighed. "I don't know what he could be hiding."

"If you did, he would not be hiding it very well, would he?"

Volle had no answer for that, and after a moment the large wolf patted him on the back. "You two can go on back to the mansion. Archie, escort them to the door, would you? Then join me back at the junction. We will need to finish the questioning quickly lest the nobles become restless." He walked off down the corridor without waiting for an answer.

"I think they're already beyond restless, sir." The weasel turned and gestured for Volle and Helfer to follow. They walked behind him, following Nero's rapidly retreating back.

"You don't have to take orders from him, Archie," Helfer said. "You're a captain of my guard, too."

"I know, my Lord."

"If it bothers you, I can have him stop."

"No, my Lord. He's brilliant. I'm proud to be working alongside him." He grinned. "I can handle him, I'm sure."

Helfer scratched his head and shrugged at Volle. "Well, all right. But bring any complaints to me."

Archie nodded. "Thank you, my Lord."

They reached the junction, where several royal guards were still guarding the various corridors. Two of them were talking to nobles, no doubt explaining why they couldn't wander the castle freely. Nero had joined one group and was gesturing back toward the corridor. His booming voice echoed throughout the chamber. "I assure you, my Lords, it will not take much more of your time, but I am authorized by the King to take these actions."

Volle ignored the voices and the general commotion, and the two weasels kept quiet until they reached the main gate. Only then did Helfer ask, "So what does the great detective think of all this?"

Archie shook his head. "He hasn't told me."

"Orders you around like a servant and he hasn't confided in you? Well, what do you think of it all?"

The weasel looked at Volle, then turned his head. "I don't know yet, my Lord."

"You think he's guilty." Archie didn't respond. "Archie?"

"My Lord," he began, and then caught Helfer's eye. "I'm not yet completely convinced. But you must admit that the alternative is certainly less credible: that he stumbled onto the body by coincidence seconds after the murder."

"What if it wasn't coincidence, Archie?" Helfer thrust his muzzle forward. "What if he were set up to be there at the murder scene?"

"Set up, my Lord?" Archie's voice was faint. "By whom?"

"Well, Dereath."

"So he killed his own witness just to put the wolf in jail?" But Archie was no longer looking at Helfer. He was looking directly at Volle, and Volle didn't like the glint he saw in the weasel's eye.

Helfer didn't notice it. "Maybe. He's done crazier things in the past."

"My Lord...my Lord, your carriage is here." Whatever Archie had been about to say, he kept back.

Renaldo was leading the small buggy up to the gate, and he waved cheerfully at Volle, but his smile died as he drew closer and saw the fox's lowered ears and tail. His own tail drooped, and he lowered his head. "Your buggy, m'Lord."

"Thank you, Renaldo." Volle turned to Archie. He wanted to protest what he thought the weasel was thinking, but he still felt numb inside, and he didn't have the energy for it. "And thank you, Archie, for your help tonight."

"Good night, my Lords." Archie bowed slowly.

They got into the buggy slowly and deliberately, sitting across from each other in the dark interior. Volle didn't say anything as the shadows of the main courtyard gave way briefly to the reflected torchlight of the gate, then to the darkness of the mountain. From his window, he watched the glow of the torches at the castle dwindle and finally disappear as they rounded a bend in the road.

When he turned back to Helfer, he saw that the weasel was watching him. He leaned forward and put a small paw on Volle's knee. "They'll find the real killer. Nero's the best, and Archie's pretty good too."

"Oh, Hef." Volle tried to keep his voice steady. "What if he did do it?"

"He said he didn't. Why would he?"

"To protect me from Dereath. Once he heard about the witness at dinner."

Helfer tilted his head. "You're innocent, right? So what could the witness have seen?"

"Nothing. But that wouldn't stop Dereath, would it?"

"I guess not." He scratched his chin. "But how would he know how to get to Dereath's quarters, or even know that that's where the witness was?"

"I don't know." Volle sighed miserably.

"You don't really believe that, do you?"

"I don't know what to believe, Hef." The clatter of the wheels outside grew louder as they traveled over some scree; the buggy bounced and then settled back into a more quiet, even ride. "He was talking about how he wanted to help, wanted to be a part of things here, and wanted to take care of me. He just might have run off to do what he thought would be a noble deed, protecting me from evil."

"What if he did do it?"

Helfer was silent. After a moment, Volle went on. "You won't mention this to Archie, will you?" He saw the weasel shake his head in the dim light. "Thanks."

"Will you be okay? If it turns out..."

That was the question Volle had been avoiding in his own thoughts. He chewed on one of his claws, trying to control the turbulent emotions inside him. "I don't know, Hef. I'll have to be, won't I?"

"I mean, after...and now..."

"After Xiller. I didn't think I'd feel that way about anyone again. I deliberately tried not to. Someone you care about is a weakness, you know? A way they can get at you." A weakness a spy could not afford. Though he couldn't say that to Helfer, he suspected the weasel didn't really understand what he meant anyway. Helfer had loved his parents, Volle knew, but he didn't think Helfer understood romantic love. The weasel wouldn't go so far as to suggest that Volle was better off without Streak; he understood how others felt and respected it. But he viewed it much as he might view the habit of bathing three times a day: an excessive indulgence.

"But we were thrown together, and then ran off together, and this last year, away from the palace, has been...nice. Peaceful, you know. I thought it might always be that way. So I didn't worry so much about what I was feeling, or what he was feeling."

Helfer's eyes gathered light from outside and gleamed as he looked at Volle. "So why did you come back?"

"You have to ask? I missed it. You, the palace, Tish, even the food... everything."

"And you told him you did."

"Streak? I think he could tell."

Helfer just nodded, but Volle knew the conclusion he was drawing: the wolf had perhaps sacrificed himself so that Volle could return to the palace that he missed so much. And Volle wanted to tell him that he was wrong, that Streak didn't care that much about him or wasn't that resourceful, but he found that he couldn't. The wolf had a big heart and was smart enough to be able to find Dereath's quarters, but what would he do then?

Could Streak actually kill someone? Volle didn't know. They'd never been in a situation that demanded killing. How many people ever were? He clutched his head, and Helfer, probably pitying him, remained quiet until they reached the mansion.

Once they were standing in the courtyard, he patted Volle's arm. "I'll walk you to your bedroom." He dismissed the waiting foot-servant with a wave. Volle followed him through the courtyard, looking up at the decorations and architecture whose small size seemed to accentuate the feeling that he was in a dream, even though he'd seen them before. They hadn't come to the guest entrance for some reason, so he had to duck his head as he walked through the beautiful wooden doors, and had to stay crouched over while Helfer led him down two corridors and out into the guest wing. The feeling that the world was closing in on him abated somewhat when he was able to stand upright.

"Listen," Helfer said when he'd walked Volle into the guest suite and closed the door so they wouldn't be overheard, "everything's going to work out fine. He didn't kill that mouse and Nero will prove it. You guys will be screwing in the rain again in no time."

"Thanks." Volle knelt to hug the weasel. "And thanks for staying with me tonight."

Helfer hugged him back. "Hey, what are friends for? And as your host, too, I felt responsible for you. Speaking of which…are you going to be okay tonight? If you don't want me to stay, I can arrange for some company for you."

The thought of another person in his bed was a jolt, but he kept his ears from betraying his surprise. "No thanks, Hef. I just want to get to sleep."

"All right. I'll call you for services tomorrow."

"Thanks." They embraced again, and then Helfer left, closing the door behind him, and Volle was alone.

He hadn't been this alone in a very long time. There had been times when he'd been apart from Streak, but he'd always known the wolf would be there when he returned. He'd been alone in the dungeons in Divalia, but that had been over a year ago, and the circumstances were different; he'd thought he would soon be dead, so he was almost relieved to be alone. And before that, he'd had Helfer and Seir and the others. But he had felt like this for a short time, he realized as he walked slowly back toward the bedroom. He'd felt like this when he'd heard of Xiller's death.

The image and scent of the cougar returned unbidden to him now, and he knew why. Xiller had died because he wanted to do something noble, something heroic, and he hadn't understood how he'd been used. And Volle was now afraid that Streak had wanted to do something noble, something valiant for him, and hadn't understood what he was getting himself into. And he was worried that it would cost the white wolf his life.

He sat down on the bed, fully clothed. He could smell Streak in the room, although the bedclothes had been changed. He found the shirt the wolf had worn the previous day, when they'd arrived—the journey seemed so long ago now. Bringing it to his nose, he inhaled deeply and closed his eyes, letting the scent remind him of the wolf.

Comforted, he lay back on the bed and let his thoughts return to that evening, and the murder. If Streak hadn't done it, then it was an extraordinary coincidence. Such a thing was possible, of course, and it was possible as well that the whole thing had been orchestrated by Dereath. His claws dug into his palm pads as he considered that possibility. Or Streak could have killed the mouse because he wanted to protect Volle. That didn't feel completely right to him, but he couldn't make himself believe that it had been a coincidence, nor that Dereath had devised an intricate scheme that involved watching Streak or luring him to his chambers somehow and then killing the witness he'd brought along, upon whom his case rested (perhaps).

Those possibilities whirled back and forth in his head for several minutes, each one seeming improbable as he examined it, but he couldn't decide which was *least* probable. He wished he knew more about the facts of the case. As it was, the one point that he kept coming back to was that he didn't want to envision Streak killing anyone.

Whatever the truth was, Volle had to face the possibility that he would be without Streak for a long time, possibly forever. Even if the wolf were not guilty, he might be convicted if no other suspect were found. Dereath would certainly do his best to see that happen. And what would Volle do then? Could he ever open his heart again?

Maybe he wasn't meant to have love. Twice he'd fallen, and twice been ripped from the one he'd fallen for. That was not a good omen. After the first time, he'd decided that his duty to his country and people was more important than his heart. Now, it felt as though the gods were reinforcing that lesson. He raised his eyes to the ceiling and the powers that lay beyond it. "Fox," he whispered, "I'm sorry. If I wasn't meant…" But he couldn't finish. He didn't feel sorry, he felt miserable and alone and the emptiness of the bed seemed to stretch on forever. His breathing quickened and he felt an itching around his eyes. Reaching up, he found that his fur was wet with tears.

He clenched his paws into fists on either side of his head, staring as if he could see the gods in their celestial homes, and cried, *"What do you want from me!?"*

The desperate passion abandoned him as quickly as it had come, leaving him crying quietly on the bed. He held a pillow to his muzzle and rubbed his eyes with the rough fabric. There was nothing he could do except lie here and mourn. He wanted desperately to see Streak, to ask the wolf what had happened, and to hold him again, but that would have to wait on Nero's ability to extract permission from Dereath. His hearing was not for several days. The only thing he could do was dream about masterminding a daring escape for Streak, followed by a cross-country flight back to their farm.

It was only fantasy, but it was a comforting fantasy nonetheless, and variations on it helped him relax still further. With Streak's shirt still clutched in one paw, he drifted into an uneasy sleep.

Chapter 6

*H*e was dreaming that Streak had picked a flower from the castle garden, but the flower was actually somehow the heart of a court noble, and while it lay bleeding in the wolf's paw, the noble died. They were coming to get him, and the wolf was looking at Volle with wide, frightened eyes, and he kept saying, *I didn't know, I didn't mean to.* Volle could see the noble, even though the body was inside and he was out in the garden; it was an indistinct form with grayish-brown fur and a medium length tail, and he thought, if only *I could see who it was, I could tell Streak that it would be okay.* He asked someone to turn the body over, but they said, *We can't move it until the hearing. It's a witness.*

Daylight intruded on his dream. He clutched at the fragments of it, trying to grasp Streak's paw as he came awake, but his paw slipped on the blood and the wolf fell away from him.

Helfer was sitting on the bed beside him, a paw on his shoulder. "You slept in your clothes."

Volle shook his head and flicked his ears back and forth, trying to wake up. He'd slept on one of his arms, and it was now sore and buzzing as he moved it about. "Yeah. Um." His muzzle felt thick and unwieldy. "Morning, Hef."

"Hi." The weasel's ears were forward, his muzzle creased in concern. "How're you feeling?"

"I'm okay. I dreamed…" He stopped and rubbed his eyes again. The dream, or sleep, had muted his anguish from the night before. Streak would be all right, and there was nothing he could do about it yet. Not until after services. "Doesn't matter. Are we going for that run?"

"I wasn't planning on it. We don't have much time before services. Do you want to?"

Volle yawned and stretched. "Might do me some good. Where are the services being held?"

"The church in Ikling. We had to do some renovations to it—bring in an Ursa statue, split up the sections, and so forth. Usually we do two services: one for Weasel, and one for everyone else."

"Have to find Cantors from somewhere?"

"Of course not. We have all six here. The other five just aren't usually that busy. They take turns doing the non-Weasel service and then they administer individually as needed. But today they'll all be doing a service. Hallis is very excited about it. He's the Canis Cantor—a fox, even. You'll like him."

Volle smiled. "Okay." He stood up and stretched again, reaching up and standing on tiptoe. Even with his arms fully outstretched, he was a foot shy of the ceiling. "So let's go run."

"I'll change and meet you back here in five minutes." Helfer got up and trotted out to the main room.

He was as good as his word. Volle had barely gotten into the short pants he'd brought, which were more like a skirt, very open and loose, when Helfer slipped back through the door, wearing a similar pair. He ran in place while Volle closed up the wardrobe and stretched his legs.

"We don't have a lot of time," Helfer said as they walked out through the guest entrance. The wind was chilly, but it felt good on Volle's bare fur. He was reminded of his afternoon with Streak yesterday, and fought the urge to get in a buggy and go up to the castle. It wouldn't do any good.

"So just once around the mansion?" Volle looked around at the sprawling structure.

"Once around the field." Helfer pointed across the road from the gate, where the grass in a large meadow reflected droplets of sunlight back at them. "We'll have enough time to get around, clean up, and meet the nobles down at the church."

"Sounds good." Volle followed him across the dirt road, watching the faint imprints of their paws in the damp ground. "Do you usually run here?"

"I used to. I don't run a lot when I'm visiting here. We could run around the mansion, but there are a couple parts where the rocks are sharp and you have to pick your way across. Don't have time for that now." He launched into a quick jog without any more preamble, setting off across the grass, and Volle joined him.

The wet grass chilled his paws at first, but he got used to it quickly. The sun hadn't quite had time to warm it, but it did warm his fur, especially the legs and arms where his black fur heated up more quickly than his body's orange or his chest and stomach's white. The breeze and the movement of air as he ran countered that nicely, as his arms and legs moved more than any other part of him. He let his tail stream out behind him, enjoying the flow of air through it, and emptied his mind, focusing on the physical sensations of running.

Part of what he'd enjoyed most about running at the palace was talking to Helfer, but he didn't feel like saying anything and the weasel didn't seem eager to break his silence. So they ran the perimeter of the meadow accompanied only by the chirps of birds and the soft, regular rhythm of their feet. Once or twice, Volle thought it would be nice to have Streak with him. Otherwise, he tried to clear his mind.

All too soon, they arrived back at the gate. Both were panting, but Volle nodded when Helfer said, "Could've done two more times around. But we're out of time." He squinted at the sun, then at the large clock inside the guest entrance. "Fifteen minutes?"

"All right." Volle nodded. "See you back here then."

Back in his bathroom, Volle dropped some scented powder in his brush, a trick he remembered from his Academy days when he woke up late after a long night and didn't have time for a full bath. He spent the most time on his tail, because most everywhere else would be covered by clothes, and tried not to miss Streak, who always enjoyed brushing his tail for him. He remembered to rub some powder just at the base of his tail, and then hurried to pull on clothes. He was just fastening his shirt when Helfer returned.

"The buggy's waiting," he said, gesturing with a grin. Volle grabbed a velvet vest from the wardrobe and followed Helfer outside.

"I'm impressed. I thought it'd take you fifteen minutes just to get that tail of yours in order."

"Jealous?" Volle slid one arm through the vest and tried to get the other in place as he jogged after Helfer.

"Hey, it's not the size, it's how you use it." Helfer grinned at him.

The familiar repartee came as naturally as if he'd never left the palace. "Believe me, I know how to use it." He couldn't find the other armhole of the vest, so he let it hang off his shoulder as they left the palace and ran to the waiting buggy.

"Where's Laya?" Helfer asked the footservant as they climbed in.

"She went on ahead, my Lord."

Helfer nodded and sat down in the buggy. When the door closed, he looked across at Volle. "Good. Whenever I visit now, she's always hanging on me, and she gets terribly upset if I don't act like I want to be around her."

"Don't you?"

"No. I don't especially like her."

"She's the mother of your son." Volle tried to contain his mild shock, looking away as he got his arm through the stubborn vest and settled it properly.

"Yes, one of them, and she never lets anyone forget it. Keeps trying to set herself apart from the others…anyway." He waved a paw. "You know what I'm talking about. You have your own wife."

"Ilyana's not that bad, really." He let his tail fall to the seat and crossed one leg over his knee, rubbing the fur on his foot. "I'm just not attracted to her."

"Of course not. But I figured if you liked her, you'd have brought her to the palace. You never really talked much about her."

Volle shrugged. *I didn't want her around to know about my spying.* "We got married so she could have my son, and she did that, and then she left. She was happy in Vinton. She's only here now because of my hearing."

Helfer stared at him. "She's here?"

"Yeah. Oh, didn't I tell you?" The weasel shook his head. "She was up at Tish and Tika's place yesterday morning when I got there. Yesterday? Yes, that's right. Seems longer."

"I know what you mean. So how'd it go?"

Volle shrugged. "She was mad about my being arrested because it put her and Volyan in danger."

Helfer snorted. "Typical. Didn't care about how it affected you, did she?"

"I...don't know."

"Did she bring...what was his name? Volion?"

"Volyan. Yes. They'll probably be at services, in fact."

"Please do introduce me."

Volle smiled, easily able to tell that Helfer was just being polite. "I will."

The buggy clattered down the road, and very soon they were passing white stucco buildings, isolated at first, then closer together. The six spires of the church were smaller than Volle had expected, but he was still able to see them from a good distance away. They surrounded a large red-tiled dome, a construction Volle hadn't seen before. Of course, he was only familiar with Caril and Divalia, cities of stone built to withstand chilly winters and warm summers. The warm climate of Vellenland had engendered an entirely different style of architecture.

As they approached, the air in the carriage became noticeably warmer. They passed the Cup and Barrel, and soon ran up against the back of another carriage, slowing to a crawl. Helfer grinned at Volle. "Guess we're not that late after all." They opened a door and poked their heads out, Volle peering over the shorter weasel, and saw four carriages waiting to enter the large plaza in front of the church.

Helfer ducked back inside immediately, but Volle stayed outside, raising his nose to the wind and drinking in the scents. Overwhelmingly mustelid, as he'd come to expect, but the warmth of the lowlands held more scents in the air than the cooler mountain air. The town was rich with the smells of produce, dust, cloth, oil, horses, and smoke. He smelled ale and cooked meat from a pub around the corner, but couldn't identify which meat or which type of ale.

The carriages ahead of them moved, so he pulled his head in before their buggy lurched forward. The door swung closed with a slam as he sat back on his seat.

Helfer grinned at him. "Sometimes I wish I had your nose, and sometimes I'm glad I don't. The streets here smell bad enough to me."

"Bad?"

"You know, all the horses and the garbage."

Volle grinned. "I can smell a lot more than that. I'm guessing that they closed the church off to most of the people, because there's someone doing laundry nearby, and the pub is serving lunch around the corner."

"There are usually two services anyway," Helfer said. "But yes, this service is just for the nobles."

The carriage pulled up again, stopped, and a wolf in the uniform of the royal guard opened the door. "Good morn, my Lords," he said. "Papers, please?"

They handed him their papers. After a cursory glance at each, he handed them back and waved them along. The buggy clattered over the paving of the plaza and stopped behind two others in front of the church. The bells started to ring just as Volle and Helfer stepped down to the ground.

The front of the church, in contrast to most of the surrounding buildings, was made of limestone, pitted and scarred with age. The seven figures over the entrance were familiar, though he noticed that the Mustela figure was more obviously a weasel than he'd seen elsewhere, and was in the favored position to Gaia's right. The Cathedral in Divalia had six larger and more ornate House statues, but they were not part of the structure, and whenever a new king was chosen, a team of workers went through the laborious task of moving that king's House statue into the favored position.

Helfer saw where he was looking. "They're fixed," he said shortly. "Alister was worried about that, but I told him there's nothing we can do about it."

Volle nodded. "It's a beautiful church, though."

"I love the Cathedral, but this has its own charm. It's smaller and closer. It is, however, very warm. I've fallen asleep more than once." He grinned.

"Try not to sleep this morning. I don't think the King would approve." The main doors of the church looked to have been newly crafted, with the same workmanship as the table in the dining hall. The reliefs depicted the Birthing in one panel, in which Gaia was cradling a litter of six cubs, and the Legacy in the other panel, in which she was instructing the six Ancestors in the care of the world she was bequeathing them. The words "Love One Another" were set above the scene in an inlaid lighter wood. Volle ran a paw along the smooth finish as he walked in under the watchful eye of a cougar guard, and admired the detail in the inlays.

"This looks like the work on the table in the dining hall," he whispered to Helfer as they walked past the door.

"Same artisan," the weasel replied. "He was delighted to be doing the work, especially knowing the King would be seeing it. He did the bureau in my chambers, too, remember that?"

Volle did, but didn't comment further as the warmer air of the church enveloped him. Though it was larger than the dining hall, it was not as well ventilated, and the scents of all the attending people, trapped inside, circulated and mingled and assaulted his nostrils. It took him a few seconds to get used to the dizzying flood of aromas, and then he was able to look about and notice the structure of the building he'd stepped into.

The room's floor was hexagonal, and there was no doubt as to which of the Houses the front segment was dedicated to. A large statue at the other end of the section depicted a cheerful, naked male weasel, about twice life size, with his paw outstretched as though he were strewing flower blossoms over the congregation. To the left and right, wooden screens hid the rest of the church, but Volle knew he'd find one sixth dedicated to each House. The wooden screens looked new and temporary, but the pews in front of them were ancient and weathered. Volle wouldn't have been surprised to find that they were the originals from the first erection of the church.

The pulpit where the Cantor stood was of the same limestone as the outside of the church, a gracefully arcing balcony set about five feet above the floor. It was vacant at present, as were about half the pews, but the rest were filled with weasels and some skunks, dots of black in the uniform brown.

"There's Laya." Helfer sighed and waved, and began trudging toward the front pew. "See you after."

"Thanks." Volle headed to his right. The Canid section was around the other side of the wooden screen, already populated with several people he knew. The pulpit at the front looked similar to the one he'd seen in front of the weasel statue, but there was no statue behind it. Instead, a lovely painting of a stern-looking wolf in a flowing robe had been placed there. The glow around the wolf's fur and the deliberate blurring of his muzzle markings made it evident that he was Canis, though Volle had never seen that particular painting before.

He made a short obeisance to the painting and then walked down the rows of pews. He caught Tish's scent before he saw the wolf, but before he could turn to join him, he caught another scent and the hiss of his name. Turning, he saw Lord Dewanne and Ilyana waving to him, and a small cub next to Ilyana looking at him with a curious tilt to his muzzle.

He slid into the space next to Ilyana, behind Lord and Lady Dewanne, and arranged his tail behind him, aware of the cub's inquisitive gaze but waiting for Ilyana to make the introductions. She did so quickly.

"Volle, this is Volyan. Voly, this is your father."

The cub got down from the pew and walked carefully around Ilyana's knees. He was wearing a simple tunic, belted at the waist, and nothing else. Volle could see Ilyana's blood in the graceful sweep of the cub's muzzle, or at least the promise that it would grow into a graceful sweep, but the large ears reminded him more of himself. The wide eyes he smiled down into held a fox's natural curiosity and the cub's own innocence, as well as poorly-hidden enthusiasm. And his scent and the cant of his ears told Volle that he was nervous, though he was controlling his tail's twitching fairly well.

"Pleased to meet you, sir." He had a slight lisp, but it was obvious he'd been practicing the speech. He extended a short paw up to Volle.

Volle smiled and clasped the paw. He'd last seen the cub at the age of one and a half, a meeting Volyan certainly did not remember. "I've been looking forward to meeting you for a long time," he said with a warm smile.

The cub's muzzle broke into an answering smile, wide and joyful. He clambered up onto Volle's knee and then hesitated, ears a-twitch, until Volle pulled him close and hugged him.

He'd never hugged a cub of Volyan's age before, but he found it surprisingly easy. He smiled over the cub's shoulder at Ilyana, and noticed that she had a strange expression on her muzzle. She was smiling, but her ears were half back and her eyes were distant. He only saw the expression for a second; when she noticed him looking at her, the smile filled out and her ears came up.

"Volyan," she said gently, "get down. It's time for services to start."

"Yes, mum." The cub disengaged his arms and leaned back, and tried to get down. When he slipped, Volle caught him and helped him down. He kept his wide eyes and warm smile on Volle as he edged back across his mother, then stopped and looked at her as though an idea had just occurred to him. "Can I sit here?" He pointed to the small space between Ilyana and Volle.

"Of course." Ilyana smiled at Volle, but her ears slipped back a notch again. She slid away from him, and only as she moved did he become aware of something in her scent that he hadn't noticed before. It was very faint, and disappeared before he could identify it. Then Volyan was climbing up onto the seat and sitting neatly between Volle and Ilyana, and he forgot about the scent.

The cub kept his tail still and kept his paws folded neatly in his lap. Volle could tell that he was trying to keep his attention forward, but his ears kept swiveling back to his side, and Volle caught him sneaking peeks backwards even after the Cantor had started speaking.

The Cantor was a tall, stately fox, and Volle was impressed by his quiet assurance as he surveyed the crowd. His voice, when he began the greeting, was light enough that Volle could hear the voices of the Mustelid and Felid Cantors on either side, but it had a musical quality that he found entrancing. He almost missed the words for listening to the cadence and rhythm of the fox's voice, but he knew the greetings by heart anyway and repeated the responses faithfully along with the rest of the foxes, wolves, and coyotes in attendance.

They sang a prayer to open the service, and then the Cantor began the reading. It was from the Book of Gaia, which Volle knew well, and concerned the Sacrifice. He told of Gaia's coupling with Skye, Lord of the Heavens, while He was bright, Her terror when She realized that He was also the Darkness of Night, and of Her determination to keep Her children with Her, safe from the Darkness. "And though each of Her children brought Her great delight, and Her loneliness was abated, so did Gaia look around and see that the world was dry. She required nothing to live, but Her children required food, and water, or they would die. And so of Her tears She drew water, and of Her flesh She drew food, and thus were Her children sustained.

"But as they grew, even Gaia's tears and Gaia's flesh could not keep them nourished. So She gathered Her children together and said, Behold, my children, I give to you the world. I must go into the world so that you and your children may thrive. Therefore, do not weep for my going, for I will always be a part of the world you live in, and you will always feel the love I bear for you."

As he spoke, Volle kept glancing down at Volyan. The cub's attention was captured by the Cantor for a few minutes, then it wandered and he glanced back at Volle, snapping quickly back to the front when he saw that Volle was watching him. Volle grinned and tried to pay attention to the sermon, but couldn't keep from looking at the cub's ears and the solemn expression on his muzzle.

The Cantor described Gaia's last walk through the world after She had bid goodbye to her children, and how She gave of Herself piece by piece. "To the bare rocks She gave Her fur. And with each hair She shed, a patch of grass sprang up, sweet and green. And the creatures that lived upon Her fur became the creatures of the grass, and they bore sweet flesh upon which Her children could dine. Bare of skin and shivering, Gaia gave of Her skin to the fields, that they might bring forth all manner of good harvests. And Her blood flowed into the valleys and became our lakes and rivers, and where Her bones fell, mountains sprang up. Her two eyes rose to the sky, where they watch over Her children still, and the tears She shed to leave them became the stars that glitter in the sky.

"And Her voice echoed to Her children, and they listened.

"And Her words were these: Lo, my children, this is your world. Love one another as I love you, and remember that you are the keepers and the tenders of the world. Do not take my gifts in vain, and do not begrudge them to one another, for they are yours to share equally. I will always be with you in love, but where there is not love, there I am not, therefore love one another and remember that this is your legacy: my fur and flesh, and my love, always."

"Blessed be Gaia," Volle murmured along with the crowd.

"And what do we learn from this?" The Cantor closed the book and looked out at them. "The nobility of sacrifice is the highest form of love, and the acceptance of sacrifice is the duty of the loved. Our sacrifices need not be on the order of our Mother's sacrifice, because our love cannot be as great and pure. But when we give of ourselves for those we love, She lives in us and Her Legacy is fulfilled. Whether that means giving up the last portion at supper," his eyes twinkled as he looked around with a smile, as though he knew that that was not an issue for most of the royal court, "or giving up a treasured possession, it is all a part of the same, and that is the acknowledgement that love is more important than any of these material things."

Volle could hear the other sections of the church already beginning the "Our Mother," and so did the Cantor. His large ears flicked straight up, and he raised his paws. "Thank you for sacrificing a little more of your time. Your love is welcomed and appreciated. But let's not fall behind, eh? Canis would want us to be at the front of the pack. But since we cannot be, let us blaze our own trail." He started the hymn from the beginning, rather than joining in with the other sections, and Volle found himself grinning as he sang along.

Volyan was looking up at him again as he sang, and Volle rested a paw on the cub's back. He was impressed that the cub knew not only the tune, but most of the words as well, considering the song was in an ancient language (its actual title was *Dicit a vocibus omnis*). They sang all six parts, one for each House, and then were sent to mingle with the Herbivores as a symbol of the unity of the Houses. Volle didn't know any of them well, but he did see the rabbit who'd been spying on them and avoided any contact with him.

"Lovely service," Lord Dewanne said outside. The Canids had largely dispersed, but the foxes had remained together. Volyan insisted on following Volle around, so they and Ilyana were talking with Lord and Lady Dewanne while Volle waited for Helfer to disengage himself from Laya.

"Oh, it was." Ilyana smiled. "He reminded me of the Cantor we had in our local church in Divalia. Very personable. Oh, hello, Cantor. We were just discussing how much we enjoyed your service."

The Cantor stood at least half a foot taller than even Lord Dewanne, who was otherwise the tallest fox there, but he didn't menace or intimidate with his height. "Thank you so much," he said in his light voice. "It is nice to be able to give a sermon to Canids. I mean, we are all brothers under Gaia, but love of pack is often lost on the weasels here."

"I imagine so," Lady Dewanne sniffed. "It's very odd to find such a uniform place."

"Many smaller communities are this uniform," Captain Nero said, walking up behind her. "Is that not so, Cantor?"

"True. But in those cases they usually share a common church with several other communities. Ikling is exceptional."

"In many ways." Nero looked around thoughtfully, and his eyes rested on Volle.

"We're integrating, slowly." Lord Dewanne sounded and looked a bit defensive. His ears were back very slightly. His wife, too, had moved to his side, slowly, but purposefully.

"Integration is a wonderful thing. It allows us to understand our brothers, no?"

"Quite." Dewanne's ears came back up, and he appeared to relax.

"Speaking of which," Ilyana said, "Where is Streak?"

She was looking at Volle, but he looked at Nero, and it was the wolf who answered. "He wasn't feeling well. He asked to remain back at the castle."

"Helfer prefers to call it a mansion," Volle said quickly.

Nero looked annoyed, but Volle couldn't tell if it was at him or at himself. "Indeed." None of the others had noticed his mistake, but his tail kept lashing. He surveyed the crowd for a moment and then said,

"Lord Vinton, I wonder if you might accompany me back to the *castle*. I think your presence there could prove useful."

"I was going to invite Lord Vinton to spend the remainder of the day at this lovely resort we've found. We're not going back to the castle." Lord Dewanne gazed at his wife, and Volle reflected that there were times when it was convenient to be married to a self-proclaimed invalid.

"Will you be there tomorrow?" Volle asked.

"Yes, of course."

"I'll join you then, if I might defer the invitation." He wanted to go, but Nero looked insistent and the reminder of Streak tugged at his guilty heart. Perhaps Nero had discovered a way for Volle to get in to see him.

"Certainly. It's the Burning Waters. I'm sure anyone local can guide you there." Lord Dewanne made as if to leave, but Volle stopped him.

"Maybe Ilyana and Volyan could spend the day there with you?" He knew that their accommodations in Ikling were less than luxurious.

Ilyana gave him a grateful look, while Volyan, who had been staring at Nero with large eyes, turned to Volle and said, "I wanna go with you!"

"Voly, dear, be polite." Ilyana rested a paw on his shoulder, but he kept staring at Volle.

"Why are you going away again?"

Volle knelt and tousled the fur between the cub's ears. "I'll see you tomorrow, Volyan. Okay? Be a strong fox and take care of your mother until then."

The cub bit his lip and then nodded. "Okay."

"Good boy. I promise I'll see you tomorrow." Volyan's tail wagged, and Volle smiled. "That's a good fox. Listen to your mother now."

"All right, Volyan." Ilyana put a paw down, and he clasped it, standing obediently by her side. She looked up at Volle. "Why do they need you at the castle? I thought your hearing wasn't until next Ursiday."

"It's not." He glanced at Nero. "But I've been assisting Captain Nero here with some of his casework, at his request, and I did promise to make myself available to him."

She raised her eyes for a moment. "All right. We'll be happy to accept your invitation, Lord Dewanne."

"My pleasure." He bowed to her.

Lady Dewanne coughed. "Do excuse my not curtseying, but after all that kneeling in church my rheumatism is bothering me terribly."

"I quite understand," Ilyana said. "We'll see you tomorrow, then, Volle."

"Bye, Daddy!" Volyan waved enthusiastically.

Volle waved back as they walked across the plaza. Being called "Daddy" still felt odd to him. He wished now that he'd made more time to spend with the cub while he was growing up. Intellectually, he knew he couldn't have, but if there'd only been some way…

Nero seemed to read his thoughts, once he'd said goodbye to Helfer and joined the wolf in the carriage. "You haven't seen your son in a year."

"More than that." Volle stared across the plaza, where the bright red of their fur was still visible. "Three years? Four years? I saw him when she had him baptized in Divalia, and on each of my visits to Vinton."

"Three times total, then. Was he baptized in the Cathedral?"

Volle flicked an ear, a little disturbed—though not surprised—that Nero knew how many times he'd visited Vinton. "No. We asked, but I'm not important enough. He was baptized in the small church her parents attend, and they did a lovely job." As an afterthought, he added, "The Cantor there is a fox anyway. The one at the Cathedral is a coyote."

"All canids. Does it make a difference? I would have thought you of all people would not hold to such differences."

"No, it doesn't make a difference. To me. But…" He paused for a moment, then realized that Nero knew he'd been raised in Ferrenis. "The Reformed Church separates each race. They don't have Families. Or rather, they do, but each Family is just one race. Fox, Wolf, Coyote."

"I am familiar with the tenets of the Reformation," Nero said stiffly.

"But in Ferrenis, I see…I mean, I didn't grow up with as much of an attitude about integration. The farm I grew up on was in a village that was primarily foxes, but we didn't ostracize the others."

"What others were there?"

Volle thought quickly. "Bobcat and hare," he said, naming the races of two of his childhood friends from the streets of Caril.

"I see."

"But here, there seems to be tension within Families and sometimes between Families."

"There will always be tension between the predator Families and the others."

"Well, yes. I don't mean that. But when was the last time there was a…a prey incident?" He was hesitant to say the word, and his ears folded back as he did.

Nero stretched out. "King Barris had been on the throne for four years. A wolf killed two mice and a hare."

"And you caught him?"

"Her."

"Oh." Volle let it drop, and Nero didn't seem anxious to discuss it any more. "So what would you like my help with?"

"I would like to visit the crime scene again. There are a few scent marks that we found puzzling, and a few items…" He trailed off, looking out the window at the mountain scenery. "As you're close to the suspect, we'd like you to take a nose around and see if you can identify his property."

"I'm sure I can. But please, while speaking to me, could you call him 'Streak' rather than 'the suspect'?"

"Of course. And I would like you to speak to Lord Fardew. Find out if there's any way he will let you talk to the sus—Streak." Volle sighed. "I am aware, at least partially, of your history. He is now my superior, though his appointment is so recent that this is the first time we have been working this closely together. I have heard his thoughts on you, but absent any actual crime, I have been left to form my own opinion."

"And that is?" Volle thought there was a slight emphasis on the word actual, but he wasn't sure. Was that a reference to the document he'd stolen?

The wolf smiled at him and shrugged. "When I have formed it, if the occasion warrants it, perhaps I shall share it."

Volle thought for a moment, then charged ahead. "You do know that I'm going on trial for an actual crime."

"As I understand it, if you are what you claim to be, then the removal of the documents is not a crime so much as a minor breach of protocol, for which you will no doubt be reprimanded. And if you are not what you claim, well then, the actual crime falls outside my purview."

"Then I will await my vindication, and hopefully that will help you form your opinion."

"I'm certain it will play a part."

Volle grinned. The large wolf's circumspect manner reminded him of Tish. "What do you do when you're not tracking down robbers and murderers?"

"I study the history of robbers and murderers. And I cultivate a small flower garden in a hothouse." He shifted his weight and stretched out again.

"History, eh?"

"I find it invaluable. Even though our city is larger than it has ever been, it is exceedingly rare that an individual finds a unique way of committing a crime that has never been seen before. The past repeats itself—not always identically, but often with the same patterns."

The image of Xiller came to Volle's mind unbidden, and he tried to shut it away. That history would not repeat itself this time, not if he could help it. He had to save Streak if he could. "And what does history teach you about this case?"

Nero looked shrewdly at him. "That I should keep my opinions to myself until I have reached a definite conclusion."

"Fair enough." But the thought of history repeating itself continued to disturb Volle, and he made no more effort at conversation until they reached the castle.

"So, should I face Dereath first?" He straightened his shirt and doublet.

"Yes, why not? I'll locate Archie and meet you in Lord Fardew's parlor, since the crime scene is there anyway."

As he wandered away, Volle heard the wolf order a servant to go find Archie for him, and he chuckled. So that's what 'locate' meant.

The castle seemed much more sparsely inhabited; probably much of the nobility had chosen to remain in warmer Ikling. He wandered the corridors and only saw two or three other nobles. In fact, he had to go out of his way to find a servant on the second floor from whom he could get directions, once he'd realized that he didn't know where he was going. "Should've asked while Nero was around," he muttered to himself. "Then he'd know I didn't know where the chambers were. But he'd probably have thought I was just pretending for his benefit."

He tsked at himself. Seir had often told him, *Don't overthink things*, and he thought that lesson applied now.

Dereath's quarters were locked, and nobody responded when Volle knocked. He sighed and looked around, but nobody was in sight. He didn't particularly want Dereath or Nero to come back and find him sitting like a servant outside the door, so he wandered along the maze of narrow passages in that area, sniffing now and then, but mostly just thinking.

He tried to stay near Dereath's quarters whenever he had a choice of passages to take, and at one point that led him to venture down a narrow side corridor when the main one would have taken him further away. Halfway down the passage, he stopped, nose held high. A scent was intruding on the air of the corridor, and though it was stale, it set his fur prickling. He must be near the crime scene, but how was he getting the scent of blood? Surely they had already moved the body, and he'd thought the crime took place in Dereath's quarters.

Further along, he found his answer. A large hole at about knee level was where the scent was strongest, and as he put his eye to it, he caught a glimpse of the room beyond before another scent made him jerk his head back.

Unmistakably, his nostrils told him, Streak had been at or near this hole in the recent past.

He knelt to the hole again. Inside, he could see a variety of simple furnishings. The bed had been neatly made, while the plain dresser stood with one drawer open. The floor was uncarpeted, covered only with a few grooming tools and several dark stains that Volle's nose told him the nature of. Sitting back on his heels, he contemplated the hole. It was too small for Streak to fit through; it was too small for him to fit through, in fact. Helfer might have been able to manage it, though he'd have lost some fur in the process.

What would Streak have been doing here? And more importantly, why had this hole been left uncovered? Unlike the hole he and Streak had slipped through, all the interior holes he'd seen at the castle had been covered with boards or sheets.

He heard noises in the corridor outside, and hurriedly stood. The noises resolved into the voices of Nero and Archie, but he managed to get back to Dereath's door before they came into view.

"Lord Vinton," Nero said by way of greeting. "It seems Lord Fardew is on his way back from Ikling, and is expected soon. We procured a key from the Steward, which Archie will have to return once it has served its purpose."

Archie was opening the door as Nero said this, and held it open for the large wolf. "I'll just take this right back, then?"

"Please." Nero strolled into the parlor, gesturing for Volle to follow him.

When he showed Volle into the small room that reeked of blood, Volle went straight for the hole. Streak's scent was even stronger on this side, which was puzzling, given that the wolf couldn't have gone through it and wouldn't have had any reason to be there—unless he was chasing the real murderer and covering for him for some reason. "You noticed this, right?"

"Of course." Nero flicked his ears, as if annoyed that Volle would even suggest he had missed something. "Despite his clear scent mark on it, it is too small for a wolf to pass through. The victim might have managed it, but it was her room anyway and she could hardly have crawled in after she died."

"Could she have been injured and crawled back here?"

"A good theory, but unsound. Her throat was cut, and the murder weapon found here. She did not live more than a minute before dying. As a matter of fact, the murder weapon is one of the things we would like you to examine." He motioned Volle over and pointed at a long pair of leather-handled scissors on the ground, the dull metal finish of the blades stained with the same black as the floor. "Are those familiar?"

Volle knelt to look, bringing a sharp, "Please don't touch them" from the wolf.

"I won't. I'm just making sure. No, I don't recognize them at all." He could smell the wolf on the scissors, though, a surprisingly strong scent even considering the leather handles.

Nero nodded. "You have your own grooming scissors?"

"Of course. Longer than these." He waved at his tail.

"Quite. As are mine." Nero swished his own tail.

Volle stood. "Quite," he echoed, and then shook his head. "Anyway, the scissors aren't mine. Or Streak's. Though they have his scent on them, that's for sure. But it's not his weapon, and he didn't do it anyway."

"Yes, it's not his weapon, and he claimed he didn't touch it. Though he could easily have picked it up when he found the body and just forgotten it." Nero stroked his muzzle thoughtfully. "He was not carrying a dagger when he was brought in. Does he usually?"

"No, never." Volle paused. "But if he were coming here to kill someone, wouldn't he bring a dagger?"

Nero nodded curtly. "That is one of the points that I am reserving an opinion on. Very good. Take a sniff around the room and see what strikes you."

Volle lowered his nose and walked slowly around the room, in the middle of which Archie returned. He stood outside the door when he saw what Volle was doing. "Were the scissors his?" Nero shook his head, watching Volle. "That rather complicates things, doesn't it?"

"Or illuminates them," said the wolf cryptically.

He tried to read Nero's expression, but the wolf was impassive, his ears straight up and not expressive at all. He couldn't see Archie from where he was, either, so he went back to sniffing. When he'd made a circuit of the small room, he sighed and shook his head. "I get Dereath, Streak, you two, and a couple females."

"The victim and the chambermaid, most likely."

"I didn't smell anyone else." Volle's shoulders slumped. He'd hoped he could've caught a scent that Nero had overlooked, even though the wolf's nose was probably a bit more sensitive than his. "That leaves Dereath as the only other suspect."

"Lord Fardew was in the main corridor a moment after the screams were heard. He came up behind the servant, according to her." Nero watched Volle's glance stray to the hole. "He could have gotten out through that hole, but it would have taken some time and his clothes would have shown the marks of the stones. I don't recall any such marks on his clothing that night. Do you, Archie?"

"I wasn't exactly eyeing his sartorial splendor, sir."

"Of course not. But you see how small details can be valuable to recollect later?"

"I could hardly miss it."

Volle looked at the doorway, where Archie wore an odd combination of a smirk and a respectful gaze. He tried to imagine Streak standing in that doorway, ears back, eyes determined, his body radiating purpose. He imagined the wolf crossing to the dresser, taking out the scissors, and—

"I can't believe it," he said, half to himself. But again, he found himself wondering, if Streak thought it would be the only way to save him, would he? Could he? When he envisioned the wolf holding the scissors, his ears were still back, but his eyes were no longer determined. They held desperation and fear, and a resolve. He pictured the wolf stepping forward, hoping to get it over with, his victim turning, seeing him, screaming, and then the downward plunge of the scissors, and Volle half-cringed at the reality of his vision.

"Believe it or don't, as you like, but whatever he can tell us—tell *you*—will be important. I know, Archie, it might well be nothing critical, but I have a hunch it is at least something that will help crystallize our thinking. I dislike having incomplete information..."

Volle had heard the scratchings a second before Nero did, and turned with him to the door. Beyond Archie, who turned as well when he saw their muzzles move, the main door creaked open and Dereath stepped through.

He took in the scene quickly; Volle saw the twitch of his whiskers and wondered if Nero also caught the flash of annoyance that melted almost immediately into a bland smile. "Inspectors. Lord Vinton. To what do I owe this pleasure?"

"Lord Fardew, we were hoping to persuade you to allow Lord Vinton to visit the—Streak."

Dereath folded his arms and smiled, just a bit. "The streak? Captain, I've no idea what you're talking about."

Volle was sure Nero could hear the hint of mockery in Dereath's reply. The large wolf's ears flicked back and then forward again. "Streak, the prisoner suspected of killing Miss Malion."

The name was new to Volle. He didn't recognize it, but filed it away as he turned back to Dereath. The rat had turned his smile to Volle. "I might be willing to consider it. But I am aware that Lord Vinton wants to see the murderer at least as badly as you want him to, Captain Nero. If he'll follow me into my chambers, I'll discuss the terms of the visit with him. Alone."

"Sir, I believe this interview could be critical to the investigation..."

Dereath cut him off with a wave. "I am aware of your beliefs, Captain. I also know this fox, and I know how likely it is that he'll provide you with a truthful account of the information he gathers."

"The Captain could accompany me," Volle said stiffly, but Nero was shaking his head even as Dereath answered.

"I hardly think your bloodthirsty friend would say anything with Nero present if he's been reluctant to so far. No, it will be you alone, so we will have to discuss terms. Come." Without waiting for an answer, he left the parlor through another door Volle couldn't see from where he was standing.

Volle took a step toward the door, but Nero's voice stopped him. "You might want to smooth your fur down, Lord Vinton."

Taking a deep breath, Volle turned around, making an effort to relax. He hadn't even noticed that his hackles were raised. "Thank you, Captain."

The wolf's eyes were calm and, Volle thought, perhaps sympathetic. "It is best to retain one's composure at all times," he said. "Most violent crimes are committed in moments of passion." He glanced meaningfully at the scissors, and while Volle bridled at the implication, he realized that Nero was only trying to help him.

"Thanks." He took another deep breath and smoothed the fur down on the back of his neck with a paw. "I'll try to keep my wits about me."

"Always the best course." Nero remained solemn, but Volle thought he saw a twinkle in the wolf's eyes. He walked past Archie, getting a pat on the back as he entered the parlor.

Dereath had brought a carpet, he noted as he walked across it to the door that led further into the rat's quarters. It was soft and plush, and dyed black, and it did not seem to belong in the sparsely-furnished parlor, alongside the plain wooden chairs. Volle watched his feet disappear into the carpet's pile and stayed at the edge of the carpet, toes flexing, while he regarded the door. It stood ajar, and he could smell Dereath's distinctive odor in the air. Through the crack, he could see the same sort of ascetic furnishings that the rat had placed in the parlor: a plain wooden table and a wooden chair. He swayed back and forth, swishing his tail, and then took a deep breath and walked in.

"Close the door behind you," Dereath drawled.

Volle swung the door shut and looked around the small room that had clearly been appointed as Dereath's study. The door on the opposite wall stood closed—probably the bedroom. To his left, a large oil painting of the King graced the stone wall alone. Dereath was sitting against the wall to his right, in a chair that was at least upholstered, if still rather old-looking. Volle reflected briefly on how large the procession carrying all the furniture to the castle must have been, then put that out of his mind. The only other chairs in the room were of the plain wooden variety, and though his legs were a bit tired, he opted to stand.

"Have a seat." Dereath shrugged when Volle shook his head. "As you wish." His muzzle rested against one paw, propped up on the small wooden table next to him.

Volle folded his arms and stared at the rat, who looked back unperturbed. He didn't want to be the first to bring up the subject, but eventually he realized that he would rather give up that slight advantage in order to get this over with. "What do you want from me?"

"You understand what a risk this is." Dereath was clearly enjoying himself. "I mean, letting a murder suspect's lover have time alone with him. I wouldn't even be considering it except that Captain Nero informs me that it might provide valuable evidence." He examined his claws. "I have my doubts about that."

"What do you want?" Volle repeated.

"Oh, Lord Vinton, one might almost think you were eager to leave my company. And here I am so enjoying yours."

"I'm sure you are." Volle felt as though a spring were winding up inside him with every word Dereath spoke. He reminded himself of Nero's admonition and took a deep breath.

"In any event, such a delicate situation requires me to put my reputation on the line. As His Majesty's highest officer and enforcer of his law, if something were to go wrong and a murderer go free…" He spread his paw out. "I don't have to tell you what an embarrassment that would be. Especially given the impact on your hearing. I know you want that to go by the book."

"Of course." Volle gritted his teeth.

"So as I'm taking such a large risk in this enterprise, and you stand to benefit—if in fact it turns out that that wolf has some information that clears him—then it strikes me that it is only fair that I receive some benefit in kind. And I believe you should be willing to…how shall I put this? Accommodate me to a large degree."

"Oh, I don't think your imposition would be very *large*." Volle looked pointedly at the rat's groin.

Dereath's ears flattened, but only for a second. He smiled a nasty smile. "You'll find out just how large it is. Here is what I want. You spend a night in my bed, doing anything I want, and the next morning, you can see your wolf for half an hour."

"A *night?!*" Volle sputtered. "You must be joking. Is this—are you that desperate?" Nero's warning forgotten, he took a step forward. He hadn't believed, when he'd made his previous comment, that Dereath would really stoop to extorting sex from him. His tail lashed against the doorframe.

"Desperate?" Dereath's eyes had narrowed slightly, but he kept his demeanor calm. "No, not desperate. Think of it more as a chance to show you what you passed up, all those years ago."

Volle shook his head. The smell of the rat, already unpleasant, was nearly unbearable now. "Ask for something else."

"Like what?" Dereath's whiskers twitched, and he showed his teeth. "A night with that wolf? I could have that now, if I wanted, you know."

Volle stayed silent, trying to unclench his paws. He didn't remember making fists. Dereath sneered at him, "No, I didn't think so." He leaned back. "My dear Lord Vinton, those are the terms and there is no negotiation."

"Then there is no deal." Volle knew he was being rash, but he couldn't help it. He couldn't let Dereath win. He wheeled sharply, swung the door open, and stalked out into the parlor.

"There will be." Dereath's words were cut off by the slamming of the door.

Archie walked out into the parlor and stopped, inclining his head curiously at Volle. "I take it the talk didn't go well," he said, folding his arms.

Volle took a deep breath, letting his ears come up and trying to relax. "You could say that."

"That's too bad. Captain Nero was counting on getting some more information."

"I'm sorry. De—" He couldn't bring himself to speak the rat's name. "Lord Fardew is being rather unreasonable."

Nero joined them. "What did he say to you?"

"He wanted…" Volle grimaced. "Physical compensation. For letting me in."

"Lord Vinton, if you're going to make up stories, at least make up credible ones." Dereath's voice purred behind him.

Volle spun to face the door, which had opened silently. Dereath stood there, leaning against the doorframe. His eyes were half-lidded and he wore a faintly amused smirk on his muzzle. "The truth isn't credible?" Volle snapped.

"The *truth*," Dereath said, "is that Lord Vinton, knowing how important this interview is to your investigation, Captain Nero, would not agree to disclose everything the wolf told him, unconditionally. When you are ready to be more reasonable, Lord Vinton, you may come see me again." He slid back into his room and closed the door.

Volle stared after him, muzzle hanging open. He turned to Nero and Archie, aware that his ears were pinned back again. "That…he…"

"Don't ask us to believe you instead of him, Lord Vinton. It's your word against his. Right now I have no reason to believe one over the other," Nero rumbled, holding up a paw.

"You *can't* believe that! I was telling you the truth!"

"And are you prepared to disclose anything he might tell you to us, unconditionally?"

"I…" Volle paused. Say yes! a voice shrieked, but he restrained himself. As a matter of fact, he wasn't willing to. "I would disclose anything that pertained to the murder." Even that, he felt, was a bit too bold. Technically, because the murder victim was a witness, anything pertaining to his hearing would also pertain to the murder.

"And who would decide that?"

"All right. Forget it." He didn't mean to snap, but the words came out that way anyway. He started to walk to the door, but Nero's soft voice stopped him.

"I would like to talk a bit more with you, Lord Vinton, if I might, about that night and your movements."

"Fine," Volle growled. "Not here."

"Of course. We can move to my chambers if you like. Or somewhere else if you're more comfortable."

By the time they reached Nero's chambers, Volle had managed to calm himself down. Archie was trying to keep a lighthearted tone in the conversation, sticking to subjects like the huge mess the King's horses had caused when the caravan stopped just outside Ikling, and it was that as much as Nero's carefully neutral demeanor that helped Volle get himself under control.

Nero's apartments were barely furnished at all. Volle stepped into the parlor and looked around with some surprise. The floor was bare, and the three wooden chairs were very plain, though the largest did have a dusty-looking cushion on it. There was no desk, no sideboard, and no table. The door that probably led into the bedroom was slightly ajar, but Volle didn't try too hard to peek into it. "None of this looks like it came from the palace."

"It didn't," Nero said. "By the time I learned I would be able to accompany the King, it was too late for me to gather any of my belongings." He sighed. "I would like to have brought some of my flowers, but I do not think this climate would have suited them."

"Why did you come along, if you don't usually?" Volle was suddenly curious.

"My doing, I'm afraid." Archie grinned. "I had met Captain Nero once before, when I visited the capital, and I tried to implement some of his policies and methods here. We keep good historical records now, at least, though our thoroughness in some cases is still lacking. I hoped to discuss some methods with him, and I thought that the two weeks' rest would let him start writing the book he wants to write."

"But you didn't come until the last minute?"

Nero, having settled his frame onto the cushioned chair, coughed as he shook his head. "The King had filled the party with invitations to nobles. The week before the retreat, Lord Ullik suffered a bad attack of gout and was pronounced unfit to travel. Lord Ikling petitioned that I be allowed to take his place, and the King was gracious enough to grant the favor. Fortuitously, as it turns out."

"That means 'luckily' to you and me," Archie said with a wink at Volle.

"Quite." Nero waved a paw lazily at Archie. "Be a good fellow and see if there's some tea in the kitchen still, would you?"

Archie rolled his eyes. "I wish you'd had time to pack a valet." He slipped out the door, closing it behind him.

Nero waved Volle to a chair. "Lord Vinton, I was hoping to talk to you about a matter of some sensitivity."

Volle sat down warily, ears perked forward. He didn't say anything, and after a moment, Nero continued. "I need to know how important the victim was as a witness in your trial."

"Ah." Volle sat back, looking at his paws as he formulated his answer. "The truth is, I don't know. I don't believe I've ever met her, but I don't know, of course. I never got to see her."

"We might be able to provide you with a chance to see her, if you think it would be useful."

"I didn't know her scent, and I don't think seeing her would change my mind one way or another. So she might have been very important, I suppose, because I don't know what she'd been told to say."

"So you doubt her testimony?"

"Of course. I am innocent, so any witnesses to my guilt must be lying."

"I see." Nero eyed the door for a moment, then went on. "Is there a chance that she saw something that could be construed as evidence against you?"

Volle threw up his paws. "Of course. Or she could have been instructed to say something. It doesn't really matter now, does it?"

"It does if her testimony was real," the wolf said, a trace of irritation in his tone. "Which is what I am trying to establish."

"I don't think it was real."

"But Lord Fardew seemed to indicate that she was crucial to his case."

"I don't know why. I told you, I've never smelled that scent before." He realized he couldn't very well say that she was nowhere around when he took the documents, so he paused and then said, "If she were a servant from the palace, I'd have run into her at some point."

The wolf nodded. "She was unfamiliar to me as well. But I don't spend a lot of time in the palace. Lord Vinton, I'm sure you can see where this is going. Do you feel your chances of winning your hearing are greater now that Lord Fardew's witness is dead?"

Volle sighed. He didn't think a lie would be credible, but he knew the truth would make him—and Streak—look bad. He looked down at the floor and then back up at Captain Nero. The wolf's squarish muzzle faced his, impassive and waiting. "Yes. Probably."

"All right."

"But I don't know what she was going to say."

The wolf tilted his muzzle. "As we said, if Lord Fardew planned to call her, it can't have been anything that would help your case."

"Then why did you have to ask me?"

"I wanted to know how much of a threat you considered her. An unknown quantity could be quite a considerable threat, and its sudden appearance could provoke a rash action."

"But it didn't."

"Not on your part, perhaps." Nero's whiskers twitched, and he brought a paw up to stroke them. "You seem to be a very intelligent fox, and one who reacts very well to unplanned situations. I don't think you would be prone to rash actions."

Volle detected the slightest emphasis on 'you.' He let it pass. "I assure you, I did not feel particularly threatened by the news of this witness. I was a bit worried, and puzzled."

"Because you're innocent."

"Yes. And I don't believe I said anything that would worry Streak."

"Did he know enough to get worried by himself?"

Volle chewed his lip and hesitated, again. The more he thought about Streak and his mood from that night, the more he seemed tense and worried in retrospect. But had he been tense before he'd asked about the witness? Or only after? He honestly couldn't remember now. Streak had certainly known enough about the case to be aware that the lack of witnesses was a large part of their defense, so there was really no reason for Volle to hesitate. Of course Streak knew enough to get upset.

He opened his muzzle to answer, and wondered suddenly if Nero were fishing for some ground to go back and question Streak himself, now that Dereath had kept Volle out. "Are you going to go ask him questions?"

"I reserve that right. But I've already asked him about the victim and he claims he'd never seen her before and didn't know her."

Volle heard Archie outside a few seconds before the weasel pushed the door open, balancing three small cups of tea on a tray. "You're in luck, Captain," he said. "They were just taking the pot off the fire."

"Thank you, Archie. Now, Lord Vinton, let's discuss your actions on the night of the murder."

Volle rehashed what he'd told the wolf the last time they'd talked, adding as much detail as he could remember. He was deliberately vague about Streak's state of mind, making him out to be generally tense, but not determined or afraid. Nero didn't ask him much about Streak's state of mind anyway, sticking more to exact movements and times. He seemed particularly interested in the time between Volle learning about the witness and dinner, and finally Volle was forced to admit that he and Streak had snuck out of the castle together.

"For what purpose?"

"Well…" Volle searched for the proper way to phrase it. "He's a young wolf, and sometimes impatient, and he thought it would be exciting…you know, he didn't want to wait until we were back at our room."

"Oh. I see." Nero flicked his ears.

Archie grinned over the wolf's shoulder and winked at Volle, then composed himself. "Can anyone else verify the time that Streak learned about the witness?"

"Lord Tistunish, maybe. He was discussing it with us."

Nero half-turned. "We've talked to him already, and he did allude to that, Archie."

"All right. I suppose it's in the notes."

"I should hope so." Nero harrumphed and adjusted himself in his chair. "Thank you, Lord Vinton. I don't think I need to ask you anything else. Will you be available tomorrow?"

Volle shook his head as he got up. "I'm going to the Burning Waters resort to spend the day with Lord and Lady Dewanne. But if you need me, you can find me there."

"I'm not familiar with that establishment."

"Neither am I." He shrugged. "I was told it would be easy to find. I'm sure if I can find it, you'll have no trouble."

Nero nodded curtly, but his whiskers twitched in what Volle interpreted as amusement. He waved back to Archie and left the room.

For a time, he wandered the corridors of the castle aimlessly. When he found himself near the north tower, he turned deliberately away from it, not wanting to confront the guard and remind himself of what was happening to Streak. A few passages later, the scents of spiced meat and roasting vegetables reached his nostrils. He followed them to the kitchen, where a servant told him dinner would be served in about an hour.

He considered seeking out Tish, but decided that he needed some time to be alone and think. Restlessness and a feeling of suffocation led him further up, until a chilly breeze that smelled of rain led him to a crumbling staircase. He navigated cautiously up it and emerged into the cold wind on a narrow parapet, with ancient stone walls to his left and the mountain falling away to his right.

Overhead, clouds massed, but the scent of rain was just a threat; the skies remained dry. Volle walked along the parapet, taking careful steps and avoiding the cracked slabs where he could. Twice he had to jump over small gaps, but apart from that, the walk wasn't difficult. When he reached the corner, he could see down the mountain, where Helfer's red-roofed mansion was just visible through a screen of trees. To his left, the walls dropped away into the main courtyard. He glanced down, but nobody was about, and when he stood against the outer wall, he felt securely hidden from any eyes below.

He rested his arms on the cold stonework, folded his ears down against the chilly breeze, and sighed. He was no closer to understanding what was going on than he had been before. Over and over, he'd racked his brains trying to identify the mouse's scent, now that he'd had a chance to smell it, and he couldn't. He knew there were several mice at the palace who served in various capacities, but he was almost sure that the scent had belonged to none of them.

It was not out of the question that Dereath had brought in a spy from outside to watch the papers. If indeed the whole scheme had been conceived as a trap, Volle thought it likely. He'd found out about the papers the night before a large banquet, and of course thought the banquet would be the perfect time to steal the papers. He went over the events in his head: the deserted corridor, the empty office, the long minutes spent sniffing the air to make sure everyone had gone, and the quick grab of the papers. The footfalls behind him in the corridor, his quick dash to the hiding place, and the subsequent arrest.

Lord Fardew's office, as he remembered it, had only a single door: the one he'd entered by. The anteroom, similarly, had only one entrance. But the palace was riddled with secret passages; just because he didn't know about one didn't mean Lord Fardew didn't have one. Could there have been a peephole through which someone could have seen him? He glumly concluded that he couldn't rule out the prospect. Dereath had listened in on the conversations in his cell as he and Streak had fallen in love, and he hadn't realized there was another conduit out of the cell until the rat had told him. If there was such a hole in Lord Fardew's office, he might not have been able to smell the mouse behind it.

That incident was tied closely to the current situation, he knew, but re-hashing it didn't help him shed any light on Streak's predicament. He knew that as soon as he talked to the wolf, he would know whether or not he had killed the mouse. Streak wouldn't be able to hide it from him. He wanted so badly to know, and just to see the wolf again. The chilly air and the breeze blowing through his fur kept reminding him of their last afternoon together, and the memory made him smile, and flooded him with melancholy. He had hoped their life could make the transition to the palace without losing the simple joys that they'd had on the farm, but the murder had changed all that.

And yet, though he didn't want to admit it to himself, there was a part of him that was enjoying being in the thick of things again. Even though he realized the danger he was in—or perhaps because he realized it—he felt awake and alive again, and the sensation wasn't totally unpleasant. Usually, he told himself, the messes he became embroiled in were not quite so dire in nature. But regardless, his feelings were similar. He felt amplified: his worry and love for Streak, usually quiet as the small creek on their farm, were as loud as a waterfall now.

And keeping him from that waterfall, the familiar obstacle of Dereath, exploiting this situation to get a cheap night of sex out of him. Though it seemed completely typical, Volle was surprised he had the nerve to do it un-der the nose of Captain Nero. He was convinced that he could find another way to get to see Streak. He wouldn't give in to Dereath. Who knew what the rat might have planned if he got Volle in his power? Mutilation, maybe? He shuddered.

But Dereath had to have known that that would be his reaction. Did he think Volle was so desperate to see Streak that he would agree to anything? Volle's tail lashed slowly back and forth as he thought about that. Had Dereath proposed that specifically so Volle *wouldn't* get to see Streak before the trial? Was there something Streak could tell him that would make a dif-ference?

Maybe Streak could tell him why he'd been in Dereath's rooms to begin with?

He was rolling a small chip of stone under his fingers as he thought, staring down at the world below, but as his thoughts carried him along this path, he turned to look behind him at the rest of the castle. The three towers stood behind the main bulk of the castle, pennants waving desultorily from their sparsely shingled tops. He couldn't see much more of the towers, but he could see that one of the towers had lost an entire section of wall, expos-ing the weathered stone inside. The other two looked more solid; his gaze flicked back and forth between them before settling on the one that he knew had to be the north tower. That was where Streak was, somewhere behind those stone walls.

The idea seized him that he could find a way in from the outside, or at least find a window he could talk through. He scanned the parapet, looking for a way over. There—but no, the other tower was in his way, and there didn't seem to be a walkway around it. Maybe he could go around the other way, through the decrepit tower.

He sidled along the parapet, aware that he was doing something dangerous, not only physically, but politically as well. If he were caught, his hearing might not go as smoothly as Tish hoped it would. He looked back every few seconds toward the stair he'd mounted, in case someone were following him or chanced to come up, but the roof remained as empty as it had been since he'd stepped onto it. He didn't dare risk a glance into the courtyard for fear someone would look up and see him.

Rounding the next corner, he saw that the decay in the walls covered more than just the tower. In addition to the side of the tower, an entire section of the castle wall was missing, and the parapet was mostly gone. He would have to walk on the wall itself to reach the tower, with a gaping hole on one side and a steep drop to the other.

Creeping closer to the point where the parapet ended, he peered down into the hole. It had been patched with boards, but half of a staircase remained, so that someone could conceivably walk up and onto the false wooden ceiling. The room didn't look used, of course, but he couldn't see beyond a bend in the corridor at the base of the stairs and he hadn't been in that section of the castle.

Gingerly, he lifted a paw and stepped up onto the wall, staying hunched over with his tail out because he felt more balanced that way. The surface was considerably less smooth than the parapet, and more than once he winced as he put his weight on a rough protrusion. He was almost to the tower when he looked up to see where he could jump onto it, and the wall fell away under his left paw as he set it down.

He felt a moment of all-consuming panic, and clutched blindly at the wall. Vertigo seized him as his body fell, but fortunately he landed squarely on the wall, not to either side. He ended up lying flat on top of it, arms and legs on either side and tail all bristled out to his left, his chest and hips stinging from the impact. The inside of his left leg gradually joined the chorus of pains as the shock of the abrasion wore off. He was sure he'd left some fur on the wall, if not blood.

The pounding in his ears subsided in a few moments, enough for him to hear voices wafting up the staircase. "...shouldn't be anybody up there..." He glanced down and saw several chunks of the wall lying on the boards, and realized that the sound of their impact, quieter in the open air and blocked out by his panicked scramble to keep his balance, must have sounded as loud as a drum in the corridors below. And in a few moments, someone would be coming up the stairs to investigate.

The tower, in front of him, offered no refuge. It was open to the staircase. He might find a place to hide while inside, but if he didn't, there would be no disguising his intent. Back? He thought he could at least get back to the parapet if he hurried. The wall was stable enough—provided he watched where he put his paws.

He scrambled to his feet, listening for footfalls on the stair below. Trying not to let panic rule his steps, he hurried back along the wall, dislodging another few chips in the process. There was a loud scrape, as of some covering being moved aside, and he saw torchlight in the shadow at the base of the stairs. The parapet was close; he leapt for it and landed squarely on it, stumbling into the wall of the castle.

"Ho! Who's up there?" he heard faintly from the hole.

The parapet was about seven feet above the top of the stairs, so Volle felt he was safe from view. But what if someone had seen him go up? Not responding could be suspicious. He agonized for a moment and then crept to the edge and peered down.

A large cougar guard, looking up, snapped his head around. Volle recognized him, and the cougar obviously recognized him, too, because he relaxed and his tail stopped lashing. "My Lord, it's dangerous up here. You should return to the castle." He looked from side to side. "How did you get up there?"

"The other way." Volle pointed. "I'm sorry, I was just angry and wanted to get away. I threw some rocks around and I guess I hit the boards. I'll come down now."

The cougar nodded. "Thank you, my Lord." He bowed and then turned and walked quickly down the staircase.

Volle lay there for another moment before getting up. He looked at the north tower again, then at the nearer tower, fixing some details in his mind. There wouldn't be a moon tonight; it was too overcast. But he might be able to navigate the wall in the dark.

He pushed that idea to the back of his mind, and padded back along the walkway. He kept close to the parapet as he walked around the main courtyard, aware that anyone might be watching. That made him think about Dereath's witness, and wonder how many times he'd thought he'd been alone and hadn't been.

As he descended the staircase, pausing for a moment to look around in the fading light at the shadows that seemed to spring from every cranny and crevice, a thought occurred to him.

He'd been in the dungeon for months. Why hadn't Dereath produced his witness then?

Chapter 7

"From what you've told me," Tish said quietly as they waited for dinner, "he wanted to get more information out of you. Producing his witness would mean a quick conviction, but the case would be taken out of his purview. As it was, nobody really knew what had happened to you apart from what we were told, remember?"

Volle nodded. "I guess that makes sense." He chewed on the small vegetable rolls they'd been given as appetizers, and looked around the table. The place next to him was empty, and Tika was on the other side of Tish. Only about half the table was full, but it was populated by small clusters who were chattering merrily to themselves. "Nobody seems really upset. Remember after Prewitt, how everyone was tense for weeks?"

Tish shrugged. "They all…" A grey fox placed a dish in front of him and then moved to Volle, and he waited until the servant was out of earshot before continuing. "They all think the murderer is locked up." He watched the King, and dug in as soon as he saw the King begin eating.

Volle didn't touch his food. "And you?"

"I'm waiting to hear what you think," Tish replied equably.

"You don't have any opinion?" Volle toyed with the chicken, and finally ate a piece. The sauce smelled just a bit off to him.

"My opinion is that there will not be any more murders."

"Then you think he's guilty."

Tish pointed a finger at him. "Wrong. I believe it was a deliberate crime, and it accomplished its goal. I do not believe that the murderer is interested in killing anyone else." He took another bite.

"Deliberate?"

"She was the witness on Dereath's list. Did I tell you I confirmed that? We still don't know who she was, but it was definitely her name. But the way it was done, Volle, think about it. She was sought out, protected in the chambers of the Minister of Defense. It wasn't a case of some crazed bloodlusting creature roaming the halls and cutting throats. It was a deliberate and planned attack."

"Captain Nero thinks Streak didn't plan it."

"Well." Tish shrugged. "If he is guilty—and you still haven't told me what you think—then the killing itself might not have been premeditated, but he certainly went to Dereath's chambers with some intention. Have you thought, for example, that he meant to kill Dereath? Rodents all smell alike, and he wasn't that familiar with the rat's scent."

"He could still tell male from female," Volle said. Hunger got the better of him, and he started in on his chicken in earnest.

"True, true. But if he were trying to disguise his scent, then his own sense of smell might have been confused."

"What would he disguise his scent with? Anyway, he wasn't. It was all over the room. And the murder weapon," Volle said gloomily.

"Well, then, you see my point. It doesn't look premeditated. Unless it was very carefully premeditated, and your wolf happened to step into the middle of it or was placed in the middle of it."

"Placed?" Volle chewed his chicken thoughtfully. "The only one who could have done that is Dereath. Would he have sacrificed his witness for a chance to put Streak in jail?"

"Maybe," Tish said. "Or maybe the witness didn't really witness anything at all, and was just bait for Streak."

Volle stopped in mid-chew, his muzzle hanging open. "She was bait," he said, and swallowed. "No, wait. How could he know Streak would..." He paused, realizing the implication of that.

"Don't forget that he knows Streak," Tish said softly.

"No, I haven't. I just think it's chancy. Not like Dereath."

"I think you're right. But it was just a thought. It's also possible that she was killed for some other reason and your wolf was just there to try to find out what she knew. Prostitutes make many enemies."

Volle frowned. "She was a prostitute?"

"That's what Alcis told me the guards were speculating."

"That doesn't make sense. Dereath doesn't like women."

"No, I suppose not. But you know how guards are."

Volle chewed and grimaced. "This makes no sense from any angle."

"It makes sense from mine."

Volle flicked an ear. "What do you mean?"

Tish lowered his voice. "I mean that without a witness, I believe that your hearing will go as smoothly as I had planned. The murder will be a distraction, but however it's resolved it shouldn't have any bearing on your case. Oh, Dereath may and probably will argue that your wolf killed his witness to give you an advantage, but even if he manages to prove that Streak is guilty, he can't prove the motive. Without a witness, his case is flimsy and I know we can beat it. And it resolves your dilemma, though not in the way you'd hoped."

"My dilemma?"

"About bringing Streak to the palace." Volle looked glumly at his plate as Tish went on. "A loved one can be a large vulnerability, Volle. Look at how easily you have been distracted by Streak's predicament. If someone offered you the chance to free him, what would you give up in exchange?"

"Not just anything," Volle snapped. Dereath's leering face appeared before him again. He looked around quickly, but the rat wasn't present at the table.

"Maybe not. But it's still a vulnerability."

"What about Tika?" Volle hissed back.

Tish glanced at his wife, who was chatting quietly with Lady Alister to her left. "Tika made a decision. She knew some of the risks."

Volle raised an eyebrow.

Tish elbowed him. "All right, all right, you impertinent pup. I don't always follow my own rules. But Tika does know the risks of being the wife of a noble, and I have been discreet and quiet enough that she's never been in danger."

Volle sighed. "Point taken."

"Besides," Tish said, "I love her with all my heart. And if I were forced to be apart from her, I would be miserable every day. So I made an exception for myself. And that's why you must be sure of how you feel." He paused. "Or had to be sure how you feel."

The servants were clearing away their plates. Volle said, "I feel more sure now than I have in a while."

"That's good. I hope it is not too late. May I have a private word?" Tish looked around, then said a soft "excuse us for a moment, dear" to Tika and got up, beckoning for Volle to follow him.

"About Streak?" Volle eyed the cream cakes the servants were bringing out as he got up.

"Indirectly." The wolf saw his look, and patted his ample stomach. "Don't worry. I've had plenty in my life. Missing one won't hurt. Besides, I don't fancy the chances of the cream not having turned at least slightly."

"I wasn't worried about missing dessert." Volle fell in behind Tish as the wolf left the dining hall. They waved to the servants outside the door, who bowed to them, and walked on down the hallway.

The castle was mostly deserted, and a few of the torches had gone out, giving it a sepulchral look in some of the darker alcoves. Tish stopped near one of these and leaned against the wall with a sigh. He folded his arms and rested his muzzle on his chest. Volle stood patiently and watched him, tail waving slowly back and forth, and was just about to speak when Tish looked up at him.

"I have been debating these last few minutes whether or not to tell you this, because it may just confuse you further. But I think you should know…" He sighed again. The grey on his muzzle was more pronounced here, away from the bright torches, there was a sag in his shoulders, and even his eyes, cast down at the floor, looked weary. That the black wolf was forty years his senior was always in the back of Volle's mind, but rarely did he remember it when he was with his friend. Tish's optimistic spirit and youthful energy usually took ten or twenty years off of his apparent age, but now they were gone or faded.

Volle waited patiently, ears perked. After a moment, Tish went on. "I told you my son never wanted to come to the palace. That is not…quite true. He did, at first. I had to be firm about it. As he grew up, of course, he resented me, and when it came time for him to come, he resisted. Again, I had to be firm, and so he is now at the palace. But he does not like it, and he does not like me.

"I did not want him around, because at the time he was born, I had only been two years into…" Working with the Ferrenians, Volle knew. He nodded in response to Tish's look, and the wolf went on. "I was young. I didn't know what I would be doing, but I knew there would be danger, and I didn't want him around to be used against me." Tish was speaking in a rapid whisper now. "I made that choice, and now I wish I could go back and undo it. But if I had to do it again, I am not sure I would not choose the same path."

Volle flicked his ears. "I'm sorry about that," he said softly. "Does this concern Volyan?"

"It might."

"And what do you think about that?"

Tish shook his head. "I cannot make your decision for you. I just wanted to tell you what you would be risking, whichever way you chose."

Volle put a paw on his arm. "Thanks. And…I'm sorry."

"So am I." The wolf smiled thinly. "Thank you for listening, Volle. There…are not many people I can talk to about this."

Volle flicked his ears, feeling awkward. "It's okay. I mean, I know it must be hard."

Tish nodded. "But it is a burden I chose, and I should not complain about it." He straightened and rubbed a paw over his ears, and when he looked at Volle, his ears stood straight up and his smile was more full. "Come on. I don't want to worry Tika."

Later, as he paced the corridors alone, Volle thought about Tish's words. The strain of his life must have been great, and the cracks he'd shown that night gave Volle pause about the direction of his own life. *Won't let it get that far with me*, he thought. *I'll get out while I'm still young. Retire to that farm.*

But the haunting voice in the back of his head mocked him. *You had all that. Retirement, a life of ease, no worries except when the frost would come or whether the rot would spread to another field…and you gave it all up to come back and plunge your head into this basket of nettles. You're just like Tish. You thrive on this, and in the end it will eat you from the inside, and you won't even realize it until you're standing in the shadows of a corridor, afraid someone will hear or see you, telling your young protégé about all the regrets you had.*

No. He pushed the voice away. *I have Streak…* He paused, night air filling his nostrils as he stood at the base of the stairs that led to the parapet. He didn't have Streak, not right now. But he would.

The torches in the hallway made the sky look black by contrast. The wind had picked up outside, making an eerie keening across the doorway that set his fur a-prickle. He pulled his vest together and started up the staircase.

The stone grew colder under his paws, and even his fur didn't keep out the chill of the night, especially when he emerged into a brisk wind with spatters of rain. He shook his fur and started along the cold stone walk. As his eyes adjusted, slitted against the wind, he could see the oppressive grey shapes of clouds overhead, and the solid grey forms of the parapet and walkway. He stepped carefully on the stone, bracing himself against the gusts of wind as they came. He thought more than once about turning back; after all, he probably wouldn't be able to get into the tower or help Streak at all. But the need to talk to him, just to hear his voice again, kept his paws moving forward.

As he rounded the corner, he opened his eyes a little wider now that the wind was blowing against his right side. Once, he slipped, and feared he would lose his balance and end up in the courtyard with a broken leg, or worse. But he recovered and stayed close to the parapet from then on, putting out a paw to hold on to it from time to time. The rough stone was comfortingly solid under his paws, and he tried to draw strength from it to go on against the wind. He no longer worried about anyone looking up from below; he just wanted to get to the other side where the wall provided at least a little shelter.

When he finally reached it, the fur on his head and tail was cold and wet, if not yet soaked. He took a moment to lean against the wall and shiver, imagining that it provided some protection from the wind. Further down the wall, the dark hole gaped, and again he considered turning around. To risk the leap with the wind and rain…

Stubbornly, he set his teeth and walked to the edge of the hole. He wouldn't risk walking along the wall this time. He waited for a brief moment in which the wind died down, and then clambered up onto the top of the wall, remaining low on his paws and knees, tail tucked under his legs and getting them wetter than they already were. Slowly, he crawled across the rough expanse, ducking his head against the wind and watching every crack and gap in the wall carefully as he put his paws down.

He almost smacked his head into the wall of the tower, so intently was he watching the placement of his paws. For a moment he just stood there, his paws becoming slowly numb. Then, slowly, he got to his feet and steadied himself against the tower wall. Below him stretched blackness; he could just make out the gleam of light on the stone stairs, but the wood swallowed the light and gave none back. The tower wall was reassuring and solid, almost bright by comparison. And the wall had crumbled away about five feet from the inner edge of the castle wall. He couldn't reach it by stretching out his arm, but he could jump to it, cling to the edge, and then…and then he hoped that the floor he'd seen inside could still hold the weight of a thoroughly wet fox.

Warm up your paws a bit, he thought. He crouched down and shoved his paws between his legs, rubbing them together until some feeling came back into them. From that position, he studied the wall.

This is crazy. I could fall. I could be killed. But he felt the need to do it, as if to prove to himself that his feelings for Streak were real. More, it was a need borne of the anger and frustration he'd felt that afternoon. He wanted so badly to beat Dereath, to get to Streak without giving in to the rat's conditions. The memory of Dereath's smirk gave him the spur he needed.

The more he hesitated, he realized as he stood, the less likely he would go through with it. He was already starting to shiver from the cold. *It's an easy jump. You've done it a hundred times (back in school, and two feet off the ground, not sixty).* A step to the edge, crouch, push off...

He took a breath, and launched himself into the rain and wind.

The wall seemed to float in front of him, getting no closer, and for a moment he panicked. Then his paws were on either side of the wall, the broken stone cutting his pads, and he was swinging his weight around and collapsing onto the remnants of a solid stone floor.

For the span of several panting breaths he sat there, back against the wall, heart thudding in his chest. He was sure that if his fur were dry it would be bristled out all over. He only moved because, upon looking up, he noticed that the tower roof on the far side was more or less intact. Getting shakily to his feet, he edged around the caved-in floor and sat on the first step of a stairway that led down three steps before it too was gone. Here, he was sheltered from both the wind and the rain.

Further along the floor, to the opposite side of the tower, the wind was blowing the rain in under the roof. He contemplated that wearily, wondering if he would have to make another jump over to the parapet. Behind him, a narrow slit of a window gave out onto the night sky, flashing with glimmers of raindrops. This was the same sort of window he could expect to encounter at the north tower—there were two still intact in this tower. He put his paw sideways into the window and moved it from one side to the other. Only about two inches leeway. He would probably not be able to see the wolf at all. This whole enterprise felt more and more foolhardy, but he couldn't stop himself. Having come this far, he had to go through with it.

Stepping back into the wind and rain was a bit of a shock, but he was prepared for it. He followed the tower wall around the other side to where it fell away gradually into nothing, and discovered that he could easily clamber up onto the broken section and drop to the walkway on the other side, which was missing some stones but seemed solid.

The wall of the castle acted as a shield on this side, so although the rain still dripped down on him, there was much less wind. His heart sank as he looked up at the blank wall of the tower in front of him. He stared again, hoping he'd just overlooked a window slit. No matter how hard he looked, the window didn't appear. In all his thoughts about getting to the tower, he'd never even considered that there wouldn't be a window where he needed one.

He turned to go back, then thought, what harm can it do to look, now I've come this far. Maybe there'll be a crack in the wall or something. He padded cautiously along the wall, noticing that out toward the parapet, the wind was still howling, driving the rain in unpredictable eddies around the raised stone barrier. As he drew closer to the tower, the far edge of it looked more shadowed and irregular, and his steps quickened as he began to make out the edge of a window.

He had to stand on the parapet itself to see it clearly. The stone was slick under his chilled paws and the wind gusted around him, but he could see the dark hole in the stone. On the other side was...

"Streak!" He called as loudly as he dared, trying to project his voice toward the hole. He cocked his ear, but the wind filled it and drowned out any reply. He called again, and this time he thought he heard a reply. Tensely, he waited, shivering and wet on the castle wall, eyes and ears fixed on the small black window slit.

After a few moments, he called again, convinced that the wind was playing tricks on him. He couldn't bring himself to turn around, but he knew he would have to soon. He couldn't stay out here all night. He—

A white finger appeared at the window, followed slowly by the rest of a white wolf's paw.

His heart stuck in his throat. He stretched his arm out, afraid that it was a ghost, but his fingers closed around a warm, solid paw. He squeezed as hard as he could, and Streak held tightly to him. Everything's going to be all right, he wanted to say. Just tell me...did you do it? He had to settle for the warm grip, the scant comfort he could give (and receive) from that touch.

It seemed hours that he stood there, muzzle pressed against the rough stone, paw holding and held by Streak's. He couldn't say which of them let go first, just that they both knew it was time. Slowly, Streak withdrew his paw, sliding it along Volle's retreating one, and then he was gone.

Volle stood there for another moment, his discomfort forgotten, then slowly slid down from the parapet. He made his way back to the ruined tower and stood there in the shelter of the wall, staring numbly down at the blackness. He'd gone through so much, and even though he'd gotten a brief touch, he couldn't help but feel that his whole ordeal had been for nothing. His heart was aching, and the pressure behind his eyes told him that the moisture on his muzzle was not all rainwater.

He looked dully over at the wall he'd jumped onto and realized that he couldn't expect to jump back. But he could easily jump down onto the wooden boards that were thrumming softly with the irregular rain. From the lowest step of the partial stair, it was about seven feet to the wood. He turned around and tried to lower himself until he was hanging from the step, but as he pushed his knees off the edge of the step, his paws slipped. He caught himself briefly, then both paws came loose from the step and he landed heavily on the boards, falling backwards onto his tail.

For a moment, he lay there, looking up at the sky, but the rain falling into his eyes and ears spurred him to get up quickly. The boards clattered a bit as he walked across them, searching out the stone stairs more from memory than sight, though as he drew closer he could see their outlines dimly. The foot of the stairs was blocked by a large tapestry that smelled of age and mildew. He paused, but couldn't smell any guards on the other side,

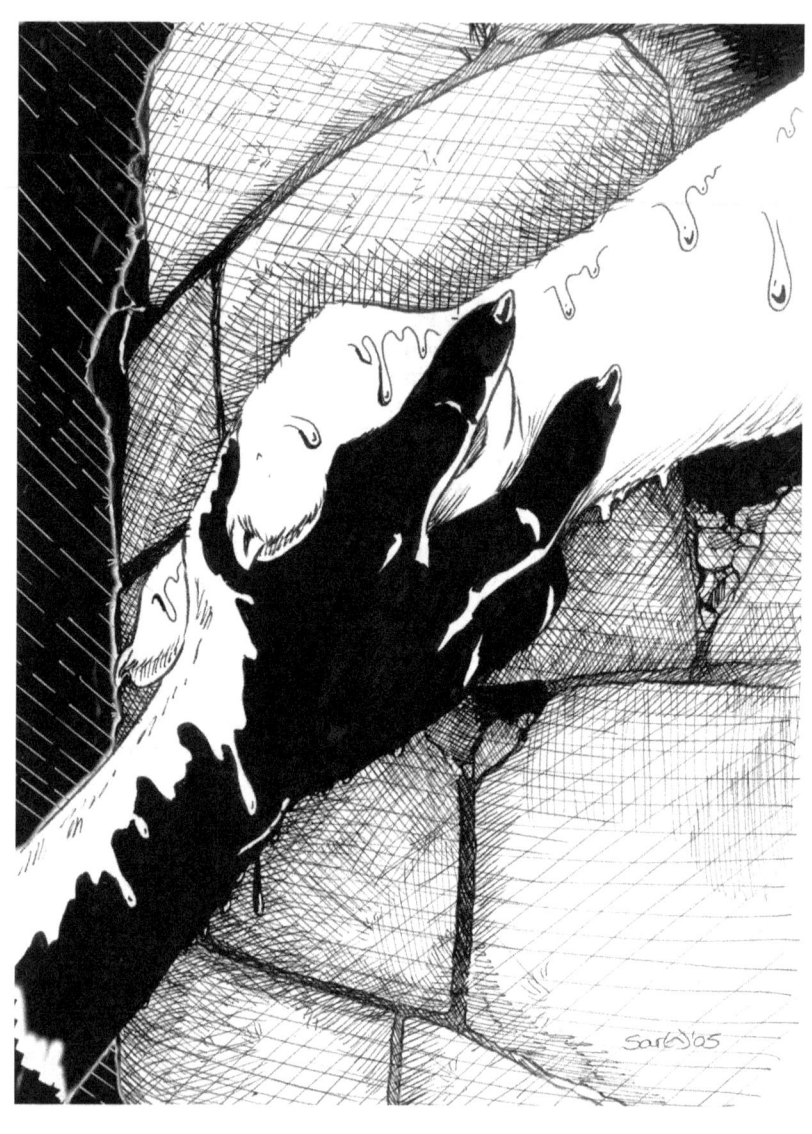

His fingers closed around a warm, solid paw.

so he pushed his way around the tapestry and made his way back through the castle.

Fortunately, it was still deserted. He only passed one couple, the Lord and Lady Villutian, who sniffed visibly and nodded to him while making a wide circuit. He realized how rank his wet fur must be, and resisted the urge to shake himself there in the corridor. Helfer's mansion awaited, with a bathtub full of soft scented powder. The thought gave him little comfort, as though the cold had reached more deeply into him and numbed him. Even stepping back outside into the chill wind and light rain didn't seem to make him any colder.

The footservant was not at the gate when Volle arrived there. He appeared a moment later, a smiling grey fox whose smile turned to an expression of horror when he saw Volle standing there. "M-my Lord," he stammered, "I'm so sorry! I didn't see…I was only gone for a moment, but you must have been waiting so long…please forgive me!"

Volle blinked at him and then realized that he was still soaked. The poor fox must have thought that he'd been waiting all this time. "No, no," he said. "I've only been here a moment. Just fetch a carriage for me."

"Immediately! Here, take my umbrella." The fox pressed the umbrella into Volle's paw, and scurried around the corner.

If he hadn't been so tired and upset, Volle would have grinned at the misunderstanding. He raised the umbrella over his head and leaned against the wall, his eyelids drooping slightly. They drifted shut, only to snap open when the fox's voice said hesitantly, "My Lord?"

"Yes?"

"The buggy will be here in a moment. It is being prepared. It is late and we had thought that everyone had left. I am sorry for the delay. Please forgive me."

Volle managed a smile, and shook his head again. "Nothing to forgive," he said. "You are doing an admirable job…" He searched for the fox's name but couldn't find it.

"My name is Mikan, my Lord."

"Mikan, then. Thank you." Volle leaned forward to get the fox's scent, whiskers twitching. Mikan smiled hesitantly and followed suit, looking relieved at the cordial gesture.

The clatter of wheels and hooves announced the arrival of the buggy. Mikan helped Volle into it and wished him a good night. Volle returned the umbrella over the fox's protests and raised a paw in response as the other fox closed the door.

He dozed off several times on the trip down the mountain, stirring groggily when the carriage came to a stop by Helfer's guest entrance. Roferro, the otter, opened the door for him.

"My Lord," he said, shocked at Volle's sodden clothes and fur, "you must come inside and dry off! You're no otter, to be playing in the rain like that."

Volle blinked at him blearily, and nodded. "I'd intended to do that." He descended from the carriage, guided by the otter's paw, and hurried into the shelter of the mansion.

Roferro walked him all the way to his bedroom, supporting him with one arm. Volle was more acutely aware now of the places he'd scraped on his legs and the places he'd landed on his back and tail when he took that fall. He could have made it without the otter's support, but he took it gratefully. When he had made it to his bed and was sitting down, Roferro left him to check the bathroom. He emerged a moment later. "Everything is stocked, my Lord," he said. "Do you need any more assistance?"

Volle shook his head. He missed his personal servant. Welcis would have had a dry towel all ready to wrap around him. "Thank you, Roferro," he said softly. "Good night."

"Good night, my Lord." The otter retreated and closed the door gently behind him.

He was tempted, so tempted, to lie back on the bed and close his eyes. But his fur was still wet, and it was when he realized that he was getting the bed wet as well that he finally forced himself to his feet. The laces of his shirt and pants were soaked and difficult to pull apart, but with fatigued patience he managed to shed his clothes, leaving them in a mass on the floor.

The bathroom had a facility where stones could be heated and then placed under the tub to warm it. But the fire was cold and so were the stones. No matter, Volle thought wearily. He was so cold that the tub felt warm as he eased himself into the powder. He covered himself with it and lay there, feeling the talc soak the moisture from his fur. I shouldn't go to sleep here, he thought as he laid his head back, and the next thing he saw when he opened his eyes was Helfer's grinning muzzle, limned with brightness from the morning sun.

"Hef?" He coughed dust out of his throat as he tried to sit up.

"Morning, sleepyhead." The weasel's cheerful grin rested on the edge of the tub. "Don't you know that's bad for you?"

"Yeah, I..." He coughed again. "I was really tired."

"I guess you were. And lonely too, I see."

Volle followed Helfer's look down his stomach and grinned sheepishly. Helfer had seen him naked before, so he didn't bother to cover his erection as he stepped out of the tub, just reached for the brush. "It was a very hard night."

Helfer laughed, though Volle hadn't meant it to be funny. "Yes, you've made your point." He grinned even more widely. "I wanted to see if you'd be up for a run."

Volle nodded. "Just let me brush off."

"I'll wait outside." Helfer slipped out of the bathroom and closed the door.

As he worked the brush through his dust-clotted fur, the events of the previous night came back to Volle. He wanted to go back to the castle right away, to try to figure out another way around Dereath, but he thought it would be good to run with Helfer first. The only question was how much of the previous day's events to tell him, and in the end, of course, he told him everything.

"You were on the roof? That place is dangerous."

Volle snorted, panting white breaths into the chilly morning air. "I'm not a cub, Hef. I was fine." He had downplayed the times he'd slipped or been close to slipping. His paw pads, slapping through the wet grass, were still sore.

The morning was beautifully clear for once; even up the mountain the usual clouds had not yet appeared. Last night's rain and wind seemed to have blown over, clearing the air but also letting in the cold. Volle only felt it in his muzzle when he inhaled, though. The sun on his fur was warm, and even the air rushing through his tail fur as he ran felt good.

Hef was quiet for a few more paces, then said, "I don't see why you had to go climbing over the roof, though. Why not just sleep with the rat? How bad could it be?"

"How bad…Hef, it's Dereath. We spent five years trying to avoid him. Six, for you. And now I should just give in?"

Hef shrugged as best he could while running. "Sure. Maybe it'll calm him down some."

"He's disgusting!"

"It's only sex. You clean up afterwards and forget about it."

Volle shook his head. "I don't know if it's that easy for me. Plus…I just don't want to let him win." It sounded petty once he'd said it.

"Of course you don't. But sometimes you don't have any choice. The longer you wait, the more satisfied he'll feel when you do go to him."

"Don't you think I can find another way around it?" He had hoped that Helfer would suggest something, with his knowledge of the area and his influence, but he didn't want to ask his friend outright.

"Sounds like you tried. If there's nothing Nero can do, then I can't think of anything else."

Annoyed, Volle lengthened his stride a bit. If Helfer noticed that he had to run faster, he didn't say anything about it. As they reached a narrow path behind the mansion, Volle relented and let the weasel run ahead of him. They ran single file along the rocky path. "I can't, Hef."

"I think you're making too big a deal out of it."

"Want me to ask if he'll take a night with you instead?"

Helfer flashed a grin over his shoulder. "If it was for something I really wanted, I'd do it."

"By getting drunk?"

The weasel shrugged. "Probably. I wouldn't want to face him sober. Or see him naked sober."

"I don't think I want to be drunk. I want to make sure I'm in control."

"I think," Helfer said, panting a bit now, "that that is just what he doesn't want."

Volle shivered at that, but saved his breath until they were back on grass. "Hef, what if he wants to…I don't know, tie me up? Or use a knife or something?"

"He won't kill you. He's not that crazy."

"I don't know. But still, he could do a lot."

"So tell Archie where you're going beforehand. If you're nervous, that's the best thing. Tell Dereath someone knows where you are."

"Tell someone else what I'm going to do?" Volle panted. "I can't even convince myself to do it. I certainly don't want anyone else knowing."

"You told me." They were running abreast again, and down the side of the mountain Volle could see the town of Ikling, red-roofed amidst the green and yellow fields. It was quite pretty, and he wished he could lose himself in it rather than go back up the mountain to the castle and face Dereath. He still wasn't sure he could bring himself to agree to the rat's terms.

The more he thought about it, the more he couldn't see what course to take. He discarded plan after elaborate plan to distract the guards and get into the cell, because he kept reminding himself that the door would be locked. He briefly wondered whether he could get in through the tower roof, then scoffed at himself. There has to be another way, he told himself, but he couldn't think of one.

By the time they finished the second circuit of the mansion, his legs were tired and he had stopped thinking. He vaguely registered that a second buggy sat outside the mansion gates, but he didn't look at it, just rested with his paws on his thighs and his head down and said, "Hef, what am I going to do?"

The weasel, likewise panting, said, "Go down to Ikling, I suspect."

"Wha—" He wondered for a moment whether he'd voiced his wish to go to the town aloud, and then he saw Lord Dewanne walking toward them.

"Lord Vinton. Lord Ikling." The fox was dressed informally for once, in a loose tunic and undyed pants. He still held his tail arched and walked like a noble, despite his casual clothes. "I thought I'd come up in person to see the mansion. I'd heard a lot about it but only saw it in passing."

Helfer looked warily at Dewanne as Volle straightened up. "I was just getting in some exercise, Dewanne," Volle said. "Let me go clean up, and I'll be right with you." He didn't want to go to the spa today, and hoped that with a little more time he could think of a way to get out of it.

"Don't be silly. You're fine, and besides, you're just going to be getting wet again. No point in cleaning up now. Here, I brought a spare tunic because I wasn't sure you had anything suitable." He tossed a tunic to Volle. "Don't want to be leaving expensive clothes lying around the spa."

Volle caught the tunic and examined it as Helfer said, "My people aren't thieves."

"Of course not," Dewanne said. "But there are thieves about."

Helfer glanced at Volle, then back at Dewanne, and didn't say anything. Volle held the tunic out to Dewanne. "I do have my own, but thank you. Let me just go get it."

"Actually, Vinton, if you don't mind, I'd prefer to leave as soon as we can. I left Delia by herself, and Ilyana had promised to be there by the time I left." His tail's tip twitched. "I told her I'd be right back."

Volle sighed and slipped the tunic over his head. "All right."

As he was pulling it down, he heard Helfer say, "So what do you think of the mansion?" His tone was slightly belligerent, but Volle wasn't sure Dewanne would notice. Even though he'd known Helfer for five years, he could barely tell.

"It's nice," Dewanne said. Volle adjusted the tunic, noticing that Dewanne was appraising the mansion as he talked. His ears were still perked up, so he wasn't reacting to Helfer's tone at all. "I don't think I've seen anything like it before. The houses in Ikling are similar, but not on that scale."

"We like it," Helfer said, less angrily than before. Volle suspected that he was having trouble staying mad at Dewanne because the fox was so blithely unaware that he was giving offense.

"All right, Hef," he said, stepping to the weasel and putting a paw on his shoulder. "I'll see you later tonight. Thanks for the talk."

"Anytime," Helfer said, patting Volle on the hip. "Just relax, okay? Don't get so overexcited about it."

"I'll try. I'm having trouble relaxing these days."

"The spa will help with that," Dewanne said, walking back to the buggy. Volle followed him and got in after him.

"So you really like this place?" He waved to Helfer as the buggy pulled away from the mansion.

"It's not the best we've been to, but it's adequate. Delia likes it."

"How's she feeling?" Volle only asked the question because he knew full well that Dewanne would spend the remainder of the half-hour ride detailing his wife's latest ailments (a small but persistent cough, headaches, and rheumatism—that last was a new one that Volle suspected was a reaction to not having visited a steam spa in many years). He listened with one ear, nodded politely, and watched the scenery going by. Whatever he might decide to do, he would have to do tomorrow. He probably wouldn't be able to get away from Dewanne until that night.

To get to Burning Waters, they drove all the way through the city to the other side, and by the time they arrived, the combination of the lower altitude and the higher sun had made the buggy uncomfortably hot. Both foxes were panting, but Volle let Dewanne exit first. The older fox nodded in thanks, waved an instruction to the driver, and padded quickly for the entrance to the spa.

Volle took a moment to look around. A low brick wall, with a large stone archway beneath which Dewanne was now passing, surrounded the resort. The ground was dusty and surprisingly bare of greenery. Or maybe not so surprising, considering the strong sulfurous tang in the air. His nose wrinkled, but the scent was not entirely unpleasant. The warm dirt felt good on his paws as he followed Dewanne inside.

"Smell takes a little getting used to," Dewanne said when Volle caught up to him. "But it's not bad."

"I've smelled worse," Volle agreed. The inside of the compound featured a number of low-sitting buildings, flat-roofed, that gleamed whitely in the sun. The heat and the brightness of the buildings and ground made Volle feel as though he had traveled hundreds of miles from the cold, rainy castle walls last night. Still tired from his run, the heat had him panting again as he and Dewanne approached one of the taller buildings. Volle saw the symbol of Canis on the side of the door, painted in some brownish tint. He glanced around at the other buildings, but couldn't make out any marks on them. The lower ones, he supposed, were for mustelids or rodents, and the tallest one, to his right, was either for the ursids or the herbivores. They weren't in the canonical order, unless he was mistaken about the heights and the ursids they had around here were all raccoons.

He expected darkness as he walked inside, but looked up to see skylights in the roof, which kept the interior bright. The smell of sulfur grew stronger too, even though he couldn't see any of the pools for which he assumed the resort had been named.

A young male weasel dressed only in shorts smiled at them as they entered. "Lord Dewanne. Welcome back. Your wife is in the third pool with her guest." He turned to Volle. "And this is your guest?" His accent was thick and marked.

"Yes. Lord Vinton."

The weasel bowed. "A great pleasure to have your noble presence grace our humble resort, sahr." He carried several towels slung across his arm that hung almost to the ground, and he offered one to Volle.

Volle took it and inclined his head to the weasel. "Thank you." The weasel grinned back at him, and Volle flicked an ear. Something in the weasel's scent told him that if he wanted them, other services could be available. He was very fit and cute, in a weaselish sort of way, sort of like a younger Helfer with lighter fur, and he was eyeing Volle with a look and a pose that said that he was getting similar messages from Volle's scent.

It was a tempting thought, considering how long it had been since Volle had had any contact (*an afternoon in the rain*), but he didn't think he really wanted to indulge here, and Dewanne wouldn't approve anyway. Normally that wouldn't bother Volle, but he was a guest of the older fox. He smiled politely to the weasel and then turned back to Dewanne, who was waiting at the doorway to the third pool. After a moment's pause to test the scents of the air and see if he recognized any of the other residents of the various pools (he couldn't make out their scents over the sulfur, though he could tell there were others there), he joined Dewanne and held the curtain aside for the other fox to enter.

The first thing Volle noticed as he walked in was the sulfurous smell, even stronger here and now bordering on unpleasant. He wrinkled his nose, but as he did he noticed that although Dewanne was standing just in front of him, he could barely smell him. Beyond the little room they had entered was a larger room in which two foxes lay in a pool of steaming water, and despite the fact that they were only thirty feet away, Volle had to guess that they were Ilyana and Lady Dewanne. He couldn't smell them at all, nor could he see them clearly through the steam. Further along the pool, a solitary wolf or coyote rested in the water.

He closed his eyes for a moment and was surprised by the sense of privacy he felt. Normally he could smell other people around him or recently near, but the sulfur overwhelmed all that, and the tiled walls and large spaces of the pool hall played with the sounds he heard, so that he could believe they were coming from far away and that there was nobody near him.

Lord Dewanne had his tunic off and was smiling at Volle when he opened his eyes. "Nice, isn't it?" he said. "Close your eyes and you're alone." He slipped his pants off without any trace of embarrassment and inclined his head toward the pool. "Come join us when you're ready."

Volle watched him walk naked to the poolside, bend and say something to a figure Volle assumed was his wife, then slide into the water opposite the two vixens. He smiled to himself. Dewanne had always seemed a little bit stuffy, but given the right environment, he could apparently loosen up some—though not all the way; he noticed that the older fox's tail was curled modestly around his waist, beneath his paunch. Volle smiled, stripped off his own clothes and left them piled on the bench beside Dewanne's.

He had barely taken two steps after Dewanne when he heard the patter of footsteps to his right. The sound stopped abruptly and he found himself ten feet from the small form of Volyan. The cub was looking right at him, but didn't seem to recognize him. Volle smiled and knelt down just as Ilyana called over, "Don't you remember your father, Voly?"

The cub took a few steps forward, sniffing the air, clearly disoriented by the sulfur, then smiled and padded the rest of the way, throwing his arms open. Even though he was clearly soaked through, Volle accepted the hug and then let go, giving him a lick on his small nose. Volyan giggled, his tail wagging. "Hi, Daddy," he said. "This place is hot and it makes my fur sticky."

"Mine too." Volle rubbed his arms and chest where the cub had pressed against him. "Why don't you go back in the water?"

"I got hot and Mommy said I had to get out for a bit."

"He was panting," Ilyana called over.

"You feel pretty warm," Volle said.

"You don't." Volyan smiled at him and then looked him up and down.

Volle noticed the cub's gaze pass over his sheath and then flick downwards to his own groin, and vague memories flashed through his mind of seeing older boys naked at the pools in the city. Back then, of course, he hadn't been interested except in how they compared to him, and he suspected Volyan's thoughts ran only along those lines. He patted the cub's ears and smiled. "No, I'm not. So I'm going to go sit in the water for a while. You can come talk to me if you want."

"Okay!" The cub padded happily behind him, feet making little wet slapping sounds on the tile floor. Volle waved to Ilyana and Lady Dewanne and walked over to where Lord Dewanne was relaxing in the water. He was sitting on a bench, it seemed, though it was a rather low one; his chin was just above the water. His head rested against the inside of a graceful arch that began flush with the pool, met the ceiling at its apex, and descended to meet the pool on the other side where Lady Dewanne and Ilyana were. A similar arch began just to the left of the entrance to the room and descended to the other side; Volle had to walk behind it to join Dewanne. In front of it sat a pair of coyotes, talking to each other in low tones; because of the arch, he hadn't been able to see them from the changing room.

"Hello, Volyan," Dewanne said as they approached. "Do you remember me?"

"Uh-huh. You're Lord D'wan."

"Dewanne." But he was smiling as he corrected the cub.

"Duwan."

"Close enough. Volle, come on in." He gestured toward the water next to him, and Volle saw the bench more clearly now. He slid into the water, gasping at first as the heat touched his pads, and again when it soaked through his fur. Halfway in, his sac hanging just above the water, he hesitated.

Dewanne chuckled at him. "Just go all the way in."

"Easy for you to say," Volle retorted, but lowered himself into the water. The heat stung his sheath at first, but that faded into a pleasant warmth all over. The bench, he thought as he sat, was probably designed to accommodate any canid. His chin actually touched the water when he sat down.

Volyan sat on the edge of the pool beside him and dipped his legs into the water. "Mommy says you're taking me to the palace to meet the King," he said without preamble.

Volle was about to answer when a voice floated over to him. "If he starts to bother you, let me know."

Startled, he looked around. It sounded like Ilyana was right beside him, but when he looked, she was on the other side of the pool waving at him.

Dewanne flicked his ears in amusement. "It's a speaking arch," he said. "So the males and females can be separate but still talk to each other."

"How interesting," Volle murmured, though really it struck him as slightly sinister. The sulfur blocking his sense of smell and the steam obscuring his sight he could handle, but that he could listen and talk to someone forty feet away that he could barely see made him a bit nervous. He edged away from the arch and sat closer to Volyan, whose wet tail slid across the tiles in excitement.

"What's the King like?" he asked.

"He's big," Volle said. "He's a bear. Have you ever seen a bear?" The cub shook his head, his eyes getting a little wider. "Well, he's this big around," he held his arms about four feet apart, "and he's very tall."

"Are you scared of him?"

"Sometimes. But he's a good King. He wouldn't hurt you."

Volyan nodded. He looked across the pool and then back. "Are there other cubs at the palace?"

"Some."

"Other fox cubs?"

Volle shook his head. "No, none of those."

"Oh."

"Do you know other fox cubs in Vinton?"

"Uh-huh." He nodded. "There's Chally, and Pikor, and Hally who came to my birthday once but she ate too much and got sick and had to go home."

"I'm sure you'll find some friends at the palace. Are you excited about going?" The cub nodded, but his ears were halfway down. "Scared?" He nodded again, more slowly. "That's okay. I was scared when I went to the palace too. And I was much older than you are now."

"Did you go to see your daddy?"

Volle shook his head. "I didn't have a daddy growing up."

"I didn't either." He blinked shyly and mumbled, "until now."

Volle didn't respond to that verbally, just smiled and perked his ears up. His neck was starting to hurt from turning to look at the cub, so he faced forward again and relaxed in the pool. The heat was soaking into his fur and body and felt very good.

Across the pool, he heard splashing and opened his eyes. The two vixens (blurry shapes) were getting out and walking toward them around the perimeter of the pool. He estimated the time it would take them and closed his eyes, folding his ears down to block out other sounds. Very faintly, he could make out Dewanne's scent, but it was distant. Volyan's was clearer, but the cub had been soaking in the sulfurous water and his scent was fainter. For the moment, Volle felt very isolated, and the sensation of privacy was not altogether unpleasant.

The water lifted his fur so that he almost felt like he was floating. Ilyana's voice wafted to him through the humid air, sounding oddly less substantial than it had through the arch. "We're going to the cooling pool. Can you look after Volyan?"

Volle opened his eyes and turned. Dewanne, he noticed, was already turned and staring at the two naked vixens. Ilyana, closer to him, was as shapely as he remembered her, with a little more plumpness that her clothes had hidden well. Her breasts had grown noticeably, but her figure was still very attractive. Lady Dewanne, behind her, was even plumper and less attractive. Her small chest did not complement her wide hips, though her fur was very sleek even when wet, and it was a rich chestnut brown, very dark for a fox. He'd noticed it before, but the color was brought out by the water.

"Volle?" Ilyana said, amused, and he realized he was staring. His sheath hadn't responded, but he heard Dewanne's movement behind him and felt certain that the older fox was at least showing some level of interest. He himself was more interested than aroused, and Volyan didn't seem interested at all.

"Yes, we'll look after him. We'll bring him to the cooling pool when we're ready to go."

"There's a separate one for males," Dewanne said, behind him. "But we'll leave him with you on our way there."

"I'm a male!" Volyan piped up.

Volle grinned. "Well, maybe you can come with us, then."

Dewanne coughed slightly. "Actually, Vinton, I was rather hoping to have a private word with you today."

"We'll have plenty of time for that." Volle turned to look at the other fox, and couldn't help glancing downward. Dewanne was indeed showing a partial erection beneath his stomach, and it occurred to Volle that Dewanne might have another reason for wanting private time. Certainly his wife's constant health complaints probably meant that his sex life was less than it could be, but in all the time Volle had known him, Dewanne had never been interested in males.

The older fox noticed his glance and crossed his legs, trying not to draw attention to it. He nodded. "All right. Just wanted to let you know."

Volle nodded and turned back to the vixens. Ilyana had knelt down and was giving Volyan a hug. "Be good," she told him. "Mind your daddy, and don't talk too much."

"Okay, mommy." He licked her nose and then she kissed him and nuzzled. Tousling the fur between his ears, she stood up, and Volle suspected she was showing off for the fascinated Dewanne, at least a little bit. She made no effort to hide the curve of her breasts and the nipples on them, nor the pink between her legs that was clearly visible through the wet fur. Lady Dewanne at least had her hips tilted to one side and her arms folded modestly across her chest.

Volle smiled and raised a paw to her. "See you later."

"Goodbye, my dear," Dewanne said.

"Bye, darling," she replied, and put an arm around Ilyana's shoulders as they walked away. Volle thought he heard her say something like "not even the *slightest* sign of interest? oh, my dear..." but the steam in the room muffled the words.

Volyan watched them leave, and then turned back to Volle. He said, with a comical gravity, "It's just us guys now."

Volle laughed, and lifted an arm from the water to rub Volyan's shoulders. "Yes, it is."

It was clear that Volyan wasn't sure why he had said something funny, but he enjoyed the attention and laughed along with Volle. His little tail wagged behind him across the tile. Volle thought he was adorable.

"What do daddies do?" The cub was still smiling, but his wet ears now had an inquisitive tilt to them.

"What do you mean?"

"Mommy said that mommies stay with cubs and take care of them until they're big. Then daddies help them grow up. But what do daddies do?"

"Well…" Volle paused. "Don't your friends have daddies?"

The cub's ears flicked back and he nodded, less happily. "They all do."

"What do their daddies do?"

"I dunno."

"Didn't you ever ask them?" The cub shook his head. "Why not?"

"I dunno."

Volle searched the recesses of his own memory, a childhood he hadn't looked back on in some time, and said softly, "Because they had daddies and you didn't?" The cub nodded, very slightly. "Did they make fun of you?"

"Sometimes." He shrugged.

Volle held the small paw in his own. "You remember I told you that I didn't have a daddy when I was your age?"

The cub's ears perked up a bit, and he nodded. "Did your friends tease you too?"

Volle nodded, though it wasn't strictly true. The other children he'd grown up with in Caril had mostly had two parents, but a few had been in his situation, and some had been orphaned. They had been picked on, but there had been enough of them that they had been able to stick together. He squeezed the cub's paw. "But I never got a daddy, and you have one now."

"I told them I did, but they said I was lying."

"Sometimes friends say that if they don't know any better." Volle couldn't think of any words that would make the cub feel better, but he didn't really have to. Volyan was already perking up, just from Volle talking to him.

"They'll see now." His tail was wagging again.

He seemed to have forgotten that he wouldn't be seeing his Vinton friends again, and Volle chose not to remind him. "Yes, I suppose so. But it wouldn't be nice to make too big a deal of it." Volyan tilted his muzzle, not understanding. "When you're right about something," Volle tried again, "and your friends were wrong, it would make them feel bad if you told them they were wrong."

"I think he's a bit young to grasp the concept of courtesy," Dewanne said with some amusement.

"I'm five years and three months!" Volyan said indignantly.

Volle let the issue drop. "What games do you like to play with your friends? Do you play, um, Ballhop?"

Volyan nodded. "Sometimes. We play Flea and Ballhop and Ring-around-the-rosy."

"What's your favorite?"

"I'm good at Flea. The flea almost never catches me." His tail wagged again.

"That's good. I was good at that too." Of course, he'd played with a group of mixed species; only the rodents were faster than he was.

Volyan launched into a story about a game of Flea he'd played that had taken place around the governor's mansion in Vinton. Volle had only seen it a few times, and he enjoyed listening to the description of the mansion through the cub's memories.

Despite his mother's warning, which had obviously lost its power with her departure, Volyan launched straight from that story into another one about when he'd gotten in trouble for breaking open a bag of flour, and by the time that one trailed down, Dewanne was getting impatient. Volle was feeling rather warm himself, so when the older fox suggested, "Maybe we should go over to the cooling pools," he agreed readily.

"Want to come with us, Volyan, or go back to your mother?"

"I'll come with you!" The cub sprang to his feet, tail wagging. He had dried off a bit, but not much, and his tail sprayed droplets of water as it swung back and forth.

"Only for a little while," Dewanne said as he started to climb out of the pool. Realizing that Volle was in his way, he stopped and waited.

Volle got up obligingly. "Don't worry, Dewanne, we'll have time to talk."

"I know, I know." The older fox waited until Volle was out and then followed him onto the tile. Volyan scampered ahead of them, and it didn't occur to Volle to warn him not to run on the wet tile until he saw the cub skid and hit the wall.

"Careful!" he called.

Volyan looked back briefly, then went on at a slightly slower pace. He disappeared into the changing room and was pawing through the clothes when Volle and Dewanne walked in. "I can't find my clothes," he said, looking up at them.

"Did you take them off here?" Volle thought Dewanne sounded faintly irritated.

"Yeah."

"No you didn't," Dewanne said. "You took them off in the other changing room with your mother." He pulled his shorts on over his wet fur.

Volle followed suit, draping his tunic over his arm as he saw Dewanne doing. "Don't worry, Volyan," he said. "Just come along."

He didn't think a naked five-year-old would attract much attention, and Volyan seemed to enjoy the freedom. He pranced around in front of them and his little tail didn't stop wagging until they reached the cool pools.

They were housed in a long, low building that looked like two squat cylinders joined together. Dewanne led him to the left hand one even as Volyan skipped toward the right. As they drew closer, Volle saw the 'male' and 'female' markings on them. Volyan finally noticed that they were going to the other building and changed course abruptly, running back to join them. Volle had the idea that Dewanne was hoping the cub would have continued on his course, but other than a revealing downward flick of the ears, the older fox didn't react even when Volyan ran right in front of him.

This building was lower and darker than the other. No arch soared overhead, and no skylights let in the outside light. In a small changing room much like the other, Dewanne slipped his shorts off again and Volle followed suit. Volyan was already splashing around in the pool inside.

As he stepped into the larger room, Volle could smell the water. Subtle oils in it combined to make a pleasant fragrance that nearly completely concealed the faint sulfur scent, much weaker here than in the hot pool. Beneath that, he could smell many different people; apparently the cooling pools were not separated by Family. As his eyes adjusted quickly to the dim light, he could see two bears, a stag, and a pair of weasels in various parts of the pool. They turned to look at Volle and Dewanne as they entered, then turned back to their own conversations.

Dewanne searched out an unoccupied part of the irregularly shaped pool and settled in, gesturing to Volle to join him. Volyan was staring at the stag and then ran over to where the foxes had settled. He jumped into the pool, but sank down to his eartips. Volle picked up the struggling form and settled the cub in his lap. Volyan had to kneel on his thighs to keep his head above water, but he didn't seem to mind that. He rested his head back against Volle's chest.

"This isn't very cool," he said, and he was right. The water was warm, but it wasn't nearly as hot as the other pool. To Volle, it felt refreshingly cool at first, but he was sure that Volyan was chilly from wandering around with wet fur, and to him, it probably felt very warm indeed. "Why do they call it a cooling pool if it's so warm? Shouldn't it be a warming pool?"

"It's cooler than the other pool," Volle said, "so that's why, I suspect."

"Oh." The cub shifted his weight and Volle felt a paw come uncomfortably close to his sheath, pressing hard into his hip. He put his arms around the cub and held him, to try to keep him from shifting around so much, and Volyan obligingly quieted. "You feel warm," he said.

"I've been sitting in a hot pool."

"What are those things on his head?" Volyan lifted a paw and pointed at the stag.

"Don't point." Volle pulled his arm down hastily as the stag turned their way. "They're part of him. He's a stag. They grow antlers out of their head."

"Doesn't it hurt?"

"I guess not." Volle nuzzled the cub's ears. "Haven't you ever seen a stag before?"

Volyan shook his head. "I saw a goat once but his horns were small and didn't have branchy things like that."

"Antlers," Volle said gently.

"Antels," Volyan repeated.

"Close enough," Dewanne said.

Volle grinned again. Between the hot bath and the chatter of Volyan, his other problems seemed little more than a distant memory. He rested his muzzle between the cub's ears and held him close, and Volyan leaned back against him. Volle felt the twitching of his tail as it tried to wag in the water, against his stomach, and then even that movement slowed. The cub's breathing became more regular, and when Volle noticed that his eyes were closed, he closed his own as well. He wasn't particularly tired, but he was very relaxed and his eyes just drifted shut.

"Vinton." He wasn't sure how much later it was that Dewanne's paw gripped his shoulder gently. "Are you hungry?"

"Uh?" He blinked his eyes open, and Volyan stirred in his lap. "I guess so." He looked around the pool. The stag and the two bears were gone. The weasels were still there, and two squirrels had come in.

"I'm hungry too." Volyan rubbed his eyes.

"But we're all wet." And naked, of course.

Dewanne chuckled. "That's okay. Usually we eat a light lunch, then go back to the hot pool and then dry off in the dust baths. You can stay down here for dinner or go back up to the castle."

The castle. He thought about Streak up there, still in prison; about Dereath, waiting with unbearable smugness for Volle to come take his offer. He felt the peace the pools had brought him disturbed, and frowned. "Maybe I'll just eat at Helfer's mansion."

"Whatever you like." Dewanne stepped out of the pool and stood, dripping, on the tile. Volle lifted Volyon off his lap and got up, placing the cub on the tile before climbing out himself. They dressed, again only in shorts, and this time Volle slipped his tunic over Volyan's head. It trailed on the ground, gathering dust, but Volyan was delighted and ran ahead of them. Twice he tripped and fell, but both times he got up cheerfully, so Volle stopped worrying about him.

Behind the buildings, under the shade of a large tent, a number of wet people sat and talked while berobed otters scurried around the tables and carried ceramic bowls to and fro. As they got closer, Volle was overpowered by the smell of wet fur, so much so that he couldn't even smell the food in the bowls.

Dewanne found the two vixens, but Volyan got there first. "Mommy!" he cried, and ran toward Ilyana, tripping and falling on the brick walk five feet from her.

"Voly!" Volle saw the concern, but she was also trying to stifle a laugh. "Where did you get that tunic? Here, put your shorts on."

The cub, unfazed by his fall, took the shorts and slipped his legs into them, but refused to take the tunic off. "I wanna keep wearing Daddy's tunic!" he said, squirming as Ilyana tried to take it off, and finally she gave up. He sprang free and immediately tripped again.

"Here," Volle said, laughing as he came up to the cub. "At least roll it up." He rolled up the hem so that it no longer trailed on the ground.

"Okay!" Volyan waited until Volle had finished, then climbed up onto the chair next to Ilyana. Volle sat on the other side, smiling at the cub's beaming muzzle as it swiveled back and forth between him and Ilyana. Lord and Lady Dewanne sat across from them. The vixens already had ceramic bowls in front of them, and now Volle could smell the food. It was simple food, some kind of fowl with fruit and a few spices in it, but it smelled pretty good, especially with his appetite.

An otter scurried over and placed two bowls down on the table, one in front of Volle and one in front of Lord Dewanne. He looked down at Volyan and then at Volle and Ilyana. "A small bowl for the cub?"

"Yes, please," Ilyana said. The otter smiled and bowed, and scurried away.

Everyone was using their paws to eat, so Volle did the same. The fruit was juicy, but overall the fowl was still slightly bland. Nevertheless, it was filling, and he'd eaten half of it by the time the otter arrived with another bowl for Volyan, about a third full. Volyan dug in with his muzzle in the bowl, until Ilyana chided him gently.

"So, Volle," Lady Dewanne said while he was still eating, "will you be returning to the palace with the rest of the nobles?"

"He doesn't know yet, Delia," Dewanne said. "The hearing is in a few days."

"Of course, I know that," she said. "But I have faith in him. Canis will see him through."

"Are you not going back with them?" Volle asked.

"I will be staying on here for a week. Possibly two." She looked around and coughed delicately. "This climate is very beneficial to my condition."

"Condition?" Ilyana looked startled. "Are you..."

"My wife," Dewanne said smoothly, "suffers from a number of ailments, and the close air of the palace is not good for her congestion and rheumatism."

"Oh, I see." Ilyana flicked her ears and certainly didn't look like she understood.

"You're going back to the palace?" Volle asked Dewanne.

The other fox nodded. "Unfortunately, my duties require me to return sooner rather than later."

"I understand you will be taking Volyan with you." Lady Dewanne leaned across the table to smile at the cub.

"Yes, if all goes well." Volle put a paw between his ears, and the cub grinned.

She turned to Ilyana. "And will you be going with him?"

"I..." Ilyana turned briefly to Volle and then back. "No."

"I see." And when Lady Dewanne said it, she did look like she understood.

When Volyan finished his lunch, they returned to the hot pool, and this time, because it was empty, Lord and Lady Dewanne sat together away from the arch. Volle and Ilyana sat together, though too far apart to touch, and watched Volyan jump in and then jump out and run around before jumping in again. For a while Volle just soaked in the water, enjoying the heat and feeling no need to talk. Ilyana didn't either, but she kept looking at him and tilting her ears. He noticed at last that she did this most often just after Volyan had been around them, and so he decided to say something.

"He's a delightful cub," he said. "You must be...you've done a wonderful job."

Her ears came up, and she smiled. "I'm glad you think so." She sounded relieved, and he knew he'd guessed right about what she'd been thinking.

"I do. I'll be...that is, I'm proud to be his father."

"He's been so looking forward to this. It's hard for him not to have a father. The others..."

Volle nodded. "He said something about it. It'll be hard for him not to have a mother, too."

"Oh, he'll get used to it." She waved a paw, but looked away as she did so. "He's starting to get impatient with me anyway. I keep him down too much."

"He'll miss you," Volle said. "But I'll try to visit you more often."

She nodded. "He has a lot to learn."

"Yes. And I think I do too."

"He's very sweet. He won't be any trouble. And you'll have a tutor who will stay with him most of the time."

Volle considered that. "I want to spend some time with him. And where am I going to find a tutor?" He knew of some tutors around the palace, but didn't know any of them personally and couldn't have begun to start choosing one for his son.

"Tish and Tika will help."

"They're retiring soon."

"Not that soon. They'll be around for a little while still. And you can always write to me. I'd…like that."

He touched her arm. "I will."

She smiled at the touch, and just then Volyan slid between them. "Mommy!" he said. "I found where the water comes in! It's over there and I can just get my paws down to it but I can't keep them there. It's really hot!"

"That's nice, Voly."

"Come see! Come see! You too, daddy!" He scampered out of the pool again and beckoned them to follow him.

Ilyana grinned at Volle. "It doesn't do any good to ignore him. He has a remarkably long span of attention for such a young cub. He'll come back if we don't go see it."

Volle walked behind her, but didn't watch the curve of her hips or the swing of her tail. He was thinking about having a son to take care of, about all the responsibilities that went along with that. He didn't know if Streak would be much help (but that reminded him of Streak's plight up at the castle, and uneasiness stirred again in him, and guilt at being at this resort while Streak languished in his tower cell). But when he saw Volyan's eager expression and perked ears, he realized that he wanted to try it. And a nasty little thought crept into his head. If Streak didn't make it—if he had really killed that mouse, or if Volle couldn't save him—then he would be alone in the palace with his son. Unless he brought Ilyana. Her naked body in front of him gave him a sense of intimacy that almost made that scenario seem plausible, and for a second he pictured the two of them walking through his bedroom at the palace to see something their son was pointing to.

He dismissed the thought. Streak was going to be fine. He would love meeting Volyan and he and Volle would take care of him at the palace. He held that thought as he knelt down next to Volyan.

The cub was pointing excitedly to a little alcove in the pool. "Try it, try it!" They each dipped a paw in the pool and remarked on how hot it was, and Volyan, happy, scampered off.

Ilyana flicked her ears apologetically. "He's adventurous too."

"I've noticed that."

She seemed very much at ease with him, despite their nakedness. He had yet to catch her looking at his sheath, and her whole posture was very relaxed. He felt comfortable as well, and the more time he spent nude, the more used to it he became, even in front of her. They walked back to their spot in the pool side by side and got in together.

The water was starting to feel uncomfortable, but Volle had thought of some questions, so he stayed in. "What else will I need to do with him at the palace?"

"I have his clothes with me, so you can take those. You'll arrange for a tutor for him, and you'll have to get furnishings—a bed and a little desk, at least. I didn't bring *those* up from Vinton. And…take him around to my family every now and then. My mother keeps asking me to bring him to visit."

"Why haven't you?" He hadn't wondered this before, but was curious about it now.

"I couldn't travel with a cub that young. And then I kept putting it off, because I was worried that…" She lowered her eyes.

"That something might happen to him?"

"That you might want to keep him in the palace if I visited."

"Oh." He could see that now, and felt like a fool for asking, especially since she *was* giving him up. All he'd done was force her to make it clear that she didn't want to.

"I heard about the…business up at the castle," she said, lowering her voice.

"Yeah." Volle tried to make it clear in his tone and with his lowered ears that he didn't want to talk about it, and she took the hint.

After several more minutes of silence, Volle got up. "I think I'll go to the cooling pool before the dust bath. I'll see you later."

She nodded. "Good bye, Volle."

"Bye, Volyan," Volle called to the cub. "I'll see you later!"

The cub stopped in mid-run and spun around quite agilely, reaching Volle in a few seconds and wrapping his arms around Volle's legs. "Easy," Volle said with a grin. "I promise I'll see you later." He noticed Dewanne getting up and out of the pool as he disengaged Volyan from his legs.

"How much later?" the cub said, and Volle knelt to nuzzle him.

"After the dust baths. You be good, now."

Volyan said a cheerful, "okay!" and ran back to Ilyana. Volle watched him, smiled, and went into the changing room.

Dewanne stepped into the changing room while Volle was trying to decide whether he wanted to take his tunic, now filthy from Volyan dragging it on the ground and falling in it. He opted not to, deciding that the cub would like it, and as he turned around he saw Dewanne pulling his shorts on.

"I'll join you," the other fox said, and followed Volle to the cooling pool.

They eased into the warm water, and Volle waited for Dewanne to begin their private talk. The other fox seemed reluctant to do so, taking a lot of time to settle in and then just leaning back and relaxing. Finally he looked at Volle.

"What do you think of the resort, eh?"

Volle flicked his ears, curious but not wanting to press the older fox. "It's very nice, very relaxing. I can see why people come here."

"It's not the best resort in Tephos, of course, but it is the best in Vellenland." Dewanne looked up. "The architecture in Earthsteam up north of the Reysfields is much more pleasing to the eye. It's been modified throughout the years, you know, in a number of various styles. This is rather drab. But functional. The arches are a nice touch. That's unique to here."

"I don't like the arches much," Volle said.

"Well, it's an interesting principle." Dewanne didn't much seem interested in Volle's views, nor in discussing the arches. "There's a nice resort up in the northern mountains, where you wouldn't think there'd be hot springs, that does some nice visual tricks with the tiles in the pools. And the water there doesn't smell quite as strong."

"I don't mind the smell. It masks everything else."

"Yes, perfect for a land of weasels." Dewanne grinned. "Of course, we foxes are used to it."

"It is nice to be somewhere where I don't have to worry about my scent," Volle agreed.

"The water up in the mountains is even clearer, even from the hot springs. And the steam fills the air because it's so cold up there. You really must try it sometime."

Volle flicked his ears again, and grinned. "Is that what you wanted to talk to me about? Inviting me on a private vacation?" He was pretty sure he was wrong. He hoped he was wrong.

Dewanne snorted at him. "I'm not going to dignify that with an answer. Although I did plan to encourage you to spend more time with your own species."

Volle's good humor dissipated. "What do you mean? Once Streak is free, he'll come to the palace with me." *Once* had very nearly turned to *if* as he said it.

"Yes," Dewanne said. "You know, it's all very well if you like males. Nothing wrong with that as long as you have an heir. But really, to go about with a wolf…there are plenty of gay foxes out there."

"Not as many as you'd think."

"Regardless. They are there. And it would be more becoming to be with one of your own kind."

Volle was starting to feel quite irritated now. "Aren't we all brothers under Canis?"

"Oh, yes, yes, all one Family. But this country has long regarded foxes apart from the others, since Bucher's time and before that. In different ways, of course," he said with a touch of bitterness. "We were among the elite once, and Bucher took advantage of that. And then threw it all away."

"Seems more like it was taken from him," Volle said. "They killed him and all his family."

"And most of the other fox nobles," Dewanne agreed. "But he exploited his standing, tried to rise even higher, and in the end fell further than he had risen. And dragged all of us down with him."

"How did your family survive?"

"My grandfather was at home at the time. He had a small infirmity of the back that made travel wearisome, so he spent a good deal of his time at home, and I believe he had an inkling of what was coming. The people in Dewanne did not subscribe to the mass hysteria that took over Divalia and other parts of the country. So our family was spared. But it was a long time before my father dared return to the palace. My grandfather never did."

Volle was silent, and after a moment Dewanne continued. "So when I heard there might be a scion of Vinton alive, I pursued the rumor and found you, and Tish was kind enough to help me bring you to the palace. Where, I might add, you have behaved rather poorly on occasion."

Volle bristled. "I've tried to do my best. It's not my fault Dereath has a grudge against me." The denial had become so that it was easy to sound natural with it.

Dewanne shrugged. "We asked you to keep a low profile and instead you get involved with Lord Ikling, of all people, and then thrown in prison and exiled. The people are feeling a lot of guilt over the murder of Bucher and his family, which is partly why you were accepted, but that only goes so far. If this hearing goes well, I hope you will learn a lesson from the past."

"Is that what you wanted to do? Lecture me on my behavior?" He felt close to getting up and walking out of the pool.

"No. Keep your fur down. I wanted to talk to you about a delicate matter, but your behavior does play a part in it." Volle settled down a little, but his ears remained flat. Dewanne didn't comment, though he surely noticed. "Because of Bucher's behavior, there are precious few foxes in the nobility."

"There's Vanadi, and…"

"Don't be silly. I mean reds, and you know it." He looked around and lowered his voice. "This isn't easy for me."

"Sorry." He'd been intentionally contrary because Dewanne had annoyed him. Now he saw that the older fox was bothered by something more personal than the general state of foxes in the Tephos peerage. His ears came up.

"You have a fine son," Dewanne said. "The kind I would like to have."

Volle looked curiously at him. "You don't have any children?"

Dewanne shook his head. "I…we don't know if we'll be able to."

"Oh. I'm sorry."

"I'd been hoping for some time, but a couple years ago…"

Volle nodded. He was silent for a moment, but Dewanne didn't go on immediately. "Surely there must be…I mean, you haven't only been with your wife?"

"I do not have any other progeny," Dewanne said stiffly.

"Okay. Isn't that…I mean, I think that if you wanted to take another wife…" Volle wasn't sure how to talk about this. He'd never been that close to Dewanne, and being taken into his confidence was unsettling. He had no idea what Dewanne was leading up to.

"I'm not leaving Delia," Dewanne snapped. "Will you please stop talking and just listen?"

"Sorry."

"Thank you." The older fox settled back against the edge of the pool. "I'm not certain…that the problem is with Delia."

Volle blinked. "Oh," he said softly. Then he blinked again. "You want *me* to…?"

"No!" Dewanne said hurriedly. "I…have a different idea. One that hopefully will not be as drastic." He took a breath. "If I die without issue, the seat will be empty and the King can assign it as he wishes. My governor is a good fox, but, alas, also childless. In fact, you might like him."

"I hardly think that would solve your problem, even if he did want to move to Divalia."

"Yes, of course. At any rate, if the King assigns it, there are few enough noble foxes that I could not be sure the seat would remain vulpine. In fact, I am almost sure it would not. So I have a proposition for you. If you and your wife have another cub, I will name him my heir and he will be Lord Dewanne. If a female, she will still inherit but she will have to find a noble fox to marry."

Volle lay back, stunned. "Really?"

"Yes, Vinton. I would rather my land pass to another fox of noble blood, even if he is not of my blood."

He thought about that for a few more seconds. "What if Ilyana doesn't want another cub?"

"She'd be foolish not to. Mother of two Lords? What other vixen could say that? What other female could say that? Besides, I see how attached she is to Volyan. She'll want another one."

"Well…that's very generous of you. I'm really touched, Dewanne."

"Don't be too touched. You're the only other fox I can turn to."

"So even if I were, say, Lord Vallerian, but still a fox…"

Dewanne chuckled. "All right. You have a point."

"So let me be flattered. I will talk to Ilyana about it, but I don't see a problem with it."

"Thank you." Dewanne heaved a sigh. "And thank you for not making that *much* more difficult than it had to be."

Volle smiled. "Sorry. I didn't know."

Dewanne shrugged, and then heaved himself up, stepping up on the bench. "I'm about ready to dry off. You?"

Volle nodded and followed him out of the pool, along the tile and into the changing room. He felt a bit odd about Dewanne's offer, but he couldn't see anything wrong with it. Clearly he loved his wife too much to let Volle father a cub on her—or else she had nixed that idea. That would be the cleanest way to handle things—Dewanne could claim the cub for his own and there'd be no trouble passing on the succession.

Unless, perhaps, he was worried that it might come to light later that he was unable to father cubs, and the cub's succession were to be called into doubt. In that case, he was taking the most certain route by bestowing the title on a noble cub in such a way that the transfer wouldn't be questioned. That made the most sense, upon reflection, and Lord and Lady Dewanne must have spent a good deal of reflection on this question. Volle was glad he didn't have to deal with their problem.

He pulled on his shorts, which by now were fairly wet despite not being worn for most of the day. Dewanne led him across the compound to a group of about ten small huts. An otter dressed in a simple blue linen skirt greeted them out front.

"Male or female?"

"Female, please," said Dewanne before Volle could answer.

"Yes, sahr. And you?" The otter turned to Volle.

"What am I choosing?" he asked Dewanne.

"Male for him," Dewanne said to the otter.

"There is a female attendant available now. For the male, there will be a short wait. I am sorry, sahr." The otter had turned to Volle and bowed slightly.

"Do you mind if I go ahead?"

Volle shook his head, though Dewanne had already taken a step forward and he suspected the other fox didn't care what his response would be. "Be my guest."

"Thanks." Dewanne followed the otter to one of the huts and disappeared inside. Volle watched him go, then walked over to the bench and sat back, closing his eyes and letting the warm sun toast his chest-fur. Out here, away from the sulfurous springs, his sense of smell was returning, though there was still a ghost of sulfur overlaying everything.

He half-dozed in the sunlight until the otter's shadow fell across his muzzle and the thick musteline scent intruded on his awareness. "Sahr? There is a cabin free."

Volle cracked one eye open and saw the otter's earnest muzzle in front of him. Blinking against the sunlight, he could just make out another figure wandering back through the compound. The scent was too faint for him to catch. He yawned, got to his feet, and followed the otter through the compound to a hut with an open door.

To his surprise, he saw sunlight streaming down inside. The roof had a large hole in the center, and a hanging canvas flap showed how it could be covered in case of rain. The hut had only one room, and in the center was a low bath filled with fine white powder scented with a mild piney aroma. To one side stood a waist-high bench covered with brushes and a few other tools, and in front of the bench stood a smiling otter in a white skirt who bowed and ushered Volle into the hut. The other otter said, "Enjoy your bath, sahr," and closed the door as he left.

The attendant otter stood patiently while Volle examined the bath. It was lower than he was used to, and included a small dust-free basin at one end that he guessed he was supposed to rest his head in. The dust was smoothed over; certainly there had been others in it earlier that day, but he would never have known it from looking at the bath. That was what two of the tools on the bench were for, he guessed. One was a small rake-like implement and the other was similar, but with a flat edge. He also saw a small ceramic bowl half-filled with lotion next to the three different-sized brushes that had been carefully cleaned of all fur.

His gaze turned to the otter, who was younger than the others he'd met but possessed of the same cheerful self-assurance. Even while waiting for Volle to finish his inspection, he wore a patient smile and held his paws clasped behind his back. His chest was firm and fluffy with a ruff of soft-looking fur, and his stomach was trim and well-groomed. He was less stocky than the other otters Volle had seen, with almost a weasel-like build.

When Volle didn't say anything, the otter spoke. He had a somewhat high-pitched voice, but not unpleasant. "If sahr would like to get in the bath?" One of his paws slid out smoothly from behind his back and gestured to the basin.

Volle started to step into the bath, then stopped and put a paw to his shorts. The otter nodded, and pointed to a small basket at the back of the hut that held several discarded garments. Beside it, another basket held a stack of neatly folded clothes. He hesitated, then slipped his shorts down over his hips and threw the wet fabric into the basket. He glanced back at the otter, who continued to watch him with the same patient smile. Volle couldn't detect any interest in his nakedness, nor was he sure whether or not he wanted to. It was more intimate in these small, confined quarters than it had been in the relatively open areas of the pools, but he reminded himself that the otter was a professional. Stepping slowly, he got into the bath.

And stopped, kneeling in the bath, the pine-scented white powder already clinging to his wet fur. "Um…on my stomach or my back?"

"Back first, sahr," said the otter, "then roll onto your stomach. Head in the head rest there." He pointed to the dust-free basin.

Volle nodded, lay on his back and rubbed his fur into the dust. Pine scent rose around him and he inhaled deeply, losing the hint of sulfur in his nose. He rolled over onto his stomach and rested his head in the stone basin, his muzzle almost reaching the bottom. There, he could almost catch the elusive scent of the people who'd been there before him, but even the gentle scent of pine was overwhelming and the stone didn't retain scents well.

The otter waited until he was settled, then began scooping dust onto his back, legs, and arms. The pine grew stronger, and the soft weight of the dust settled into his fur, warm from the sunlight. His eyes drifted shut and stayed closed as the brush first touched him.

The bristles moved through his fur in long, even strokes, and the otter's gentle paw followed behind, smoothing the fur down. The effect was relaxing, very soothing, and any tension that was left in Volle's body drained away.

When the otter had brushed out all of Volle's fur, he paused. Volle heard the soft click as he put down the brush and picked up another, and then he started brushing Volle's tail with a longer-bristled brush. It reminded him of the way Streak liked to brush his fur, and this time rather than push the memory away, he let it enfold him. The scents were blurry enough in his nose that with his eyes closed, he could pretend that the white wolf was there brushing his fur, that it was his rough, strong paws and not the otter's soft, delicate ones that smoothed down Volle's russet fur and gently caressed him. He tried to focus on the happiness of the memory and not their current situation, and while the brush ran through his tail he almost managed it. He knew Streak's scent so well that he could fool himself into thinking he could smell it there.

"Turn over please, sahr," the otter said, dispelling the illusion Volle had nearly lost himself in. He sighed and rested for a moment, working his paws through the dust, and then turned over onto his back. The otter placed a cushion across the head rest to support the back of his head, and then set to brushing his tail again.

Volle closed his eyes, but he couldn't convince himself that Streak was there any more. The sight of his paw covered in white powder, still wet, reminded him with an almost physical pain of the paw he had clutched in the rain only last night. He might as well open his eyes, he figured.

The otter seemed to know. He turned and smiled a moment later, then continued his brushing. He was pleasant enough to look at, and Volle felt a stirring. He tried to quell it, but when the otter switched to a shorter brush and carefully groomed his chest and legs, it grew stronger. The more he tried to ignore it, the more aware he was of it. The stirring spread to a swelling in his sheath, and as his member slid free, he thought about apologizing.

But the otter just kept brushing, his expression changing only through various shades of concentration on his task. When he'd finished brushing Volle's arms, he switched to a small, fine brush and carefully brushed the fur around his sheath and sac, and then gently brushed those as well.

By this time, Volle was fully aroused. Must happen fairly often, he thought, and indeed the otter's muzzle and ears showed little surprise when he put his small brush away and looked at Volle. "I can perform other services, sahr, if you wish."

It was tempting, very tempting, and Volle considered for several seconds before shaking his head. "No, thank you. I appreciate the offer." He smiled. "Just thinking about someone." His body pleaded with him to accept, but Streak's memory and the otter's businesslike attitude had made him hesitate just long enough. How long had it been since anyone but Streak had touched him like that? He wanted it, very badly, the more so because it had been so many days, and in fact the moment he said no, he regretted it. Streak wouldn't mind, he told himself, or maybe it was his arousal telling him that.

The otter nodded, with that same smile. "Of course, sahr. When you are ready, you may stand." He stood attentively.

Volle raised himself to his elbows and glanced down at his length, still very full. "About those 'other services,'" he said hesitantly. "Um, how much…"

He was trying to figure out how to ask "how much are you allowed to do," but the otter jumped in when he paused. "The charge will be added to your bill, sahr. There is no need to worry about paying now."

"Charge?" He felt his arousal start to flag.

"Yes, sahr. For the other services, there is a small additional charge."

"I see." Dewanne was treating him, he supposed, because he hadn't been asked to make any sort of payment or promise as they entered, and now he remembered the weasel asking Dewanne if Volle was his guest. That meant that if he did anything, the charge would be billed to Dewanne, and Volle was sure it was just what Dewanne expected of him.

He sighed. He didn't particularly want Dewanne to be able to hold that over him, not after their discussion earlier. The other fox had irritated him with his self-righteous judgment of Volle's behavior, and Volle didn't want to give him any more ammunition. And besides that, he was now facing the practical concern that his erection had already slid partway back into his sheath.

He smiled at the otter. "I'll pass, for now, I think."

"I'm sorry, sahr." The otter's whiskers had drooped, and as much as his small ears could, they were swiveled down. "I should not have mentioned the cost."

"No, no." Volle got up carefully, trying not to raise clouds of dust. "The moment had passed, that's all."

"If you say so, sahr." The otter held his brush ready as Volle stepped out of the bath, and started with his back.

Volle sighed inwardly at the otter's gentle touch, regretting the missed opportunity somewhat, but thinking more of Streak. He had to see the wolf again. And down here, away from the castle, with Dereath a more distant memory, the price didn't seem too high after all. Not that he suspected they would allow him any length of private time in the tower cell, but at least it would be something.

The otter switched to the longer brush to touch up his tail, then moved to his front. He used the smaller brush delicately on the inside of Volle's thighs and up near his sac, cleaning the dust out, and then stood up on a small stool to clean his muzzle of the traces of dust it had picked up. As he put the brushes down, Volle felt his fur and found it to be only mildly damp.

Holding out one of the folded clothes from the basket, the otter bowed slightly. "As sahr leaves, there will be basking areas should sahr wish to dry in the sun."

Volle smiled and took the shorts, pulling them on with a bit of regret over his smoothly brushed fur. He hadn't felt this clean in a long time. "Thank you. You did a wonderful job."

"Thank you, sahr. If you are here tomorrow, I would be greatly honored if you returned to my bath." The otter moved to the door and opened it for him.

"If I am here, I certainly will." He patted the otter's head and walked out.

The basking area, when he found it, was rather crowded. Dewanne and the vixens were there, but he pretended not to see them and instead took a solitary bench near two weasels who were chattering back and forth. He lost their words in the rhythmic murmurs, closed his eyes in the warm sun, and thought about his decision. To give Dereath what he wanted—did he really want to go through with that?

He couldn't think of anything else to do. It had now been two days, and he had to see Streak, had to be sure he wasn't guilty, had to assure the wolf that everything was going to be okay. Nothing was as important as that, not Dereath, not Nero, not anything. And as long as he took enough precautions with Dereath, and remained on guard...well, it was just sex, wasn't it? Even if the thought did make him faintly nauseous.

To quell the unpleasant feeling, he thought about Streak, imagining that the sun's warmth was the white wolf's body on top of his. He smiled, picturing how their reunion would feel, and the relief they would feel when Streak was cleared of the murder. The visions relaxed him so much that although he hadn't felt tired, he was asleep in moments.

Chapter 8

*H*e heard Ilyana's voice as if through a haze, calling his name. Then a huge weight landed on his stomach, shocking him awake and leaving him gasping for breath.

"Voly!" Ilyana sounded like she was trying not to laugh as she scolded the cub, and as Volle's vision came back into focus, he saw that the weight on his stomach had orange fur, a tail, and a big smile.

"Hi, Daddy," it said.

"Hi," he wheezed, and reached out to move the cub off his stomach. Volyan was dressed now, he saw, at least in a small pair of yellow shorts, if not a shirt or tunic. "You're pretty heavy, aren't you?"

"Just when he jumps." Ilyana smiled and took the cub's paw, helping him down from the bench. "We're going to dinner and wondered if you'd be joining us." She had dressed in a simple tunic, belted around the waist. It looked good on her.

He rubbed his stomach and sat upright. "If I still have anywhere to put it."

The dinner was served at the lunch pavilion in the same informal manner, and was largely composed of the same type of food. "Where are Lord and Lady Dewanne?" Volle asked as they sat down, bowls appearing in front of them almost instantly.

"They're eating over there with some other nobles who came down this afternoon." Ilyana helped Volyan sit up to the table and reach his bowl. "They said they thought we might like a little time as a family."

Volle's ears flicked back before he could help it. He saw Ilyana notice, and said, "Sorry. Dewanne was giving me a hard time about Streak today. Wants me to stay with my own 'kind.'"

"I haven't known him very long. Has he always been like that?"

Volle shrugged and talked around a mouthful of fruit and poultry. "Dewanne? I don't know. I wasn't seeing Streak until this year."

"Is he going to be okay?" She said it softly, but he thought there was an edge to her voice as well.

"If I can help it." Volle kept his voice low as well. Volyan was absorbed in his food and didn't even look up.

She took another mouthful, swallowed, and kept her eyes on her bowl. "If...you know. I mean, if it turns out that..."

"We'll worry about it then." He said it quickly, not wanting to think about that possibility right now, much less discuss it. His earlier thoughts were still swirling around in his head, but he pushed them aside and tried to keep a clear perspective. He had to go save Streak.

"Right." She dipped her ears apologetically and took another bite.

Volyan looked up after a moment of silence and said, "I had a streak on my knee. It hurt a lot."

"Scrape, dear. You had a scrape." Ilyana patted him on the head.

"Oh yeah. I scraped my knee."

"How did you do that?" Volle intended to distract the cub, and got his wish, as Volyan launched into the story of how he had been running across the stone floor trying to catch a mouse and had fallen on his knee and scraped it. Volle suspected that some of the story was embellished—he doubted that the stones had been covered in blood, for example—but the cub clearly enjoyed telling it.

They made small talk for the rest of the dinner, and when it was over, Volle hugged Volyan and said he had to leave. "I want to see if I can get up to the castle before it's too late." He eyed the sun, already near the horizon.

"We'll walk you to the front, then, if that's okay." Ilyana took Volyan's paw and guided him through the tables to the edge of the pavilion, then let him scamper free across the ground.

She and Volle followed behind at a more leisurely pace, and he thought again of how nice it was, but pushed the thought back. If Streak were here, he told himself, it would be just as nice, if not more. That thought made him feel worse, because he wanted to show the wolf this resort. To distract himself, he told Ilyana what Dewanne had proposed.

"Really?" She said it thoughtfully, looking at Volyan.

"Yes. So if you do want another cub, well…"

"Of course I do. I was going to ask you about that before this visit is over."

"All right. Well, I'll be glad to be of, you know, service."

"As long as you don't throw up again."

He smiled wryly. "I'll think of something. Maybe I'll get drunk on something smoother than blackberry mead."

She didn't say anything, but her tail drooped at that remark. He touched her shoulder. "It's not you. I think you're very pretty. It's just the way I am."

"I know." She smiled, stepped close, and he put his arms around her. She slid hers around his waist as well, and they hugged for a brief moment until Volyan leaped into them.

"Mommy! Daddy!" He wagged his tail. "There's a weasel outside and I'm almost as big as he is!"

"You're a big cub, I told you that." Volle smiled and knelt down. "I have to go, but I'll see you again soon."

"Aww. Stay with us tonight, Daddy!" The cub threw his arms around Volle.

"I can't." Volle nuzzled him gently. "But I'll be back, I promise."

Ilyana helped to disengage Volyan over sniffling protests. Volle smoothed his head fur and ears, and nodded to Ilyana. "Thank Dewanne for me, if you see him."

"All right." She touched her nose to his. "Good night, Volle."

"Good night, Ilyana." He watched her walk out of the gate and down the street. He thought about offering to pay for a carriage for them, but realized that he didn't have any money, and also that the town was not too far away. He asked the weasel about a carriage, and was told that one would be along directly to take him back to the mansion.

He watched the sun sinking and looked around to see the mountain the castle stood on. It was shrouded in clouds; he couldn't see any of the castle. He thought about Streak up there, thought about Ilyana walking back to town alone, and it was clear to him where he needed to be, no matter what the price. When the carriage pulled up, he jumped in, and almost told the driver to take him directly to the castle, until he remembered that he was wearing only a pair of plain shorts, and should probably change first.

For the whole ride, he grew more and more anxious. Having resolved to give Dereath what he wanted, he now wanted to get it over with as quickly as possible. Darkness had fallen by the time they pulled up to the guest door at the mansion, so Volle hurried past the footservants into his chambers. He'd stripped his shorts off and was hunting through his wardrobe when he heard a familiar cough.

"You could knock," he said, flicking his ears back without turning around. "Do you *try* to come in while I'm naked?"

"Just a side benefit," Helfer chuckled. "Maybe if you wore clothes more often, people wouldn't walk in on you naked so often."

Volle selected a pair of trousers and slipped into them, then pulled down a soft cotton tunic. "You know, I'd argue with that, except that I spent most of the day naked."

"Really?" Helfer sounded more interested. "Anyone I know?"

"Dewanne." Volle hesitated between a deep blue doublet and a light green one.

"Really. I never would have guessed. Was he good?"

"And Lady Dewanne. And Ilyana."

"You know, I didn't think you were into that kinky stuff."

"And Volyan."

"Your cub?"

"We were at the Burning Waters resort." Volle finally turned and grinned at Helfer as he slipped on the light green doublet.

"Whew!" Helfer smiled in mock relief. "Glad to hear you still have good taste. Did you enjoy it?"

Volle nodded. "It was very relaxing. There are good attendants down there, too. But you must know that."

"I've only been once. But it was good, yes." He eyed Volle's clothes. "If you're dressing for dinner, you're late."

"I'm going up to the castle. I'm going to give Dereath what he wants. I need to get to Streak."

"I don't think you should do that tonight."

Volle stared at Helfer. "You told me this morning that I should. You said it was just sex." He held up a paw as Helfer started to talk. "No, you did, and you were right. I realized that today. There was this adorable young otter down at the spa, and he was brushing me, and I wanted him, Hef. And he would've done it, or done something, anyway, but I wanted Streak more. And I thought, you know, how bad can it be with Dereath? However bad it is, it'll be over and then I'll get to see him. I have to. I have to know whether he did it or not. If not, I have to be at his side. If he did…"

Helfer just watched him struggle for words. "If he did," Volle went on, "then…then I have to figure out what to do. I have a wife and a cub, and a life, and if I survive the hearing, I'll have to start worrying about that. So you see? I have to go. I have to get it over with."

"That all makes sense, Volle. I just don't think you should do it tonight, because Dereath's not at the castle."

"What?"

"You remember how I told you I was going to take some people down to the orchards?" Volle nodded. "Well, I had to go down there with Alister and Villutian and Dereath and a bunch of others and take them around, because we hadn't had it approved…" He rolled his eyes. "Anyway, they're all still down there. I came up early because I wanted to have dinner here, and they didn't need me anymore."

"Oh." Volle crossed to the bed and sat down. He folded his arms in his lap. "Will they all be down there tomorrow?"

"Most of the nobles are going, but not until the afternoon. They'll be up there in the morning." Helfer walked over and patted him on the shoulder. "Glad I could help. Though it sounds like the cute young otter was more help."

"He sure helped put things in perspective." Volle smiled. "Though in a way, he didn't help, if you know what I mean. Of course, I would've had to pay him to."

Helfer whistled. "I hadn't thought…you don't have access to any of Vinton's funds, do you?"

"No. Not until I'm cleared. I don't really need them, but…"

"Say no more. And don't think about paying me back for staying here, if you even were. It's my pleasure to have you here."

"Thanks, Hef. I already owe you a lot. I'll just add this on."

The weasel grinned. "That's what friends are for. Tell you what. I'll ride up with you in the morning and if you don't feel like telling Archie what you're doing, I will. I feel like at least he should know."

"Why? Is he into that sort of thing?" Volle wasn't at all sure he wanted Archie to know.

"To make sure you're safe. I don't think there's anything to worry about, but I wouldn't have said anyone could commit a murder here, either. So just to be on the safe side."

"Thanks, but I think I'd prefer to tell him myself. I'm not sure how much of the truth he needs to know."

"Enough that he realizes you might be in some danger."

Volle nodded. "Yeah. All right. Though I don't know…he already doesn't know whether to trust me or Dereath."

Helfer snorted. "Then he's not half as bright as I gave him credit for when I told Burren to go ahead and appoint him."

Volle looked up with interest. "I didn't think you took that active an interest in local affairs."

The weasel grinned again, tail swishing. "I don't. But I assume I must have approved his hiring, so I must have thought he was pretty intelligent or Burren would never have told me to sign the approval."

Volle laughed, and it felt good to laugh. He hadn't realized how tense he'd become until he felt himself relax. "All right, Hef. I promise I'll tell him."

"Good."

"So are you taking all the nobles around tomorrow, or do they have someone to do that?"

The weasel sat on the bed and snorted. "No, it's my job. I tried to convince them that Huster could do it, but they said I have to be the one. So I'll be leaving in the afternoon and probably we'll have dinner down there. You can come along too, of course."

The empty castle might provide another opportunity to see or help Streak. Dereath surely wouldn't want to collect on his promise until that night. Volle shook his head. "Sorry. I think I'll stay around the castle."

"Tish is going, and Tika too."

"I've just got too much on my mind, Hef."

"All right." The weasel shrugged. "I'll bring back some fruit for you."

"Thanks." Volle yawned and leaned back, and Helfer stood. "I should let you get to sleep. We'll get up for a run tomorrow?"

"Wouldn't miss it." Volle smiled and held his arms out to his friend. Helfer smiled back and stepped into the embrace. "Good night, Hef."

"Night, Volle. See you in the morning."

"Unless you want to stay and watch me undress."

The weasel winked. "Seen it." He waved, and left, closing the door behind him.

Volle grinned and shook his head. He slipped the doublet off and stood up, carrying it over to the wardrobe and replacing it. Slowly, he shed the tunic and pants as well, and walked back to his bed. He got in and lay down, staring at the ceiling. Tomorrow, he thought. Tomorrow he would take care of it. He would endure whatever Dereath had in store for him, and then he would demand to be taken to Streak immediately.

Perhaps because of his earlier nap, perhaps because of his restless thoughts, it took him a long time to fall asleep.

He dreamt that he was in Dereath's quarters, standing naked in front of the bed. Captain Nero was lying on the bed, also naked. He didn't look like Nero; his fur was covered in a white powder and he was slender. But he had Nero's voice: a low, deep growl that in his dream was strangely seductive. *Come on*, he said, *get your sheath up.*

Volle looked down and saw his erection. *It is*, he said.

Then come here. This is what you wanted, isn't it? The white Nero sat up and Volle saw his shaft, similarly erect and pink against the white fur. He patted his lap.

Volle was on the bed, then, and he felt the wolf hard under his tail. The wolf's paw stroked him up and down. *We have to do this*, he said, *until the truth comes out. You're not afraid, are you?*

He became aware that Dereath was standing by the bed watching them. The sensations were familiar but didn't build to a climax, and after a little while Dereath took him by the paw and led him off the bed. *That's enough. You can go.*

He was in another room then, a door closed behind him, and it was Streak's tower cell, but he was standing in the rain. He turned to see who had closed the door, but only Ilyana's scent came to him. He knew he was standing in Streak's cell, but when he turned back around, it was the small hut with the bath in the center, and the young otter stood there, naked and dripping. He smiled tentatively, and Volle knew he was waiting to be paid. He handed him three coins that he found in his paw, and the otter put them down, then sat in the white powdery bath, which seemed to be sheltered from the rain. The dust crept up his fur as he beckoned to Volle. *This is what you wanted, isn't it? You're not afraid, are you?*

The scent of otter was strong in his nostrils, and his sheath thrummed with desire. He took a step toward the bath, put his paw down, and felt the white dust envelop him like a blanket. The otter put a paw on his dust-covered sheath. *Lord Vinton?*

The dust was more and more thick atop him. He tried to push it aside. "Lord Vinton?"

Slowly he blinked into wakefulness. He had his paws full of blankets and a voice was whispering his name. His nose was still full of the scent of otter, and as he turned to the bedside, he saw the young otter from the bath house kneeling there, one paw on his stomach. "Lord Vinton?" the otter whispered.

"Wha—? How did…?" he said blurrily.

"Lord Ikling sent me," and Volle realized as the otter said it that he was older than the otter from the bath house. His chest was broader and his voice was deeper.

"For what?" He was still trying to shake the sleep from his eyes.

"He was worried you were lonely." The otter smiled, his paw slipping down to the bulge that covered Volle's hardness, very tight and very full. "I suppose he was right. You do feel lonely."

"Listen," Volle said, brought more awake by the touch, "I…"

"It's all right." The otter stood in a fluid motion, so Volle could see his large sac and maleness, hanging between his legs. He let Volle have a good look as he slowly pulled the blanket back. "It's what I'm here for."

His fur was silvery in the night, though there wasn't much light. Either the moon had gone behind a cloud, or it hadn't risen yet. But the otter had definitely risen. His maleness was sleek and full, and despite the dim light, Volle could see it clearly in the reflected light from the otter's ivory white chest and stomach-fur.

His protests ebbed away. The otter smiled again and knelt on either side of his legs, pinning them down. He bent down and applied a large, soft tongue to Volle's sac. As hard as it was, Volle's erection still jumped and shivered at that touch. He clutched the blankets and gasped softly as the tongue lapped over and over, dampening the fur, describing the roundness and caressing it, pushing against the hard base of his erection that lay behind his sac. The tongue moved up and slowly slid along his length, as lovingly and familiarly as if they had been lovers many times before.

The scent of otter was too strong for Volle to imagine anyone else. He tried pressing one of the pillows to his nose, but Streak's scent on it was old. All it did was muffle his moans as the otter's touch made his knot swell larger. His body felt as though it were on fire. He knew it was only because he had been celibate for several days, but knowing didn't diminish the pleasure, or the undertone of guilt. So he left Streak's memory behind and cried out in pleasure as the otter's paw gripped his knot, taking his length fully into the warm muzzle.

This is what you wanted, isn't it?

His legs tensed and gathered as he felt his release building, but the otter did too, and stopped abruptly. Volle threw the pillow aside and looked up at him, unable to form words, his body so close.

"My, you are lonely." The otter smiled. "I was told to give you the full treatment." He moved forward on Volle, straddling his stomach, and lifted Volle's slick erection before settling down.

Volle's whole body convulsed as the short fur brushed his shaft, soft and yet not as plush as the only other fur to touch it in the past year. And then the otter's tight tail hole and rear had surrounded his shaft, slid down its length slowly, and had pressed up against his knot. Volle gasped and moaned, anticipating the fire he would feel when the otter pushed down further, but the otter was in no hurry. He slid up and down, keeping Volle on the edge, and if the fox thought he couldn't get any closer without coming, he realized he'd been wrong.

The otter's erection waved up and down in front of him, and when he put a paw on it, the otter made a soft chirring noise. He kept stroking, barely aware of the slick pre dripping from the end, mostly just occupying his paw. His soft pads stroked over the thick length, registering that it was shorter and thicker than he was used to; his strokes kept sliding off the end. It felt wrong to him, but he adjusted.

His knot felt as though it were going to burst. The otter was moving faster and faster, and the fire was building in him even without the pressure on his knot. The otter's shaft was quivering beneath his paw and seemed already on the edge. "Nice...fox..." he panted, his breaths becoming heavier and deeper. And then he pressed his rear down against Volle's hips.

Volle's knot seemed to explode. The otter kept his tail hole tight as he forced Volle's knot into it, and Volle arched his back as the explosion spread throughout his body. He moaned loudly as the convulsions forced his seed out into the otter in spasms, each one a bright wave of pleasure rushing through him. It had only been a few days, but it was as if he hadn't had a climax in weeks, or months. He was aware that he was still moaning, and he closed his muzzle as he sank back onto the bed.

He kept his paw moving, and moments later the scent of otter grew sharper and stronger. He felt a warm splash against the fur of his ear, then another on his chest, and the otter's pants became moans of passion. He tugged on Volle's knot as his body shook, and Volle clenched his teeth, yelping between them at the pressure on his sensitive member.

His paw was sticky when he drew it back. He felt serene, but as the pleasure subsided, the undertone of guilt remained. He convinced himself that Streak wouldn't care. Then he convinced himself again. It didn't seem to take.

"Lord...Vinton," the otter panted. "I hope you feel...less lonely."

"Yes," Volle lied. "Thank you. You were wonderful." That part, at least, he could be sincere about.

The otter smiled, whiskers twitching. "Well," he said, "you obviously needed it, my Lord."

"Yes, I did." He felt sleep stealing up on him again, but held it off for the moment. He had needed it, and as he thought about it, he didn't want his first time in that many days to be with Dereath. He might have enjoyed it too much. "What's your name? How did Helfer know you?"

"I'm Ellitt, my Lord. Lord Ikling knows the establishment where I work. He sent Huster down tonight specifically looking for an otter, and since Jillick was off tonight..." He shrugged and smiled.

"You can tell Lord Ikling that you performed admirably."

"Thank you, my Lord." The otter smiled and wriggled. Volle's knot was subsiding, but he was still tied to the otter.

Volle knew mustelids and knew Ellitt would be ready for more in a few minutes, but thankfully, he didn't feel any obligation to take care of it. He would probably be up for another round soon, since it had been so long, but he thought sleep was going to win out. He wished it were Streak sitting astride him, Streak brushing his chest's fur, Streak's thick, (*fluffy*) muscular tail lying on his legs, but the best he could cling to was that tomorrow, he would take the first step toward seeing the wolf again.

Sleep overtook him then in short waves. He came fully awake when Ellitt lifted himself up, letting his shaft slide free. The otter gave it a short caress and then covered Volle with the blankets again. Seeing Volle's eyes on him, he smiled and gave a short bow. "Good night, Lord Vinton." The moonlight gleamed off his fur in a way that made it look wet. Through the filter of his dream, Volle saw him almost glisten.

"Night," he murmured, lifting a paw.

Ellitt bent to pick up a garment from the floor, stepped into a pair of shorts, and then slipped from the room. Volle didn't see him go.

In the morning, he smelled the otter scent all over his bed, dispelling any thought he might have had that the episode was just a dream. Lying in bed, he tried to sort through the chaotic whirl of his feelings. He felt guilty, but he didn't know why. He and Streak had never talked about being exclusive to each other, but they'd never had the opportunity not to be. Streak's reaction upon hearing about Volle's prior escapades had been caution, with some amusement, as though he weren't worried about it happening again. But they'd never discussed it. Volle realized that one thing making him more tense than anything else was that he didn't know how Streak would react when he found out about the night with Ellitt.

If he found out.

He pushed that thought aside and flicked his ears, suddenly aware of the encrustations on his left. He got up and walked to the bathroom, still brooding. It hadn't been wrong, what he did, but he felt bad for having enjoyed it so much. Maybe it was that he felt he'd replaced Streak—but he clearly hadn't.

But was he worried Streak would see it that way?

With rough strokes, he brushed the dried semen from his ear and chest, adding some scented powder so at least he wouldn't be carrying the same scent on him. He watched the fur settle to the floor. How long had it been since he'd brushed someone else's scent out of his fur? In an odd way, he missed that, and the little voices inside his head were growing louder, more seductive, telling him that he could have Ellitt or someone like him every night. Someone different, every night. A wife to look after his son and leave him free to gather intelligence and seduce young males over at the Lonely Cock.

A return to the past he'd thought had slipped away.

Avery and Tish would be happy about that—one less liability to worry about. And his duty to Fox said he should look after his family, his pack. Who was more his pack than his wife and son? But the thought of sending the young wolf away brought a new kind of ache. Like it or not, he couldn't bring himself to do it. He loved Streak, and while he'd been in love before and not worried about being with other people, this time was different. "I'm not twenty any more," he muttered to himself. "And I'm not a weasel."

Helfer had no concept of a time when he wouldn't be able to wander down to a bar and pick up a young rabbit. Or maybe he did, but the money his estate brought him would mean he would always have a bed at the Jackal's Staff, the all-male brothel in Divalia near the palace. But Ellitt had driven something home to Volle; that as much as he might long for another one-night-stand, he longed for a familiar touch even more. Streak was his pack and his family, and he knew Fox would understand.

He only hoped Streak understood too, when Volle was forced to tell him about Ellitt. If only Helfer hadn't hired him. Volle had been doing well enough on his own; yes, he'd been tempted by the otter in the bath house, but conscience and fate had prevented him from giving in there. Last night, he'd been sleepy and he hadn't really had a chance to say no. And he'd enjoyed it. A lot. He felt guilty even as he replayed some of the memories in his head, and he knew that just the fact that he felt guilty meant it had been wrong on some level, and he threw the brush to the floor in frustration.

And of course, it was just at that moment that Helfer walked in.

"You ready yet?" The weasel poked his head into the bathroom, lifted his nose and smiled. "I can tell you and Ellitt enjoyed yourselves. Was he cute?"

Volle grunted noncommittally. Helfer seemed so proud of what he'd done, and completely oblivious to the anguish Volle was going through because of him. Normally Helfer's shortsightedness wasn't a problem, but this time was too much.

"What? Didn't it work out?" Helfer's smile faded.

"It was fine. He was cute. Let's just go." Volle brushed by the weasel and out of the bedroom.

Helfer followed him out of the room and down the hall, "Didn't you like him? I was just trying to help you out. I mean, I can tell something happened there. You said yourself you wanted that otter at the resort."

They were outside before Volle answered. "Yes, I did. But I didn't do anything about it and I should have left it that way." He started to jog.

Helfer ran alongside him. "You can't have it both ways. If it's just sex with Dereath, then it was just sex with Ellitt."

"That's totally different," Volle said after a minute. "The thing with Dereath, that's…I have to do it. For Streak. This was something else."

Helfer sighed. "It's sex or it's not."

"It's not that easy!"

"Only if you make it harder."

"I'm not the one who made it harder!" He ran faster, leaving the weasel behind.

"Hey! Don't run away from me! Listen, I know you're having a rough time here, but I'm not exactly having it easy either. I've had to spend days and days working out plans until my head is sore, I have to go all over creation working things out, and to top it off, everything that happens here reflects on me."

Volle stopped and stared at Helfer. "Oh, come on. You don't care what anyone thinks about you."

A look passed across Helfer's muzzle then; his ears went back and his eyes shifted to one side. Volle didn't understand the look then, but he remembered it and later he would think about it. "No, I don't," he said. "But I want this vacation to go just badly enough that I never have to do another one, not so badly that I lose income." He started running again, and Volle followed.

"Lose income?"

"Maybe. There's never been a murder before. Alister said some things yesterday that…well, anyway, I've still stuck by you, and I was just trying to…"

Volle's chest felt a chill that had nothing to do with the morning air. "What is that supposed to mean?"

Helfer looked at him again, then down at the grass. "Nothing," he muttered.

"You think I had something to do with it."

"You did, didn't you? Whatever the motive was, it's your wolf who's the prime suspect, and he was a guest in my house."

Volle stared at the weasel for five steps, and then he didn't want to look at him any more. He sped up, and this time he didn't wait for Helfer until he'd reached the far side of the mansion. There he stopped, turned around, and rested with his paws on his thighs. Helfer was his best friend around here, and he couldn't afford to alienate him. Besides, he was under a lot of stress and he probably hadn't meant what he said. Volle thought he'd appreciate the chance to apologize. He was even ready to apologize for his own outburst—after all, Helfer *had* meant well.

But Helfer never rounded the corner.

After fifteen or twenty minutes, Volle finished his run around the mansion. Helfer wasn't waiting for him at the front gate, but Roferro was. He stood stiffly at attention as Volle walked up to him. "Lord Ikling said that you should proceed to the castle without him, Lord Vinton. A buggy will be here when you are ready."

The sight of the otter brought the memory of the previous night flooding back again, and with it his conflicted feelings. He'd never felt guilty about sex before, and he didn't like it. Without Helfer there, the desire to apologize faded. He said, "Fine," and went to his bedroom to change.

The bedroom reminded him of Helfer's hospitality, and he thought as he bathed and dressed that the weasel was really risking a lot by having him here. And the otter was a misguided gesture, but well intentioned. And besides that, he himself wasn't certain that Streak wasn't guilty. Helfer was probably feeling as bad as he was. He lingered around the front of the mansion for several minutes, hoping Helfer would come down, but the weasel didn't make an appearance. Finally, he said to Roferro, "Could you please tell Lord Ikling that…that I'm sorry. I know he's having a bad time. I just…I want him to know that…I'm still his friend, and…"

Roferro waited while Volle struggled to find a way to finish, and in the end, Volle just said, "That's all."

"I will convey the message, my Lord." The otter bowed. "Oh, I nearly forgot. There was a merchant here yesterday morning to see you. He brought samples of glassware and seemed rather distressed that you had gone out."

"Merchant?" Volle's confusion lasted only a moment. *Reese.* "Oh. I completely forgot. Did he say whether he would be back?"

"He said he would hope to see you at the castle today or tomorrow. I told him I would deliver the message."

"Thank you, Roferro." Volle looked around one last time for Helfer, then climbed into the buggy. Roferro bowed and signaled to the driver to go ahead. The buggy clattered out of the courtyard and onto the road.

He brooded for about a third of the way up. Not only had he been having a wonderful time while Streak was in prison, even having *(really good)* sex with someone else, but he'd now possibly distanced himself from his best friend. As the buggy mounted into the fog, he forced himself to look forward rather than backwards. He would track down Helfer at the castle and apologize (and hopefully Hef would, too), and he would atone for his missteps by doing whatever Dereath wanted him to, and that would let him see Streak again.

He had to admit to himself that he felt more relaxed, at least physically, than he had in days. Whether it was the day at the resort or the night of passion, he'd been rid of a lot of the tension that had driven him the past few days to do some foolish things. He rubbed his thigh; it still stung where he'd scraped it, though the rest of his bruises from that night on the roof were fading. Today, he told himself, he would not proceed rashly.

By the time he reached the main gates, he was filled with a grim determination to get through Dereath as fast as possible. It occurred to him that probably half an hour would be enough, and maybe he could even get in to see Streak today. He brushed past the footservant who helped him down from the buggy and walked quickly into the castle.

The corridors were as busy as he'd ever seen them. People were chattering happily about the upcoming trip, most of them sounding delighted to be getting out of the castle and into the sunlit warmth they'd been promised. He strode past Lord Alacris and his wife, and when they called a hello to him, only waved back cordially without stopping.

At the foot of the stairs, a voice called out, "Hey! Lord Vinton!" He recognized Archie's voice and waited until the weasel had made his way across the floor.

"Thought that was you. Hard to mistake." He grinned.

Volle smiled back tautly. "How's the investigation going?"

"Stalled for the moment. Nero asked me to go along with the nobles this afternoon while he stays here and searches up leads." He cocked his head. "You don't have any, do you?"

"I'm going to see Lord Fardew," Volle said tightly. "Then I'm going to see Streak. After that I'll talk to you."

Archie perked up considerably. "Really! So you've decided to agree to his…" He paused. "His terms?"

Volle nodded. "Listen," he said. "I know you don't believe me, but I'm worried. I'm putting myself in his control and…Helfer thought it would be a good idea if you knew where I was."

Archie considered that, his small ears flattening back briefly. He walked around Volle and up two steps so he could look the fox in the eye. "You really believe you might need to be rescued?"

Volle took a breath and nodded. "I really do."

The weasel's dark eyes searched his, and then Archie nodded. "I'll tell Captain Nero. You're going there right now?"

"Yes, but only to tell him. I don't think he'll want to…see me right away. Probably later tonight."

Archie's whiskers twitched. "Come see me when you know when it will be. All right?"

"But if you're going on the trip…"

"We're not leaving for a couple hours yet. Tell you what. I can come with you."

"No, thanks. I don't think…" Then he paused, an idea forming in his mind. "Yes, actually, that would be helpful."

"Good." The weasel turned and skipped up the stairs, and Volle followed.

At the door, Archie allowed Volle to knock. The rabbit answered the door, and surveyed the two of them, eye level with Archie and looking up at Volle. "Good morning," he said. "Is Lord Fardew expecting you?"

"He'll see me," Volle said.

"And you are…?"

Volle glared at the rabbit. "You know who I am."

The rabbit held his stare for another moment, then nodded curtly. "One moment."

"I'm only asking," Archie said quietly, "because I've never been. Is it customary for servants to be rude to nobles at the palace?"

"No." Volle wanted to say more, but decided against it. He waited patiently for Dereath to appear.

It seemed to take forever, and when the rat did appear, he sauntered into view and was smiling with more than his usual smugness. He glanced at Archie briefly and then addressed Volle. "Just you. Come on in."

"I don't need to come inside, and Archie doesn't need to leave." Volle folded his arms.

Dereath shrugged. "Fine. Come back when you're ready to be more reasonable." He turned to go.

"I'm willing to give you what you wanted." Volle hoped those words would be enough.

The rat stopped, but didn't turn. Volle waited, and then added, "But this is the only time I'll offer. You turn me away now and you'll never get another chance."

He turned then, the smugness fading. His pointed muzzle was still set in a smile, but his eyes looked angry. After another glance at Archie, he fixed Volle with a stare. "Tonight, then."

"I figured you wouldn't have the 'agreement' ready now." Volle stared right back. "But I don't think it will take me that long to read and sign it. Shall we say an hour before dinner? That will give me half an hour to review and sign your 'agreement,' and then you can take me directly to Streak afterwards."

Dereath narrowed his eyes. "Why don't we say an hour?" he said silkily. "Just in case there are any…sticking points that need to be…worked out."

"Oh, I don't think you could put together anything that would take me more than about fifteen minutes." Volle was starting to enjoy himself, though he wasn't sure that infuriating Dereath was good for him.

"You might be surprised at what I could put together," Dereath said. "One hour, and let's make it mid-afternoon. So you have time for your interview before dinner."

"An hour after lunch, then," Volle said. "I'll be back here then."

"I'll have everything very ready for you." Dereath glanced again at Archie and turned without saying goodbye. He disappeared into his bedroom, and the rabbit came back to bow to them and close the door without another word.

"I don't know if I quite believe you, but he certainly lacks charm," Archie said as they walked away. "Okay, I'm going to go find the captain. I know where you'll be, and I'll make sure he knows. Feel better, m'Lord?"

"Yes. Thanks, Archie." Volle couldn't stop his whiskers from twitching. He was committed now.

When Archie was gone from sight, Volle set off to find the merchants. He got lost twice, and wasn't helped by the fact that nobody else seemed to know where they were either. Finally, he found a passageway he'd missed the first time and emerged in a courtyard crammed with tents and noise. It took him ten minutes of squeezing through merchandise and edging around people to find Reese, and another fifteen minutes to get him out of there.

Reese had been making small talk about how pleased he was to see the esteemed Lord Vinton and how honored that the Lord came and sought him out, but as soon as they had entered a small deserted room with half a ceiling and closed the door, he rounded on Volle.

"I broke three samples on the ride down and you weren't even there."

"Reese, I'm sorry," Volle whispered. "I told Dewanne I'd go to the resort with him and he picked me up early."

"Could've sent word up, spared me a trip, but no…"

"Hey, you're just a merchant. I'm a noble, remember? I don't have to justify myself to you."

Reese glared at him. "I remember when I picked you up out of the gutter," he whispered, "and carried you back to our room. You never thanked me."

Volle was as certain as he could be that nobody could hear them when they whispered, but talking out loud about their past still made him nervous. He broke off the banter. "Listen. Something's going to happen today and I might need to talk to you tonight." Briefly, he told Reese about Dereath's ultimatum and his acceptance.

Reese whistled. "You mean you're going to go have sex to get what you want? By the Hare, Volle, you *have* changed!"

"Shut up," Volle said, caught between amusement and annoyance. "It's Dereath, remember? I'm not exactly looking forward to it."

"Sure, but then you get that wolf later on, and…okay, okay. So what do you want me to do?"

"Lose the attitude, for one." He sighed at Reese's grin. "Yes, I know that won't happen. Just keep an eye out, and be around later tonight in case something happens that Avery will want to know about. You have a way to get word back to him, right?"

Reese nodded. "Me. It's not the safest, but we couldn't bring any of the couriers from Divalia and not seem suspicious."

"All right. I've told Archie what I'm doing, and he's telling Captain Nero. In case Dereath…tries something."

For the first time, Reese looked more alarmed than amused. "Like what? You think he's going to try to hurt you?"

"I don't know." Volle laid his ears back. "It's possible. I can defend myself, if so, but…I don't know. He knows that Archie knows I'll be there, so I don't think he'll try anything drastic."

"Yeah, but…" Reese looked definitely nervous now. "He could do something to you that you couldn't see coming. One cut…you wouldn't even know to defend yourself until it was over."

"I remember that class too," Volle said tightly. "Let's just hope he didn't take it."

"You'll be all right." Reese squeezed his shoulder. "If you're not, I'll take care of the rat myself."

"Get in line," Volle said, but with a smile. "Thanks. I'm sure it won't be necessary."

Reese nodded, letting go. "Anything else you want me to take care of?"

Volle shook his head. "I don't think so. Just be ready."

"I can do that."

"Thanks again. And Reese?" Volle grinned. "Sorry about yesterday. I really am."

Reese waved a paw at him. "It's not the worst thing you've done to me." He grinned back.

Volle flicked his ears. "I apologized for that about a hundred times."

"We have long ears and long memories." Reese chuckled and changed his tone as they approached the door. "So, my Lord, I may call on you at the palace?"

"Yes, provided I resume my residence there." Volle slipped easily into the conversation.

"Thank you. I have already made two other contacts in the palace and I hope to expand my influence there."

"I'll be glad to help as much as I can." They emerged into a corridor where several people were rushing toward the gates. Volle stepped aside to let them pass. "I see the coaches for the orchards must be leaving."

"Ah, yes." Reese smoothed his vest down. "I was going to go along. Lord Quirn wanted to use one of my goblets to sample mead from."

"That would be a good connection to have. I won't stand in your way."

Reese bowed to him, and said in a low voice, "Good luck."

Volle nodded, and watched the hare walk quickly but with dignity down the hallway. Reese had really taken to the role of merchant, one that he hadn't expected to have to keep for any length of time. He enjoyed it, Volle could tell, and what's more, he seemed to be getting good at it. He was well on his way to becoming one of the palace merchants. He also had a family, with a kit on the way—no, that had been last year; his kit would have been born by now. Probably that's why his wife hadn't accompanied him.

Over the next half hour, the palace cleared out. Volle scanned the departing crowd for Helfer, but didn't see the weasel anywhere, even when he went to the front gate and watched the coaches leave. He did think he noticed the large form of Captain Nero sitting in one of the departing coaches, and peered after it, but couldn't say for sure. He stood there for a few moments after the last coach had left, wishing he'd seen Helfer and wondering if the weasel was avoiding him. He finally went back into the castle when the same footservant who had called the coach for him two nights ago started to walk toward him with a worried cast to his ears. Volle didn't want to explain what he was doing there.

Lunch had been served early, but Volle convinced one of the palace staff to bring him some of the leftovers and he sat alone in the large dining hall, eating quietly and watching the staff clean up. The talk with Reese had heartened him, especially after the fight with Helfer, and he supposed that in some way he knew he'd needed the reassurance, and that's why he'd sought out the hare. Archie had helped, too, so he was dreading the appointment with Dereath less than he had been that morning.

Not much less, but at least a little.

Even after he'd picked at the last scraps of his lunch and made it last as long as possible given his suddenly poor appetite, he still had an hour or so left. The servants were trying not to obviously hover over him, but he could tell they wanted to finish cleaning up, so he smiled and left the room.

His paws carried him almost without him realizing it to the north tower, where he turned a corner and found himself facing the staircase that led to the tower. Two guards stood there talking quietly, a large puma and a stag. Volle recognized them, and decided to try to circumvent Dereath one last time.

"Afternoon, my Lord," the puma said as he approached. He and the stag both bowed.

"Good afternoon," Volle said. He studied their wary countenances, the cautious tilt to their ears. "I was hoping I might convince you to let me see the prisoner. I'm about to visit with Lord Fardew later, and it would be very helpful if I could see the prisoner first."

"Has Lord Fardew authorized that?" The puma was obviously the one in charge.

"He will," Volle said. He'd briefly considered lying, but he wasn't sure the puma would believe him and it would probably just make things worse.

The air was tinged with a slight scent of fear from both of them as the puma shook his head. "We can't disobey Lord Fardew, my Lord. The last guard who did…" He exchanged a fearful glance with the stag.

"What happened to him? Discharged?"

"Not just discharged, my Lord. He was thrown in jail, so they say. Never heard from again." The puma lowered his ears. "My Lord, I have a family…"

"All right," Volle said, raising a paw. "I apologize for asking." He began to walk away, then tilted his head curiously and came back. "That guard…Dereath's only been Lord Fardew for a month, hasn't he?"

The stag answered this time. "Yes, my Lord. The guards, we all thought…well, he had a reputation but we didn't understand the proper respect that had to be shown him. So that guard was made an example of."

"What did he do?"

The stag and puma looked at each other. "Nobody knows," the stag said. "But he's gone, all right." The scent of fear got slightly stronger.

Volle nodded, and walked away quietly, leaving the two guards to their conversation and their anxieties. Their words had only increased his own worry; if Dereath wielded that much power and influence already, he would be a formidable opponent, not just at the hearing, but for the foreseeable future.

He wandered through the nearly deserted castle without much sense of purpose, feeling like a prisoner under sentence, until he found himself near a familiar courtyard. It wasn't raining outside; in fact, he could see breaks in the clouds. He padded slowly over to the break in the wall and began to ease himself through it, then stopped and let his eyes adjust to the darkness.

There was nothing there. He'd hoped to find a tuft of fur, something to remind him that their afternoon here had been real. It seemed years away now. He sighed and pushed himself through to the outside of the castle.

The ground was damp there, and the wind a bit brisker. It was clean and fresh, though, and he closed his eyes just for a moment to breathe in the scents of dirt, of trees, the hint of rain that never quite went away. Keeping his eyes closed, he stood against the wall, nose lifted, and only after several deep breaths did he lower his muzzle and open his eyes. The mountain below was even more beautiful than it had been in the rain. The clouds threw shadows across the trees, and down below, he could see a bright patch of sunshine. It seemed so far away that he just sat and watched it for a while, wondering how long it might take him to reach it.

He sat down, back against the wall, and remembered standing while Streak knelt in front of him. He smiled as he did, and felt warmth building in his sheath. *Why not?* he thought, and undid his pants, letting his paw inside. *Might as well wear myself out before Dereath gets to me.*

Closing his eyes, he drew his fingers up and down his swelling sheath, brushing his tip when it poked out into the air. He imagined Streak's tongue flicking along it and stroked harder, and then Ellitt floated into his mind, unbidden.

He forced the image of the otter away, pausing in his strokes and then resuming again. He'd lost the fantasy, and now he couldn't help worrying about Dereath as his paw slid up and down his slowly hardening member. He kept stroking because he felt silly stopping once he'd started, but the desire kindled by the memory of his last afternoon with Streak had been extinguished—not so much by the memory of Ellitt, but by his reaction to it.

He wondered what Dereath could possibly want. He suspected it would involve his humiliation somehow, and he thought the rat wasn't above trying to produce some evidence of his treason. He would have to be careful not to say anything. *Probably he'll want to top me,* he thought sourly, and wished he'd brought something to lubricate his rear with. He didn't think the rat would be gentle.

But at the end of it, I'll get to see Streak again.

He held onto that thought, imagined the muzzle of the white wolf and the smile in his eyes when he saw Volle, imagined the tight hug he would give him and the beautiful scent of his fur, and he smiled. His erection, finally brought full by simply the physical act of stroking, perked up more, and he felt warmth building at the base of it. His paw moved more quickly now, but it was Streak he was stroking in his imagination, holding the wolf's body against his, moving together with him.

The rubbing of his paw against his taut, warm skin fed the images in his mind. He could almost smell Streak's thick musk through the cool mountain air. It sang through his body until he pitched forward on his knees, gasping for breath and panting, his paw working at his shaft, sliding up and down with greater and greater urgency. He felt it building in him finally, and as he moaned, he hunched over and watched the white spurts of his passion fall to the ground, his body convulsing in pleasure.

The heat of his climax dissipated quickly in the cool air. It seemed like such a huge, enveloping thing that he was always surprised to see it reduced to a spattering of white on the ground. From a few feet away, he might not even notice it, if not for his strong musky odor. He breathed it in, letting himself relax slowly, and licked a drop off his paw before tucking his sheath back into his pants.

When he stood, he pondered covering up his 'tracks,' but decided to leave them. They would be gone in a few hours, and the scent wouldn't last much beyond that. He crawled back into the courtyard and made his way back through the silent castle. He'd certainly accomplished his goal, he thought as he mounted the stairs. He didn't feel remotely interested in any sort of sex at the moment.

At Dereath's door, he hesitated. *Last chance*, he told himself. *You can still back out now. Go back down to the resort and stay there with Dewanne and Ilyana, take that life and make it yours*. But the voice was faint and its call no longer as appealing as it had been the previous day and night. Even without any desire for sex, he still wanted Streak's companionship and love. He visualized the muzzle of the white wolf smiling at him, and knocked on the door.

Chapter 9

*H*e waited, and then knocked again. Still no answer.

Paws curled into frustrated fists, he was about to knock again when he heard voices in the corridor. "…waste of my time… things I shouldn't have to deal with any more." A low voice responded, and then Volle heard Dereath clearly.

"It's the responsibility of the captain of the guards. I've told him that a dozen times." Inaudible response. "Oh, that's right, he's down in the orchards. Well, it couldn't have come at a worse—ah." They had rounded the corner, and Volle saw that Dereath's companion was his personal servant, the rabbit. Dereath's teeth showed in a nasty smile.

"Why, look," the rat said, clapping his paws together, "it's my pet fox, right on time. I like punctuality. He's obviously eager to get started."

"Eager to be finished," Volle said as Dereath unlocked his door.

The rat turned and gave him a nasty smile. "You shouldn't count on finishing," he said, leering, and then motioned Volle inside.

Volle looked at the rabbit. "He stays outside."

"Oh, don't be that way. He won't come in and watch, but I can't very well ask him to go entertain himself outside for an hour."

"Why not?" Volle folded his arms and glared at the rabbit, who seemed unruffled by the attention.

"It would be rude. This is his home, too. Besides, what if you try to overpower me?"

"I still need you to get me past the guards. I wouldn't do that."

"I just feel safer with him here. He'll stay out of the bedroom, I promise. I want it to be just you and me." Dereath's triumphant mood showed in his tone. The bitter edge he usually had was replaced by an eagerness that Volle found slightly nauseating, and not only because it concerned him directly.

He debated whether to press the point, and decided that the longer he argued, the longer this would take, so he followed Dereath into the parlor without another word. The rabbit followed quietly behind him and closed the door, locking it.

"Just a minute," Dereath said. "Let me straighten up first." He slipped into the study, leaving the door ajar so Volle could see him go through the next door into the bedroom.

Volle didn't want to look at the rabbit, so he looked around the room, and his eye fell on the parlor door where the mouse had been killed. He hadn't smelled blood before, but now he fancied he did, and his fur prickled. He could still leave, could unlock the door and run out before Dereath got

170

back.

You're not afraid, are you?

"No," he murmured to himself. "Fox will protect me. I'm doing this for my pack." The scent of blood faded as he turned away from the door, replaced by the ratty, dusty smell of the parlor. The rabbit, he noticed, had a very subtle scent that was hard to pick up, and he suspected that was one reason he disliked the creature so much. Someone without an obvious scent was someone hiding something. Of course, it was perfectly possible that he was just a weak-scented person, but in Dereath's employ, Volle assumed the worst.

The rat pushed the door of his bedroom open, breaking Volle's train of thought. "I'm ready for you now, Lord Vinton." He was smiling that same nasty smile.

Volle took a breath, and tried to sound confident as he passed through the study. "I'm ready for you, too."

"We'll see about that," Dereath said.

Volle walked into the bedroom and folded his arms as Dereath shut the door, then watched the rat walk around to the other side of the bed and sit on it. The bedroom was actually rather large, about fifteen feet, he estimated. Against the far wall stood a large wardrobe, flanked by a chest of drawers on one side and a footlocker on the other. Beside the dresser was a door that undoubtedly led to a bathroom. Faintly, he could smell a palace scent: sandalwood, he thought.

The bed had been placed lengthwise across the room about halfway down, headboard against the left hand wall, leaving only a few feet between the foot of the bed and the right hand wall. A large linen sheet covered the whole bed, trailing down to the floor; only a lump at the head showed where the pillow was.

"All right," Dereath said. "Now take off your clothes and get on the bed. Your hour doesn't start until then." He was fiddling with an hourglass that stood on a small table next to the bed, but his eyes were on Volle.

Volle noticed a basket next to the hourglass and wondered what was in it, then thought grimly that he would know soon enough. He pulled his shirt off quickly and dropped it to the floor, then hesitated only a moment before slipping out of his pants as well. When he reached for his pendant to take it off, Dereath said, "No, you can leave the jewelry."

Volle let the pendant drop into his chest-fur. He made no attempt to hide or show off his nakedness, though he tried to avoid looking at the gleam of lust in Dereath's eyes as he walked toward the bed. He sat on the near side, facing away from Dereath. At least the rat smelled clean. The sandalwood scent was stronger on the bed and seemed to be on his fur. "Start the hour," he said, looking over his shoulder at the hourglass.

"In a minute." Dereath leered at him and leaned back so he could see Volle's lap, keeping one paw on the hourglass and reaching the other toward Volle's sheath.

Volle grabbed the rat's thin wrist. "You don't get to touch me until you turn that over."

Dereath's dark eyes turned sour. Without a word, he turned the hour-glass over and placed it on the table. Volle watched the grains of sand sift through the small opening, and reluctantly released Dereath's paw.

It closed none too gently around Volle's sheath, rubbing it firmly before sliding down to cup his sac. "I've waited for this for a long time," the rat whispered. Volle didn't answer. He tried to keep his mind on Streak as his sheath was fondled, but he felt the stirrings of arousal and shifted his thoughts to the stark beauty of the mountains, the earthy smell of his farm, and the sandy earth of the resort. Streak kept creeping back into his mind, though, and much to his annoyance, he found he could not stop his sheath from swelling.

"That's right," Dereath murmured. "Enjoy it while you can. Let me see...let me see..." He kept stroking hard and tight, almost to the point of being painful. Volle wondered if he would have to endure a whole hour of this. That wouldn't be so bad, he thought.

There was more, of course. He estimated it was maybe five minutes before his erection pushed its way tiredly out of his sheath, and when Dereath saw it, he grabbed the tip between two fingers. Volle squirmed involuntarily, which made the rat twist his fingertips. Volle gasped, and Dereath grinned. "Good. Now lie on your stomach."

Here it comes, Volle thought. He gets to pound away at my rear for an hour. Well, fifty-five minutes, anyway. He got up onto the bed and lay on his stomach, head resting on his arms.

"Oh, no. Paws under your tail."

Volle smelled the worn scent of leather and knew what Dereath had gotten from the basket. "No, please..." he said, and then bit his lip. Of course Dereath wanted to hear him beg.

"Paws. Under. Your. Tail." The rat was growling, but couldn't disguise the glee in his voice, and Volle hated him in that moment more than he ever had before. Slowly, he reached his paws back and clasped them under his tail.

Dereath wound the leather strap around Volle's wrists and then looped it around his tail's base before cinching it tight. Volle instinctively tugged at the strap, feeling his heart race faster when his paws wouldn't come free. Settle down, he told himself, but his body was crying at him to struggle as hard as he could, to get free of the restraint. He chewed on his lip again, trying to distract himself, trying not to let the stone walls of his prison rise up in his head. He flexed his paws, making and releasing fists, not caring what the rat thought.

He didn't seem to notice. Rummaging in the basket again, he removed a small wooden ring, polished smooth. It almost looked like a napkin holder, but it was larger and not as long. "I'll bet you can guess what this is for." He held it in front of Volle and turned it back and forth before saying, "Open your muzzle."

Volle paused a moment before obeying. The position strained his neck, as his head had to lie flat on the bed, but he figured that wouldn't be the worst thing he was in for. He tried to adjust his back so the strain was spread out more. While he did that, Dereath put the wooden ring into his mouth and pressed down. "Now just hold still," the rat said as his paws took a strip of cloth and wound it around Volle's muzzle, tying it off at the top after pulling it tight.

Instinctively, Volle struggled against it. He couldn't close his mouth around the ring, and he couldn't open it further to let the ring out. If he let it slide back further into his mouth, he was worried he would choke on it. He slipped his tongue through the hole experimentally, then retracted it when Dereath said, "Ah, you *do* know what that's for. Good boy, I knew you would."

Volle closed his eyes as Dereath fumbled with the catch on his pants. He couldn't see the rat's expression, but he could see the trembling of his paws and assumed it was excitement. The thought made him sick, and he didn't want to look any more. After a few moments, when the smell of rat was getting stronger and the movements on the bed more noticeable, he thought he'd better take a look so he knew what he'd be in for.

Dereath was in the process of removing his pants. He tossed them to one side and knelt low in front of Volle, presenting his groin as if for inspection. Volle tried not to study the rat's erection, but he got enough of a glance to see that it was already full, stiff and dripping. It was small, but well proportioned for Dereath's size, and Volle actually wished it were uglier; it would seem more fitting.

"Now," the rat said softly, and Volle noticed he was already panting, "let's see that tongue again."

Volle hesitated. It was almost not a conscious decision, that pause. He knew he was delaying the start of things, and the longer he dragged it out, the less he would have to do, but he also knew that he'd made an agreement and he didn't want to give Dereath any reason to reneg on his part of the bargain.

"I said…" the rat began, but Volle slid his tongue obediently through the wooden ring before he could finish. "Better," Dereath grumbled. He pushed the pillow under Volle's muzzle, lifting his head and putting even more strain on his neck, then positioned himself and held the wooden ring with one paw. Slowly, he guided his shaft through it with the other.

Volle felt the slick length against his tongue and tasted the rat's rather foul musk for the first time. He almost gagged. Dereath didn't make it any better, releasing his shaft once it was through the ring and using that paw to grip the back of Volle's head by the fur. He thrust hard into Volle's muzzle, pressing his fur right into Volle's nose as he did.

Thick musk filled Volle's head, and he closed his eyes again, determined to bear it until it was over. Knowing Dereath, he suspected there would be more, but he could get through this. He could.

It didn't even last as long as he thought it would. Dereath's legs were shaking so much that the whole bed trembled. His paw gripped Volle's fur even tighter, and he dislodged the wooden ring as he slammed his erection against the fox's tongue, over and over. His harsh panting and prolonged grunt were the first clue Volle had that he'd come; then he felt the spurt and tasted something near the back of his throat. It was hot and rancid, and he imagined it was the essence of Dereath himself. It seemed to burn.

Dereath was panting, "Oh Rodent...oh, that was good." He leaned back, not completely out of Volle's muzzle, but the fox couldn't wait any longer. The dislodged ring no longer held his muzzle open. He jerked his tongue back and used it to push the ring out of his muzzle as he wrenched his neck to one side, coughing and spitting onto the sheet.

"Ow!" Dereath sprang back and pulled the ring off his dripping shaft, throwing it to one side. "You bastard!" He cuffed Volle hard across the head, bringing stars to the fox's eyes, then shook his head roughly with the paw that still held fur. "That hurt!"

Volle coughed again. He couldn't open his muzzle all the way because of the loose loop around it, but he mumbled, "Couldn't...help it."

"Couldn't what??" Dereath jerked his head up painfully.

"Couldn't help it!" Volle panted. *If I could have, I'd have bitten harder.*

Dereath held his head up for a few moments longer. Volle could see his snarling visage clearly. Breathing was getting harder through his bent windpipe, and eventually Dereath either realized this or got tired of holding his head up. The rat let him drop to the bed, then slid off it. He walked around behind Volle and pushed up on his hips. "Up on your knees. I'm not done with you yet."

Volle looked desperately at the hourglass, but it wasn't even half gone. Sighing, he worked his knees up toward his midsection, lifting his hips off the bed. Dereath fingered his quiescent sheath. "Aw, that little adventure didn't excite you? I'll have to try harder." He pawed it back and forth. "It will be a little while before I'm ready again, so maybe I'll let you have a little fun. Wouldn't you like that, Lord Vinton? Let me give you a little pleasure."

His voice had softened to a croon as he stroked. Volle closed his eyes and tried to keep his thoughts as far from anything sexual as he could. He thought about the murder in the next room, about the scent of blood and mouse and rat and wolf in the room, and that reminded him that he was totally under the control of someone who was involved in a murder, which just made him nervous. He tried to clear his mind, but the persistent stroking, even with Dereath's spindly fingers, was having an effect.

"Ahhhh." He heard Dereath's exhalation and felt ashamed as his sheath swelled. He hated responding, but he couldn't stop his body. The best he could do was to send his mind away from it, think about the hourglass and the sand drifting down at a snail's pace, the only thing now that stood between him and Streak.

"If only you'd let me do this all those years ago," Dereath was saying quietly.

Volle clenched his teeth together and said nothing. Dereath's spidery fingers were working over his shaft as it emerged, sliding over the skin, and one paw was caressing his sac almost tenderly. "I can be a considerate lover, you know. When given the opportunity. But you turned me away. And you took my big, stupid warrior away."

That was too much. "He was not stupid, and he was never yours." Volle's voice was harsh from the coughing, and from the memory that statement spurred.

"He was more mine than yours." Dereath's voice was growing harder, his paw's grip firmer.

Just keep quiet. Volle ignored his inner voice's advice. "Never. You would have just thrown him away."

"He was *mine!*" The rat stopped stroking for a moment. Volle imagined him standing, quivering with rage. He didn't look back, and deliberately cupped his ears forward, away from Dereath.

After a moment, the rat started to stroke again. "It doesn't matter now, anyway. He's dead, and good riddance."

Volle's paws clenched into fists at that, and he pulled painfully on the straps that bound him to his tail. If he'd been untied, he would have strangled the rat then and there. Slowly, he calmed down. *Just make sure the same doesn't happen to Streak,* he told himself. *Stay calm.* And this time, he listened. He slowed his tail's lashing and relaxed his paws.

He was quite hard now under Dereath's paw, and slightly sore. He'd been rough on himself earlier, and Dereath was none too gentle. At some point, he abandoned the strategy of not thinking about it as his body took over his mind, and he started to thrust into the rat's paw.

"There's a good fox," Dereath murmured. "Nice and ready and obedient. If only you could be like this all the time. If only I could stop time and keep you here." His voice was dreamy now, and Volle glanced at the hourglass to be sure it hadn't stopped, keeping up his thrusts. He was still sore, but the warmth of arousal was building slowly in him and overriding the soreness. He chose to answer Dereath's words with panting and harder thrusts.

His nerves were singing inside him, and he felt himself about to stain Dereath's sheets further. He groaned softly, and—

—and Dereath's paw released its grip abruptly.

Volle thrust forward into empty air, the climax so close he growled in frustration and tried to press himself into the bed. Dereath grabbed the leather straps around his tail and held him back with surprising strength. "Oh, no you don't," he said, his voice still soft, but now dripping with venom. "Now you know what it feels like to be so close and be unable to get what you want, to be thwarted at every turn. I told you the pendant of fortune swings back, didn't I? And now, here's something else to remember me by." He drew a finger along Volle's taut shaft gently, then gripped the tip and drove his claw into it.

Fire erupted through Volle's shaft. He cried out at the first spike of pain, unable to help himself. Tears filled his eyes and he tried to buck away from Dereath's paw, but the rat held on. Even when he withdrew, the sharp pain remained for several moments before becoming a throbbing fiery soreness. "Uh…unh…" He tried not to cry, despite his quickened breath and the tears that were now soaking into his fur. Slowly, he regained control of himself, feeling a wetness on his shaft that had nothing to do with arousal.

Dereath's breath ruffled the fur inside his ear. "Don't forget," he hissed softly, "that I know what you are. Even if you've fooled all the rest of them." Volle flicked his ear and turned his head slightly so he could see Dereath's eyes gleam. "And I know about the other one, too."

Tish? For a moment, Volle panicked, then he noticed that Dereath's eyes had a curiosity behind the gleam, and he was certain the rat was bluffing. "You don't know anything."

He said it more out of spite than anything else, and he'd meant to say more, but his voice had threatened to give out. The pain was still occupying most of his awareness, though at least it had taken his mind off his sore neck and shoulders. But it had an effect on the rat; his eyes narrowed and he shot a paw back to squeeze Volle's sore member, sending more waves of pain through him. "I know *everything*," he hissed. "Don't you ever forget that. I know secrets you could not possibly begin to dream of. I know enough secrets to bring down half the nobles in this realm. Why do you think a common-born rat was able to take the most important bestowed title in the land? Once that fool Rallish was out of the way, there was nobody who dared oppose me. You would do well to remember that. In the end, fox, I always get what I want."

This is what you wanted, isn't it? Volle fought to keep from crying out at the pain. "You just wanted me in your bed," he whispered through gritted teeth. "You wouldn't care about anything else otherwise."

The rat's grip relaxed, and his muzzle relaxed into an ugly smile. "Maybe that's true," he said. "But it's too late for that. You humiliated me, nearly cost me my position twice, and I will not let that go."

Volle pressed the point. "You only used information to get back at me." He kept his voice to a whisper, for fear it would break if he spoke louder.

Dereath laughed. "Oh, Lord Vinton, of course I did. What else would I use it for?"

Volle had no answer for that. He moved his head to look forward again and glanced at the hourglass, which was now about two thirds finished.

Dereath must have followed his glance, because he chuckled softly. "Fortunately, I'm ready to finish your lesson." He disappeared from Volle's peripheral vision, and a moment later Volle felt him climb up on the bed behind him. A paw grabbed his tail and held him; he braced himself as he felt the rat move into position. Nothing applied to make it easier, as he'd

He swore that he would get even with the rat for this.

suspected. He gritted his teeth.

He heard the rat inhale, then felt a burning pain as he was penetrated. He tensed, and he felt his tail bristle, but he tried not to react otherwise. With excruciating slowness, Dereath pushed and pulled. *He can't be enjoying it much,* Volle thought, tensing his legs to keep them still. The pain was getting worse, but compared to what had come before, he could take it. It was the humiliation that was almost worse, that he was just being used. That was all Dereath had ever wanted from him, he was sure. He fought the pain and the shame with anger, and swore that whatever happened, he would get even with the rat for this. That thought held him as Dereath's thrusts got faster and more ragged, and his breath came in short moans.

Beyond a point, Volle noticed distantly, the pain didn't get much worse. When the rat grunted again and yanked at his fur, pushing all the way into him, he almost gasped in relief. The hourglass had maybe five or ten more minutes to go.

"Ahhh…unh…" Dereath moaned and then straightened up, remaining inside Volle. He traced his paw around Volle's rear. "I…uhh…don't want to forget this view."

Volle closed his eyes. *Fox, please don't let me remember this too clearly. I did it for my pack.* As he said the short prayer, he relaxed, and the pain receded ever so slightly. Or maybe he was just going numb.

"Well. You've held up your end of the bargain." Volle could almost see the rat's smirk as he put a paw under Volle's rear and pulled himself out in an abrupt motion. Inside, Volle could feel the uneasy heat of the remains of the rat's passion, and he fought to hold it in for a bit longer. "Now I should go and keep my promise."

Volle kept his muzzle pressed into the pillow, easing the strain on his neck, while Dereath went into the bathroom. The rat emerged a moment later, the smell of sandalwood stronger around him. "Can't have the guards knowing what I do in my private time," he said with a sneer as he pulled his pants on. He fastened them and then gave Volle's now-soft sheath a squeeze, smiling as the fox winced in pain. The paw slid around from there, rubbing him beneath the tail and gripping its base. "You just sit tight here, and I'll be right back."

"You're going to let me in to see Streak." He tried to make it a statement and not a request, but wasn't sure whether he'd succeeded.

"You've been rather mean," Dereath said tauntingly. "I thought first I might round up a few guards, a few Lords…whoever's left. Bring them in here to show them my little fox toy."

Volle turned to look at the rat, now standing by the door. "You promised."

"Oh, don't worry. I got what I wanted. I'm only going to show him." He opened the bedroom door and indicated the rabbit, who was standing just beyond it.

Volle felt his fur prickle in shame, and he turned away from the rabbit's eyes. "You said he wouldn't..."

"I said he wouldn't come in, and he won't." He heard the rat say, "Keep an eye on him. I'll be back soon." Then the opening and closing of the outer door, and then silence.

He couldn't hold back any longer, nor did he want to. He lowered his rear and fouled Dereath's sheets, gasping as he ridded himself of the rat's semen. Then he fell—forward—onto the bed.

For several minutes he lay there still, not wanting to look at the rabbit, watching the hourglass instead. The last few grains were taking a long time to fall. He let his body relax, trying to ignore the various pains he felt in his groin, and rolling his shoulders and neck to alleviate the stress there. The room was quiet enough for him to hear the faint hiss of the sand, and then even that faded away as the last grain fell.

He began to struggle with the leather straps that bound his paws. If he twisted them around, he could almost get a grip on them, and if he could only get a grip, he might be able to loosen them. He thought he heard a noise from the direction of the wardrobe, then there was a definite noise from the front room. He turned his head, and saw the rabbit walking toward him.

Holding a long, wicked-looking knife.

"Hey," he said desperately. "You're not supposed to come in here. Listen—ow!"

The rabbit had grabbed his paws, ignoring him, and with a smooth flick of the knife, cut the leather. Volle collapsed onto his side, bringing his paws in front of him and rubbing his wrists, then his sore tail base. He looked at the rabbit, who shrugged. "I don't go for this sex stuff," he said simply, and walked back into the front room.

He'd left the door open, but Volle was beyond caring. He got down carefully off the bed, ignoring his protesting hips and arms, and padded to the door to retrieve his clothes. The rabbit was in the front room, watching him with no more than casual interest. Volle met his gaze briefly, then turned and went to the bathroom. As he entered, he thought he caught a faint scent, but it disappeared beneath the sandalwood aroma before he could identify it. He closed the door behind him and sagged back against it.

There. It was over now. He'd made it to the other side of the hour, and if Dereath didn't keep his word now...well, he would take care of that when the time came.

He deposited his clothes on a nearby stool and went to examine the available fragrances. The whole room reeked of sandalwood, so he inspected the other jars and found one that smelled of cinnamon. The exotic spice was strong enough to cover the unpleasant scents on him, so he applied it liberally to the fur under his tail and around his sheath, wincing as he did so. Both areas were still sore. There was blood on his sheath and on his abdomen just above it, too, from where Dereath had wounded him. *That*, he thought, *I will repay him for. Even if he keeps his bargain.*

The rat didn't have any decent brushes, and Volle didn't want to use something with rat fur on it anyway. He combed his fur as best he could, aware that Dereath could return at any moment, and cleaned up the worst areas. After he saw Streak, he would need to take a bath. Preferably a long water bath.

He pulled his clothes on and went back out into the main room. Clothed, he felt more in control and more assertive. He would go see Streak now, before Dereath could…well, do anything other than what he'd promised.

The rabbit stood as he crossed the front room. "You're to stay."

Volle shook his head. "I can't. You can try to stop me if you want." He paused, the door half-open, and said, "Thank you."

The rabbit didn't seem inclined to respond to any of his words. He shrugged again and followed Volle out the door.

On the staircase, they met Dereath coming back the other way. The rat was holding one paw inside his shirt and looking down, so he didn't see them until he was about to run into them. When he looked up, he stopped, startled, then shot a nasty look at the rabbit before turning his attention to Volle. "Eager, aren't you? Well, come on, then. I've given the guard his orders, and at least he knows how to follow them." This last was accompanied by another look at the rabbit.

Volle had to pause for a moment before following. His first impulse had been to grab the rat and choke him to death. After a moment, he thought he might settle for knocking him down the stairs, as long as he got to kick him repeatedly at the bottom. But when Dereath turned and actually began heading to the north tower, the revenge fantasies faded slightly—Dereath was actually going to take him to Streak. Besides, they were both dressed now. If not for the pains over his body, it would be hard to believe the previous hour hadn't been a bad dream.

They walked through the corridors in silence. The castle was still nearly deserted; the only people Volle saw were servants walking quickly around on errands. Dereath's mood had shifted, Volle noticed; he was no longer garrulous and thrilling over his own power. He seemed to be walking under an odd sort of tension, with a restrained haste, as though he were worried about something but couldn't resist the lure of it.

Volle, himself, was feeling sore. Walking made it worse, especially as his sheath was rubbing against the leather of his trousers and aggravating the wound unless he walked carefully. But inside, he was feeling nervous and elated, and couldn't keep his tail from wagging despite the soreness under it. He didn't even want to kill Dereath any more. At least, not right away. Streak was so close now…and maybe, he thought, unable to stop himself from wondering, that's where Dereath's tension was coming from. Could he be worried about what Streak will say? Or…did he have another nasty surprise planned?

All the way to the tower stairs, he harbored these thoughts. But when they reached the tower and the puma standing guard attentively (he stood much straighter in Dereath's presence than when Volle had seen him earlier), Dereath made his remarks short and to the point.

"Lord Vinton is permitted one visit to the tower, beginning right now. If he isn't out before dinner, you are to go in and remove him. Otherwise, do not disturb him in any way." He turned to Volle. "There. We're even now."

Oh, hardly. The resentment flared up in him again; he felt the residue of his torture anew. But he controlled himself. A look up the stairs reminded him that Streak was waiting for him, so he nodded curtly to Dereath and watched the rat walk away, flanked by the rabbit. Only when they'd turned the corner did he nod to the puma and put a paw on the stairs.

"Just a minute, my Lord," the guard said. "I'll unlock it for you. Please stay down here while I do." He produced a large key from his waist pocket and climbed the stairs. A moment later, Volle heard the sound of a lock being drawn back, and then the puma reappeared, glancing over his shoulder. "Go ahead, my Lord," he said, taking his position again.

Volle nodded and climbed the winding staircase slowly. Turning around at the top, he could no longer see the puma below him. The door facing him was large and ancient, but solid for all that: reinforced wood that had stood the test of time in the castle. He wrapped his paw around the large metal handle, and felt a sudden shiver of trepidation. For a moment, he hesitated. Then the scent hit him, and he pulled as hard as he could, throwing the door open wide.

Chapter 10

They stared at each other for a heartbeat. Streak was standing, waiting by the door in his disheveled and dirty clothes, but the shock in his eyes showed that whatever he'd been prepared for, it wasn't this. "Volle?" he whispered, and then they were wrapped in each other's arms, and Volle didn't care that the wolf was squeezing him so hard it hurt. He drank in Streak's scent like wine, running his paws up and down the wolf's broad back, and then his nose touched Streak's and they were kissing, tongues pressing fiercely against each other. For a moment, Volle forgot to breathe, and his body's aches and pains were gone. There was nothing but the wolf in his arms and the glow in his heart that felt like a fire returned to a long-dead fireplace.

They fell apart by mutual agreement, almost at the same time, and Volle couldn't hold back a smile at the way each of them knew just what the other was about to do. "Close the door?" Streak said as Volle's paw was half-way to pulling it shut.

Volle was about to smile, but he saw the wolf's ears lay back and the wet tracks through the fur of his muzzle. "Streak?" he said softly, wincing as the aches returned one by one.

"Sweet Canis, Volle...I...I thought..." the wolf sniffled loudly and gulped at the air, falling to his knees. There was no furniture in the small cell, and now that Volle didn't have his nose buried in Streak's fur, he could tell that there wasn't a toilet anywhere either. He filed those impressions away and sank to his knees, putting an arm around the wolf's shoulders.

"What? Tell me, what?"

Streak lowered his head and pressed it into Volle's chest, sobbing loudly now. He spoke in stuttering gasps punctuated with sniffles and guttural cries. "You came...for me. I...the other night, I thought it was...I thought I was dreaming." Another round of sobs shook him, and before Volle could think of a response, Streak went on.

"I didn't know...if you'd ever come. They said...they said I would hang, and I thought maybe you just thought you'd...you'd be..."

"Hush." Volle cradled the wolf's head to his chest, his own eyes tearing up. "I tried to get to you the other night, through the rain. I was going crazy."

"Why didn't you come sooner?" Streak looked up, tear-filled eyes meeting his.

"Dereath wouldn't let me. I wanted to. I tried to get in that night, but I was too late."

"That's what Nero said, but...I thought you'd find a way."

"I tried." He pushed away the guilty memories of the day at the resort (*the night with the otter*) and held the wolf close, kissing his ears and nuzzling him. "I finally…talked him into it."

Streak's sobs had been fading slowly, and now trailed off altogether, though he still sniffled. He nuzzled Volle and sighed, and finally spoke. "You smell funny. Lots of cinnamon, and…" His nose was right at Volle's stomach.

Volle tugged his muzzle up and licked his nose. "I wanted to try something different." He was sure there was still some scent of blood on him, and he didn't want Streak to get close enough to smell it. "You like it?"

The wolf smiled tentatively. "Not really."

"Never again, then." He sat down on the stone floor, winced, and resituated himself to keep his weight off his rump. He held Streak's paws in his, rubbing the fur and pads with thumb and forefinger, remembering the night in the rain.

Streak squeezed his paw, his eyes showing that he was remembering as well. Then he said, abruptly, "I didn't do it."

Volle exhaled and brought his ears all the way forward. "I was hoping you'd say that."

"Did you think I had?"

His heart ached at Streak's confused words. "I wondered. You might have thought you were saving me from the hearing, if you thought the witness could really hurt me," he said quietly. "It felt almost like the sort of silly, noble thing you would try to do for me."

The wolf smiled, and sniffled again. "She really was the witness, then?"

Volle nodded, and looked back at the wolf, who was shaking his head. "I didn't kill her. Maybe if she were threatening you…but not someone helpless, just like that."

"I didn't really think you did. Do you know who did, then?" Volle smiled, and Streak smiled back, but with an odd waver.

"Volle…" He took a breath. "I guess I should tell you what I was doing there."

"Since you won't tell Nero," Volle began, and then saw the hurt in Streak's eyes. "All right." He sat back and waited.

"He came to see me," Streak whispered. "Dereath. While you were at the castle that first night. He knew me, from when I was a guard, and he told me that I had to come see him after dinner that night. He said…he said that he…that I owed him for deserting, and that he was going to give me the chance to pay him back and save you at the same time."

Volle held his paw sympathetically and listened as Streak went on. "He said he had a witness, someone who had seen you commit treason, and he said that if I came to see him and did what he said, then he would make sure she didn't testify."

"Was anyone else around while you were talking?"

Streak shook his head, and Volle sighed. He'd suspected Dereath was too clever for that. He nodded to the wolf to continue.

"So I thought, he's just bluffing. But then I heard you and Tish talking about the witness, and I...I had to go."

"Why didn't you tell me?" Volle said softly.

"He told me I couldn't, or the deal was off. I couldn't tell anyone."

"Why didn't you tell Nero this? I mean, the witness was dead."

"He said if I told anyone but you, he'd..." Streak swallowed and said the last words in a whisper, "have you killed."

"Why didn't you tell me before dinner, then? Before you went there?"

"No..." Streak waved a paw and laid his ears back, looking confused. "That was after dinner, that he said that. Before, he said I couldn't even tell you because you wouldn't let me."

"He's probably right. What did he want?" Volle thought he could guess.

"He wanted me to...to sleep with him. But we never did anything," he said hurriedly. "He put his paw down my pants, but that was all. I heard the scream before I went into the bedroom."

"Where was he when you heard the scream?"

"Outside. He told me to wait in the bedroom, that he had to go make sure we wouldn't be disturbed." Streak kept touching Volle's fur with his free paw, sliding his fingers under the sleeve of Volle's shirt as though he didn't even want the cloth to separate them. His words came more and more quickly. "I didn't know if I could go through with it or what you'd think of me, but I had to do it, you understand? And then I heard her scream and I had to go take a look. She was dead when I opened the door. There was nobody else in the room. I couldn't move. The servant found me, and De—he was right behind her."

"Okay, okay." Volle rubbed the fur on Streak's paw gently and looked into the wolf's eyes. "I understand. I wouldn't have been mad at you. You were just trying to help me. I'd—" *I'd have done the same for you. I did.*

Streak looked relieved, then he searched Volle's eyes in return and read his unspoken words as easily as if Volle had said them. His ears folded back again. "That's what you did, isn't it?" he whispered. Volle didn't say anything. "You did that to get him to let you in here—oh, fox, I'm so sorry. That bastard." He growled softly.

"I'll get him back," Volle said. "I've sworn that by Fox. And we're together now, anyway. I was worried he might have done something to you."

Streak shook his head and started to reply, but was stopped by a knocking at the door. The puma's voice followed. "Lord Fardew says you have to step outside in five minutes, Lord Vinton."

Volle folded his ears back and called, "No."

"But Lord Fardew..."

"Lord Fardew can take his five minutes and be damned." He was almost trembling now, and if Dereath had come into the room, Volle would certainly have attacked him.

"Yes, my Lord. He told me to tell you, my Lord." In the ensuing silence, Volle heard the scratching of claws on the stone as the puma descended.

He sighed as he turned back to Streak, whose ears were pressed back. "Don't worry," he said. "He's through with getting what he wants. I'm going to stay with you for a while longer."

Streak looked down, a low growl in his throat. "I still wish you hadn't had to…"

Volle shook his head. "It's over now. And I know you didn't do it."

"But we still don't know who did."

"We have a suspicion. But…" Volle rubbed the wolf's paw. "Did Nero tell you your scent was on the scissors?"

"Yes. I said I didn't handle them."

"How else could your scent have gotten on them?"

Streak shook his head. "That's what I don't know."

"Scent transfer…wait…" Volle searched his memory for one of the classes he'd taken at the Academy. They'd done a piece on scent transfer, and as he recalled pieces of it, his fur prickled. "When Dereath put his paw down your pants," he said slowly, and didn't finish.

"It was down the back, under…under my tail," Streak said softly.

"I'm an idiot," Volle snarled. "If he'd grabbed you in the front, it would have smeller muskier, but I assumed that…"

"Volle, what?" Streak looked bewildered.

"Just under the tail, for canids," Volle said. "That's where the scent is strongest and it's really the only place you can pick up enough to transfer. We never think about it, we just brush more scent into it. He got your scent and put it on the scissors before he stabbed her."

"You think Dereath did it?" Streak's eyes were wide and round. "But he didn't have time. And he didn't go into the room anyway. He was outside in the hallway."

"He could have squeezed in through the hole in the wall." Volle's fists were clenched, and then his ears lay back flat as a memory shivered back to him.

Dereath's paw slid around from there, rubbing him beneath the tail and gripping its base.

"Don't worry. I got what I wanted."

He could feel his tail bristling out to twice its size. Streak noticed too, and his eyes and scent betrayed his alarm. "Volle?"

"Stay here. I have a very bad feeling. I think I may have done something very stupid." He stood abruptly and squeezed Streak's paw before releasing it.

"What?" Streak stood up.

Volle turned to him, one paw on the door. "I hope I'm wrong." *But I'm not.* "Please, it's best for you to stay here. Don't get into any more trouble."

Streak looked hurt, but stepped back. "Sorry," he mumbled.

Volle flicked his ears up and softened his tone. "I'm not blaming you," he said. "Dereath's up to something and I don't want you to get mixed up in it. If you leave the cell, you could be in a lot of danger."

"Okay." Streak looked a bit less upset, though he was still far from happy. "Come back and tell me, even if you have to shout through the door."

"I will." Volle threw the door latch, opened the door and slipped through.

The silence outside the door enfolded him. It almost seemed that the castle was holding its breath, waiting for something to happen. He stopped at the top of the staircase, letting his nose look ahead for him. He smelled the puma, traces of other people, and then, as he breathed in deeply, the unmistakable tang of blood. He searched the air, but there was nobody else close, so he descended the stairs cautiously.

The puma lay sprawled at the base of the stairs, blood pooling below him. It trickled down his jerkin in a slow trail that began at the leather-handled knife planted in his chest. Volle stared at the body, heart pounding, and walked slowly down the stairs, unable to stop himself. The knife looked familiar, and as he drew nearer he realized where he knew it from. It was the knife from Dereath's chambers, the knife the rabbit had used to cut him free.

He knelt down beside the puma. The scents were all clear to him now: the puma's own scent, the thick, acrid tang of his blood, and another scent working its way to the surface. He bent over, cautiously, and brought his nose inches from the handle of the knife.

His scent was all over the leather.

Uttering a choked cry, he sprang back and stumbled, sitting down hard on the stairs. His sore rump hit the stone hard, and he yelped at the shock of pain. That sound seemed to bring the silent castle to life. He could hear footsteps in the corridor outside, and the thunk of the latch in the door above him. "What's the matter?" Streak called.

"Stay back!" Volle couldn't take his eyes from the puma. He'd walked right into the setup. Dereath had engineered it brilliantly.

No sooner had he thought that than he heard the rat saying "This way! Before we're too late!" He looked wildly back up the stairs, then down at the corridor. Neither option offered any relief, but he thought he would rather see Streak one more time. He tried to stand up, but his legs were wobbly. He'd just levered himself upright when he heard the wolf behind him.

"What's going on—Volle?" Streak was far enough around the corner to see the dead guard now. He gasped and stared at Volle.

Before Volle could frame an answer, Dereath and the stag guard appeared at the bottom of the stairs. Both were panting, and the stag had drawn his sword. They stopped cold when they saw the puma's body on the bottom few stairs.

Dereath looked at the puma with a pretense of sadness, then up at Volle. "Look! He's trying to escape with his lover."

The stag, too, stared at the puma, but Volle thought his grief was genuine. When he looked up, his eyes were narrowed in hate. "Did you do this?"

"No!" Volle said, but Dereath had bent to the knife and was gesturing to the stag to do the same.

The guard did, only taking his eyes from Volle for a second, and when he straightened, his gaze was murderous. "You whoreson. I'll see you never come to trial." He set a foot on the bottom stair.

Volle backed up just as Streak rushed down the stairs, and he had to hold the wolf back with one arm. "You'll have to get through me first!" Streak shouted defiantly.

"Hush," Volle told him, and then two other guards came into view, a wolf and a goat.

Their arrival seemed to slow the stag, but when the goat grabbed his arm, he resisted. "He killed Arnie," he protested roughly.

"Let the King sort that out," said the wolf, but his look told Volle that he'd already worked it out for himself. "You don't want to be executed for killing a noble."

"Too right," said the goat. "He's not worth it, Rog. Let it go."

"I believe the other tower would be suitable for a cell," Dereath said. He seemed to be enjoying himself immensely. "Why don't you accompany Lord Vinton there, Forrin? Rogis, you put the white wolf back in his cell."

The wolf guard nodded. "Lord Vinton, if you would accompany me?"

Volle jerked his muzzle at the stag. "Get him out of the way first."

The stag glared at him and didn't move. "Lord Vinton," Dereath said, "you are hardly in a position to dictate terms, are you?"

"I think Rogis should move aside," said a new voice, and Archie strolled into view at the bottom of the stairs. "After all, we don't want to risk yet another tragic incident, do we, Lord Fardew?"

Dereath whirled, and for the first time registered true surprise. Archie returned his stare blandly, and after a moment Dereath said, "Rogis, stand down."

Reluctantly, the stag stepped down off the staircase and back out into the corridor. He continued to glare at Volle.

"I'll see you soon," Volle whispered to Streak. "Promise."

Streak squeezed his arm. "I'll be okay. I know you didn't do it."

Volle nodded and smiled, and descended cautiously to the corridor, keeping his eye on the stag, whose sword was still drawn. The wolf, Forrin, put a large paw on his shoulder. "Come on, my Lord. Are you carrying any weapons?"

Volle shook his head, and then turned to all of them. "I didn't kill him," he said. "Just so you know." The goat looked away, and the stag spat at him. The wolf didn't react at all.

"I think I'll go with you," Archie said. "Just to make sure nothing further happens."

"You don't need to do that, sir," Forrin said.

"I think you had better stay here and examine the crime scene,"

Dereath said smoothly.

Archie considered that, and then nodded. He stepped over to Volle. "I'm going to look around here. I'll be in to see you presently."

"Please, smell this first." Volle held out his paw, which had Streak's scent as well as Dereath's cinnamon on it. The knife, he was sure, held neither.

The weasel looked at him curiously, but obliged. Volle couldn't help but notice that the smell of sandalwood, which he'd attributed to Dereath, was also hovering around Archie. "Mm," Archie said as he stepped back. "I'll remember that."

"Thanks." Volle nodded to the wolf, who set off down the corridor. He followed, and it took him a moment to realize that the sandalwood scent wasn't getting weaker. He turned his head and saw Dereath following him.

Seeing his look, the rat chuckled. "You finally slipped up this time, fox," he said. "You think you're so clever, waiting until the castle is deserted to try to break your lover out of prison. Now you're both going to be tried for murder. Don't worry, though. I'll make sure you make it to the trial. I'll assign you only the best guards."

Volle noticed the wolf's flat ears and thrashing tail, but he couldn't think of anything to say that would help his case. If he told Dereath that he knew how he'd committed the murders, Dereath might not let Archie back in to see him, or he might decide that Volle was too big a threat and get rid of him right there, somehow. So he held his tongue, and resisted Dereath's taunting until he was marched up a staircase similar to the one he'd just left, and thrust into a bare room.

"Enjoy your new accommodations," Dereath sneered, and closed the door. Volle heard the lock turn, and the slow march of paws down the stairs, and then silence again.

He let out a deep sigh, and started to pace the confines of the cell to distract himself from the furious anger building in him. The only windows were slits that he could get his paw into only if he turned it sideways. He stalked over to the ancient stairway on the opposite side of the room from the door, and mounted it quickly.

It led him to another small room, this one littered with debris from the roof, half of which had fallen in. He blinked up at the overcast sky and the soft light, and it took him a moment to realize that it was not dawn of the next day. So much had happened that he felt he'd spent an entire night since his stroll outside that afternoon.

The walls were about ten feet high, and even at their most broken down, he could not get to the top of them. He stomped about the room, growling in frustration, running the events of the past few hours over in his head. *Scent transfer!* How could he not have seen it?

Because nobody ever does it, he reminded himself. It only works with mustelids and canids, and to pull it off successfully requires such an intimate touch that the field of suspects is narrowed down almost immediately to one. And yet Dereath had made it work.

But he wouldn't get away with it, Volle vowed grimly. Even if he stopped Archie and Captain Nero from visiting, Volle would get a chance to talk at the trial. He could see almost perfectly now how Dereath had done it. The witness *was* just a decoy, a piece of bait to lure Streak up to the room so he could be set up for murder. And Streak in turn had been bait to get Volle—and let Dereath have a bit of fun while he was at it. And the poor guard and the poor mouse were just pawns in Dereath's game.

He growled again, realizing he needed to relieve himself and that he would have to do it here, in the debris, as no doubt Streak had done in his other cell. Feeling dirty, he did so, and marked it up as one more grievance Dereath would pay for—in addition to the painful wound, which started bleeding again as he urinated.

With the open air, the smell wasn't so bad, but the knowledge drove him back downstairs, where he waited for Archie, pacing, standing, and finally sitting on the stone floor, back against the wall next to the staircase. His rump was still a bit sore, but it was bearable now, and except for the pain in his sheath, his other injuries seemed to be healing well. His neck and shoulders were still stiff, but if he kept his head tilted forwards, they didn't bother him much.

The light from upstairs waned and finally vanished, replaced by a chilly wind, but the weasel didn't visit him, and neither did anyone else. Some hours after darkness had fallen, he heard noises on the other side of the door. He remained sitting, but braced himself cautiously, ears perked forward.

He couldn't make out what was being said, if anything. He thought he heard some chuckling and a splashing sound, and then the door latch was drawn back. The door opened slowly, and a paw pushed a tray through the opening. When it was all the way in the room, the door was quickly closed.

Volle's stomach rumbled as the scents from the tray reached him, but immediately he caught another scent and he realized what the splashing he'd heard must have been. His stomach went from hungry to nauseous in a moment, but he forced himself to check. Halfway across the room, he stopped, ears and tail drooping. The tray of food he'd been brought had been fouled, wolf urine sprayed across the entire dish.

He walked back to the wall and sat down, breathing in the fresh air from outside. For hours he waited for the door to open again, and he didn't realize he'd fallen asleep until he opened his eyes and realized that the staircase to his right was brighter, and that this time it really was dawn.

His muscles were stiff from sleeping in a sitting position, and his neck and shoulders were even more stiff. He went upstairs to see the sky and relieve himself, and noticed that the pain from his wound wasn't nearly as great as it had been the previous day. It had stopped bleeding; he could brush dried blood carefully off of it, but it was still very sore to the touch. When he came back downstairs, he was just in time to see the door closing and hear the chuckle of the guards. Another tray lay on the floor, wisps of steam rising from it in the early morning chill. It took him only a sniff to tell that it had been treated the same as the last one. His stomach growled in protest. Ignoring it, he occupied himself with a series of exercises to stretch his sore muscles. All he could do now was wait.

He stayed downstairs so as not to miss any visitors. Around midday, he got his first. His ears pricked up as the door latch was thrown, and the door creaked open to reveal Dereath. He smirked down at the tray and kicked it back outside, then closed the door behind him.

"Why, Lord Vinton, you don't look pleased to see me."

Volle looked away and didn't respond.

"And you haven't been eating the delicious food they've been serving you. No appetite? I do admit the guards were reluctant to feed you at all, since they're still convinced you killed one of their number. Lord or no, they don't like that one bit. Now, if you were a Lord in good standing, they might not be as vocal about it, but someone's been reminding them that you're on trial for treason later this week." His voice oozed false sympathy. "If you aren't already in prison for murder, that is. You'll probably not hang unless you lose the treason trial too, and the King may decide it's not worth the bother to try you for treason, since you're already a murderer."

Volle curled his tail tighter around his feet and tried to ignore the rat. Dereath was gloating now, but he hadn't won yet. Volle brushed his pendant with a finger and stared fixedly at the stones.

"I just thought I'd come by to see how you were doing," Dereath went on. "Sore at all? I'm feeling most wonderfully refreshed."

Volle clenched his teeth and stayed quiet. Dereath stepped closer to him, and Volle looked up, baring his teeth. "Careful. I'm already branded a murderer. One more body won't change that, and it would make me feel so very good."

Dereath sneered at him, obviously trying to gauge Volle's sincerity, then took a step back. Volle savored that minor triumph.

"In case you were waiting for your weasel friend," Dereath said, more sharply, "he won't be coming. I would expect you will see Nero, to tell you when the trial has been scheduled for. With all this evidence and the guards in the state they are, I expect it will be soon. Maybe even tomorrow. Do you know what tomorrow is? Tomorrow is Rodentiday. Sometimes things really do work out nicely." He turned and walked for the door.

Volle watched him go, wishing he could think of something to say that would make the rat uneasy and let him feel a bit more of that minor triumph. In the end, he decided it would be wiser to remain silent, especially if Nero would be coming later. He would have a lot to discuss then.

Sometime after midday, he was sitting in the upper room looking at the sky. His moods rotated between worry for Streak (muted, since he'd seen the wolf), anger at Dereath, and slight apprehension for his own fate. The dilemma of Ilyana had been pushed back into his mind, so much so that he never even thought to wonder whether she was expecting him at the resort today. He did wonder about Helfer, no longer angry at the weasel. He wondered whether Helfer had been told of what happened, how much he knew, and what he thought.

Mostly, though, he tried to remain in a mood of calm resignation. At this point, there was little he could do except wait, and he preferred to wait under the sky, even if it meant sitting with the reek of his makeshift toilet in his nostrils when the wind swirled into the tower.

His ears caught noises from downstairs. He had found a fist-sized piece of rubble, and laid it near him, in easy reach. They obviously hadn't put a lot of thought into this prison, but he supposed nobody had guessed that they would need to imprison even one person, let alone two. Lucky he wasn't actually inclined to violence, though if Dereath showed his pointy muzzle, he wasn't sure he could keep from throwing the rock at him.

He was mildly surprised to hear Nero's voice huffing and grunting as the wolf climbed the stairs. "I suppose I can't blame you for wanting to be up here," he said as his head came into view. Volle saw his nose wrinkle, but he didn't mention the smell. "It's hard on an old wolf's legs, though." As he stepped up to the floor, he looked around for somewhere to sit, finally gave up, and sat on the top stair.

"I didn't kill the guard," Volle said.

"No, I gathered as much from Archie. He seemed to believe that you had been set up, and he provided a most convincing argument. I fear that argument carries little weight with the victim's comrades, though."

"I guess not." His stomach growled. "Do you think you could bring me some food tonight?"

Nero nodded. "I'll do that, and speak to the guards." He shifted his weight and sighed. "I have spent the morning talking to Streak. He has been more forthcoming than he was previously, for which I gather I have you to thank."

"He told you what happened, then?" Volle leaned forward eagerly.

"He did. And he told me several other things, the importance of which may have escaped him." Nero tapped the floor with one claw.

"So you know who did it?"

Nero looked sharply at him. "I have formed several theories which have rather different likelihoods of being true. I cannot say for certain that I have narrowed down that list to one."

"But Dereath did it," Volle said softly, insistently. "He got the scent from me and Streak. Scent transfer doesn't happen accidentally. He had to have planned it out, because the scent wouldn't stay on his paw for long."

The wolf narrowed his eyes again, but didn't speak immediately. When he did, he was no longer looking at Volle. "Accusing a highly ranked Lord, even one not born to the peerage, is a difficult business. Circumstantial evidence—as convincing as it may be—will probably not be enough. Not when it comes down to your word against his."

Volle growled. "But at least the evidence should be enough to free me, right?"

"Perhaps. Streak certainly stoutly defended your innocence, but he admitted that he didn't know the puma guard's voice for certain. You could have had a collaborator knock on the door after you'd killed the guard just to make Streak think that the guard was still alive."

Volle gaped at him. "How would I even think of that?"

"It is my job," Nero said, "to imagine all the possibilities."

"Is there a possibility in which you killed the guard?"

"Doubtful, as I was in the orchard having dinner at the time." Volle's stomach growled at the mention of dinner. "But I'm certain there is a scenario under which I could have arranged for it to happen."

"Why did you go to the orchards?" Volle suddenly remembered seeing the wolf in one of the carriages. "Archie said you were staying here."

"Circumstances arose that made it more convenient for us to swap places," Nero said. "Archie was rather peeved at being deprived of a nice trip, and I am less than enthusiastic about taking trips in general, but I dare say it worked out for the best."

Volle flicked his ears curiously. "Why is that?"

Nero smiled. "Because I was treated to the best dinner I have had in a long time, and Archie, well…Archie had quite a rewarding afternoon." He shook a paw at Volle. "You are lucky he was around."

"I have a feeling it was not quite luck."

"Well, you may be correct. But remember that the fortunate often make their own luck. Now, apart from getting you an unmarked dinner, is there anything else I can do?"

Volle's tail swished against the rocks restlessly. "Get me out of here."

"Your trial will be tomorrow. I think I can safely say that there is very little chance you will be convicted, but I would ask you to remain quiet during the proceedings. It will be a very delicate thing, however it happens."

"Tomorrow…" Volle thought about Dereath's words. "Do you believe in omens?" he asked softly.

"I believe that the astute person can perceive small details, sometimes without realizing it, that may give him insight into the larger picture."

"I mean, do you believe that Canis, and Gaia, send us signals sometimes?"

Nero looked at him curiously. "I believe that they provide the small details. The astute person…"

"All right, all right." Volle didn't know whether to frustrated or amused. "Don't you even want to ask me what happened with the guard? Or…with Dereath?"

Nero smiled a toothy smile. "If you would like to tell me any relevant details, small or no, I would be happy to hear them, but between Streak and Archie, I think I have compiled an adequate picture of the proceedings." He placed just the slightest stress on the word 'relevant.' "I regrettably did not have the chance to examine the body of the guard, but I am not sure I needed to."

"What would you have been looking for?" Volle tilted his head curiously. "Archie or I might have seen it."

"I am not looking for anything in particular. It might have been instructive; that is all."

Volle sat back and nodded. "The puma was alive when I went into Streak's cell. I'm almost sure it was him knocking at the door. He said Lord Fardew wanted me to come outside in five minutes. I wasn't going to go, but then...I was talking to Streak and he mentioned Dereath putting his paw under his tail, and I remembered that he did that to me too." Volle put his ears half back. "Earlier."

Nero nodded, not seeming curious as to how that had come about, so Volle gratefully went on. "So I went outside to look. I had a feeling something was wrong. I found the puma dead. Only a few minutes later, Dereath and another guard came running up. The other guard seemed about ready to kill me. But I smelled the knife handle that was in the puma, and my scent was on it, but not the cinnamon I'd put on my paws. I'd just done it that day, just, er, trying it out. If I'd killed him, I couldn't have helped getting cinnamon on the knife, and I know there wasn't any there."

"That is what Archie told me." Nero nodded.

"Did he smell Dereath's paws?"

"I don't believe so. In any case, I doubt that would have revealed anything. If Lord Fardew did as you said, he would certainly have washed before returning."

"I don't know if he would have time," Volle said thoughtfully.

"He has certainly washed by now." Nero's voice held a trace of amusement.

"I'm sure he has." Volle flicked his ears back. "And Streak was in the bedroom when that mouse was killed. She was dead when he opened the door. It had to have been Dereath, getting out through that hole in the wall."

"I am still convinced," Nero said, "that Lord Fardew never passed through that hole. In fact, he may have found it a touch larger than he would have liked."

"What do you mean?" Volle was getting tired of asking Nero that.

"Your Streak did tell me that he was waiting in the bedroom, but he also said that he got to the parlor door a couple of moments after the scream. That's very quick. Even someone who was ready to act at a moment's notice would be hard-pressed to get from the bedroom to the parlor door in 'a couple of moments.' When I pointed that out, he admitted that he was in the parlor when he heard the scream, and I asked him why he had left the bedroom. He said that he heard a noise in the parlor, but the ensuing excitement had driven it completely from his mind."

Volle listened, ears perked, as Nero continued. "I asked him what kind of noise, and the best he could recall was that it sounded as if something had fallen. Something small and metallic."

"The scissors."

Nero nodded. "That is my guess."

"So she dropped the scissors, then someone picked them up? No, that doesn't work." Volle stroked his chin, frowning as he tried to work it out. A moment later, his eyes widened. "She wasn't the one who screamed. She was already dead."

"Exactly." Nero seemed pleased. "The murderer stabbed her with the scissors, then put your wolf's scent on them later, threw them into the room and screamed through the hole in a passable imitation of a female mouse."

"Dereath."

"So it would appear. But again, we have no proof."

Volle growled again, softly. "He can't get away with it."

"He can. It is my job to see that he doesn't. I don't anticipate needing your help, but I may ask you some questions. Please remain quiet otherwise."

"You said that already." Volle nodded grimly. "I can do that."

"Good." Nero smiled and heaved himself to his feet. "I'll bring some food as soon as I can. Get a good night's sleep tonight, Lord Vinton."

"Thank you, Captain Nero." Volle smiled and felt his tail wag slowly. He got up as well. "I appreciate all your work."

Nero gave him an enigmatic, thoughtful smile. "I wonder if you do." He shook his head and waved a paw. "Please forgive me. I am in a frightful mood today."

Volle watched him leave, and then curled up amidst the debris, keeping his growling stomach as compressed as possible. He watched the clouds in the sky and tried to find peace there, and he did find calm for a time. The clouds rolled and turned like his thoughts, but much more slowly, and he found himself lulled into their graceful rhythm. The hours drifted by, and he'd almost forgotten his hunger when he heard a noise downstairs.

Nobody appeared at the stairway, so he descended cautiously to investigate. Nero—if it had been him—had come and gone, but he had left behind a tray piled high with food, steaming from its own warmth and nothing else.

Volle fell on the tray, attacking the plate and gorging himself, pausing after a few mouthfuls to carry the tray to the other side of the room. His hunger returned with a vengeance as he grabbed the warm bread, the steaming pieces of chicken, and the roasted vegetables that filled the plate. He knew he was spilling food on his fur, but he didn't care for the moment.

His stomach protested finally, and he slowed down, letting himself taste the food. He really needn't have bothered; it was similar to what he'd eaten at the castle before, but the chicken and vegetables were older and only the bread was really fresh. He finished about two thirds of the tray and then pushed it aside, feeling bloated and a little queasy.

Mindful of Nero's advice, he walked slowly back up to the upper room and stretched out in the open space beneath what was left of the roof. He'd gotten used to the smell there, and didn't mind the chill in the air. As darkness set in, he wanted to lie awake and think about the trial, but the food in his belly made him sleepy. He found himself yawning, and thought, "I shouldn't go to sleep just yet," and a moment later he was blinking in the morning light.

The door downstairs opened about an hour later, and he heard the gruff voice of the wolf guard. "Lord Vinton? Time to go."

He got up and stretched, and made his way down the stairs. The wolf guard and another he didn't recognize, a raccoon, were standing at the door, both looking grim. Volle paused at the foot of the stairs. "Where's Captain Nero?"

"He's better things to do this morning than waste his time playing escort."

Volle stood firmly. "Get Archie, then. I'm not going without one of them."

The wolf bared his teeth. "We are allowed to bring you there by whatever means we need to use, Lord Vinton."

"And it will be a lot easier if you get Archie." Volle folded his arms. He certainly wasn't inclined to make things easier for the wolf.

The raccoon tugged on the wolf's jerkin, and the two held a hasty discussion that ended with the wolf slamming the door shut. Volle sat down on the bottom stair and waited, tail twitching nervously. He didn't really think the wolf would've harmed him on the way to the trial, but he wanted to be sure he arrived safely, and at the moment there were few people he trusted.

He stood up again when the door latch clicked a few minutes later, and Archie stepped in. "What's this all about?" His ears were back and he looked annoyed.

Volle shrugged, feeling a bit foolish now that the weasel was facing him. Archie obviously would have had other things to worry about. "Sorry. I just felt like I needed a bit of extra protection."

Archie considered that, and nodded. "All right, let's go."

The wolf and raccoon flanked them as they walked through the corridors. Volle essayed a question about the trial, but Archie cut him off, and he took the hint. For the rest of the way they walked in silence, until they came to the throne room. The guard at the entrance, a scruffy-looking rat, pulled one of the doors open for them to enter.

The hall had been reconfigured drastically. The large throne was gone, replaced by several smaller tables on the dais at one end and about ten rows of chairs on the end closer to the door. Half of the chairs were occupied by nobles, all of whom turned to look as Volle was led into the room. He saw Tish and Tika among them, but refrained from acknowledging them, just as they made no signal to him. Their presence was a comfort, anyway. Helfer was there too, but Volle didn't respond to his encouraging smile. He noticed that in addition to the guards escorting him, there were two at the table where Streak was already seated, two more behind Nero, seated at the opposite table, and no fewer than ten more scattered throughout the audience.

Archie led him to the table where Streak was sitting and gestured to the remaining empty chair there, then walked across the room to join Nero as Volle seated himself. The guards remained behind him as he did. To his right, the King and Queen sat at a table with Alister and Lord Alacris. The King met his eye as he looked in that direction, but if he intended to communicate anything with that look, Volle didn't understand it. He gave Streak an encouraging smile, and the wolf responded weakly. His ears were back and his tail was lashing agitatedly. He did reach out and take Volle's paw in his, and squeeze it hard.

When Archie had seated himself, Alister stood up and the murmur of voices died down. "Attention, please. I hereby call to order this inquest into the murders of Jatha Malion and Arnut Xefor. His Majesty King Barris presides."

"Thank you, Alister," the King said. The coyote bowed his head in reply and consulted his papers.

Volle whispered to Streak, "That's good. It's an inquest, not a trial. That means we're not formally accused." Streak nodded in understanding, and his ears came up a bit.

"The principal investigator in these matters has been Captain Nero of Divalia Law Enforcement." Alister had selected a paper and was reading from it. "He will present his findings to the King. After his presentation, he may call witnesses to support his conclusion. Any member present may then present an alternate conclusion or a challenge, supported by witnesses, and Captain Nero will have an opportunity to rebut. When there are no more challenges, the King will make his decision. Which is final," he added, glancing about the room.

Nobody spoke. Alister waited for a moment, and then said, "Captain Nero, you may proceed." He sat down.

Nero levered his bulk out from the chair and stood. "Your Majesties, gracious Lords, fellow children of Gaia," he began. "I had hoped that this retreat would be a welcome holiday. Instead I find myself hard at work. Fortunately, I enjoy my work." He paused, as if expecting a response, but when none came, he proceeded smoothly.

"Here are the facts of the cases as I understand them. Five days ago, Jatha Malion, a guest of Lord Fardew, was murdered in the chamber she had been given in his quarters. The murder was committed with a pair of scissors that, as best I can determine, belonged to the victim. The first to discover the body, the wolf known as Streak, was also accused of the crime and imprisoned.

"Three days later, Streak's host, Lord Vinton, negotiated with Lord Fardew to visit Streak in his cell. As Lord Fardew returned, he discovered that the guard, Arnut Xefor, had been killed with a knife from Lord Fardew's quarters. Lord Vinton, the first to discover the body, was accused of the crime and imprisoned." After this speech, there was a great deal of muttering from the guards, so much so that Alister had to stand and call for silence again.

"Thank you," Nero said, bowing to the steward. "On the face of it, both cases seemed very simple, as indeed they proved to be. The scents of the accused were found on the murder weapons. They were among the first to see the victims dead; whether they were indeed the first is the matter to which I turned my investigations."

"They proved to be simple?" Streak whispered to Volle, a note of panic creeping into his voice. "He's going to arrest us."

Volle just shook his head and cocked an ear toward Nero. Streak looked uneasy, but did the same.

"I will discuss the cases separately. The matter of Miss Malion seemed very simple at first. Streak had known that Miss Malion was to be presented as a witness in a hearing to decide the fate of Lord Vinton. Because of their relationship, Streak was quite agitated by this. The witness was a heretofore unknown quantity, as I understand it, and the only witness Lord Fardew intended to present. It is not hard to imagine the passion of youth, ignited by the noble desire to protect his Lord, driving him to do away with the single obstacle to his Lord's reinstatement in one quick spontaneous blow. That, in fact, seemed to be the prevailing opinion among those aware of the case."

Volle couldn't be sure whether Nero's glance at him then was intentional or not. He felt ashamed of any doubts he'd ever had of Streak. A paw squeezed his knee, and he looked over to see the wolf smiling gently at him. He returned the smile, abashed, and held Streak's paw as they listened to Nero continue.

"I ran into obstacles when I first questioned Streak. His demeanor did not fit with the 'noble act of heroism' theory. One would have expected him to be proud and defiant, or perhaps scared of what he'd done. He was neither. The story he presented was simple and equally convincing. I left unconvinced of his guilt or innocence.

"Which raised the question of how else the murder could have happened. By Streak's own account, there was nobody else in the chamber with him. He heard the victim scream, and opened the door a few moments later. The only possible exit from that room that he would not have seen—if he were telling the truth—was a medium-sized hole in the wall.

"The victim could have fit through that hole, but the idea that she was pushed in there across the room after being stabbed was ludicrous. The room was clearly hers. Lord Fardew could have fit through it." Here Dereath sat a bit straighter, and his eyes gleamed warily. "But I met Lord Fardew shortly after the murder. He had been in the company of one person or another nearly since the murder, and would not have had the chance to change clothes. His clothes, I noted, were clean of any marks that might have indicated he had gone through the hole.

"Adding to the confusion was the presence of Streak's scent on the scissors. I was prepared to believe that he had picked them up out of confusion when he discovered the body, but he denied that. A curious denial, for I would have expected him to clutch at that explanation. I believed, more strongly, that he was telling the truth. But he would not explain why he was in Lord Fardew's quarters. Lord Fardew professed no knowledge of the reason, and so it remained a mystery. But Streak told me he would talk to Lord Vinton."

Nero faced Volle. "Lord Vinton, who will later this week be facing a hearing on the charge of treason if he is not convicted here. Lord Vinton, whom, I learned, was imprisoned for six months recently by the current Lord Fardew before he held the title—without the knowledge of the King. The more I investigated, the more bad blood between the two of them was uncovered. In my experience, when a murder occurs in proximity to a long-standing feud such as this one, it is nearly always related.

"I tried to convince Lord Fardew that letting Lord Vinton talk to the prisoner would be beneficial to the case, but he refused, saying that he didn't trust Lord Vinton. This seemed reasonable in light of their history, so I pressed Lord Vinton to agree to Lord Fardew's terms—a signed agreement that he would reveal any information gained from the prisoner. Lord Vinton, for his part, was reluctant to accede to those terms, but two days ago, he finally did.

"He was taken to see Streak, and the two of them talked. While they were talking, Arnut Xefor, who was guarding the prison, was killed. By Lord Vinton, it would seem, in the course of helping Streak to escape. A plausible theory: he had motive and opportunity, and his scent was on the knife. But again I remained unconvinced. There were small discrepancies that did not seem to add up."

Volle found himself kneading his paws on the table. He knew where Nero was going, but he still felt tense. He didn't know what could still go wrong, but he was trying to remain aware of everyone in the room, so that nothing unexpected could creep up on him.

Cautiously, he looked around the room. Dereath was staring fixedly at Nero, rigid in his chair. His smile could have been one of anticipation, or it could be masking anxiety. Volle couldn't see his tail clearly, but his ears were half-back. Tish caught his eye as he looked and gave him a nearly imperceptible nod. To his right, the King was absorbed in Nero's narrative. He probably had heard very few details of the crimes up to now. Nero was obviously aware of this and enjoying the attention. Archie was the only person in the room not fixed on Nero; he was tapping his fingers impatiently on the tabletop.

"Lord Vinton had washed with cinnamon just before visiting Streak. There was no cinnamon on the knife, nor anywhere near the cell, and he had none on his person. It was impossible for him to have killed Xefor and then applied it to himself, and he could not have handled the knife without some trace of cinnamon remaining on it—which was not the case."

Dereath shot a look full of hate at Volle then. It was clear he hadn't realized the significance of the cinnamon. Volle caught the motion and looked back without changing his expression. He noticed behind Dereath that two large guards, a bear and a puma, had moved closer to where the rat was sitting and were watching him closely.

"Therefore, I began to question whether the scent on the knife had come from his paw at all. Scent transfer is a rare practice, but not unknown in the history of crime. It is most often used between people whose relationship is intimate, but it was famously used by Pierrine in the Onyx Crest murders, recorded nearly a hundred years ago." The expressions and half-cocked ears Volle saw throughout the audience told him that to most of them, like him, the crime was anything but famous.

Nero turned to his assistant. "Archie?"

The weasel sprang to his feet. "Lord Vinton was worried about what might happen when he negotiated with Lord Fardew to see Streak. He told me about it so that I would know where he was. Captain Nero asked me to do more than that. So I had one of our guards call for Lord Fardew and his servant on a trivial matter, and I slipped into his chambers through the hole that Captain Nero mentioned a little while ago." He looked very pleased with himself.

Dereath's tail was lashing audibly now. Volle looked over and saw the tension in his slender frame. He also noticed that the two guards were now right behind him. Dereath hadn't noticed them yet.

"Lord Fardew favors a sandalwood perfume," Archie continued. "So I slipped into the bedroom and helped myself to a bit of it to cover my own rather distinct scent. I fit comfortably into the large chest in the room, covered myself with some clothes, and waited. The chest lid didn't close quite properly, so I had a clear if limited view of what went on."

Volle folded his ears back. He wanted to tell the weasel to stop, but he knew the only way for the truth to come out was for the weasel to tell everyone what had gone on. It was worth the humiliation. Looking at Dereath, he saw that the rat was not at all displeased at the prospect of their activities together being revealed.

"Lord Fardew and Lord Vinton came into the bedroom at the appointed time." Archie was looking at Volle, and his eyes were soft. "Lord Fardew presented the agreement he had worked up, and Lord Vinton read through it. They argued over it for nearly an hour before Lord Vinton signed it."

He smiled at Volle's slowly rising ears and look of disbelief. "And I saw Lord Fardew press his paw under Lord Vinton's tail, under the guise of making a pass at him."

Nero cut in. "The area under the tail, of course, is the strongest scented in both canids and mustelids. Anyone planning to perpetrate a scent transfer would want to draw the scent from there."

Archie nodded, but didn't have a chance to continue. Dereath stood up and said, "Your Majesty, I would like to protest this invasion of my private chambers." He glared at Archie. "I would like this weasel taken into custody immediately."

All eyes turned to King Barris, who waved a huge paw. "Sit down, Lord Fardew. We will consider additional charges when this inquest is over."

The bear behind Dereath put a paw on his shoulder, and only then did the rat notice the beefy guards behind him. He sat down, but Volle thought his expression was more calculating than worried.

"What else did you see?" The King spoke to Archie now.

"Lord Fardew left to inform the guards that they needed to prepare for another visitor. Lord Vinton grew impatient with waiting, washed with cinnamon—to be clean for his visit, I presume—and then left along with Lord Fardew's servant. When I was sure they would not be returning, I slipped out of the chest and out of the chambers, and headed to the north tower. I was too late to see Lord Vinton enter, but I saw the guard Xefor at the entrance." He paused dramatically. "And then I saw Lord Fardew approach him. They walked up the stairs together, and on the way down...Lord Fardew produced a knife and stabbed him in the chest."

The tumult from the crowd was almost deafening. Volle saw Dereath spring from his chair faster than the guards could catch him, shrieking, "Liar!" as he charged at Archie. Several of the nobles gasped, and all the guards in the room, including the ones behind Volle and Streak, growled and ran after Dereath. He reached Archie a second before the guards did, despite the weasel ducking below the table. The wolf who'd been guarding Volle was the first to pull Dereath out from under the table, and then the others joined him, pinning the rat down.

Dereath was still screaming at the top of his lungs, "He's lying! He's lying!" Archie emerged from under the table, smiling despite the blood oozing from his ear. Nero bent over the table, extending a paw, but Archie waved him off as he took his seat.

"Silence!" Alister was standing and pounding the table. "Silence." Gradually, the noise died down, and Dereath too stopped struggling and screaming.

The King looked at Nero. "Captain, is this your conclusion?"

"Yes, your Majesty," Nero said. "In an attempt to frame Lord Vinton, Lord Fardew committed two murders. He killed Jatha Maison before Streak ever entered his chambers. He used a similar sexual overture to gain the wolf's scent, put it on the scissors, and threw them into the room through the hole. Immediately afterwards, he imitated the victim's scream to bring Streak to the door. After he had sent Lord Vinton to the cell at a time he knew about, he made sure there would be only one guard there, killed that guard, and then conveniently 'discovered' the crime with another guard later."

King Barris leaned over the table to look at the restrained rat. "Lord Fardew?"

"I didn't kill anyone," Dereath spat the words at Nero.

"Do you wish to present any witnesses or make an argument on your behalf?" Alister said formally.

Volle was watching Dereath, and saw a canny look enter his eyes. "No, I do not."

"Very well. Then King Barris will make his ruling."

"Let him up," the King said to the guards.

They got off of Dereath, letting him get to his feet, though two of them kept a secure hold on his wrists, the wolf who'd been guarding Volle to his left and the large puma to his right. He shook himself and then stood upright, lifting his muzzle haughtily.

"Lord Fardew," King Barris said, "I am deeply disturbed at the betrayal of the trust this crown and this country have placed in you. I find you guilty of two instances of murder, and sentence you to be hanged when we return to Divalia." Dereath nodded his head curtly, but didn't seem overly disturbed by the sentence. "Captain Nero, thank you for your tireless efforts on behalf of truth and justice. Guards, escort Mister Talison to the cell formerly occupied by the wolf Streak." He sat back in his chair and nodded to Alister.

"This inquest is now concluded," the steward said. "All those having further business with the King must wait for another time."

Dereath shot Volle a wicked-looking smile as the wolf and puma pulled him toward the exit. Volle watched his progress across the room and noted that twice, Dereath stopped to whisper into the ear of a noble. First Lord Whassel, a youngish beaver, and then Lord Wallen. Both lords looked discomfited by Dereath's words.

"I did tell you I would get you out." Nero had paid his respects to the King and wandered over to stand next to Volle.

"You said you would try," Volle reminded him with a smile. He felt an odd reservation about the whole thing. He couldn't believe it was over that easily.

"Congratulations, Lord Vinton." The King stopped on his way out to lay a paw on Volle's shoulder. It was heavy and regal, and a significant touch.

"Thank you, Your Majesty." Volle smiled. "I owe Captain Nero a large debt."

"I always enjoy a good puzzle." Nero seemed slightly distracted when he said it.

Volle looked behind him. "Is Archie okay?"

"I'm fine." The weasel padded cheerfully up to the table. "Justice prevailed and all that. A little rip to the ear can't take the shine off that."

"It certainly did no good to his case."

The King shook his head. "Indeed not, Captain. Once again, our sincerest thanks. You have never failed to justify our faith in *you*. Despite your occasionally unorthodox methods. You really should keep your helpers out of troublesome and dangerous situations." He sighed. "Now, if you will excuse me, I believe Alacris and I need to begin discussing the appointment of the new Lord Fardew."

He strode down the side of the room and swept out, flanked by the queen, three guards, and Lord Alacris. The rest of the nobles began to filter out of the room once the King had gone. Tish caught Volle's eye and smiled, and gestured upwards toward his rooms. Volle smiled back and nodded.

"Notice I didn't get any of the praise there?" Archie said. He and Nero had walked over to where Volle and Streak were standing. "I only risked my neck getting into Lord Fardew's chambers, that's all."

"You did what I told you to," Nero rumbled. "The King handed out praise where it was due."

"Easy for you to say. You didn't have to hide in a chest stinking of sandalwood and rat for two hours."

Volle was following their discussion with an ear, but the other was turned to Streak, who'd remained quiet but wore a huge smile. He stepped forward at the same time Volle did, and a moment later they were hugging each other warmly. Volle's sheath protested when pressed against the wolf, and his nose twitched at the smell of the prison cells on them both, but the rest of him was so happy, he decided to ignore it. Besides, he didn't want to advertise his wound. Streak would find out soon enough, and it was nobody else's business. But that, and Archie's remark, reminded him that he wanted to thank the weasel for his discretion.

Archie was just nudging Nero and saying, "Maybe we should leave 'em alone."

Volle grinned at him. "Actually, Archie, I'd like a word alone with you before I go off with Streak, if I could?"

The weasel gave him a knowing smile. "We don't need to talk now. I know you appreciate all the work I did, even if this wolf doesn't."

"Yeah. I just wanted to thank you particularly."

"You're very welcome. I think you were pretty brave yourself, what you went through and all."

Volle smiled and leaned against Streak. "I had to."

"Yeah." Archie smiled and took Nero's arm. "Come on, boss. I hear they're serving lunch over in the dining room."

Helfer had come up to the table, and shook Archie's paw as he and Nero turned to leave. "Great job, Archie. You did us proud here."

"Thank you, my Lord." Archie grinned and looked at Nero. "Nice to know someone appreciates what I did."

Nero rumbled amusedly. "Come, before your head gets too big to fit through the door." Archie laughed as the two of them walked out.

Helfer smiled and then threw his arms around Volle. "Hey," he said, and wrinkled his nose. "Phew! Well, you smell better than last time you got out of prison."

"Ow. Careful." Volle winced, but hugged back. "Hi, Hef. Listen, I—"

"No, let me go first." Helfer looked around Volle at Streak. "I'm sorry. I should've asked you."

Volle smiled down at the weasel. "I'm sorry too. I was tense and had a lot on my mind. I shouldn't have snapped the way I did."

"What happened?" Streak nosed up next to Volle curiously.

"I'll tell you later. We just had an argument right before I came to see you."

"I have a lot to ask you about," Helfer said, chuckling. "But it'll wait."

"Yeah. I think Tish wants to see us." Volle smiled. "He's probably been pretty worried."

"I hope he has. I know I have."

Volle gave Helfer another hug, carefully, and then looked beyond him. The wolf guard had returned from escorting Dereath and had joined the stag who had apprehended him. Both were standing respectfully below the dais, looking down at their feet, obviously waiting for Volle and Helfer to be done. Volle moved Helfer aside and nodded at the guards. Helfer saw them waiting and stepped back, waving to Volle. "I'll see you back at the mansion for dinner?"

"Definitely." Volle watched Helfer slip past the two guards. They turned their ears to follow him and then stepped up to the dais, dropping to their knees in front of Volle. The wolf's tail was curled down between his legs, and both his and the stag's ears were down. The stag was trembling slightly, and Volle could get a faint whiff of the anxiety they both were feeling.

"My Lord," the wolf said shakily, and then didn't continue.

The stag glanced at him and said in a throaty voice, "My Lord. We have behaved disgracefully. We are here to ask you to accept our resignation from the palace guard as punishment for our treatment of you."

They both looked down, waiting for his response. Flush with his triumph, Volle couldn't recall the anger he'd felt at them earlier. He couldn't bring himself to dismiss them. "I appreciate your gesture," he said, "but you were only expressing your feelings for your fellow guard. I can't say I blame you. Your resignations are not accepted."

The stag gave him a grateful look and stood, bowing deeply. "Thank you, my Lord." He stepped back.

The wolf remained on his knees. Volle bent down, paws on his thighs. "Is there something else?"

"My Lord," the wolf said. "I wonder if you would do me the honor of accepting my services as your personal guard."

Volle blinked, and flicked his ears. "Your services?"

"Yes, my Lord. I feel it is only just that I atone for my behavior, and it sounds as though some extra protection would not be unwelcome." He swallowed, still avoiding Volle's gaze.

Volle glanced at Streak, who just looked bewildered. Helfer, who had lingered behind the wolf and listened in on the conversation, gave him a smile and nodded his head enthusiastically.

Gently, he rested a paw on the wolf's shoulder. "What is your name?"

"Forrin Macleith, my Lord."

"Forrin, I would be honored to accept your services."

For the first time, the wolf's ears came up. He didn't smile, but his eyes looked determined now, rather than ashamed. "My Lord, none will harm you for the remainder of this retreat. And I will bear witness to your actions should any question them."

"Thank you, Forrin." Volle extended a paw. "I am truly and deeply honored. Please rise."

The wolf did so, slowly. He was half a foot taller than Streak, and much broader across the shoulders than the slender white wolf. His muzzle was the more traditional grey, but had reddish tones that crept up to the backs of his ears and covered them in dark reddish-brown. His darker grey tail also had brownish hints to it, but Volle couldn't see whether the rest of his fur followed suit, below the neat guard's uniform. Golden leather wrist bracers and vest set off his red shirt, and his pants were of the same leather, trimmed with a red stripe down the outside of each leg.

"Thank you for this opportunity, my Lord." He stepped around behind Volle and stood there imposingly, waiting for Volle and Streak to move.

"Forrin, will there be a problem with you leaving the palace guard?"

"My Lord, personal guard duty for the nobles of the palace is one of the duties assigned to the palace guard whenever a Lord requests it." He paused. "I believe that even though I asked your favor, it still counts as a request."

Volle smiled. "All right. We're going up to Lord Tistunish's quarters. He's a good friend of mine and we won't be in any danger from him."

"As your personal guard, my Lord, I will remain wherever you ask me to, but I will respond immediately as I see best if I perceive a threat or danger."

That sounded ominous, but Volle chose to believe that Forrin was sincere and would do his best. "Very good. I've never had a personal guard before, so please let me know if I'm doing anything wrong." He smiled, trying to elicit a response, but Forrin only nodded.

Tish seemed surprised to see the large wolf, but nodded at Volle's explanation without registering any surprise. He welcomed them all into the parlor; Volle and Streak sat down next to him, while Forrin waited by the door, arms folded. Alcis seemed unsure how to deal with the large wolf; the servant ended up straightening the dishes on the sideboard, casting nervous glances at the guard as he did so.

Tika was effusive, hugging Volle and Streak both despite their protests at their filthy state. "My dears, how frightening! How wonderful that the culprit was caught. Are you both all right? We've been so worried and there was nothing we could do. It's been a terrible time."

"We're fine." Volle lied only a bit; the day alone in prison to recuperate had left him feeling almost fine. Only his member still ached noticeably, and he still had stiffness in his neck and shoulders. "It was a rough few days for us, too."

"Of course it was." Tish drew Volle aside while Tika fussed over

Streak. "My boy, I think you can finally relax. Without Dereath, without a witness, your hearing should be just a formality."

"I was hoping you could just get it canceled."

Tish laughed. "No such luck. I do have to find out who is taking over the prosecution's case, though."

Forrin cleared his throat. "Excuse me, sir?"

Volle and Tish both turned to look at him. "Yes?" Tish was tall enough to look the guard straight in the eye.

Forrin's ears flicked. "My Lord, I believe Lord Wallen will be taking over those duties."

"How do you know that?" Volle asked.

"While we were escorting Lord—the former Lord Fardew from the room, he bent to Lord Wallen and said something about getting the papers from his desk. I regret that I did not hear more."

"Thank you, Forrin." Volle stroked his whiskers. "Wallen doesn't like me."

"No. I rather thought it would be either him or Villutian."

An idea occurred to Volle, and he turned back to Forrin. "Did you happen to overhear what he said to Lord Whassel?"

"I only heard one name, my Lord. He said 'Angeline.'"

Volle frowned, his ears sliding back and then up again. "That doesn't mean anything to me. Tish?"

The black wolf shook his head. "Nor to me."

Volle sighed. "I don't trust him. Even in custody."

Tish put a paw on his shoulder. "You should be prepared to realize that he may not face punishment for his crimes. Nobles rarely do, and even though he is not born a noble, he will benefit from having had the title. In addition, those in his position are often privy to delicate information with which they can leverage favor—at least enough to avoid the gallows."

Volle's ears lay back, and he was vaguely aware of Forrin's doing the same. "We'll see," he said.

"He won't be involved in the Defense Ministry any more, you can be sure of that." Tish was trying to reassure him, but Volle didn't feel comforted.

"Who will be running it now?"

Tish shook his head. "I am not part of those deliberations, thank goodness."

The obvious insincerity of that sentence made Volle grin. "Oh, I thought you knew everything that went on at the palace."

"We are not, you may have observed, at the palace." Tish looked back at him loftily, but with a twinkle in his eye.

"You have an excuse for everything." Volle shook his head. "All right. I hope we can at least assume Dereath will be in prison for the next few days."

"I suspect he will remain in custody until the King returns to the palace. I would not be surprised to hear of an escape somewhere along the way back." The old wolf shrugged. "It has happened before and will happen again."

"Mm." Volle considered that. "But not always."

"No, not always." Tish met his eye.

"What are we talking about?" Tika was pulling Streak up to join them.

"The next Minister of Defense," Tish said smoothly.

"Oh? Who will it be?"

He put an arm around her. "Nobody knows yet, dear. I believe the King will delay his decision until he returns to Divalia."

"Most likely. He has time. Did they send a messenger back to the palace with the news?"

"I would imagine so."

Tika changed gears. "Listen, dear, I was thinking that we might take a stroll around the castle for an hour or so. See some of the battlements, perhaps. I understand that some of the original reliefs are still there."

Volle started to shake his head, but Tika silenced him before he could say anything. "And it might be nice for these two to have a little privacy."

Tish grinned. "I have been wanting to visit the battlements before we go."

Streak slid a paw around Volle's waist, but the ache in Volle's sheath made him say, "Actually, I think I would rather have some lunch. Aren't they serving now?"

Tish and Streak stared at him, while Tika said, "Yes...I believe they are."

Volle looked back, trying to pretend that he didn't understand why they were all shocked. "Maybe we could just freshen up a bit in your bathroom?"

In the bathroom, as they daubed themselves liberally with a pine-scented powder and then brushed it out, Streak whispered to him, "Are you all right?" Volle nodded, not feeling inclined to talk about it. Streak persisted. "What's the matter?" Then his eyes widened and his voice dropped to a whisper. "Is it something about...Dereath?"

"I'll tell you later," Volle said quietly, and then raised his voice. "Actually, I would really like a nice water bath."

"We're going down to the resort to visit Dewanne tomorrow. Would you like to come along?" Tika offered from the next room.

"I think I'd really like to, thank you." Volle smiled at Streak. "You'll love this place."

Streak nuzzled his eartips. "If you're there, I will."

Lunch was dried fruit and dried meat with fresh bread, but Volle thought it was the best thing he'd tasted in days. He kept looking at Streak sitting beside him and wondering how he could ever have had doubts. Even through the pine scent, he could smell Streak's strong lupine scent, and it was sweet to his nostrils. Nobody else seemed to mind or notice that they smelled a bit stronger than nobles were used to. Several nobles stopped to greet him and wish him good fortune, or express their disbelief over the way the inquest had turned out. Lord Alacris shuffled up to him and said gravely that the kingdom appreciated what Volle had gone through.

You have no idea, Volle thought as the bear walked further down the table.

Forrin didn't eat with them. Volle asked him about that, but he said that his job was to guard Volle during meals. Indeed, he scrutinized everyone who approached, and some of the smaller nobles were visibly intimidated by his presence. Volle decided that he didn't mind that so much, and so he took a cloth napkin and wrapped up some bread, fruit, and meat, and presented it to Forrin when they rose at the end of the meal.

"From now on," Volle said, handing the package to the surprised guard, "I would like you to eat with us. I think you can be as effective a guard sitting down, and certainly more effective than on an empty stomach."

Forrin blinked, but accepted the food and the command. He bowed. "As you wish, my Lord."

"There are some groups going to do outdoor painting this afternoon," Tika said, coming up behind them, "or you could go practice archery or swordfighting with some of the others. You're free to do what you want." She wagged her tail and smiled as she said it.

Volle looked at Streak, who shrugged and smiled. The fox turned to Tish and Tika. "I think perhaps we'd just like to take a walk together. It's been a while."

Tika smiled, and Tish said, "Good idea. We'll see you tomorrow at the resort, then?"

Volle nodded. "Sometime in the morning."

"Not too early." Tish grinned, and patted them both on the shoulders. "Today went well. I hope the rest of the retreat goes as well. I have a feeling it will."

They waved as he and Tika left the room, and wandered out themselves a moment later, with Forrin preceding them. "Where are we going to walk?" Streak asked.

Volle smiled. "I don't know. It's just nice not to have any obligations, and to see you again."

"Yeah." Streak pulled him close and nuzzled him. "I was really worried when they took you away."

"That's when I stopped being worried about you."

They emerged into the large confluence, where a crowd of people milled about, talking. Volle's ears flicked around, catching pieces of the discussions; most of them concerned the morning's hearings, those who'd been there filling in the ones who'd missed it. Nero and Archie stood at the base of the staircase, talking quietly with a trio of bears. Volle recognized Lord and Lady Barclaw, and Lord Quirn, as he drew nearer, and he would have passed on by if Lady Barclaw hadn't seen him.

"Vinton!" The large bear turned and scooped him and Streak into the gathering with a warm paw. "We were just discussing your harrowing adventures. Are you feeling better?"

"Much. Thank you." He smiled. "We really owe our thanks to the captain here. He believed our stories and found the proof to back them up."

Nero harrumphed. "As I have said in the past, belief is not my job. I simply noted that your stories seemed to concur more closely with some of the minor details of the crimes that perhaps others might have overlooked."

Lord Quirn ignored Volle completely, making a show of listening only to Nero. "What sorts of details?"

Nero quickly gave up any pretense of being reluctant to speak. "For example, although the scissors were lying on the floor, they had clearly been thrust deep into the throat. There was no reason for the murderer to have pulled them out again unless he was intending to dispose of them—which didn't fit with the pattern of an impulse murder."

"What if it were premeditated?" Lord Barclaw said.

"Then the murderer would have brought his own weapon." Volle chimed in. Glancing past Nero to the staircase, he saw Dereath's rabbit servant leaning against the banister, listening to them. There didn't seem to be any malice in his expression, but Volle kept an eye on him anyway.

"Quite right." Nero nodded. "Additionally...well, there is a forensic expert in Divalia, name of Macey, a coyote. He's doing some wonderful things with murder investigations. I'm sure he could have made more of the scene than I could have, but I did notice that the wound appeared to have been made at an acute upward angle. That suggested an attacker more rat-sized than wolf-sized. And lastly, there was no scent of fear on her body. A mouse, surprised by a wolf one and a half times her size, could hardly help a burst of fear. Yet there was none on her body—suggesting that her attacker was someone who knew her."

"Brilliant." Lord Barclaw smiled. "Delighted that you're working for us in Divalia, captain. We can rest easier at night."

"I only wish I could prevent as many crimes as I solve," Nero said, and his eyes when Volle met them seemed to be very sad. "If I had trusted Lord Vinton sooner, the unfortunate guard might still be alive."

Volle shook his head. "You had no reason to trust me."

"Looking behind you just leads to chasing your tail, boss," Archie said with a grin.

Nero sighed and nodded. "True."

"Where are you boys off to?" Lady Barclaw asked Volle.

He looked at Streak and smiled. "We're just going to take a walk and spend some time together. It's been a while."

"Very nice. Don't let us keep you any longer." He patted them both on the back and then looked across them to Lord Barclaw. "Why don't you ever take me for a walk?"

Lord Barclaw smiled. "We go for walks all the time."

"Oh, how could I forget? We walk to dinner, to lunch, to the King's hearings…"

Volle grinned and extricated himself from the group, waving to everyone as he did. Forrin, who had waited patiently outside, set off again, but before they'd gone more than ten feet, the large wolf guard whirled to meet a figure who was running after them. He didn't draw his sword, but he dropped to a defensive posture, and the figure, little more than half his size, drew up short.

It happened so quickly that Volle had only seen it out of the corner of his eye, and not until he turned did he recognize the rabbit. He didn't call Forrin off, but he did say, warily, "What can I do for you?"

The rabbit, eyes fixed on Forrin, stepped back. "I, er…" He took another step back. "I just wanted to…you see, I don't have a Lord any more, and I don't particularly want to go back to Divalia."

"Why not?"

The rabbit shuffled his large feet. "I heard that he's a murderer. I won't be able to get another job in the palace. And I rather like it here. I know you're staying with Lord Ikling. I was wondering if you could ask him if maybe he needs another servant for his mansion."

Volle chuckled softly. "I'll ask. Are you staying here until then?"

The rabbit nodded. "In Lord Fardew's quarters. I mean—"

"What's your name?" Volle asked, realizing he didn't know.

"I'm Terril," he said, and then took another step back as Forrin growled, his ears dropping. "What?"

"You'll address Lord Vinton as 'my Lord' or 'sir,'" Forrin snarled.

"I'm…sorry, my Lord," Terril said.

"It's all right." Volle patted Forrin. "Thank you, Forrin."

"So you'll ask him? My Lord?" Terril added the last part quickly with a glance at Forrin.

"Yes." Volle waved a paw. "I should see him tonight, so I'll send someone up with an answer tomorrow."

"Thank you, my Lord." Terril turned and walked slowly back up the stairs.

"I don't trust him," Streak muttered. "Anyone who worked for that rat…"

Volle shrugged and flexed his wrists, remembering the slide of the knife blade across them and through the leather straps. "But Helfer likes rabbits," he said with a grin. "Though I'm not sure he'd be a good match, actually." Someone who "wasn't interested in that sex stuff" might hold little interest for Helfer.

"I wouldn't think so."

"I'll mention it to him, anyway."

"I don't trust him either, my Lord." Forrin turned his head partially as they made their way through the crowd.

"Why not?"

"He didn't have any respect for you. And his scent was weak."

"I noticed that too." Volle shrugged. "Some people are born like that."

Forrin looked doubtful, but didn't say anything else.

As they made their way to the main gate, Helfer caught up to them. Forrin's ears turned at the sound of running footsteps, but he relaxed when he saw who it was. They stopped just before the large doorway.

"Volle, Streak," Helfer said. "And...Forrin, right?"

The wolf nodded. Volle grinned. "Why in such a hurry?"

"I ran into Tish, he said you were taking a walk. I was going to ask where."

Volle looked at Streak and let him answer. "No plans," the wolf said.

"Might I suggest a trail down the mountain to the mansion? It should take you a few hours and you'll arrive in time for dinner." The weasel's eyes glinted brightly.

Volle canted his ears. "Why?"

Helfer shrugged and grinned. "I'm about to take a buggy down and put together a little evening celebration for you. It's a nice scenic walk, and as pretty a day as you'll get up here. And it'll give me time to arrange everything. It's not easy pulling this off at the last minute, you know."

"Hef, you don't have to do that."

The weasel raised a paw. "Hush. Don't you think I'd jump at any excuse to throw a nice party?" He grinned, his little tail wagging. "Besides, it'll look good. I can invite the nobles and maybe that plus the orchard visit and the brewery sampling next Caniday will salvage this visit. It's hard to get over two murders."

Streak grinned at Volle and gave a small nod and shrug. "All right," Volle said. "If it means that much to you..."

"Great!" Helfer clapped his paws together. "I'm off now. Roferro's here, he can take you to the trail head. He'll go with you if you want."

"Might be best," Forrin rumbled. "To have someone who knows the way, I mean, my Lord. If you trust him."

"You can trust Roferro," Helfer said before Volle could respond. Forrin looked to Volle for confirmation, and Volle nodded.

The trail Roferro led them to was wide enough for two to walk side by side, so Forrin accompanied the otter while Volle and Streak walked some distance back. For the first hour or so, they wound their way through boulders and loose scree, and more than once Volle had to stop and pick a pebble out of his paw. The slopes were occasionally steep, but all were easy to navigate; the problem was that conversations tended to be interrupted, and eventually they stopped trying to talk.

He had to admit that the rocks were pretty. The primary material was a grayish-black rock veined with white quartz, but scattered throughout the area were smaller rocks of reddish and orange sandstone. Streak found a small rough rock that was bright white: a piece of pure quartz crystal, and he gave it to Volle with a smile. Twice they saw small rodents scurrying for cover behind rocks, but other than that, the place was devoid of life.

The rocky path opened out onto a large meadow, and here the trail became less distinct. But Roferro pointed across the meadow, explaining, "There's a spring on the other side. We used to come play here as kits." He jogged across the soft, springy grass.

Forrin looked back at Volle, his tail wagging slightly, and Volle waved him on. The grass was smooth on his paw pads, and on the other side of the meadow he could see trees and hear the burbling of the stream. Birds chirped, and small animals rustled through the grass and bushes. In contrast to the rocky part of the trail, the meadow smelled and sounded alive.

The pastoral setting lifted his spirits and he supposed the others felt the same. Forrin jogged after Roferro and he and Streak followed at a more leisurely pace.

"I suppose you have to go through the harsh place to get to this one," Streak said.

"I'm glad we're through our harsh places." Volle slipped an arm around his waist. "I was beginning to wonder if there would be an end."

"I know what you mean."

They walked in silence for a few more paces, and Volle could tell Streak was struggling with something. He let the wolf sort out what he had to, and perked his ears when the wolf's white muzzle opened.

"You know, for all the time I was in the cell, I mostly thought about how I'd let you down. I wondered if you'd come back for me or just let me go."

"Let you go? Why would I do that?" He said it somewhat uneasily, trying to forget the temptations he'd had, telling himself that he'd never really considered them.

Streak lowered his head. "We hadn't even been around a day and I managed to stumble into a murder and get thrown in jail."

"So? That wasn't your fault."

"We didn't know that until today. And anyway, you think that makes me feel better? I got tricked like some backwoods farm wolf." His ears drooped. "Which is what I am."

"That's the wolf I fell in love with, and I won't hear a word said against him."

Streak smiled then, but weakly. "You know what I wanted more than anything, there in that cell?" Volle shook his head. "I wanted to be back with you on the farm, away from all this. There's just…so much." He brought his paws up, then dropped them back to his sides.

"We don't have to go back to the farm now, though. As soon as my hearing is over, we can go to the palace." Volle was fighting back the crawling sensation at the back of his neck. He suspected he knew where this was leading.

Streak didn't talk for while, just looked down at the grass as his paws shuffled through it. "This is nice, here," he said finally. "We don't have mountains back at the farm."

Volle lowered his ears. "You don't want to go to the palace."

"I don't know." There was an undertone of anguish to his voice. "I want to be with you, but now I'm...I'm frightened."

"I can protect you there," Volle said. "I have friends, and..." He trailed off, as Streak was shaking his head.

"I'm frightened that I'll let you down," the wolf said quietly.

They had almost reached the spring, and Volle stopped to look into Streak's eyes. He touched his nose to the wolf's and breathed softly. "You won't let me down."

For the span of several heartbeats they stood eye to eye, and then Streak managed a smile. He licked Volle's nose and nodded. "All right, then," Volle said, and walked with him to the spring.

Roferro was drinking from the spring, and Forrin was wiping his muzzle. As they approached, Roferro scooped a paw into the water and flicked some water at the wolf, grinning mischievously.

Forrin blinked at him, then shook the arm the water had landed on and walked deliberately a little ways away. He looked around and then sat at the base of a tree, looking back toward the spring.

"Yoicks." Roferro stood up, saw Volle, and shrugged. "Just havin' a bit of fun, my Lord. No harm meant."

"It's been a tough few days for him," Volle said softly. "Just leave him be." He bent to the spring and drank. The water was very cold, but wonderfully refreshing, and he didn't stop drinking until his tongue started to tingle from the chill of the water. He straightened and watched Streak drink.

Roferro was looking down the mountain, arms folded. While Streak lapped at the water, Volle followed the otter's gaze and saw only trees and grassy hills. "How far is it from here?"

"A few hours, my Lord. There's not really much of a trail from here on, but it's hard to get lost." He gestured and grinned. "Just keep going downhill."

"Which way is the mansion?" Volle asked, and followed Roferro's pointing arm. "Can't see it from here?"

"No, my Lord. In about an hour, you should be able to."

"All right." He turned to the large wolf. "Forrin, are you ready?"

Forrin levered himself to his feet. "Yes, my Lord." He raised an eyebrow at the otter, who grinned at him.

"Sorry," he said, and extended a paw. "No harm done?"

"None," Forrin rumbled, but he didn't take the paw. After a moment, Roferro shrugged and started off down the hill.

This portion of the walk was much more animated than the previous one. Squirrels chattered in the trees, rodents scurried about the grass, and the birds sang back and forth overhead. Volle and Streak walked with clasped paws behind the other two, breathing the fresh air and occasionally exchanging smiling looks. Volle was trying to think of ways to convince

Streak that life at the palace wouldn't be anything like the past week had been, but every time he started to say something, he felt as though he were protesting a lost cause, so he closed his muzzle again.

Roferro led them through the woods, closely following the stream. They stopped to rest twice, once at a bend in the stream where there was a large flat rock, big enough for them all to sit on. The second stop came at a small clearing where a fallen tree had made a makeshift bench, and it was while they were sitting there that the clouds parted and the sun appeared for the first time. Volle leaned back, letting it warm his fur, and closed his eyes, sighing happily.

A scent tickled his nose a few moments later, and he opened his eyes to see a bright blue flower being waved under his nose by a smiling Streak. The scent of the flower was delicate and fragrant, and he liked its soft blue color. He tried to take it from Streak, but the wolf pulled his paw away and worked the flower into Volle's collar.

"You'll wear it, won't you?" He nuzzled Volle as he said it.

"Of course." Volle could still smell the flower, but more faintly. He touched its soft petals with a paw. "Is this to tell everyone at the party tonight that I'm taken?"

Streak grinned. "No. I'll tell them that myself. This…is just because it looks pretty on you."

Volle kissed him and wagged his tail from side to side. "It's so nice," he murmured, "not to have to worry about anything. Just being here with you."

Streak's tail brushed against his as it wagged. "Yeah. It's nice." The wolf slid an arm around Volle's side, hugged him, and sighed deeply.

The sky was already darkening by the time they reached the mansion, but a bright glow rose from a spot just in front of the large building. They emerged into the meadow through which Volle and Helfer had run a few times, but it was no longer bare.

Paper lanterns had been hung from the trees and mounted on ribbon-strung poles. Two weasels were just scurrying about lighting the last of them. A makeshift platform had been erected to one side of the meadow, upon which a group of weasels was setting up instruments. On the other side of the meadow, two otters and a weasel heaved large barrels into place. Volle didn't have to see the wooden cups placed alongside them to know what they contained.

Several bears, wolves, and raccoons were wandering about the meadow already, nobles and guards alike, and Volle saw another pair of bears and a familiar pair of antlers walking up from the main gate of the mansion. "I wondered how Helfer would hold a party in his weasel-sized house," he murmured to Streak.

Streak nodded. "This is great. It looks like the weather should hold." He turned his muzzle briefly to the sky, where a multitude of stars was just beginning to join the bright few already visible.

Tish and Tika weren't anywhere that Volle could see in the crowd.

Two more carriages pulled up, but before he could see who was getting out of them, Streak tugged him over near the barrels, where tables of fruit and cheese had been spread out. "I can smell the oranges," he said. "Oh, fresh fruit...There!" A large tray of orange slices sat to one side of the table, and the wolf made a beeline for it.

Volle chuckled softly and took a few pieces of fruit himself, watching the wolf's blissful expression as he licked and then chewed the juicy orange. "Mmm," he said, and then lowered his voice. "I can only think of one thing I missed having in my muzzle more."

"Goat cheese?" Volle grinned and held up a small piece of white, fragrant cheese.

Streak laughed. "Not quite. I'll show you later."

"It's really good with these apples." Volle bit down and smiled, watching a small shape thread its way through the crowd toward them. "Helfer knows his food and drink, that's for sure."

"Thank you." The weasel grinned and bowed. "How did you enjoy the trail down?"

"It was beautiful," Streak said, his tail brushing the table as it wagged back and forth. "I can see why someone would want to live out here."

"So what does that say for me spending most of the year in Divalia, eh?" Helfer pretended annoyance.

"Helfer likes scenery of a different sort," Volle said. "I'm surprised you don't have the Young Gay Rabbit dancers here."

The weasel swatted at him. "Not enough of them in this area to form a group, I'm afraid. But look." He pointed over in front of the stage, where a young rabbit in very few clothes was dancing to the music provided by one of the musicians on a set of pipes. The drummer had just started to join in with a subdued beat.

"Very nice." Streak sighed. "I wish I could dance like that."

"He's my gift to myself," Helfer said happily. "After the party, I'll take him inside and keep him up all night."

"Oh, that reminds me," Volle said. "Dereath's assistant, that rabbit, was asking if you had any jobs down here."

Helfer turned away from the dancing rabbit and looked skeptically at Volle. "Dereath's assistant?"

"He doesn't seem too bad. He doesn't want to go back to Divalia, with what happened at the hearing."

"I wouldn't, either." Helfer stroked his whiskers. "Is he cute?"

Volle held out a paw and wiggled it back and forth. "He's not bad. Sort of plain. But I don't think he's really interested in working under you in *that* way."

Helfer shrugged. "Well, maybe he can find work at one of the resorts. I really don't need any more servants at the mansion. At least, that's what Huster tells me. He's always trying to get me to let one or two of them go."

Streak looked visibly relieved.

Tish and Tika showed up half an hour later, and Dewanne and Delia some time after that. Volle and Streak talked to them about the hearing, about the retreat in general ("I can't remember a more exciting one," Tika said brightly, "now that everything's turned out okay, that is."), and about the party itself. Once the music really got underway, several pairs of nobles began dancing immediately. The singer, it turned out, was a female mink, and her voice was beautiful, equally capable of the powerful trills of a rollicking dance number or the soft, sultry tones of a traditional ballad.

Volle drank enough wine to build a nice warmth in his stomach that spread slowly through his body. There weren't enough informal parties like this at the palace, he reflected, and Dewanne, who happened to be nearby when he made the observation, agreed.

"By the way," Volle said, "Where is Ilyana?"

Dewanne glanced at Streak and lowered his voice. "She's, er, indisposed, I believe."

"I hope she's better before the end of the retreat," Streak said, returning Dewanne's glance defiantly. "I'd like to get to talk to her more."

"Yes, do you know what's the matter?"

Dewanne shook his head and changed the subject immediately, remarking on the song the musicians were now playing and how it shared the same tune as a traditional fox's ballad even though they'd changed the words. They chattered on for a while and then Streak pulled Volle away to dance slowly as the band started another ballad. As the song started, some of the guests started to leave; Volle saw two bear couples pay their respects to Helfer and walk back toward the main entrance, where a line of buggies waited.

"Can you believe him?" Streak whispered as they held each other and danced. "As if I'd be threatened by your wife. I thought she was sweet and charming."

Volle smiled. "And you know where my heart is."

"Other things, too." Streak reached down and gave Volle's sheath a squeeze through his pants.

The rough leather pressed against him and the sudden wave of soreness made him wince. He tried to recover, but Streak was already looking at him with concern. "I'm okay," he said, but the wolf's ears went down as he said it.

"Come on." He stopped dancing and walked away from the music. "We're going to bed, and you're going to tell me what that rat did to you."

"Wait." Volle tugged the wolf toward Helfer. "We have to say good night to the host. He did put this on for us."

Streak paused, then nodded and fell in behind him.

"Not leaving already?" Helfer said as they approached. The young rabbit was at his side, one paw draped across the weasel's thigh.

Volle realized suddenly that he hadn't seen Laya all night. He wondered if she'd come to the party and left, decided not to come, or—not been invited. He didn't feel this was the appropriate time to ask Helfer, so he put on a smile. "We haven't had any private time since the inquest."

"What? You smelled of pine, I figured you'd washed...go, go!" Helfer waved them away with a grin.

"Thanks for the lovely party, Lord Ikling," Streak said, bowing. "The food and mead were wonderful."

"Welcome to Vellenland, youngster." Helfer was most likely on his fifth or sixth cup of mead, but Volle could only tell that because he saw the slight list to the cup the weasel was holding, and because Helfer never called anyone "youngster." Maybe he was feeling his age. More likely the rabbit was feeling it, judging from the way his paw was creeping up Helfer's pants. "It's always like that here."

"Good night, Hef. Enjoy the rest of the evening."

"Oh, I will." He patted the rabbit between the ears.

Forrin had been near them for most of the dance but keeping a respectable distance. As he saw them leaving, he hurried to catch up, and insisted on preceding them into the mansion. When they reached the guest chambers, Forrin made them wait in the parlor while he inspected the bedroom and bathroom, making sure they were empty and had no other entrances or exits. He emerged and nodded. "Go ahead in, my Lord. I'll sleep out here, across the doorway."

"Wouldn't you be more comfortable on the couch?" Streak asked.

"Pull the couch across the doorway," Volle suggested. "We'll knock in the morning to make sure you're awake."

They helped him drag the heavy wooden couch over to the door, despite his protests that he could manage it alone. When it was in place, they bade him goodnight and slipped into the bedroom, closing the door behind them.

Streak looked at the door for a moment. "Does that make you feel weird? Him being right on the other side there?"

Volle, who had slept next door to a personal servant for five years in the palace, shook his head. "Not particularly."

"All right." Streak smiled and put both paws on either side of Volle's muzzle, bringing him close.

Volle parted his muzzle as the soft fur of the white wolf's touched it, and felt a familiar warmth and taste as their tongues brushed each other. He pulled his muzzle closer, pressing it against Streak's, keeping their teeth apart with expert care. Their bodies slid closer together as well, and this time the soreness when Streak pressed on Volle's sheath was easy to ignore. He felt his tail swing back and forth as a wave of euphoria washed over him. This was what he had missed, this was what he had gone to all that trouble for, this was what he wanted.

Streak felt the same, he could tell. The wolf's tongue thrust insistently against his and his arms tightened as though he wanted to pull the fox into himself. Volle pressed against him without protest and returned the embrace until he felt they were just sharing one breath, back and forth.

Finally, with a sigh, they let their muzzles slide apart. Streak brushed Volle's whiskers with a tender smile. "I missed that."

"Me too." Volle nuzzled the wolf's paw softly.

"All right. Now come over here," he tugged Volle toward the bed, "and tell me what happened that day."

Volle sighed and sat down on the bed. He debated whether to hold anything back, but decided against it. He kept his voice low, so that if Forrin were listening he couldn't hear, and told Streak what Dereath had done. The only details he left out were their conversations; it would have needlessly upset Streak to hear some of the things Dereath had said.

When he reached the part where Dereath had drawn blood, he hesitated and found it hard to describe. Streak took a second to understand, and when he did, his eyes widened in horror.

"Oh, merciful Canis! No wonder..." He chewed on his lip. "Is it...healing? Can I see?"

Volle was reluctant to show Streak, but he knew he'd have to eventually. "I don't know how much you'll be able to see in the dark. It is healing. It's just sore now. I don't know if it'll leave a scar."

Streak tried a smile. "It could be interesting." His ears were still down. "What else?"

Volle finished the story, and Streak sighed. Volle reached over to pat the wolf's leg, and then realized that his paws were clenched into fists and that what he'd thought had been a sigh had been a low, strangled growl. "It's okay," he started to say, but Streak cut him off.

"It's not okay." His voice was trembling. "You went through all that for me, because of my stupidity. And that...son of an outcast did it to you. And he enjoyed it! If he weren't in prison, I'd go up to the castle and wring his neck right now."

Volle took the wolf's fists in his paws and looked into his muzzle. "What's important is that we're here, together. Let him be. He can't hurt us now." Something gnawed at him as he said that, knowing he wasn't being quite truthful, but he pushed it aside.

"If he does anything like that again. If he ever *touches* you again..."

"He won't." Volle looked into Streak's eyes. "I promise."

Streak relaxed slowly, his paws uncurling. "I feel like it's my fault," he whispered.

Volle shook his head. "You didn't make him do those things. Blame him."

"Oh, I do." His whisper regained its edge.

"But not tonight." Volle kissed Streak gently, surprised to find himself swelling with arousal despite the soreness that accompanied the feeling. "Tonight let's just celebrate being back together again."

The wolf's ears came up slowly. "All right. You're right." He kissed Volle back. "But I still want to see."

"Okay." Volle stood and started to undo his pants. He wanted Streak to be happy; in a way he felt like he was protecting the young wolf from the extremes of emotion that could get him in trouble at the palace. Distracting him with sex seemed to be working, and, Volle admitted to himself, it had its side benefits as well. He let his pants fall to the floor and shed his shirt a moment later.

Streak knelt in front of him, eyes close to Volle's sheath in the dim light. He sniffed the fur after examining it and then licked gently. "You'll have to take it all the way out," he grinned, nosing at the top of Volle's sheath.

"I trust you can remember how to do that." Volle chuckled softly.

"Mmm." Streak bent to licking again, and Volle shuddered. While he remained in his sheath, the pleasure of the licks countered the pain nicely, but as the wound slid past the tight ring at the opening of his sheath, a sharp pain made his knees buckle and brought a gasp to his lips.

"You okay?" Streak was on his feet, holding Volle and looking anxiously into his eyes.

"Yeah," Volle panted. "Just…a bit of pressure on the wrong spot." The pain was fading quickly.

Streak examined him worriedly for another few seconds, and when Volle smiled reassuringly at him, he nodded and dropped to his knees again. He caressed Volle's emerging length with gentle pads and brushed his nose and tongue along it. Volle felt a twinge as his tongue brushed past the wound, and then heard a growl and an exhalation of breath.

Worried that Streak was going to get upset again, Volle reached down to pet his ears gently. "It feels better when you lick it," he said.

"Does it?" In the moonlight, Streak's eyes shone up, but Volle could still see the spark of a smile in them. He nodded.

"I guess it's my duty to keep licking, then." He leaned forward and bent his tongue to the task.

Volle gasped; after a few licks it really was more pleasure than pain. The aching subsided, replaced by urges and a rush of blood he hadn't felt in days. "Oh…" he moaned softly.

"Mmf. 'Sbetter," Streak mumbled around his shaft. "Like old times."

"I missed you…wolf…" Volle panted.

Streak responded by sliding his entire muzzle over Volle's erect, trembling shaft and holding it there, letting his tongue rub gently up and down. Volle closed his eyes, his knees weakening, paws sliding to Streak's shoulders and resting there.

Still Streak kept licking, sliding his muzzle back and forth, careful not to press too hard on the small wound. Volle felt two days of chastity and nearly a week of frustration and tension melt away from him, drowned in waves of arousal that crested higher and higher. He heard himself moaning and felt his paws clench more tightly on the wolf's shoulders, and then felt a shiver as the wolf stopped and gently drew his muzzle back.

"I want to be part of this too," he said. "I don't think you can mount me tonight, so if you're not too sore…?"

Volle grinned and clenched his rear experimentally. "Not a bit of it, dear."

Streak's tail wagged quickly as he divested himself of his own clothes, in what seemed to Volle like record time. He found the small pot of lubricant and sat down on the bed with it, patting the space beside him.

Clambering onto the bed, Volle dropped his muzzle into Streak's lap and nuzzled the warm sheath, sighing happily. Streak reached around behind him and applied the cream, more gently than usual, though Volle could have told him not to worry. It actually felt cool and quite good, and he was amply distracted with the growing length under his tongue. He drew his tongue along it, and the familiar shape and taste were like coming home.

He hardly realized he had Streak in his muzzle and was sliding his muzzle vigorously up and down until he heard the wolf's harsh panting and smelled the musk of his arousal, stronger even than the pine smell now. He grinned and lifted his muzzle. "Okay. I think you're ready."

"Oh, sweet Canis…this is going to be the quickest mating we've ever had, I think." Streak panted, his eyes wide with desire as Volle lay on his back, head on the pillow. The wolf knelt between his legs and held his stiff member with one paw while the other guided his own erection under Volle's sac. Volle felt the pressure, a moment of discomfort, and then the warm hardness covered by cool lubricant, sliding into him as neatly as it ever had.

He panted himself then, so close to his climax that he tried to keep Streak's slick paw away from his shaft, sure that the least touch would push him over. Streak's motions almost did that anyway; the wolf's knot was already as big as it would get, and his quick thrusting motions were making Volle shudder all over.

"Oh fox…" he whined, "I can't hold on…" Then that knot was pressing against Volle's rear, and he was grabbing Streak's paw and rubbing it quickly up and down his shaft, because the sensations were too much for him, too. Streak's howl was cut short by a series of moans as his knot popped into Volle and his hips worked back and forth, his body shuddering as it released its passion into the fox.

The noise had barely died down before Volle had begun panting and moaning himself, the touch on his member like fire. Dimly, he felt some pain from the wound, but it was thrust back far away where it didn't matter. He was exploding, bright spots danced before his eyes, and his back arched as he finished with a deep, loud moan. He felt the splashes of warmth on his chest first, then on his stomach, and finally on his paw. For a long moment, he held the tension, and then he collapsed on his back, pulling Streak down with him.

They shared a deep, warm kiss, stroking each other's fur as the feelings subsided. Volle was aware of a small ache on his member, but much less than when he'd been squeezed at the dance. He sighed happily. In a few days that too would be gone.

Streak nuzzled him and pressed his muzzle into the pillow. "Phew," he said. "Fox, that was so…Mmm."

"Yeah," Volle said, and stroked a paw down the curve of the wolf's back, playing with the base of his tail. "For me too. Wow."

"Mmm. Say…"

"Hmm?"

"Why does the pillow smell like otter?"

Chapter 11

*V*olle froze for a moment. He'd completely forgotten about Ellitt. But Streak didn't seem disturbed at all. "'Sa matter?" he mumbled into the fabric. "Prob'ly just some of the servants had a good time in here. Musk's pretty strong."

For a moment, Volle realized he could skip the whole episode. He could let Streak believe that and go to sleep, warmly tied together, their own musk the overpowering scent in the room, and in the morning he would tell Helfer never to mention Ellitt.

But that wouldn't be right. He could do it, but he would always know, and one day Streak would probably find out. There were enough lies in his life, and he had promised to keep Streak free of them as much as he could.

"Listen," he said softly into Streak's ear.

"Hmm?" The wolf was half-dozing already.

"Streak." Volle nosed him gently. "I have to tell you something."

One blue eye opened and looked at him. With an effort, the white wolf lifted his head. "What's up?"

Volle took a breath. "This is what Helfer and I fought about."

As objectively as possible, he told Streak about Ellitt. He left out the parts about how good it had been, and emphasized that Helfer had called him, that Volle himself had been half-asleep, and that it hadn't meant anything to him.

He watched Streak's expression go from curious to guarded, and kept his paws on the wolf's sides. "The thing is, afterwards, I realized that…I don't want anyone else. I know you were worried about that, but that night…it just made me miss you more."

"You did that here? In this bed?" Volle nodded cautiously. Streak searched his eyes. "Was he better than I was?"

"Course not," Volle said. "Didn't you hear what I said?"

"Yeah." The wolf shrugged. "You just have so much more experience. I wonder how I measure up sometimes."

Volle squeezed Streak's shrinking knot playfully, making the wolf yelp. "You're the best."

"Now I know that's not true." But Streak was smiling now, leaning forward to lick Volle on the nose.

"Sure it is. I've spent a whole year training you." Volle looked up innocently, ears askew on the pillow.

"Training…" Streak giggled and tugged on Volle's rear, his knot small enough to let him slide out. He lay flat on the smaller fox, pinning him gently to the bed and nibbling at his muzzle. "Is that what you call it?"

Volle giggled, squirming. "That's what I just called it."

"Maybe you need some more training yourself." He couldn't stifle a huge yawn, though. "You're lucky I'm too tired to give you a lesson now."

"I wouldn't call it lucky. Maybe I'll get luckier tomorrow."

"Maybe. Good chance, I'd say."

"Mmm." Volle licked his muzzle gently. "So…are you okay? I promise I …" *Won't do it again?* That sounded insufficient, somehow.

"Hmm?"

The words came to him smoothly. "I promise I won't be with anyone but you. Ever."

A blue eye opened again and looked at him. "What?"

He held Streak tightly. "I won't be with anyone else."

The wolf hugged back silently, then rolled off him and rested a paw on his stomach. "I feel the same way," he said quietly. "But…I can't hold you to that."

"Why not?"

"Not yet. If…"

Volle reached across his stomach and covered the white paw that lay there. "If you come back to the palace, you mean."

Streak looked at him and his whiskers twitched. "Or if you come back to the farm."

Volle sighed and nodded slowly. "Okay." He nuzzled Streak gently. "We're together *now*."

"Yeah." The wolf snuggled closer to him, and before either of them could think of anything else to say, sleep had overtaken them.

In the morning, Helfer woke Forrin, or at least that's what Volle assumed had happened; he woke to the low murmurs of conversation outside. Streak yawned and turned to him a moment later, eyes opening and muzzle stretching into a smile as he woke. They lay in bed for a little while, waking up and stroking each other's fur. Volle marveled at how he felt he'd never really appreciated how lucky he was to have been waking up next to this wolf for the past year. He thought by the shine in Streak's eyes that he felt the same way, and he was glad that there weren't any lingering doubts from the previous night.

"Think we should get up?" he said finally.

Streak brushed a paw over his sheath, carefully avoiding the wound, and grinned. "Feels like you're already up."

Volle smiled and kissed him. "I'm not the only one. But we shouldn't keep Helfer waiting."

The wolf's paw slowly slid off him, making the fox shiver. "I suppose you're right," he said with some regret.

Volle resisted the urge to curl up and take Streak into his muzzle just to tease him. He had a pretty good idea that if he did, things would keep going. So he just kissed Streak and climbed out of bed, showing off as he stretched, wiggling his hips from side to side. Streak made a grab for the swaying erection, but Volle took a step back and stayed just out of reach. With a growl, Streak lunged, and ended up nearly on the floor as Volle stepped back again.

"Not as quick as a fox yet, are you?" Volle teased, padding to the bathroom, then running as Streak chased him.

They ended up sprawled together on the floor of the bathroom, Streak pinning Volle down and tickling him until the fox yelped for mercy. Then they just sat and giggled together for several minutes, kissing lightly before starting their daily grooming.

Fifteen minutes later, smelling more of vanilla than of musk, they cracked open the bedroom door. Helfer and Forrin were talking quietly, and both looked up at the opening of the door. "Finally," the weasel grinned. "In another ten minutes, we would have had to burst in on you."

"Sorry to disappoint you." Volle stepped around the couch and into the room. "Forrin, are you coming on our run?"

"Of course, my Lord," the wolf rumbled, standing up. "I would be remiss in my duties otherwise."

"All right," Helfer said with a mischievous look at Streak and Forrin, "let's see if you wolves can keep up with us."

For the most part, they acquitted themselves well. Forrin was in better shape than any of them, but clearly was not accustomed to running long distances with his sword, and he refused to leave it behind. As they rounded the mansion and started the second lap, he started to fall back, and so that he wouldn't feel as though he were neglecting his duties, Volle fell back and paced him while Streak and Helfer ran on ahead.

When they met again at the gate, Helfer was wagging his short tail. "Ah, size isn't everything, is it?" he chuckled, rubbing his paws together. "At least, not with legs."

Forrin smiled good-naturedly. "I suppose not, my Lord."

"Well, I think I'm going to take a bath and spend the day relaxing around here, supervising the cleanup maybe." The weasel gestured toward the meadow, though they had all seen while running through it that it was already mostly clean.

"We're going to the resort to get a proper bath." Volle sighed at the thought.

"Burning Waters, right?"

Volle nodded.

"All right. Come on back up for dinner if you can."

"We will." They waved a goodbye and climbed into a waiting buggy. Forrin didn't join them inside, but sat up front with the driver.

They spent most of the trip talking softly about the resort, neither one willing to broach the serious subjects they knew were looming only a couple of days away. Volle told Streak about the sulfurous fumes and the sense of isolation, and the blissfully hot and cold pools. He mentioned the dust baths and massages, getting a curious look when he told Streak about the young otter ("not the same one," was all he said), but he did not mention the whispering arches. He wanted to surprise the wolf with them.

When they arrived at the resort, the weasel at the front gate greeted them with a deep bow and a hesitant look. "Welcome to Burning Waters, my Lords. You are the guest of Lord Dewanne, yes?"

"Yes," Volle said. "Though I believe we may be guests of Lord Tistunish today."

"Quite so." The weasel nodded and the hesitation was replaced by a smile. "Enjoy your day at Burning Waters."

"When I have my estate back," Volle muttered to Streak, "we won't have to be here as guests."

Streak smiled and nuzzled him. "It's okay," he said. "Either way, you'll be taking those clothes off soon, won't you?"

"Mm. And so will you." Volle wagged his tail as they approached the hot baths.

Tish, Tika, and Volyan emerged from the house just as they were walking up to it. Volyan squealed and ran at Volle, flinging his arms around Volle's legs. "Daddy!"

Volle knelt to hug the dripping wet fox cub, getting quite wet even through the cub's tunic. Tish and Tika strolled up, also wet, but keeping their distance. All three reeked of the sulfurous water they'd been in. "Hiya, kit," Volle said, nuzzling him. "How've you been?"

"I'm here all by myself!" Volyan said proudly. "Mommy said I was old enough."

"You sure are. You're just walking around with Tish and Tika because you like them, right?"

The cub nodded and whispered to him, "Mommy said I should keep a eye on them."

Volle saw the grins on the wolves; the cub's whisper was not exactly secretive. "As well you should," he said. "You never know what trouble they might get into."

Volyan's eyes widened. Then he nodded and wagged his tail. "I won't let 'em get in trouble."

"And we won't let you run on the wet tile." Tika put a paw on his shoulder.

Volyan rolled his eyes to Volle, in a gesture so reminiscent of his mother that Volle had to stifle a laugh. "Who are they?" he said, pointing at Streak and Forrin.

"Don't point, dear," Tika said, and Volyan lowered his paw.

"This is Streak," Volle said, and Streak knelt down.

"Hi," he said. "What's your name?"

"I'm Volyan." Volyan examined the wolf and then said, "Are you white all over?"

"Almost." He grinned at Volle and the fox grinned back.

"I never met anyone who's white before." The cub craned his neck around to look at Streak's white tail. "Were you always white?"

"Always." Streak held out a paw. "But my fur still feels the same as yours."

Volyan reached out and brushed the fur, and then grinned. "I know that. It's fur. It's just a color."

Volle laughed, and gestured to Forrin to come forward. "Volyan, this is Forrin. Forrin, this is my son."

The guard didn't kneel, but bowed deeply, and said, "A pleasure to meet you, young master."

Volyan looked up at him with wide eyes, and only when Volle nudged him did he say, "Pleased to meet you."

Volle smiled, holding the cub's paw, and looked up at Tish. "So are you all off to the cool pools?"

"Yes," Tish said. "You'll meet us there?"

"Or we'll meet you at lunch. We got sort of a late start."

Tish and Tika just grinned at him, and he rolled his eyes at them, imitating Volyan's gesture. The cub giggled and nodded back.

"We'll see you later, then. Come on, Volyan."

"I wanna stay with Daddy," the cub said.

Volle leaned close to him. "You'd better stay with them and keep an eye on them, like your mommy said. I'll see you later." He ruffled the cub's wet head fur.

"Okay." Volyan nodded and licked Volle on the nose. "Bye, Daddy!"

Volle waved as the cub walked away with Tish and Tika, skipping over the dusty ground. Streak waved, too, and then smiled as they walked toward the hot baths, Forrin shadowing them alertly. "He's cute. Very bright."

"Mostly his mom," Volle said. "This is the first I've seen of him in a while. He hasn't had a chance to pick up any of my bad habits."

Streak chuckled as they entered the steamy, sulfur-scented room. "Hopefully he won't. Phew, it does smell in here."

"Yeah. But it's a nice way to get away from the world." Volle put his muzzle into the crook of the wolf's neck. "And you can still smell someone if you're right up close."

Streak giggled and turned to kiss Volle on the nose. "So this is where we take our clothes off?"

"I would prefer to remain clothed," Forrin said. "If my Lord permits." He moved to the far doorway and stood there, watching the interior of the pool.

"Certainly." Volle nodded, and stripped his tunic off. "Streak, we can leave our clothes here." When he had folded his pants, he noticed that Streak had only his tunic off, and was watching him. "Careful," he grinned. "We're still in public and you want to stay presentable."

"Just admiring the view." The wolf smiled and dropped his own pants, and still managed to goose Volle under the tail as they walked past Forrin into the large room.

Volle jumped, but didn't turn around. "Careful! You don't want to make me slip." Streak snickered.

They could see three other shapes in the pool, but Volle was glad to see that the whispering arch in front of them was empty. He guided Streak around in front of it and pointed to the submerged bench below the arch. "Sit there," he said. "I'll be right back."

Streak tilted his ears curiously, but lowered himself into the water, gasping at the heat as he did. Volle smiled and then padded quickly around the pool, waving courteously to the two otters he passed. They waved back, eyes fixed on him, and he reflected that they must be locals who hadn't seen foxes around much, probably used to using the Canid pool when the others were too crowded. That led him to wonder where Dewanne was. Already made it to the cool pools, most likely.

He seated himself under the opposite end of the arch, lowering himself carefully into the water and sighing blissfully as the heat soaked through his fur. He slid down up to his neck, tilted his head back, and breathed softly out, watching the eddies in the steam as his breath passed through it.

"Can you see me?" he whispered, and heard a splash from across the pool that traveled along the arch and sounded as though it were right beside him.

"Volle?" Streak's voice sounded confused.

"I'm right here." Volle closed his eyes. "Right next to you in the water."

"How..." Streak lowered his voice to a whisper. "How are you doing that? Can you hear me?"

"Yes. It's the arch. It carries sound."

"Oh." There was a short pause. "No one else can hear us?"

"No." Volle smiled. "I could talk about how much I'd like to have my paw on your creamy white sheath, stroking it and feeling it grow warm and hard..."

He heard a strangled gasp and then a slow exhalation, or maybe it was just the movement of a tail through the water. "Are you sure they can't hear us?"

He glanced at the two otters, and though he couldn't see them clearly, he could see that they were engrossed in conversation. On the other side of the pool, nearer to Streak, a female coyote was just getting out of the pool. "Positive. They don't know I'm talking about my paw stroking your nice long wolfhood."

Streak's voice came ghostly to his ears. "And they can't hear me tell you I'm pressing my rump back against your sheath, feeling your swelling and rubbing against it."

Volle grinned. His sheath *was* swelling as he talked and listened. "Mmm. I'm rubbing it up under your tail. Running my paws all over your lovely body."

"I'm pressing back...wanting you inside me. All nice and hard under your paw." He paused and then giggled. "I am, too."

Volle grinned. "Me too," he said softly. "All hard, under your tail, pushing up and inside you."

"Ooh."

"Stroking you with my paw."

"Feeling you inside me, squeezing and pressing back against you."

"My arms around you, paw sliding up and down your wolfhood, pushing in and out of you."

Another pause. "Volle?"

"Mmm?"

"If we don't stop, I'm gonna come in the water. And I think they'll notice that."

Volle laughed. "Okay. Me too, actually." His member was rigid, fully extended from his sheath. The hot water felt good on it, and he realized that he had only felt a slight twinge from the wound Dereath had given him.

"This is neat, though."

"I thought so. I didn't really like it at first, but it's better with you."

"I'd prefer it if you were here."

"All right. Be there soon." He stood, grateful for the low bench that kept his sheath under the waterline, and kicked off, swimming rather awkwardly across the pool. He'd never been a great swimmer, but he could get to where he was going, albeit with a lot of splashing. The otters, he was sure, were smirking as he made his way across to Streak.

The wolf had moved away from the listening arch to another bench nearby, and Volle joined him there. Though the water wasn't completely clear, he could see the effect their talk had had on the wolf, and he settled down beside him, spreading his legs to show off his similarly hard member.

Streak grinned and nuzzled him, looking down, and slid a paw through the water to feel his hardness. "Mmm. I'd better not…"

Volle resisted the urge to thrust into the wolf's paw and wrap his paw around the erect wolfhood. He just nuzzled back with a smile and said, "I don't think I have the willpower to stop you."

"It's up to me, then." Slowly, Streak withdrew his paw, trailing his claws through Volle's fur in the warm water. "I'll make it up to you tonight."

Volle kissed his nose. "Not if I get to you first."

They relaxed for a little while longer, until they were presentable again, and Volle was just about to suggest that they move to the cool pools when he heard a voice behind him. "Lord Vinton."

Volle flicked an ear back. "Lord Dewanne." He turned slightly. "I was wondering where you were."

The other fox smiled. "Delia and I had some business to attend to." His gaze flicked to Streak, who had turned as well. "I heard that you and the wolf were acquitted. Congratulations."

"Thank you," Volle said. He couldn't smell Dewanne's disapproval, but he could hear it in the polite lack of enthusiasm.

"Thanks," Streak added, but Dewanne didn't turn to him.

"Well, I'm going to have a soak. I'll see you later." He waved a paw and strolled around to the other side of the pool.

"You'd think he would be more friendly, being another fox," Streak remarked when Dewanne was out of earshot.

"He was." Volle sighed, not sure he wanted to tell Streak about Dewanne's sentiments. "Maybe he's just out of sorts today. You ready to cool off?"

Streak nodded, and together they left the pool, dressed with a little groping and giggling, and walked over to where the cool pools were situated, Forrin at their side. Tish and Tika were no longer there, but after a brief bath, Volle and Streak found them at the lunch tables, eating with Delia.

Volyan bounced off the table and ran over to Volle when he saw them approaching. He skirted Forrin warily and tugged on Volle's shorts. "I gotta secret," he whispered. "Mommy told me to tell you a secret."

Volle smiled at the nearby weasels and bear who had turned at the cub's loud whisper. Streak and Forrin, looking amused, walked on and joined Tish and Tika. "I've got big ears," Volle told the cub, squatting down beside him. "You can talk quieter. What's your secret?"

"Mommy gave me a secret message for you," Volyan said, more quietly. "I couldn't tell you before 'cause the wolves were there. She said it was only for you."

Volle nodded. "What did she say?"

"She said she wants you to come see her this afternoon."

"By myself?"

The cub's ears flicked back, and his eyes drifted downward. "I dunno."

Thoughts clicked together in Volle's mind. Ilyana had been 'indisposed' for a couple days, and now she wanted to see him. She was in season; that's what was going on. And she wanted him to come breed a new cub. He didn't know if he was ready for that, but he supposed she must have an idea of the proper time. "All right. Was I supposed to bring you?"

Volyan shook his head. "No. But—oh! She said..." He wrinkled his little muzzle, trying to remember. "She said...you don't hafta bring the blackberries."

Volle grinned. So she'd known he might guess, and was reassuring him. "All right. Maybe I'll bring Streak instead."

"Do you have blackberries?" The cub's tail wagged as he looked up hopefully.

"No."

"Oh. I thought if you didn't hafta bring them, maybe I could have some. I like them."

"It's the wrong time of year," Volle said, ruffling Volyan between the ears. "Though maybe around here...who knows? Tell you what. If we can't find any, then when you come back to the castle with me, we'll have some blackberry jam. I know they keep it in the kitchens there. Okay?"

"Yeah!" The cub hugged him and then scampered off to the table, saying, "Tika, Tika! I'm gonna have blackberry jam!"

Volle joined the lunch table, and a moment later was chewing on a fresh chunk of bread. He enjoyed the relaxed atmosphere of the luncheon; since everyone was wet, there was no real point to observing proper table manners. Volyan was taking full advantage of this, eating directly off his plate and not even using his fingers. Even Forrin relaxed somewhat, smiling and joking with the other wolves.

Dewanne joined them halfway through lunch, sitting next to Delia and nodding hello to everyone. He didn't talk much, and so when Tish and Tika rose and announced that they were planning to return to the hot baths, Volle stood too. Streak, who had finished eating some time ago, stood with him, and Forrin did the same, adjusting his scabbard.

"Coming back for a bath?" Tish asked

Volle shook his head. "We need to get back up to the mansion. I think, if Streak doesn't mind, I'd like to dry off and walk into town."

"No, that's fine." Streak smiled and extended his muzzle to Tish and Tika. "It was nice to see you again."

Tika grabbed him into a hug and wagged her tail enthusiastically. "We're delighted to see you again, too. So nice to see you enjoying yourself out here."

Tish nodded, touching muzzles. "We'll see you at services tomorrow, if not before." The sparkle in his eyes belied his serious tone.

"Goodbye, you two," Volle said, but if he thought he could avoid a wet wolf hug, he was mistaken. Tika squeezed him too, the wet press of wolf and sulfur assaulting his nostrils as he hugged back. Tish smiled when he'd been released and touched muzzles with him.

"Pity they aren't younger," Streak mused as they walked toward the dust baths. "They would have been fun to go out with, I think."

"I think they still are."

"They are," the wolf agreed. "But they won't be staying around."

"No." Volle tried to forget that whenever he thought about returning to the palace.

Streak seemed to sense his reluctance to think about that, and dropped the subject. They reached the dust bath area and waited behind another couple. "They dry you off here," Volle explained, "and get the sulfur out of your fur. Feels really good."

Streak nodded. "What are we doing in town?"

"Oh. Ilyana wanted to see me. But she didn't say I couldn't bring you." He flashed a smile. "So I'm going to."

Streak smiled and nodded as they advanced to the weasel, who bowed and smiled. "Male for you, sahr?"

"Female this time, I think." Volle grinned and pointed to Streak with his thumb. "Male for him."

"Very good, sahr. We have a female ready. The male will be a moment longer. And for him?" He indicated Forrin.

The guard shook his head. "I'll come with him."

"Er…" The weasel looked slightly discomfited. "Only one allowed in bath house at a time, sahr."

"Then I'll wait outside," Forrin rumbled.

The weasel shrugged. "As you like. Come?"

"I can wait until his is ready too," Volle said, but Streak nudged him.

"Go on," the wolf said. "I can wait."

Volle chuckled and nodded. "All right." He followed the weasel back amongst the bath houses.

"Listen," he said, bending down to talk softly in the weasel's ear. "If it's possible, could you give the white wolf the otter I had last time?"

The weasel smiled and nodded. "He is working today. You liked him, sahr?"

"Very much. I would like my friend to see him too."

"Very good, sahr. But today you want female?"

Volle nodded. "I just want a massage. It's easier for me to be restrained if it's a female."

"Ah, I see." The weasel nodded enthusiastically. "You will like Daira. She has strong paws." He held aside the curtain in the doorway of the cottage they'd reached. Forrin poked his nose in, looked around, and then came back out and nodded to Volle, taking up a position just outside the door.

"Thank you." Volle ducked under the curtain and stepped inside.

"Good afternoon, sahr." The high-pitched voice that greeted him belonged to a small female weasel standing beside the familiar shape of the dust bath. Even for a weasel, she was small, and her scent indicated she was young, though still mature.

Volle nodded. "Good afternoon." He slipped his tunic and pants off with less reservation this time, since he knew what to expect. She took the wet clothes and brought a dry set to her workbench while Volle lay down in the dust, his head in the basin. He could feel her in the air currents as she moved around the room, and then felt the sprinkle of dust as she covered his back and legs.

There was a scrape of claws on stone, unexpectedly, and then he felt her press down on his back from an odd angle. A moment later, he felt all four paws on him as she kneaded and walked her hind feet down his rump and legs, expertly hooking her claws into his fur so she wouldn't slip. The added weight lent a pressure to her strokes that even the male otter hadn't had, and soon Volle was groaning in pleasure.

It was a pleasure of one sort only, however; her scent and body, while attractive, held no allure for him, and when she asked him to turn over, his member was discreetly quiescent in its sheath. She didn't seem disappointed or surprised, but continued her massage, and finished it without asking if he wanted any other services.

He smiled, dressed, and thanked her. Blinking in the bright afternoon sun, he squinted his way back to the waiting area and stretched out on a bench, closing his eyes while Forrin sat alertly nearby.

Some time later, a paw on his shoulder broke through his doze. Volle blinked and yawned, looking up at the white-furred muzzle blocking the sun. "Nice massage?"

Streak trailed a paw across the fox's ears and glanced at Forrin. "I…see what you mean about otters." His tail was wagging, and as he turned, Volle could see the grin on his muzzle.

Volle feigned surprise. "Oh, I had one here last time. Young, cute, shy?" Streak nodded. "Hard to resist?"

"Mm. Yes, that's the one. How much do 'other services' cost?"

Volle swung his legs off the bench. "I don't know." He grinned and lowered his voice. "But if you can wait for a fox, you can have them for free."

"That sounds like too good a bargain to pass up."

"Well, come along, then." Volle took the wolf's paw and walked with him through the resort and out the front gate, pausing to ask the greeter the quickest way to Ilyana's lodging house. He offered a buggy to take them there, which Volle was about to decline until Streak pointed out that the day was warm and the street was dusty, and they didn't want their recent baths to be all for naught. They clambered inside while Forrin sat up top with the driver again.

Some twenty minutes later, the buggy stopped in front of a small, tidy house in a secluded street. As the driver, a tall weasel, held the door for Volle and Streak, he asked, "Sahrs need me to wait?"

Volle looked down at him. "How much to wait? I can pay you once we get to the mansion."

The weasel shrugged. "No need to. I am employed by the resort. They pay me to take guests wherever they need."

"All right. Yes, please."

The weasel nodded and walked around to his mount, taking the opportunity to feed it while Volle and Streak walked into the house, preceded by an alert Forrin.

A female weasel greeted them. "Ah, noble sahrs, you are here to see the lady, yes?"

Volle nodded. "Yes."

"One moment. I will tell her you are here. She is sleepy."

She disappeared up a small flight of stairs, leaving Volle, Streak, and Forrin to look around the room. Their heads nearly touched the ceiling—Forrin actually had to bend his neck slightly—so Volle could see that most clearly; it was made of wood beams, smoothed and nearly polished, although they were still new enough to hold some of the smell of the tree. He reached up to brush a finger along one.

To his left, a small bureau held a number of variously colored bottles, but he didn't smell alcohol in any of them. They seemed to be fruit juices and other flavored tonic waters. To the right, he saw Streak eyeing a small couch that had been carefully upholstered with a nicely patterned fabric. He grinned. "I don't think it would hold you."

"I'm not that heavy," the wolf retorted, grinning back.

"Sahrs?" The weasel had reappeared on the stairs. "She is awake. She will see you. But you, sahr, only." She pointed at Volle.

"Thank you. I'll be right back," he said to Streak, and then walked carefully to the stairs, ducking his head and almost tripping on the small stairs.

The upstairs was very dark, shutters drawn, candles extinguished. It took his eyes a moment to adjust to what light there was, but they weren't the first sense to register. As soon as his head moved above the floor level, he caught a bewildering array of smells, flooding his nose and overwhelming him for a moment before he made sense of them.

*Vixen in season…sickness…a strong herbal smell…soap, wet fur…*blood?

"Ilyana?"

He could see curtains drawn around what he assumed was the bed, now. She stirred behind them. "Volle?" Her voice was low and weak, rough-edged as though her throat was sore or congested.

"Are you all right?" He took another step up.

"Just stay there. I'm fine."

He sat at the top of the stairs, only five feet or so from the curtains. "Is there anything I can do?"

"That's what I'm about to tell you. Dewanne—"

She stopped and coughed, and his ears shot up. "Did he do this to you?"

Her coughing fit stopped. "I did it to myself. Listen, Volle, please. Dewanne came to me a few days ago. He knew about your hearing and that I was worried…he asked if I wanted to make sure of having a noble cub."

"Oh." Volle's fur had risen; now it settled. "I know. We talked about that the other day."

"You don't know all of it. He said that he would propose that to you. But he told me something different. He said that if you lost the hearing, if you were disgraced, that I would have nothing. He offered me refuge in his lands if I would carry his cub."

"*His* cub?" He felt his fur rise again.

"Yes. If you were disgraced, he would take me to Dewanne and I would raise his bastard son, who would eventually inherit the peerage. If you were not, then he'd struck a deal with you and I was to ask you for another cub after he'd already…" She trailed off.

"So I would think the cub was mine, when…"

"Yes."

He growled softly. "But he told me…he said he can't…"

"He told you what he needed to tell you to get you to agree."

"Why doesn't he have a cub of his own, then?" He realized he was raising his voice, and he clamped his muzzle shut.

"He wouldn't tell me. At first he said that his wife couldn't bear cubs, but I think that's a lie, too. I think she just doesn't want to."

"It's not a pleasant business."

Volle shook his head. "She wouldn't be that selfish." But replaying the few times he'd met her in his head, he couldn't dismiss the notion. "That's a wife's duty."

"She's deathly afraid of disease. Bearing a cub is dangerous at her age."

"Still…" He couldn't believe Dewanne would do that to him.

"He was here this morning, Volle. I used some herbs to fake the onset of my season. He took me to his rooms and took me there. His wife was in the next room."

His head was spinning. "Why do I smell blood?"

She paused. "I had to get some more herbs. I'm…washing him out of me. It's not a pleasant business."

"Let me smell him."

Another pause, longer. "All right."

She sounded hurt, and he knew immediately why. "I trust you, Ilyana," he said softly. "But I need to be sure. I thought I could trust Dewanne, too."

"Who do you believe?"

"I believe you."

"Come here, then."

He walked around the curtain and held it aside. Ilyana lay on the bed, naked, her tail curled demurely over her midsection. The white of her chest stood out in the dark room, and her eyes gathered the dim light and gleamed at him. "Over there," she said softly, indicating a pot.

Slowly, he knelt and brought his nose close to the pot. The herbal smell was very strong, making his nose wrinkle. Beneath it, he could smell her musk, some blood, and a male fox. He recognized Dewanne immediately.

"Why are you telling me this?" He took her paw gently.

"Because," she said, "I want the cub to be yours."

He shook his head. "It would still be yours."

"Yes. But I'm your wife."

Her paw squeezed his, and he squeezed back, unsure what to say. "Even though…"

"Even though you would rather be with your lovely young wolf, yes." He thought he saw the hint of a smile. "We still vowed to be true to each other. And I know you've not been with another female, let alone another fox." She coughed again.

"I haven't. I wouldn't."

"I hope you can forgive what I did. I could have said no to him. But I wanted…" She fell silent, and he let her gather her thoughts. "My father used to tell us stories about our ancestors. They were noble foxes and held land, he said, though he never said where the land was. My brother and sisters…they never cared much for those stories. They thought he was making them up. You know, every cub wants to be of noble birth. But I believed them. I thought someday it would be wonderful if a son of mine held a peerage. And now…" She smiled, and her voice gathered strength. "Maybe two of mine will."

She looked at Volle directly. "So now you know, my husband. Can you forgive me for lying with another fox?"

Touched by her story, Volle nodded. He felt ashamed for taking for granted the title that he didn't deserve. To Ilyana, it meant the world; it was her most desperate dream. At that moment, he would have forgiven her just about anything. "Of course. I know I don't perform my duties to you…"

"You gave me one son. I ask for another cub." He heard her tail twitch in a small wagging motion. "And perhaps an invitation to the palace balls once in a while."

"Any time." He squeezed her paw again. "But you could have borne Dewanne's son. I wouldn't have known."

"But I would have. And besides…" she paused to yawn, her voice getting more tired. "When I think of my son growing up to be like his father, I like the idea that I think of you. I don't want to worry that my son will grow up to be like a desperate fox, who would rather betray a friend than demand honor from his wife."

Volle couldn't think of anything to say to that, so he remained silent, stroking the back of her paw. Eventually she stirred again, and said, "I'm sorry. I shouldn't speak so of Dewanne. He no doubt thought he was doing me a service. And you, when it comes down to it."

"He did betray me," Volle said bitterly.

Ilyana sighed. "I'm afraid so."

"Thank you," Volle said. "For telling me, and for doing what you did. I promise, whenever you want me, I'll do my best to get you another cub."

"Tomorrow after services? I feel very sleepy right now. The herbs are still taking effect. By tomorrow I should be ready again." He heard her yawn. "I hope you won't have to get drunk this time."

"I'll figure out something." He nuzzled her paw. "Sleep well, and thank you again. You've done more than I would have expected from a wife."

She murmured dreamily, "That's because you're not used to one."

He rested her paw on her stomach, and carefully slipped around the curtain and down the stairs.

"I did not know there were this many foxes in Vellenland," the weasel was telling Streak as Volle came down the stairs. "Three come today alone!"

"They're all with the King's retreat," Streak said, his muzzle barely over his knees. He had managed to wedge himself into the small sofa, and struggled to get up when he saw Volle. Forrin was crouched near the door and got to his feet, stooped over so as not to bump his head.

"But they do not stay at the castle?"

Volle smiled tightly, holding back his desire to get out as quickly as possible. He felt trapped in the small house, very nervous at the recent revelations Ilyana had made. With an effort, he managed to be polite. "I'm a guest of the governor. The other foxes are staying at the Burning Waters resort, for their health."

"Oh, I see." The weasel nodded, and he could see her whiskers and fingers twitch with the repressed desire to ask about his relationship to Ilyana. "Will you stay for a juice, sahr? I do not have large glasses, but you are welcome to what we have."

"No, thank you very much." Volle bowed to her and nearly hit his head on an overhead beam when he straightened. "We have to be going. But I will be back tomorrow."

She bowed as they left. "Good day to you, sahrs!"

In the buggy, Volle took a moment to compose his thoughts while Streak watched him worriedly. "What's the matter?" the wolf finally said softly. "What did she say?"

Volle told him the story in a few sentences that he didn't think did justice to the convoluted nature of the whole affair. He hadn't intended to tell Streak about Ilyana's history and personal ambitions, but he found himself unable to stop, and that whole side of the story came spilling out as well. After finishing, he said, "Dewanne was the one who brought me into the palace. Into the peerage. I thought—he wanted more foxes in the nobility. I thought I could trust him."

"It doesn't sound like you can trust much of anyone." Streak was sitting back in his seat, arms folded.

"I guess not. You, Tish, and Tika." And Helfer, he started to say, then remembered the otter, and then thought that it was petty of him to hold that against his friend, so he said, "And Helfer," anyway.

"And Ilyana."

"She's not at the palace," Volle pointed out.

"She's a good wife. She has your welfare at heart."

"And her own, too."

"Yes, but she could've played this either way. She still gets another noble cub. She chose a more dangerous way to stay true to you."

Volle nodded. "She's a good vixen."

They sat in silence while the buggy clattered up the slope of the mountain, leaving the town behind them. "So," Streak said, "tomorrow after services you're going back to do your husbandly duties?"

Volle saw a twinkle in the wolf's eye, though he was keeping a smile from his muzzle. "I guess I will. I can't get drunk this time, though."

Streak laughed. "You'll figure out something. I guess I'll find some way to keep myself amused."

A thought crept into Volle's mind. He grinned at Streak. "What if I could figure out a way and keep you amused at the same time?"

The wolf looked shocked at first, his ears flicking back and then forward. "What do you mean? You want me…"

"Well, you'd certainly inspire me." Volle rubbed a paw across the wolf's knee as his tail thumped the seat. "And I'll have room for you."

Streak looked at his tail, and the wolf's blue eyes widened. "You'd want me to…while you're doing it to her?"

"Mmm. Maybe not all the way in—if I were tied to her and you to me, it could be uncomfortable. But otherwise…would you do that?"

"I…" Streak thought about it for a moment.

"It would be a big help." Volle took the wolf's paw. "And it would make you sort of another father to the cub. Not officially, but…"

Streak laughed. "It's the only way I'm likely to father a cub." He looked into Volle's eyes and nodded. "All right. I'll do it. It'll be a story to tell the cubs when they're older."

Volle grinned, giving the wolf's paw a kiss. "Much older. If ever. I don't think I'd want to hear that about my parents."

"No, I don't suppose I would either."

The banquet hall at Helfer's mansion had been garlanded with flowers and ribbons, and all the servants wore flowers in their fur or on their clothes. When Volle, Streak, and Forrin walked in, the room was bustling with activity such as Volle had rarely seen. Weasels and otters dashed here and there, scooting around the canids to bring decorations and food into and out of the long hall. Flower petals littered the floor, brushing their paws as they walked up to the head of the table.

Helfer waved them to a pair of seats across from himself and Laya, who was sitting next to him with their son in her arms. An otter couple was talking to Helfer and to the weasel on the other side of him from Laya, whom Volle assumed was his governer, Burren. The otters were smiling, the female especially, and they bowed several times to Helfer and scurried further down the table as Volle and his companions approached.

"I didn't know there would be three of you," Helfer said. "Sorry."

"I told Forrin he could eat with us," Volle said.

"I can stand."

"Nonsense." Helfer waved a paw and caught the attention of a servant. "Another chair?"

The servant nodded and scurried away. Helfer grinned. "There. We'll just squeeze another place in. Nobody will care."

"Hef, what is all this?"

Helfer spread his paws. "It's the annual festival of my visit. The servants and some of the people—as many as can fit—come and have dinner with me. They like to talk to me and it turns into a big party. I thought you'd like to be here too. Hello there." He smiled as a pair of female weasels in formal gowns approached him, whiskers flicking shyly.

Though Forrin had his chair soon enough, they noticed that very few people actually stayed seated. They would sit, eat, and then get up and move around to talk to other people. The 'servants' Volle had seen carrying flowers and dishes were not simply servants; they were everyone. The table had been laid out more like a buffet than a dinner, they realized after a few minutes of waiting for someone to bring food. Forrin offered to get Volle's dinner for him, but in the end all three of them got their own, moving through the crowded mix of smells and sounds and back to their original places with simple, but delicious, food.

Helfer asked them if there was anything else they needed, but he was constantly getting pulled aside by people who wanted to talk to him, or touch their muzzle to his paw, so they talked mostly with each other, and a little with some of the weasels around them. Everybody seemed happy, and the atmosphere got even livelier once the mead and wine was brought out—they were brought in big barrels from the storerooms by a few muscular otters and weasels, who lined up to be the first served after they plunked the barrels down.

About that time, a chorus of minks started singing some raucous songs. Volle didn't know the tunes, but Helfer obviously did; he and everyone at the table joined in—except for Laya, who sat rocking her cub. Volle smiled at her, and she smiled back but didn't talk. Two weasels started dancing, and more joined in, congregating in the open area of the room between the table and the doors. Volle watched them, his paw tapping the floor to the music.

Streak touched his shoulder, smiling. He was wagging his tail and swaying his shoulders to the song. "This is nice," he said, gesturing around at the party. He'd brought two glasses of wine, and handed one to Volle.

It was nice wine, not the best, of course, but still good. Volle sipped it. "Thanks," he said. "Want to dance?"

Streak grinned at him, taking a drink. "Do you?"

"Not really."

The wolf laughed. "Then why did you ask?"

"I would, if you wanted to."

Streak smiled and put a paw on his shoulder. "That's sweet. Lucky for you, I don't want to."

"I wouldn't have minded." The wine was making him tired, especially after the long relaxing day. He leaned against Streak and watched Helfer dance with one partner after another.

The weasel had barely had ten seconds to himself all night. Volle felt an odd twinge of envy—he was a Lord, too, and yet he'd never felt this kind of adoration from his people. On the few occasions when he'd visited, the people had been respectful and polite, but rarely effusive. Probably, he thought, it's because they never got a chance to know me. They know Anton, the governor, and now they know Ilyana. And they'll know Volyan, when he's Lord. That thought comforted him.

"Nice to be loved by your people," he said, watching the dancers.

"This climate is good for love." Streak nuzzled Volle's ears.

Volle grinned up at the wolf. "You want to get away?"

"I am getting kind of tired," Streak admitted, "but you have to be ready for your husbandly duty tomorrow. I'm not going to take the blame for your cub being weak and sickly."

Volle laughed and nuzzled back. "All right, all right. How about we just curl up together and sleep?"

They said their goodnights and returned to the bedroom, the sounds of the party following them all the way back. It wasn't until they'd closed the door to their suite that they could no longer hear it. Forrin checked their bedroom and bathroom again before settling himself down on the couch, leaving them alone in the bedroom.

And even though they went to bed naked, and there was a good deal of groping and giggling, Streak was true to his word, and they fell asleep hard and unreleased.

Chapter 12

Volle woke with his erection pressed into Streak's rump. The wound on his tip didn't hurt until he wriggled, and even then it was only a mild soreness. He inhaled the warm smell of the wolf, cracking one eye open to see the motes of dust drift through the sunbeam that crossed over his head. With a happy sigh, he closed his eyes again.

A few moments later, Streak stirred. He yawned, and Volle waited patiently while the wolf stretched and slowly became aware of the world around him. He felt the fluffy white tail wag slowly between them, and then Streak turned his muzzle and murmured sleepily, "You're all ready for this afternoon."

"More than ready." Volle nuzzled his shoulder.

"Think you can make it through services?"

"I'll have to, won't I?"

Streak rubbed gently back. "You sure will."

Volle pressed forward and stroked a paw down his side, claws trailing through the fur. "Maybe a run with Helfer will help work off some of this energy."

"You'd better hope so, or else it's going to be a very interesting service."

"The Cantor is cute. Wait 'til you see him. He's a fairly young fox."

Streak rolled over and pinned him, grinning. "I have all the fox I need."

They kissed and embraced, and then both their ears perked at a light tap on the door. "My Lord?" Forrin's muffled voice came through from the parlor. "You're awake?"

"Yes," Volle called.

"My Lord, Lord Ikling said he would be leaving for his run in about ten minutes, and that if you were not ready, he would see you on the way to services. I chose not to wake you, but I heard your voices."

"Thank you, Forrin," Volle called. "We'll be out in a few minutes."

Streak got off Volle and out of bed, and the fox followed him. Streak picked up the pants he'd worn last night and looked at Volle, who chuckled softly. "Forrin?" he called.

"Yes, my Lord?"

"Could you, er, find our running shorts and toss them into the bedroom?"

"Yes, my Lord." And a few minutes later, the bedroom door opened a crack and a bundle of cloth was tossed in.

They pulled on the shorts and met Helfer in the parlor. The weasel gave a huge yawn as he walked in. "Morning."

"Late party last night?" Volle grinned.

Helfer nodded. "It always is. But they like it, and I like it. Good enough reason to keep doing it. Come on," he said, "or we'll be late for services."

They didn't talk much on the quick run around the mansion. Helfer was too tired, and Volle and Streak kept their thoughts to themselves. Once, Streak did ask Helfer how many people he knew at the party, but Helfer's answer was so clipped that he and Volle were both discouraged from asking anything further. The day was clear and hot, further encouraging them to conserve their breath, and by the end of the run, all three were panting heavily.

Volle and Streak wanted to take the time to brush each other's fur after applying their vanilla powder, but Forrin interrupted their ablutions with a reminder that the buggies would be leaving for services imminently. "At least we smell decent," Volle said as they pulled on the clothes they'd brought in from the parlor.

Streak gave Volle's tail a few last brushes. "You always smell good," he said, which got him a kiss as they walked into the parlor. Forrin had changed, too, into a slightly nicer vest.

"I didn't see you bring any clothes down," Volle remarked as they walked out the guest door and around to the front.

"I didn't. Lord Ikling was kind enough to send to the castle for my effects."

"Very nice of him," Volle said.

"He is a gracious host," Forrin agreed, in a tone that indicated he hadn't expected such courtesy. "Lord Ikling," he said, bowing as they reached the main gate and saw Helfer, "thank you for sending for my things."

"Well, I thought you might need them." Helfer smiled, and indicated a waiting buggy. "Ready?"

Forrin rode in his usual place up front, and the other three climbed into the carriage. Once the door was closed, Helfer leaned forward. "Actually," he said, "whoever let you in last night told Huster we have a new guest, and he arranged it all. But I don't mind taking credit for it. I did hire Huster, after all."

Volle smiled. "It comes out to the same thing in the end. Please thank Huster on our behalf."

"I will. So what do you have to do after services? Going back up to the castle? Your hearing is tomorrow, right?"

Volle nodded. "But no, we're going to visit Ilyana." He hesitated. A year ago, he would have cheerfully told Helfer all the details of his intended visit and they would have chuckled ruefully together over the necessity of sleeping with females. But with Streak involved, Volle felt as though he'd be betraying a confidence by telling Helfer, or at least diminishing the intimacy of Streak's participation. He glanced at Streak, and kept quiet.

"Oh? Invite her back for dinner. I'd like to spend more time with your son."

"You'll see him enough once we're at the castle."

"*If* you win your hearing."

"With Dereath in prison, I think my chances are pretty good."

"Yeah, I still can't believe that. I mean, I knew that little prick was annoying, but I never thought he'd actually have the guts to kill someone. Did you?"

Volle shrugged, but Streak spoke up. "I guess you never really know if someone could be a killer unless they have a really good reason."

"Good point. Me, I don't think I could ever do it. I hate the smell of blood."

"Doesn't everyone?" Volle tapped a paw on his knee. "It makes me ill."

"I guess so," Helfer said. "Did you get sick when you found the guard?"

"Almost." Volle tried to remember. It seemed so long ago. "My mind was on other things."

"Yeah." Helfer drew his knees up onto the seat and sat against the wall of the buggy. "It's certainly been an interesting retreat."

"It's not over yet." Volle watched the terrain go past the window as they rolled down the road. A few minutes later, he saw the house that he'd come to recognize as the first sign that they were entering town, a small cottage with a tile roof that had partially fallen in. He was looking forward to services again, looking forward to the singing and the slow, measured recital of the books. He was looking forward, too, to sharing the experience with Streak.

When they arrived in the queue of carriages outside the cathedral, they could hear the bells that signaled the start of services. Helfer opened the door and called out to the young weasel driving the buggy, "We'll walk from here."

Forrin hopped down and helped them out of the buggy, then walked in front of them the two blocks to the cathedral. Several others, hearing the bells, had made the same decision, so there was a small crowd at the doors and it took them a little while to get through. Helfer waved as the other three headed for the Canid section and found seats in the back. Tish, Tika, Dewanne, and Delia were already there, sitting in the front. Volle couldn't see Volyan at first, then saw a pair of ears bobbing between Tika and Delia and smiled as he sat down.

The Cantor was walking past the pews and nodded as he came to theirs, acknowledging them. "We are joined in a silent prayer for the souls of those who have left us over the past week," he said softly. "I will begin in another minute. There may be some late arrivals."

Volle, who was furthest from the Cantor, saw Forrin and Streak's heads dip in prayer. Forrin's ears went down as well, and Volle knew he was thinking about his friend who'd been killed. Streak's whiskers were moving slowly, making Volle wonder what he was thinking about. Volle dropped his own muzzle and closed his eyes, and prayed that Felis and Rodenta would take care of the souls of the two that had been slain in the last two weeks.

He felt motion in the pew and smelled the distinctive scent of Captain Nero. Glancing to his left, he saw the large wolf settling himself in the seat. Nero looked over at him and nodded briefly before bowing his head in prayer.

"Welcome all children of Gaia, children of Canis," the Cantor said some five minutes later, and everybody's muzzle rose. "Let us sing the Joy of Canis."

It was a different prayer than he'd begun with last week, but it was one of Volle's favorites. He hadn't heard it often in Divalia, because in the large echoing chambers of the Grand Cathedral, the extended notes of the song that were almost howls tended to annoy the other Houses. Here, the sound was slightly more muted, but he still felt the joy in the song, even if he couldn't quite howl. Streak and Forrin's voices complemented each other's nicely, he noticed. Whereas he and Streak were both baritones, Forrin was definitely in a lower register.

"Thank you," the Cantor said, and Volle could see his tail wagging behind the lectern. "That prayer introduces one of my favorite stories, which I will share with you today: the story of the First Pack.

"When the world was new, and there were only the Six, they remained together for a time, out of habit. Rodenta and Herbivora began to build, and Mustela agreed to help them, for He had always loved his older sisters. But Canis, Felis, and Ursa felt the urge to wander and discover. They agreed to wander for one year and then return to tell the others what They had found.

"Felis had loved to play with His Mother's hair, and Her hair had become a thick, lush jungle, and so Felis went south to the jungles. Ursa had loved to climb on Her Mother's knees, and Her knees had become the great mountains to the north, and so Ursa went north to the mountains.

"Canis had loved most of all to curl up on His Mother's stomach, and Her stomach had become the great plains of the west, and so Canis went west to the plains. He traveled for ten paws of days and nights until He reached a place where the river sang, the grass grew tall, and the stars dipped close to the earth at night. And when He reached this place, a great peace filled His heart and He howled His pleasure to the moon and stars.

"But the Darkness heard His howls and was jealous. He knew that the children of Gaia together were strong, but here was Canis alone. He wanted Canis to create more life so that He could twist it to His own ends, for the Darkness could not create life without the essence of Gaia, which Canis possessed and He did not. So the Darkness quenched the other noises of the night, so that Canis became lonely. And the Darkness sent a breeze to bring the scent of red clay to His nostrils, clay from the riverbed. And Canis stirred there in that Dark night and decided that He would make a companion.

"On the first night, He worked at the red clay and fashioned a companion. But the clay was insufficient to make His companion as large as He was; the wet clay all ran down to the tail so that it became large and long. And He lay with her that night and when she took His divine essence, she opened her eyes in light. And she was the first Fox.

"On the second night, Canis slept with Fox at His side, and her tail covered Him, but she could not cover His ears and toes. So the Darkness sent a breeze to chill the parts of Canis that were exposed, and Canis woke. He decided to create a larger companion, so He gathered the red clay of the river and coated it with the sand of the shore, so that it would hold its shape better. And He lay with His second companion that night and when she took His divine essence, she opened her eyes in light. And she was the first Coyote.

"On the third night, Canis slept between Fox and Coyote, and Fox covered Him with her tail, and Coyote slept at His feet. But His ears remained exposed, and again the Darkness sent a breeze to wake Him. And Canis saw that He would have to create a third companion, larger than the others. So He took the red clay of the river, covered it with sand from the shore, and rolled it in the grass of the plains. And He lay with His third companion that night, and when she took His divine essence, she opened her eyes in light. And she was the first Wolf.

"And Canis taught His companions to love one another, and the children they bore loved each other as well. And when a year had passed, Canis lived with a pack of ten times two paws, and all His children adored Him and loved each other. And He kept the Darkness far from their hearts, as His Mother had taught Him."

He closed the book, looked out at them, and said, "Blessed be Gaia."

"Blessed be Gaia," Volle and the others murmured in response. He was a little surprised that the Cantor had stopped there. The rest of the story concerned the intrusion of Darkness into the pack and the naming of the first Cantor, who reminded the Pack of Gaia's message when the Pack became too large for Canis to be with all the time.

Instead, the Cantor looked up at them and smiled. "And the lessons we take from this are many. Most important is that we all long for a pack, we children of Canis." He spread his paws. "For most of us, our pack is our family. For some of us, our packs are the people we choose to be with. This congregation is a pack, of sorts, though most of us are visitors to this church. The second lesson is that we must always be wary lest the Darkness turn our desires against us. But remember that if Darkness had not spurred Canis's loneliness, none of His children would have been born. And so thus the third lesson: that sometimes the thing is separate from the cause, and Light can come from Darkness. But also can Darkness come from Light."

He opened the book again. "So let us begin with a prayer to guard us from the Darkness."

He had selected three prayers for them to sing, the "Ward Against Darkness," the "Song of the Pack," and the "Forest Path," a prayer Volle had sung often to himself while in prison. It was about being lost in a dark forest and Canis arriving to show the way out. It reminded him of prison, which reminded him of Streak, and as they sang it, he reached out to clasp the wolf's paw in his own.

They concluded with the "Our Mother," in unison with the other Houses this time, and were sent to greet the Mustelids. Volle and Streak found Helfer and Laya amidst the sea of weasels, and greeted them appropriately. They stood around talking about the service, and were joined by Tish, Tika, and Volyan, who hugged Volle and then Streak. The wolf seemed surprised, but hugged back.

"I know all about Darkness," Volyan said without preamble. "Darkness is like a big black panther except it doesn't have any scent and it comes up and whispers things to you and runs away before you can see it. And you have to not listen to it."

"That's right," Volle said. "But black wolves are okay."

Tish grinned. "Foxes, on the other paw, you want to watch yourself with."

Volyan put his paws on his hips. "Silly! I *am* a fox!"

"Of course you are." Tika patted his head. "And you're a big young cub, too! Out without your mommy all day!"

The cub's tail wagged at that, but the wagging slowed. "I miss my mommy," he said, and Volle was reminded of the first time he'd been sent away from his mother when she came into season. He'd been about the same age, and he hadn't understood either. And Volyan would be leaving her for good in a couple of days.

"Maybe you can see her tonight," he said. After a mating, the scent and moods of her season would fade in a few hours.

The other canids understood the reason for those words, and Tish and Tika gave him encouraging smiles. Tika's was especially wide, and accompanied by a sudden wagging of her tail. "That would be very nice, for him to be able to see his mommy tonight."

"Yes," Volle said deliberately. "After all, he won't be seeing her much at the palace."

Streak was momentarily confused by Tika's attitude, then Volle saw his ears flick as he understood that they'd figured out what Volle meant. "He will be lonely at the palace," he said. "Maybe he'll have a playmate in a bit."

"Are there other cubs at the palace?" Volyan asked, and they all laughed.

"We should be on our way," Volle said. "Hef, is there a place you'd recommend for lunch? I think we'll take some over to Ilyana."

Helfer, who didn't really understand canid seasons, looked relieved to be discussing something he did understand. "There's a place on the other side of the square that sells dried and fresh fruit. They're pretty good."

Laya chimed in softly. "There's also a place a little further down that that has good drinks, fruit, and bread. They might be able to make up a lunch basket for you."

Helfer looked put out by Laya's contribution, so Volle smiled and said,

"We'll try both places. See you all tonight or tomorrow."

Both shops offered tasty options, and so they made up a small basket for Ilyana and ate a lunch themselves on the way over to the house, buying lunch for Forrin and their buggy driver as well. The bread was slightly stale, but the fruit must have been picked freshly that morning or the previous evening. Volle and Streak ate as much as they could, and were pleasantly full by the time the buggy pulled up outside the house.

"Should I wait outside, my Lord?" Forrin asked as they climbed out.

"Probably," Volle said. "Do you want to check the house first?" He was starting to understand the way Forrin liked to operate, and he was becoming accustomed to the idea of having a personal guard.

"Yes, my Lord," Forrin said. He mounted the stairs and knocked, then stepped inside, and a moment later he emerged nodding his head. Volle and Streak walked forward.

Volle remembered the last time he'd climbed a flight of stairs to do his ancestral duty—or rather, he remembered that he'd done it. He didn't remember much about the actual stairs. Or about the actual mating. He mostly remembered waking up that night with a hangover.

The old weasel bowed to them as they came in, and was speechless when Streak handed her the basket of food. "This is for you and your boarder," he said, and she wrung her paws and then disappeared with the basket into what Volle assumed was the kitchen.

He and Streak looked at each other, and the wolf shrugged. "Should we, um..." He nodded toward the stairs.

"I suppose." Volle took a step. He didn't feel very aroused, but he trusted Streak would take care of that. He tried imagining the wolf's paws on him while he climbed the stairs, then grinned at himself—in a moment he would be feeling the real thing.

The scent of vixen in season was much more overwhelming than it had been the previous day. He glanced back at Streak and saw the wolf wrinkle his nose. The scent wasn't unpleasant to Volle; in fact, it was slightly alluring, but not really arousing. He wondered if Dewanne had sent his wife to pick up Ilyana, or if he'd come himself, and if he'd come himself, whether he'd managed to keep from mounting her in the carriage on the way over.

Those thoughts set his fur to bristling, so he set them aside. Ilyana hadn't betrayed him, and she was here now and needed him. He heard her before he got to the curtain.

"Volle?" Her voice was not as rough as it had been the previous day, but it had a guttural quality to it. "I can smell you...get in here."

"Just a minute," he said. He started unfastening his pants. Streak was standing still, ears back.

"No. Now!" She swept the curtain aside and stared at them both with hungry eyes. It took a moment for her to notice Streak. "Who's that? What's he doing here?"

"I never liked Mom when she was like this," Streak whispered.

"He's here to help. Just wait." Volle pulled Streak down to kneel with him, and whispered, "Don't think of your mother."

"I don't want to wait!" She lunged off the bed, and Streak scrambled around behind Volle, who backed up as much as he could.

Streak pressed against him. "I can't go back any more," he said. His voice held a note of trepidation. For a fleeting moment, Volle regretted bringing him.

"It'll be okay," Volle whispered, trying to keep Ilyana from ripping his pants as she clawed at him. "Hey, careful, that's—"

He managed to get the fasteners away from Ilyana and undone without much damage. She pulled down the front of his pants and pressed herself up against him, growling in frustration at his limp state. "Sorry," he mumbled. Her scent was stronger now, but the aggressive thrusting against him was definitely not arousing. She was aroused, though; he could feel the dampness on his sheath as she pressed her lips against it. He had to admit it was a little disconcerting to see her like this. Was this how mating always was for normal couples?

"Maybe I should help." Streak seemed to have recovered some confidence now that Ilyana was occupied with trying to press Volle's retracted member into her. The wolf slid down the back of Volle's pants and cupped his rump, then slid a paw underneath to tease his sac.

Volle shivered at the touch and turned his head to get more of Streak's scent. That helped the arousal more than anything else. He held Ilyana's squirming body against him and focused on the touch from behind, the strong male smell in his nostrils. It was difficult to distract himself from Ilyana, especially since she kept moaning, "Mate me!" into his ear. It wasn't until Streak pressed a paw under his muzzle and Volle drew in the thick scent of his musk—he must have been rubbing his own sheath with it—that he felt a strong surge of arousal.

Then he felt more like a participant than a sex toy; then the rubbing against his sheath became more pleasurable, adding to his arousal instead of diminishing it. He felt a pressure under his tail and lifted his rump enough to let Streak's paw rub there. It was slick, but he didn't know with what, and he didn't much care. It was working. He abandoned himself to the sensations and grinned at the thought that he was doing Fox's and Canis's work, building a pack for his mate—both his mates.

Ilyana's growls changed from frustration to pleasure as his sheath hardened against her. Volle could feel the warmth of her arousal, and when he got hard enough to slide out of his sheath, the slickness made him tremble. He hadn't thought her musk could get any stronger, but it did; he had to turn his head again to smell Streak.

Her muzzle was on top of his, pressing his nose into her neck fur when he turned around again. She was squirming wildly, gasping and moaning even though he hadn't quite entered her yet. But he was close, halfway out of his sheath, and if she weren't pressed so close to him, he would have.

It took a lot of effort for him to keep still for Streak, until the wolf pressed up behind him and held his thighs down, slipping his paws under Ilyana's constantly shifting legs. Volle gasped as he felt a pressure under his tail and pressed back, clutching tightly at Ilyana as he felt Streak's erect member slide into him.

"Ohh!" He shuddered, moaning through the vixen's fur, and then shivered again as his movement created enough space between him and Ilyana for his now-hard member to drop between her lips. Warmth surrounded it, slick and tight, and she matched his moan as she felt him in her. She struggled to push harder against him, and for a moment he felt himself overbalance and was afraid they would all go tumbling down the stairs. But Streak pushed back confidently, his arms holding Volle as his wolfhood slid all the way in, and Volle wanted to cry out, the warmth and pressure and stretching and movement through his tail hole all making his legs go weak. If he hadn't been kneeling before, he would have been by now. It felt as though it had been months since he'd made love, not just days. His body was afire with the pressures and scents, and he couldn't stop moaning his pleasure, though he did manage to keep his moans quiet.

Ilyana had no such restraint. She managed to hook one of her legs over Streak's arms, putting most of her weight on Volle's hips and driving him even further into her, and she let out a loud moan when she felt that, throwing her head back. He was trying his best to thrust in and out, but it was difficult to time his thrusts with Streak's, especially when his body wanted to go in both directions at once. He pressed himself back into Streak, feeling the wolf's growing knot under his tail and remembering dimly that for some reason it wasn't a good idea to take the wolf all into him, but his body was nearly beyond the control of his mind now. And then he pressed forward, and the fact that the lithe body rubbing against him was female mattered a bit less as she took his length into her, punctuating their collective gasps with yelps and clinging to his shoulders, her smooth labia stroking him up and down.

He couldn't get into any sort of rhythm, but it didn't matter; the more she thrust herself onto his trembling foxhood, the harder he wanted to press back and the more wolf he wanted inside him. His head was swimming from the musk in the air, his nerves thrummed with delight, and he could feel a knot of tension growing at the base of his erection, pressing harder to get into the vixen in his lap—but it was the wolf behind him that excited him more.

Behind him, Streak's hind paws were scrabbling at the floor. He seemed to be trying to pull back from Volle's thrusts, but Volle wanted to feel the knot inside him, to feel the wolf he loved close to him. In this odd configuration, when he could barely think coherently for the flood of sensations, he wanted to be close to Streak, and the wolf stopped fighting it and gave in.

The knot sliding into him grew larger and larger with each thrust, and Volle could hear Streak's whimpers behind him, the paws on his thighs curling and gripping the fur. He felt his own legs slipping, toes curling at the shivers coursing down his legs and back, and his paws slid down further, pressing on the small of Ilyana's back and pulling her toward him. He was all the way inside her now, his knot so tight it was almost painful, and as she pulled back and couldn't disengage, he realized that they were already tied, and that the sensations were very close for him now.

For her, too: she let out a low, guttural moan, followed by a series of short, bark-like "Ah!" noises. Volle held her tightly against him and felt her body shudder as her barks became more urgent and higher in pitch. He himself was on the edge until her convulsions squeezed at his knot, rubbing and stroking it, and then he felt the rush of release starting and taking over his body, forcing a moan out of his throat as it tightened all his muscles.

He squeezed Ilyana, the long moan and the moment of tension seeming to go on and on, Streak's long wolfhood sliding in and out of him in ever more quick and hard strokes, and finally he felt the tension uncoil explosively in his groin, contracting all his muscles and sending his seed into Ilyana in a rush of pleasure. The convulsions pressed him back hard against Streak, and the wolf's knot, just as full as his by now, pressed through him and then settled inside him, sending new shivers of excitement through him. He wouldn't have thought his second spurt could be better than the first, but oh it was. "Oh—ahhhh!" he yelped, and Ilyana yelped with him.

The knot inside him kept moving, and Streak's paws gripped him more tightly. Ilyana was relaxing against him while he was still shuddering in the last throes of his climax, and before he'd quite finished, Streak growled and then howled behind him, pressing hard into him and shaking all three of them with the force of his orgasm.

They did topple over then, but forward rather than back. Volle cushioned Ilyana with his paws so she didn't hit the floor too hard, and then tried to brace his arms so she didn't take Streak's weight. He wasn't quite in time.

"Oof!" Her breath whooshed past his ears as he landed on her, and Streak on him. Her legs were still up at his sides, her feet brushing Streak's shoulders. Slightly worried, Volle squirmed around to look at her muzzle, but she wore a blissful smile and her ears were relaxed, flat against the floor.

"Ilyana?" She turned her head slightly and looked at him. "Are you okay?"

"Mm. You have no idea…thank you, Volle." She closed her eyes.

Streak lifted his weight slightly off Volle, then tried to pull backwards gently. Volle yelped softly as Streak's knot tugged on his rear, and tried to move back. "Careful," he said with a giggle. "I'm caught here."

"Sorry." Streak slipped his arms around Volle and hugged him. "Are you okay?"

"I'm fine. I feel good. That was really good." He curled his tail against Streak as much as he could. He felt sleepy too, but not overwhelmingly so. Mostly he felt warm, and the ties around his shaft and inside him gave him a warm sense of belonging. "Thanks for being part of it."

Streak's paws rubbed gently through his fur. "Glad I could help."

"Are you okay?"

"Yeah. It feels a little weird." He nuzzled Volle, and Volle sensed rather than saw him looking down at Ilyana, who was already most of the way to unconsciousness. "Did it...work?"

"I think so. It usually only takes once." He chuckled. "Thank Fox."

"And Canis."

"Him too." Volle turned his muzzle to lick Streak's. "And thank you, my wolf."

"You said that already." But Streak said it playfully, licking back.

"I really mean it." He pressed one of Streak's paws over his own. "I couldn't have done this without you. Well, maybe I could. But it would have taken a lot longer and I think she'd have clawed one of my eyes out."

Streak giggled softly. "Is she going to sleep for long?"

"I don't know. Last time I did this, I passed out too." Volle reached down and brushed a paw along Ilyana's muzzle and down her chest. She stirred and turned her head, but didn't wake.

"The weasel heard us."

"I'm sure she did."

"No, I mean, I know she did. I heard her footsteps on the stairs, then she went back down quickly."

"She had to know Ilyana was in season. Do you think it would be a surprise?"

"I don't know." Streak nuzzled him. "She hasn't come back with anyone, so I guess it's okay."

They sat quietly for a little longer. Volle thought about the cub that would be born, and then about raising Volyan at the palace by himself. And that led him to wondering whether Streak had made a decision. Finally he had to ask.

"Wolf?"

"Hm."

"Do you still want to go back to the farm?"

There was a pause. Streak rested his muzzle on Volle's shoulder. After a moment he said, "Well, fox, right now it's hard to imagine being separated from you."

Volle giggled softly, squeezing Streak's shaft with his rear. "I'm serious."

"Yip! I know." He sighed. "I couldn't talk you into coming back to the farm, could I?"

"I can't. I have to look after my son."

"And you have other things to do, I know." Streak nuzzled his cheek ruff. "I just worry that I'd be a distraction. Or worse, you know, a burden."

"Don't be silly." Volle kissed his nose.

"I'm not. I really don't want anything to happen to you because you're worrying about me. Like...like it almost did here."

"It won't." Privately, he was recalling Tish's words. He knew Streak would be a complication, but he felt certain that he could handle it. "Just tell me if anyone tries to frame you for murder again, okay?"

He'd meant it to be funny, but Streak didn't laugh, and as soon as the words were out, Volle regretted saying them. "I mean," he added lamely, "just trust me. And I'll tell you more. We should be able to talk about things."

"You're right, I know you're right." The wolf sighed again. "I know you're smarter than I am and you can figure things out better. I should just trust you."

"I'm sorry for bringing it up," Volle said. "You still have time to decide. But you are part of our family now. Sort of a second father to this cub. So you have some responsibilities." He made sure Streak could see his grin.

The wolf grinned back, and wriggled his shaft inside Volle, making the fox squirm. "Right now I'd say you're more like a second mommy to the cub, my dear fox."

Volle yelped and tried to pull back, and then yelped again as his knot slid out of Ilyana. Her legs dropped to the floor, making a loud thump, but she just turned over, draping one paw over her sticky groin. Volle and Streak watched her for a moment, and then Streak drew a paw along Volle's shaft. "Mm. You did good work here today," he said, teasing the tip.

"Hey!" Volle squirmed and grinned. "I'm still sensitive."

"So I see." The wolf clasped his shaft in a paw. "And still rather hard, I notice."

"Streak, don't," Volle moaned. "I'll be sore."

The wolf stopped, his fingers having brushed the small scar on Volle's shaft. "Sore…oh, I'm sorry. Does this still hurt?"

"No, I mean…twice in an hour? My poor—yowp!" He yelped as Streak rubbed the other side of his tip.

"Oh, you'll be fine, fox. I feel bad for having made you wait so long. And this time," he whispered, "I get you all to myself." Slowly, he slid his paw up and down Volle's shaft, pulling the fox back until he was kneeling again.

"I…I mean it…ohhh…" Volle's protests died away as the wolf's paw caressed him up and down, bringing back the arousal he'd felt. He noticed that Streak's knot wasn't shrinking; the wolf was still tied to him as tightly as when he'd first come.

"I mean it, too." Streak kissed his neck and shoulders, his paw rubbing up and down Volle's slick shaft in a firm rhythm.

Volle gave up and just leaned back, placing a paw on the wolf's knee, tightening his rump and loosening it, feeling the warm presence of the wolf around him and pressed up inside him, locked to him. The passion rose in him gradually this time, not surging; a warmth building in his groin that spread outwards to his belly, his chest, his legs, his toes, until all of him was suffused with it. Ilyana's scent had faded and now Streak's was all around him, mingled with his, strong male musk arousing him.

He tried to lift himself up and down off Streak's thick wolfhood, but the wolf stopped him with his other paw and said, "I'm all right. Just let me do this." And Volle subsided without complaint, his knot already growing again as the wolf's skilled and familiar fingers danced up and down it.

The leathery paw pads took their time, pressed against the skin, and Volle closed his eyes, feeling the wash of each stroke go through him. It was warm and personal, and he couldn't help thinking, as his tail and feet began to twitch, that it was much more filled with love than the previous act had been.

His muzzle sought Streak's and found it, clumsily exchanging licks when they couldn't kiss. He was panting again, and shivering, but it took a lot of paw strokes to bring his orgasm around a second time.

Fortunately, Streak was patient.

Volle tried to keep his yelps quiet, moaning and pressing back against Streak as he came again, dripping onto the wolf's paw. He pulled on Streak's knot, sending more shivers through himself, and after several throaty moans, he collapsed back against the wolf. Streak licked him tenderly and hugged him, and Volle nuzzled back, panting.

"I am going to be sore," he said, but he was smiling. "It was worth it, though."

"I could have waited until tonight, but..." Streak teased Volle's dripping shaft again.

"Ow! Definitely no more, okay?"

The wolf giggled and kissed his shoulder. "Well, all right. I need to clean off this paw of mine, though." He brought it to his muzzle and licked it until the fur was shiny and damp.

Volle watched through half-lidded eyes, and stroked the wolf's fur where he could reach it. "I guess we don't have time to stop at the resort for a bath."

"Probably not," Streak agreed. "We should clean up at the mansion and get to bed early. Important day tomorrow."

Volle nodded, and wriggled his rear. It felt looser, and when he pulled gently, Streak's knot slid out of him. Streak gasped and panted, his shaft bobbing between his legs as it came free. Volle stepped over Ilyana and turned back to the wolf, cupping his wolfhood in his paw, his fingers slipping along the slick surface.

Streak grinned at him, still panting. "I'm not up for more. And we don't have time anyway."

"I know." Volle squeezed him and he gave a soft yelp. "I just wanted to tease you back a bit."

"Oh, well, if you must." The wolf closed his eyes and panted.

Volle slid his paw slowly up the still-stiff length and then let it drop. Like his own shaft, Streak's was starting to slip back into his sheath. He pulled his pants up carefully around it. "All right," he said. "Can you help me get Ilyana back to bed?"

It was difficult in the small room; they had to be careful they didn't bang their heads as they carried the sleeping vixen across the room and set her on the bed. He placed one paw gently on her lower abdomen and smoothed the fur down, still damp from their mating. He nodded to Streak, and they walked quietly down the stairs.

The old weasel was waiting for them, looking uneasy. Volle thought he would ask her to look in on Ilyana in a bit, but as soon as he approached her, she pointed to the door.

"You go now. Take her too."

"We can't take her. She's asleep. Why…?"

Her voice was growing stronger and more angry. "I run a nice house. Not a brothel. And both of you…it is wrong. You all go."

"She's asleep!" Streak said.

The old weasel considered this. "Fine. You leave now. She leave tonight."

"She doesn't have anywhere to go." Volle was half-worried, half-exasperated. "She's in season, she can't help being like this."

"I don't care about season. She invited you. And you come yesterday and nothing happen."

"That was different. I—"

"You go now," she repeated firmly. "She go tonight."

"All right." Volle sighed. "Tell her to come to the mansion when she leaves."

The weasel nodded, and glared at them until they left.

"I thought she would have told her," Streak said ambiguously as they walked down the stairs slowly.

"Ilyana?"

"Yeah. Wouldn't she have known she was coming into season?"

Volle nodded. "I don't know. Maybe she thought we wouldn't be that loud. Or…" Or maybe the old weasel was shocked that Streak was participating. He kept that thought to himself. "Or she thought…that we'd take her somewhere else."

"Like Dewanne did."

"Right," Volle growled as they reached the carriage and climbed inside quickly, not wanting to give Forrin a chance to sniff them.

"Sorry," Streak said, and then, because the driver was waiting, he reached out the window and tapped the board. "Mansion, please."

"It's all right," Volle said. "I'm still angry about it, but that doesn't mean you can't mention it. You're right."

"Maybe," Streak said, "she just didn't think to mention it."

Volle smiled, leaning back in the seat. "It doesn't matter. I'll have to make sure she can stay at the mansion, or the castle. I don't know what else to do. If she stays at the mansion, she'll have to stay in our suite. Nothing else is big enough."

"That house wasn't particularly big."

"No, true." Volle shrugged. "She could stay with Tish and Tika, too. I just feel bad for getting her in trouble."

Streak put a paw on his knee. "It's not your fault. You gave her a cub, and that's what she wanted more than anything else."

Volle thought about that, and slowly his muzzle curved into a smile.

That evening's dinner was a quieter affair, with fewer people. Volle and Streak, having found a water bath, felt clean and fluffy and had scented themselves with vanilla, leading Helfer to ask what kind of day they'd had that they had to bathe in the middle of it. Volle skirted the question, though he answered it indirectly when he asked Helfer if Ilyana could stay at the mansion. Helfer grinned and replied as Volle had thought he would: he offered a low-ceilinged room, or said she would have to share Volle and Streak's suite.

"She can stay in our suite tonight," Streak said.

"I'll ask Tish and Tika if she can stay with them tomorrow." Volle patted Streak. "You're sure you don't mind?"

Streak waited until Helfer was occupied with his dinner and then said, softly, "After this afternoon?"

Volle grinned. "I just wanted to make sure."

Ilyana didn't arrive until later that night, and when she did, she was rather distraught. Volle, Streak, and Forrin were in the guest quarters when she was shown in, and they saw her clutching her bag to her as a weasel servant held the door. She looked around nervously, then saw Volle and dropped the bag. She looked as though she wanted to run, but kept some measure of dignity in walking quickly to him.

She threw her arms around him when she reached him. "Volle," she said, "Martika, she said I had to leave. I'm sorry, I didn't know what...I thought they knew about being in season."

He shook his head. "I'm sorry. I should have had you come up here."

"No, it's okay. It's done. Thank you for offering me a place to stay. I..." She looked around. "Is there another room?"

"Just the bedroom."

"You can sleep there," Streak said gallantly. "I'll stay on the couch."

She turned to him and smiled, slowly, as if just recognizing him. "You were there too, this afternoon," she said softly, and then turned to Volle. "Wasn't he?"

Volle folded his ears back, unable to read her expression. "He's better than blackberry mead," he said by way of explanation.

"I see." She nodded, and turned back to Streak. "No, I couldn't take your bed. You've done so much for me. For us."

Streak flattened his ears, but in gratified embarrassment. Volle still wasn't sure about her tone, but he nuzzled Ilyana and was happy to see the action bring a hesitant smile to her muzzle. "We only have the one couch, but Helfer said there's a room with a bed, if you don't mind a low ceiling."

"I can sleep on the floor, my Lady," Forrin said. "I've done it before. I'm used to it. There's a rug."

"No, I couldn't." But her protest was less forceful than it had been.

"I insist." He bowed. "It is the least I can do for my Lord's wife."

"If you're sure…"

"I am."

She smiled. "Thank you, then, er…"

"Forrin," Volle said.

"Thank you, Forrin." She bowed to him, and when she straightened, she seemed a bit more relaxed.

"You see, it'll be all right." Volle nuzzled her.

"I know, I know. It was just a shock, finding myself homeless. I didn't know what Volyan would do. Thank Canis he was with Tish and Tika."

Volle held her closer with one arm. "I wouldn't let you be turned out into the street."

"I know," she said softly, working her muzzle under his.

He looked at Streak, and saw the wolf smiling at him, but the smile with tinged with a sadness he couldn't quite fathom.

Chapter 13

When he'd put Ilyana to bed later that night, covering her with a blanket on the couch and sitting with her until she fell asleep, he padded back into the bedroom. Streak was already in bed, but when Volle slipped in beside him, he stirred and nuzzled the fox.

"Everything okay?" he whispered.

Volle nodded. "She's asleep now. She'll be fine in the morning. I think it was just a shock, getting turned out like she did."

"Mm-hmm."

"Are you okay?"

"Me? I'm fine." The wolf licked him.

"All right." He wanted to ask if Streak were jealous, but he couldn't think of a way to say it. "Streak?" he said finally, determined to say something.

"Hmm?"

The words seemed silly now, and irrelevant. Volle pressed up to him and held him close. "Nothing."

Streak licked his ear. "I love you too, silly fox."

"Okay." Volle smiled, and carried that smile into his sleep.

In the morning, he declined Helfer's invitation to run. Despite Tish's assurances, he was still nervous about the outcome of the hearing. There had been enough going on that he'd been able to distract himself from it, but now that the day was here, he was beginning to realize that there was a chance, however small, that he would be waking up the next morning in prison. There would be no running away, no miraculous rescue; if he were arrested at his trial, he would be marched to prison in Divalia.

He thought Streak might not want to come, but the wolf showed no signs of hesitation, dressing with Volle and smiling encouragingly whenever Volle paused, lost in thought. To his surprise, Ilyana decided to come along, too.

"It will be good for Dewanne to see me, if he's there. And it will be good for me to be there to show support for you, even if he isn't," she reasoned, and Volle could find no fault with that.

They rode up in a buggy with Helfer, all four of them crammed inside while Forrin and the driver shared the top. They talked quietly on the ride up about how they were all getting back to Divalia, the others implicitly reassuring Volle by assuming he would be traveling with them.

Later, the buggy ride would all blur into one long moment for Volle. It seemed to last forever, and as they drove up into the thin fog, he conceived the idea that if they just kept driving, he would be safe. He had his best friend, his mate, and his wife all here and safe, and if he could just keep them in the buggy, nothing bad could happen to any of them. The fancy became so strong that when they did pull up outside the castle, and Helfer sprang out of the buggy, Volle nearly grabbed at him to stop him.

But then they were all outside, standing in the chilly fog, where the vulpine footservant who'd been aghast at Volle's wet fur several nights ago directed them into the castle. Its stone corridors were barely warmer than the fog outside, until they approached the great hall where the inquest had been, and saw that now a fire had been lit, warming the room from behind the dais where the King would be sitting. Once again, Volle was led up to the table he and Streak had been seated at, but this time Streak was shown to a chair in the audience, and Volle was seated alone. Forrin didn't seem to know quite what to do; there were already guards on either side of the dais. He settled for standing near one of them, and was soon talking in whispers with him.

Across from Volle, at the prosecutor's table, Lord Wallen was conferring with a younger stag Volle didn't recognize. They had a stack of papers in front of them and were shuffling through them. The older stag barely spared Volle a glance as the fox was seated.

Tish and Tika were already in the audience, with a number of others, and when Volle was shown to the table, Tish came up to see him. Volle scanned the audience and saw his friends outnumbering his enemies; only a few of the senior Lords had any enmity towards him. Wallen, of course, was chief among them. Many of the Lords in attendance, as far as he knew, had no particular leaning one way or the other. He supposed this was the best entertainment available at this time.

Tish examined his neck as he approached. "Got the pendant? Good," he said quietly, tapping it. "Just let me do the talking for the first part, m'boy."

"All right." Volle nodded. "Tish?"

The wolf had begun to step away. "What is it?"

"I'm nervous."

White teeth flashed a smile in the black muzzle. "Don't be. You'll be back in your old chambers by this time next week." Volle flicked his ears, but managed a smile in return. "That's a good lad. This will be over before you know it."

The minutes dragged on, each one giving Volle ample time to imagine the horrible surprises that might be awaiting him. *Fox protect me*, he prayed silently, going back to an old prayer of his childhood. *Give me the wit to avoid my enemies, the speed to outrun them if I cannot avoid them, and the strength to fight them if I cannot outrun them*. There would be no running and no fighting here; only his wit would save him if he needed it. That and Tish, he remembered. Volle scanned the audience, finding Helfer, Tish, Tika, Ilyana, Nero, Archie, and Streak. The white wolf was seated next to Tish, and Volle was struck again by the vivid contrast between the black and white fur. Tish seemed to be whispering reassurances to Streak; the white wolf was looking relaxed and confident. Volle drew some strength from that, and relaxed himself.

Still, it was a relief when the King was announced. He lumbered up the dais with as much dignity as a bear could muster, and took his seat behind the table. The entire room stood with heads bowed until he was seated, and then they took their seats again.

Movement at the back of the room caught Volle's eye; he saw Terril slip in and take a seat near the back. Were commoners allowed in the hearing? He felt a momentary flash of guilt for not carrying Helfer's answer back to the rabbit, but he hadn't been to the castle since then.

And then the King cleared his throat, and everything else was driven from Volle's mind.

Alister was standing next to the King, and he announced to the now-silent crowd, "My Lords and Ladies, we are ready to begin."

The crowd watched attentively as the coyote picked up a scroll and read from it. "His Majesty is present today to rule in two matters brought forth by our, er, former Minister of Defense; first, that the fox named Volle, currently holding the title of Lord of Vinton, was not born to that office and should be removed from it, and second, that said fox did knowingly steal confidential and important documents from the office of Defense with the intention of delivering them to a foreign monarch."

Intention, Volle noted. Clever wording, and hard to prove, but also hard to disprove.

"Who is speaking for the defense?"

Volle stood. "I will present my own defense, your Majesty, but I reserve the right to call upon members of the audience as needed."

"So noted." Alister gave Volle a quick smile as the fox sat again; they'd always gotten along well. "And who is speaking for the prosecution?"

Wallen stood. "I have the honor of presenting the case against the so-called Lord Vinton," he said evenly.

"Thank you, Lord Wallen." Alister looked down at his parchment again. "You may make your first argument for the first case, the matter of the legitimacy of Lord Vinton's claim to his title."

The stag rose as Alister said down. "Thank you," he said. "It is our intent to demonstrate that the fox who presents himself as the scion of the Vinton family line is no more related to them than I am."

"Surely a *little* more related," the King rumbled.

The audience tittered. Wallen was taken aback, and Volle couldn't help but grin. He felt a little better, knowing that even if the King were impartial, he wasn't averse to throwing the pompous Wallen off balance.

"It—it's a figure of speech, your Majesty." The King merely nodded, and Wallen continued. "This fox presented himself to an investigator as the son of a Tephossian noble whose whereabouts were unverifiable for the last few years of his life. Based only on this recommendation, he was welcomed into the palace and subjected to the most trivial of supervision. An attempt to uncover his past was discarded even though it turned up several disturbing questions."

Volle took advantage of a pause to say, "Could you tell us who made that attempt, Lord Wallen?"

Alister extended a paw toward him. "Please, Lord Vinton, wait your turn."

Wallen was glaring at him, and took a moment to continue. "As I said, several disturbing questions were raised."

"Excuse me, Lord Wallen," the King said. "Who did make that investigation?"

The stag had the grace to look uncomfortable as he coughed. "It was the junior deputy Minister of Defense at the time, your Majesty."

"His name, please, Lord Wallen. We don't care for the accusation that we casually dismissed potential threats to our kingdom, and we would like to know the full facts behind these accusations."

"Dereath Talison," Lord Wallen said in a low voice. The audience murmured.

"Thank you." The King settled back.

"In any event, further facts have been brought to light. Interviews with people who knew the old Lord Vinton—regrettably, only two, who are unable to make the trip—have brought certain facts to light that—yes, what?!" He snapped at Tish, who had stood in the front row and cleared his throat repeatedly during the previous sentence.

"I believe I could save his majesty a considerable amount of time, if given the opportunity." Tish looked directly up at the King.

"We would be greatly interested to hear that," the King said, beckoning him with a paw. "You are speaking for the defense, I assume."

Tish didn't answer until he had stepped up onto the dais and reached Volle's table. "Give me the pendant," he whispered.

Volle pulled the leather strap over his head with a little difficulty, and handed it to Tish. The wolf closed his paw over it and turned to the King. "Actually, your Majesty, I believe I can prove the prosecution's case conclusively."

Another surprised murmur rose from the audience. Lord Wallen, who had gathered himself up to object, suddenly sat down. Volle felt his fur crawl as he went numb. First Dewanne, and now Tish? If Tish was against him, then he was lost. He felt that morning's despair creeping back, and then Tish caught his eye and unmistakably winked at him.

The King had sat up and looked interested. "Go on, Lord Tistunish—if you are amenable, Lord Wallen?" The stag nodded, slightly suspicious but evidently willing to take a chance.

"I must beg his Majesty's indulgence, and the audience's, if in the interest of saving a lot of time, I spend a little of it."

"I have never known you to be brief about anything, old friend," the

King said with a smile.

"I will attempt to restrain myself, your Majesty." Tish smiled and began to walk back and forth on the dais, alternately facing Lord Wallen and Volle.

"Many of you know that I was born near the end of King Bucher's reign." Volle glanced quickly to Wallen in time to see the stag's grimace at the mention of the name. "My family was not one of the most favored, but being children of Canis we were naturally favored to some degree. I was of an age with King Bucher's youngest son, Archer, and was allowed to play with him. We became fast friends—as fast as cubs of four years old can be. We explored the castle together.

"His nurse was an old coyote who took care of us both during lessons and playtime. She brought us treats from the kitchen…" Tish paused. "I'm sorry," he said, and Volle thought he detected a quaver in the wolf's voice. "That isn't pertinent. She loved us both.

"She came running into the playroom one day. We thought it was a game, but she was frightened. I just remember her hustling us into a wardrobe, covering us with clothes, and telling us to stay there. I could smell the fear on her and I wondered what could possibly have made her so scared.

"You all know, of course. We'd heard the shouts outside the window, but they were far below and we felt so safe in the palace that it never occurred to us that we could be threatened.

"We lay there trembling until we heard a commotion. Someone had run into the playroom and was begging the nurse to hide him. I had to hold my paw over Archer's muzzle when he recognized his older brother's voice.

"Our nurse wouldn't put him in the wardrobe. She said it was locked and that she'd thrown the key away. He begged her, but she said all she could do was dress him in her robes. Perhaps he could pass for the nurse.

"The rioters broke in ten minutes later. They weren't fooled. We heard them yell, heard the nurse scream, heard Archer's brother's terrified yells and heard them stop abruptly."

Volle shivered, and even Lord Wallen seemed mesmerized by Tish's story. The wolf paused and then went on. "They threatened to kill the nurse. She said she wasn't a fox, that she didn't know any foxes, that she didn't know where any foxes were. They left her alone. Eventually.

"When they'd gone, she whispered to us through the door not to worry, that we'd be all right now, that we had been very good and had to wait just a little longer. It was hours later that she opened the wardrobe, and the sky outside was dark.

"She had a small cloak with her and she gathered Archer up in it. 'We have to leave,' she told me. 'Your mother and father will be here soon.' She kissed me, and Archer and I held paws until she lifted him in her arms and left. And that was the last I saw of him.

"My parents didn't come until later. I was too scared to go anywhere but the playroom, even though the body of his brother was lying there, getting cold. It was savaged almost beyond recognition. But there was something left on it—a small gold pendant."

Volle made the connection then, and his jaw dropped at Tish's audacity. Tish had stopped in front of the King, and had started talking again by the time Wallen jumped to his feet. "The same gold pendant that everyone in his family wore. The same pendant that Archer wore when his nurse smuggled him out of the castle." He turned to look at Volle. "The same pendant he passed on to his son."

He laid the pendant on the table in front of the King as the audience erupted in disbelief. Volle heard Lord Wallen yelling, "This is impossible!" and someone in the audience yelling, "Noble blood!" The rest of the remarks were lost in the tumult.

Alister was on his feet, paws in the air, shouting, "Quiet! Quiet!" After a few minutes, his words had some effect and the people who'd been standing sat down, except for Lord Wallen. The stag was trembling with fury, but restrained himself until Alister looked at him and nodded. "Lord Wallen?"

"This is preposterous," the stag thundered. "This story is even less probable than the last. Lord Tistunish—I mean no disrespect, of course, but it was on his recommendation that this fox was brought into the castle to begin with! And he promised conclusive proof. I hardly think that a childhood memory retold by the oldest active peer is conclusive. No disrespect intended," he repeated as he sat down.

"Lord Tistunish?" The King had bid Alister sit with one motion of his paw. His dark eyes seemed to sparkle as he looked at the old wolf.

"None taken, Lord Wallen," Tish said. "What my junior peer says is quite true. I would not accept the story on my word alone. That is why I brought this."

He pulled one paw from his pocket and placed a worn wooden box on the table, then opened it in front of the King. "This is the pendant I took from his brother's body that night in the playroom, because I wanted to remember. I never told anyone I had it, at first because I was scared of being a thief, and later because Bucher and his family were so unpopular, it seemed pointless to raise old ghosts."

The King lifted a small piece of gold from the box and examined it, then compared it to the pendant Tish had taken from Volle. He looked up. "Would you like to examine them, Lord Wallen?"

"I certainly would!" The stag stomped around his table and joined Tish in front of the King. He reached out and then drew his paw back, as though the pendants were something dirty. Instead, he peered closely at the two pendants for several long minutes. Finally, he placed them carefully down and marched back behind his table, without a word.

"Lord Vinton," the King rumbled, turning to him, "or rather, Volle. How long have you had this pendant?"

"As long as I can remember," Volle said truthfully.

"And where did you get it?"

"My mother said it was all my father had left us."

The King nodded, slowly. "Lord Tistunish, you never noticed it until this retreat?"

Volle stood. "If I may, your Majesty?" His mind was working furiously to figure out what he could say that would be enough of the truth without being too much. The King nodded to him. "I did not wear it when I first came to the palace. I didn't know what it was and I feared that it might be inappropriate, coming from Ferrenis as I was. I didn't even bring it, in fact. I left it with a moneylender who was a friend of my mother's." That was all true enough. "When I returned to Ferrenis recently, I retrieved it from him, and upon returning here, I felt more comfortable and I knew that it wouldn't cause any trouble, so I wore it. Lord Tistunish was very surprised the first time he saw it, but I didn't know why."

Tish gave him the barest of nods, and turned to listen to the King. The large bear was looking back and forth between Volle and Tish, and then turned to Lord Wallen. "Do you wish to mount a challenge to this before we enter my deliberations?"

"I don't believe I can, your Majesty." The stag rubbed his antlers. "Unless there is someone else present who was alive during Bucher's reign. But if this fox is indeed descended from that—"

"Very well," the King said firmly, cutting off the stag's words. He picked up the pendants and examined them, then looked at Tish. "Lord Tistunish, you admit you were mistaken about Volle's parentage?"

"Our information said that his father was a Tephossian noble who had disappeared. He fit all the information about the former Lord Vinton, and I had no idea Archer had survived. I never saw the pendant, and those who did had no idea what it meant." Tish spread his paws. "I regret my mistake, but I think it is an honest one."

"We would tend to agree." The King shuffled both pendants back and forth in his paw, rubbing his chin with the other. Slowly, he dropped Tish's pendant back into its box, and held out the leather strap to Volle. "You may have your pendant back," he said.

Volle walked forward and took it, trying to read the King's expression. Tish picked up his box as well, and they stood side by side, waiting. The King faced them, but Volle had the impression that he was looking through them rather than at them. Finally, he spoke.

"We can find no reason that Lord Tistunish's story should be false, nor any other logical reason that these two should be in possession of identical pendants. Our decision is to accept this account of the fox Volle's ancestry."

"Thank you, your Majesty," Volle said, and walked back to his table, feeling suddenly very important. Tish returned to his seat, tail wagging. Lord Wallen looked blackly across the dais at Volle, but Streak and Helfer were smiling broadly. It occurred to Volle that he had never known his father, and it was possible that he was related to a royal Tephossian house. He wondered to himself whether that would make a difference.

"And our decision," the King said, looking sternly at the stag, "is final."

Alister quelled the scattered applause from the crowd. "We have one more matter to resolve," he said. "Lord Wallen, are you also presenting this case?" The stag nodded. "Lord V—Volle, you are handling your own defense?" Volle nodded. "Lord Wallen, go ahead."

The stag rose as Alister sat. "My Lords and Ladies, your Majesty, it is our intention to show that the fox known as Volle appropriated some highly confidential documents from the office of the Minister of Defense and intended to bring them to a foreign power."

He picked up one of the pages from the table. "Just over a year ago, plans were made to move our army into a strategic zone near Ferrenis—or so it was rumored. A set of plans was drawn up detailing these movements, and was left in the office of the Minister of Defense. They were stolen.

"This fox was apprehended running away from the office. He was the only one nearby. It is true that the plans were not discovered on him, but there was no other possible suspect. He was placed in prison and interrogated, but he refused to reveal where he had hidden the plans. After a few months—"

"Six months," Volle snarled.

"Lord Vinton…Volle, please," Alister said.

"After a few months," the stag continued, "he managed to escape with the help of a duplicitous guard. He fled immediately to Ferrenis, a foreign power. Obviously he has been working for them all along." He shifted slightly, looking around, and then sat down quickly.

"Volle?" Alister smiled.

Volle stood. "My Lords and Ladies, your Majesty…" His mind whirled, making sure that what he would say would refute all of Wallen's arguments. "It is true that I was near the office of the Minister of Defense. I had heard about the war plans and was worried. When I got to the office, I saw the plans, but I didn't get close enough to see very much. I heard movement and was worried about being caught, so I ran. Next thing I knew, Dereath and some guards had cornered me and I was being hauled off to prison." He emphasized Dereath's name. Wallen winced slightly as he did.

"My escape from prison was orchestrated by Dereath. He was hoping I would lead him to the place the documents were hidden. He was, of course, disappointed, and even more disappointed when I managed to slip through the trap he'd set. Upon finding myself free, I couldn't imagine returning to the palace, where I'd be considered a criminal. The only place where I knew I would be safe was at home in Ferrenis. So that's where I went.

"Lord Tistunish, who had always been my friend, believed I had been framed. He pleaded with me to attend this retreat so that I could make sure my case was heard. And that is why I am here today."

He sat down after that, and bowed his muzzle to the King.

"Thank you both," the King rumbled. "Lord Wallen, have you any rebuttal to Volle?"

"Your Majesty, without the documents, there is little we can offer in the way of proof. But we did petition your Majesty for the right to call a witness, and we would like to do that now."

The audience stirred slightly. Volle shot a look at Tish, who looked bewildered; beside him, Streak looked incredulous. The King, if he knew that the witness was dead, didn't react. "Go ahead, Lord Wallen."

"I would like to call Bayard Lilian." He looked expectantly out at the audience.

Volle followed his gaze. Most of the audience looked bemused and were looking around at each other. Except for one.

Slowly, Streak stood and walked up to the dais.

The room fell silent. Volle stared at the wolf, who avoided his gaze until he stood before the King, and then he glanced quickly over at Volle, his ears down, tail limp behind him.

"Bayard Lilian?" The King glanced at Volle, then back at Streak.

Streak nodded.

Alister said, "Respond to the King when addressed, please."

Streak looked up. "Yes, your Majesty," he said so softly that Volle barely heard it.

"You are aware of your duty to your King and your gods, and you will tell the truth?"

"Yes." The wolf's voice was barely a whisper. He cleared his throat and spoke a bit louder. "Yes, your Majesty."

"Lord Wallen, proceed," the King ordered, sitting back.

Volle tried not to betray his nervousness as the stag prepared his papers. He didn't think Streak would give him away, but the wolf would find it hard to lie to the King. Tail curled under his chair, he watched and said a quick prayer to Canis.

"Mister Lilian, where did you first meet the defendant?"

Streak glanced at Volle, then turned to face Lord Wallen. "In prison."

"You were working as a guard?"

"Yes."

"And how did you meet him?"

Streak paused. Volle couldn't see his muzzle, just the set of his shoulders and his tail, which had lifted slightly. "I was sent. To torture him."

"And did you?"

Volle couldn't see how that was relevant, but he couldn't interrupt. "No," Streak said softly.

"Why not?"

"I just couldn't. He was helpless. He'd already been tortured." And now the wolf's voice held a trace of rebellion in it.

Also, Volle remembered, Streak had been told to rape him, and in order to throw him off balance, Volle had begged him to. He'd been confused and hadn't been able to perform.

"I see." Lord Wallen looked down at his papers. "Did you ever talk to him?"

"Yes."

"What did you talk about?"

"My childhood. His childhood."

"Is that all?"

"We talked about a lot of things," Streak said. "I don't remember them all."

"Did you ever talk about his political views?"

"I…" The wolf glanced briefly at the King, and stopped.

And then King Barris leaned forward. He said, "Mister Lilian, your attachment to the defendant is well known. Please be assured that he will not be returned to prison if he is found guilty based on your testimony. He will be sent back to Ferrenis, and you will be free to go with him. We only want the truth."

Volle's heart sank. The King had given Streak exactly what he wanted.

Streak turned further and looked at Volle. In the white wolf's blue eyes Volle saw all the pain of the past few days, the fear of being questioned in front of the King, and, behind it all, the love that the wolf felt for him. The only thing he could not see was what that love would lead Streak to do. He tried desperately to communicate that whatever happened, he would still return that love, but he knew he couldn't hide his deep desire to return to the palace, to be a part of the court again. Guilt made him lower his ears, and as he did, Streak turned to look back at the King.

"All right, your Majesty," he said, and returned his attention to Lord Wallen, though his left ear remained cocked in Volle's direction. "Yes, we did."

"Can you tell us whether he at any time said that he had planned to take some important documents to a rival power?"

Streak thought for a moment, while Volle agonized. "I don't believe he said that."

"Did he ever say that he was in the pay of a foreign power?"

"No, I don't think so."

"Did he try to convince you to work for a foreign power? Maybe retrieve some documents for him?"

The answer came immediately this time. "No!"

Lord Wallen was beginning to look exasperated. His ears kept flicking back. "Did he ever say anything that would have made you believe he was not loyal to his Majesty the King?"

This was it, Volle thought. He cupped his ears forward, barely able to bring himself to listen. Streak was taking a long time, holding his muzzle in thought.

"It's hard to say," he said. "I mean, he was in prison. Of course he wasn't very happy about it."

Volle clamped his paws together to keep their nervous movements to a minimum. Streak was dodging the questions. For some reason, he had decided that he didn't want to give Volle up.

Lord Wallen looked annoyed, and paused for a moment before going on. "You helped him escape, is that right?"

Streak glanced at the King again. The bear said, "Answer truthfully. If Volle was innocent, then your action will not be punished."

"Yes, I did. They were going to kill him!" he said, showing passion for the first time.

"That is as it may be," Lord Wallen said. "Certainly it would have saved his Majesty some valuable time. How did he convince you to help him escape?"

"He didn't," Streak said. "It was my idea."

The audience murmured, and Lord Wallen struck the table in front of him, hard. "You may have thought it was your idea," he said, louder, "but isn't it possible you were tricked into thinking that?"

Right idea, Volle thought, wrong culprit. Dereath was the one behind the escape. The white wolf, obviously remembering that, matched Wallen's passion in his answer. "They stopped bringing him food!" he cried. "He could barely stand up when I found him! He couldn't even walk!"

Alister raised a paw to Streak. "Please, calm down," he said, and then turned to the stag. "That goes for you, too, Lord Wallen."

"My apologies." The stag took another moment to gather himself, appearing to get his temper under control. "Mister Lilian. After he escaped, you went with him." He leaned forward on the table. "Did you see him with those documents at any time?"

Streak barely hesitated. "No."

"Did he leave you to go get them? Did he tell you where they were hidden and make you go get them?"

"No!"

"You swore to tell the truth," Wallen growled, ignoring the warning looks from Alister.

"I remember what I swore," Streak said. "I never saw him take the documents, I didn't get them for him, I never saw him with them—I have never seen those documents you're referring to."

The stag stared at him coldly. "Of course you'd lie to protect him."

"Lord Wallen." The King himself stepped in, the reprimand clear in his tone.

"I apologize, your Majesty." He looked around the room desperately, as though hoping someone would tell him what to ask.

The King waited for nearly two minutes before speaking again. "Are you finished?"

"Yes. Thank you, your Majesty." Lord Wallen sat down heavily. He covered his eyes and lowered his antlered head to the table. Beside him, the younger stag looked extremely uncomfortable.

"Volle, do you have any questions or rebuttal?"

"No, your Majesty." Volle was fighting to keep a grin off his muzzle. His tail was tightly wrapped under his chair, but the tip was still wagging.

266

"Thank you for your service to this court, Mister Lilian. You may step down."

Streak bowed. "Thank you, your Majesty." He ventured a small grin to Volle and stepped back to take his seat in the audience.

The King nodded to Alister, who stood. "Lord Wallen, have you any other evidence to present?" The stag's antlers shook from side to side. He didn't look up. "Volle?" When Volle shook his head as well, the coyote continued. "There will be a brief recess while his Majesty deliberates the evidence presented. Lords Alacris, Villutian, Barclaw, Quirn, please approach."

He sat down, and as the four bears rose and walked to join the King, some of the other audience members rose from their chairs to talk. Volle saw Tish and Streak waiting for him, reluctant to follow the bears onto the dias. He looked at Alister and gestured in their direction.

"Go on," the coyote said with a smile. "Just stay in the room."

Volle nodded and walked down quickly, into a huge embrace between the two wolves. He grinned and hugged them back, tail wagging freely now. "He hasn't decided yet," he reminded them, looking at the King's meeting with his advisors. Lord Quirn, whom Volle knew disliked him, was arguing the loudest, while his allies, Barclaw and Alacris, were smiling.

Tish patted him on the back. "Don't worry about them. They're just there for show. I know the King. We've won." Tish kept his voice down, but his ears were perked and his manner was as jubilant as Volle had ever seen him.

"What—" Volle was about to ask Tish about the pendant when he noticed Streak's expression and half-tilted ears. "What's the matter, Bayard?" he said teasingly.

Streak winced and grinned. "Don't call me that. There's a reason I never told you my name."

"I like it, though." Volle nuzzled him. Tish stepped back and put his arm around Tika, who had joined them. Forrin had approached and was smiling as well, though he kept a respectful distance from the group. Volle could see Ilyana and Volyan a couple rows back in the crowd; the cub was chattering something at his mother, and she was replying with a distant expression.

"Congratulations, Volle!" Helfer slapped his rump with a paw, grinning. "Where you gonna stay at the castle now? Hey, if you don't have land, maybe you could be Lord Fardew."

"Even if for some reason the King went mad and offered me the job, I'm not sure I'd want it," Volle chuckled, hugging the little weasel with his other arm. "But I don't know what I can do. I was just going to ask Tish about that."

"I'm sure the King will find a place for you," Tish said.

"I hope so." Thinking about staying at the palace reminded him that he wasn't going back to the farm, and that reminded him of Streak, and then he thought he understood what was behind the wolf's mixed emotions.

He squeezed Streak around his shoulders and then released him. "Want to talk?"

Streak nodded. Volle looked around. "Could you all excuse us for a moment?"

The others nodded and stepped back as Streak led Volle to the side of the room, away from most people. Forrin took two steps toward them, but stopped far enough away that he wouldn't be able to hear what they were saying. Streak looked at him and then whispered to Volle, "I was so nervous."

"You were perfect," Volle said.

"I was afraid he'd ask a hard question." Streak's ears folded down. "I don't know if I can be around you all the time waiting for someone to ask something hard like that." Volle could barely hear his whisper.

"That won't happen again," he said.

"Not for this time, but..." Streak paused, and looked over Volle's shoulder.

Volle didn't smell anyone nearby, but when he turned, Terril was standing a few feet behind him. He took a step forward when Volle turned. "I'm sorry to interrupt," he said. "I have something I think...I mean, I think you'll want to hear it."

Volle glanced at Streak, who looked as puzzled as he was, and then nodded. "What is it?"

"Well..." The rabbit approached and lowered his voice. "I was going through Lord Fardew's things yesterday and I found where he'd written down some of the conversations he overheard you two having. I thought you might want to have those transcripts."

Streak and Volle exchanged apprehensive glances. "What do you want in return?" Volle said warily.

"You did offer to get me a job," the rabbit said. "I don't really want more than that. I mean, I think you should have them."

Volle was about to say that he had been ordered not to leave the room when Alister called down from the dais, "Volle, his Majesty requests your presence."

"I'll go," Streak said quickly. "I want to. If that's okay." He smiled at Volle. "I know what he's going to say anyway."

The rabbit hesitated a moment, then nodded. He led Streak out as Volle stepped back up onto the dais and stood in front of the King.

King Barris was standing himself. He turned to Alister. "Is there a nearby room where we might talk to Volle privately?"

"Of course, your Majesty." Alister led what turned into a procession of King Barris, Volle, Forrin, and two of the King's guards out of the room and a short way down the hallway. The King motioned Volle inside and told the guards to wait at the door.

Volle looked around the relatively small room. It looked like it had been used as a staging area for some of the banquets; a smell of food lingered in it and there were several small tables scattered around. The bare stone walls were solid and windowless except for two small slits at the top that let in the daylight; if there had been no slits, a hole in the ceiling and a trench on the floor, Volle would have been reminded of his prison cell.

The King closed the door, leaving the rest of the group outside; apparently it had been a royal 'we.' He gestured for Volle to take a seat on one of the small tables, while he himself leaned his ponderous bulk against a wall, and regarded Volle for several long seconds. When he spoke, his tone sounded more amused than anything else.

"Our mother had a saying she used quite often, Volle. 'The buzzing of the bees means honey in the trees.'" He folded his arms, tapping one paw onto the opposite arm before continuing. "Esteemed fox, there has been an inordinate amount of buzzing around you ever since you arrived at the palace."

Volle blinked, but kept quiet. King Barris continued in his deep, measured voice. "It was not long after you arrived that a small group of activists put into motion their plan to bring us to war with Ferrenis, believing the time to be right. Soon after that, a leading noble was assassinated." He looked sternly at Volle. "Despite the very likely possibility that he was a part of or even the leader of that group, we do not look kindly on assassinations within the peerage, much less inside the palace. It was quite a disturbing time.

"We recall that Dereath first began his campaign of allegations against you at that time, too. He didn't do a very good job, did he?"

Volle shook his head and started to reply, but the King held up a paw. "No, don't say anything. Then there was the matter of the raiding party, two years later. They were slaughtered, you remember, by a division of the Ferrenian army that had no reason to be defending that town. We do not believe it was a coincidence that they had just reported their movements and intentions to the palace the previous month.

"You married, and your wife has not been to the palace since then, we believe. Which, again, fits with your life, but also gave fuel to Dereath, Whassel, Wallen, and the others who were beginning to share their suspicions of you. Yes, it wasn't only Dereath, though he was the most vocal. We daresay Wallen might now be beginning to wonder whether he has been led astray by a murderous lunatic, though unfortunately, your newly revealed ancestry will do nothing to endear you to him even so.

"But we can do nothing about that. We are recalling the events of the past year."

He left the wall and started to pace back and forth in front of Volle. "The plans you referred to were the result of a year and a half of work—more than two years, if you count the time Dereath spent convincing us they were necessary. You see, while we could fit those incidents into a pattern that coincided with your arrival, Lord Alacris pointed out that there were other incidents—or rather, lack of incidents—that did not fit the pattern. We will

"Esteemed fox, there has been an inordinate amount of buzzing around you ever since you arrived at the palace."

give you two examples." He held up a single finger. "Firstly, the trade agreements with the northern tribes. You are likely aware that neither Ferrenis nor Tephos owns the valley that is the most convenient entrance to the northern lands. They are a fierce and independent people there, unwilling to bow to any king. We had planned an embassy to the north for two months, and they spent another month traveling there. There would have been ample time to communicate a message to Ferrenis to sabotage the party. We would have assumed they had been killed by the barbarians.

"But the embassy succeeded."

He held up another finger. "Example two. Two years ago, the heavy rains rotted the grain in the storerooms around Divalia. We kept it secret, but you were on the Agriculture Committee. You had to have known about it. We bought some grain from the Reysfields that saved a number of lives, not to mention grain that we requisitioned from some lands bordering Ferrenis. Again, it would have been a simple matter to have directed the Ferrenian raiding parties to burn down grain silos, or to raise the price on the Reysfields grain harvest by offering them more.

"But neither of those things happened."

"Rallish, who was a very sensible wolf, sat down with Alacris and ourself after Dereath had presented yet another plea for us to investigate you, and we decided that there were three options: either you were not a spy; or you were a spy but not a very good one; or you were a spy but your aim was not in and of itself to be a threat to our kingdom."

"We agreed to Dereath's plan, finally, in order to be sure. Alacris felt that in none of the three cases would you be a serious threat, but Rallish made the point that your first loyalty being to another power could be a threat under the right circumstances, no matter what your aim. So we ordered some troop movements, discreet ones that could not be read as an overt sign of war. We drew up a single set of plans that showed an aggressive intention to take over the Reysfields. We let some rumors spread in the right circles. And we left the plans in Rallish's office."

Volle was holding one paw in the other; both tightened at hearing this. So now he knew: it really had been nothing more than a trap, and he had fallen right into it. He couldn't keep his ears from folding back, but he brought them forward again immediately.

Barris didn't seem to notice. He shook his head angrily, his voice acquiring a distinct growl, but his anger was aimed far outside the room and long ago. "The worst possible thing happened. The plans disappeared without anyone being caught. Dereath claimed that you had gotten away, and we were furious. The plans had to look authentic in order for the trap to work. They would be believed if they reached the palace in Caril, in Ferrenis. Our countries could, and very likely would, go to war. Over nothing.

"We were afraid to pull our troops back, lest they leave precious areas undefended against attack. We were afraid to move forward and attack preemptively in case the plans had not made their way to Caril. There were proponents of both actions in our inner council, but we could not act without knowing the fate of the plans. We spent months wondering if the dawn would bring a rider from the Reysfields with the horrible news that war had begun."

Volle shuddered. The King nodded. "If Rallish had had any other competent help, we would have dispensed with Dereath then and there." He paused. "Looking back, we admit the possibility that his other assistants were discredited or displaced by Dereath himself, which is regrettable. In any event, the rat stayed. And six months after the theft, when we all had begun to breathe more easily, he came crawling to us with another confession. You know what this one was."

"That he'd lied to you about me getting away."

"But that it was no longer a lie. Yes. And we went through it all again. He had some excuses about there being another spy in the palace, that you had to have handed the plans to someone else or had some associate—perhaps because he still believed you were responsible for Prewitt, and you were unmistakably elsewhere at the time, if we recall." This time, he actually smiled at Volle, and Volle smiled boldly back.

"I was with my wife." The first mating they'd had. Well...the first fruitful one.

"Precisely. So he had to confess that he'd tortured you, devised a cunning plan to get you to reveal the identity of your conspirator, and that it had all gone wrong. We were tired of his cunning plans by then, but his knowledge was invaluable, so again he was kept on, with stern warnings this time. We hoped he had learned his lesson."

The King paused and looked at Volle. "I am about to tell you certain things that not even your friend Tistunish has heard."

Volle nodded. King Barris dropping the royal 'we' made him very aware of how important and personal this was. "Yes, your Majesty. I swear by Canis and Gaia that I will keep your confidence."

Barris waved a paw. "They will not be secret for long. I would not be telling you if they were. I fully expect that your friend *will* have heard them within the next few hours." He gave Volle a knowing smile, and continued. "We decided that we did not want to endure another six months of waiting and wondering, so we sent an embassy to Caril with an entreaty to open a channel of diplomatic communication."

His brows lowered as he continued. "We are Ursid, Volle. We do not embrace change quickly. Ferrenis and Tephos had existed peacefully for years by ignoring each other and sending raiding parties back and forth across the border periodically. We saw no reason for that to end, except that we grew very tired of watching our eastern border, tired of wondering whether we would soon be embroiled in a meaningless war. And in the end, that was reason enough.

"We found the Ferrenians open to discussion. They did not express any knowledge of our false war plans. Negotiations are currently proceeding well, which is to say slowly and deliberately, just as we like. It would be a terrible blow to them if a Ferrenian spy were to be discovered in our midst." He didn't smile as he said that, just stood with arms folded and looked at Volle.

Volle tried to match the bear's serious expression. He was buoyed by the King's story, delighted at the turn things had taken. "I can see where that would be an impediment to negotiations."

"As for you," Barris said, "we are left with our original three options, though we think we can eliminate one. A spy who was not very good would not long leave us in doubt about the other two options. So we are left with the question of whether you are a spy or not."

He shrugged. "We believe that you took the plans. It may be that you just picked them up to look at, were alarmed when you heard movement, and hid them so you would not be accused of stealing them. When you escaped to Ferrenis, you simply left them behind. Or it could be that you stole the documents because they presented an imminent threat to Ferrenis, took them with you when you escaped, and did not turn them in to the monarchy there.

"Or. It is possible that you took the documents and presented them to the monarchy. In that case, you would almost certainly have been consulted as to their authenticity, and as to the need to act upon them." His dark eyes studied Volle, who could not think of a single thing to say.

"Still, it appears now that you are of royal Tephossian blood, and that changes some things. If you are the kind of fox we believe you to be, you are an observer of Canis's creed to care for your pack, and you will not be able to deny that in some small respect, your pack includes the land of Tephos. You have rendered a great service to this monarchy by exposing the murderous nature of its Minister of Defense, and you have rendered good and faithful service as the Lord of Vinton for five years. Your governor recently attested to that in a letter sent to the Crown on your behalf."

He smiled, a full, broad smile now. "It occurs to us that such faithful service should be rewarded. And here we have a fox in need of reward, and a land traditionally ruled by foxes that is bereft of a Lord. One does not have to be as clever as a fox to see the solution."

Volle's ears flicked in surprise. He certainly hadn't expected to be Lord Vinton again this soon. He was surprised not only by King Barris's offer, but by how much he realized he wanted the title. The unexpected support of Anton, his governor, touched him deeply. His voice cracked as he said, "I…would be most greatly honored, your Majesty."

"Of course you would. But I think this is something everyone should see. Let us return, and," he fixed Volle with a dark eye, "remember what we have spoken of here."

"Yes, your Majesty," Volle said. His tail swished with excitement as he followed the King back to the room, Alister and the guards escorting them.

The crowd had not diminished in the hearing room, except that Volle noticed that Lord Wallen was gone, and Streak was not back. He felt a sharp pang of disappointment; he wanted the wolf to see this. But he couldn't very well ask the King to wait while he went to find him, and he didn't have time to send someone else. He sighed. He would have to tell him about it, and Streak would be sad that he'd missed it.

They returned to the dais, where the King raised a paw to the crowd. "We have made our decision," he said. "The fox called Volle is innocent of the charges of treason that have been brought against him." He quelled the brief spatter of mixed applause with another motion of his paw. Volle noticed several members of the audience who looked less than pleased, but he had no time to worry about them now. "And because, in the course of this hearing, the province of Vinton has been left without a Lord, it occurs to us that a fox of noble blood is just what is needed to fill that vacancy."

King Barris turned to Volle and drew the long, glittering, ceremonial sword at his side. "We know that you swore an oath of fealty to us six years ago," he said more quietly, "but we hope you will understand if we require you to swear it again."

Volle dropped to one knee, bowing his head. "Of course, your Majesty."

The sword shone as it ascended to the top of its arc, then descended to his shoulders, tapping each one in turn. "We hereby award to thee the title Lord of Vinton. Let Gaia, Ursa, and the assembled peers recognize that henceforth, you shall be the servant to the people of Vinton, their voice to the King, the foundation beneath their paws, and the fur that protects and keeps them warm. This title shall be yours and your cub's, and your cub's cub's, in perpetuity."

"I swear fealty to you, King of Tephos, and I pledge to you my loyalty and the loyalty of my people," Volle said. He didn't remember exactly how the oath was supposed to go, but Barris apparently found it acceptable, because he tapped Volle's shoulders with the sword once again.

"Rise, Lord Volle of Vinton," he said.

Chapter 14

The room filled with cheers and applause, both genuine and otherwise. Even the younger stag at the prosecutor's table was clapping, though his expression was anything but pleased. As the King stepped back and Volle got to his feet, he was greeted by a beaming Tish, who tried to shake his paw around the weasel hugging his waist. Volle hugged Helfer back and then Tish, and then walked down into the crowd, still feeling rather dazed. He looked around for Streak, but still didn't find him.

The King stepped down as well, beaming, and joined Tish and Volle briefly. Tish bowed his head. "Your Majesty never ceases to amaze me."

"On the contrary," Barris laughed. "You amazed us today. And everyone else, we dare say."

Tish's ears flicked. "I was as surprised as you were, I assure you. But your Majesty has shown excellent judgment here today."

"We hate to lose a good servant, and we hate to pass up the opportunity to welcome a new one." Barris laid a heavy paw on Volle's shoulder. "We believe in Lord Vinton, here. He won't let us down."

"No, I don't believe he will." Tish smiled.

"Please excuse me now," King Barris said, stepping back. "Well done, Lord Vinton."

"Thank you, your Majesty," Volle replied, bowing as the King wandered off to mingle with some other nobles.

"They're going to be serving lunch over in the banquet hall," Tish said. "Will you join us?"

"I think I'll wait here and see if Streak turns up," Volle said. He was hungry, but already he was starting to worry, remembering the last time the wolf had disappeared. "Maybe I'll go look for him…but I don't want to miss him in the hallways if he comes back a different way."

"He's probably worried about having to testify against you," Tika said. "He'll be all right."

Lord Whassel, a beaver, was talking to Lord and Lady Quirn. As they drew closer to Volle, the beaver pitched his high voice so that the fox and wolves could hear him. "…don't know what the King could have been thinking, when there are at least three bears waiting for a peerage. What about Funia, your friend?"

Quirn shook his head, without looking at Volle. "Regrettable," he said in a deep bass voice. "But we must resign ourselves…" They passed on by and out of the room.

Volle looked darkly at their backs. Tish put a paw on his shoulder. "Don't worry. There is only so much they can do."

"Oh, Volle!" Ilyana had made her way forward and now threw her arms around him. "I can't believe it!"

Volyan hugged his leg at the same time, saying, "Hi, Daddy! Hi, Daddy!"

Volle smiled and nuzzled Ilyana, patting Volyan on the ears. "It's going to be okay," he said. "In a couple days, you and I will be leaving for the palace. Are you excited?"

"Yeah!" Volyan's tail wagged back and forth. "Can Mommy come?"

"I've told you I can't, Voly." Ilyana smiled. "But you'll be able to come see me."

"You'll be so busy," Volle said. "You're going to have a lot of fun."

"With Daddy Streak?"

"Yeah..." Volle looked around the room, but the white wolf was still nowhere to be seen.

"Mommy," Volyan said, bored as soon as the focus of attention was away from him, "I'm hungry."

"Go ahead and eat," Volle said. "I'll be along soon."

"All right. Congratulations again," Ilyana said, though her smile was much more relieved than excited. She took Volyan's paw and followed Tish and Tika out of the room.

Much of the crowd was leaving with them. Helfer stuck by Volle and said, "Want me to go look for him? Or wait here while you go?"

Volle shook his head. "No, I'm sure he's fine. He had a lot to think about. Maybe he just wanted to take a little time." The wolf had certainly been eager to go with the rabbit. Volle started to wonder if he'd taken that opportunity to just slip away, so that Volle wouldn't be burdened with the decision. He hoped not.

"All right. Then I'm going to eat too. Hi, Archie." Helfer grinned as the other weasel walked up.

"My Lords." Archie emphasized the plural, smiling broadly, and bowed. "Congratulations, Lord Vinton, you seem to have come out on top."

Volle waved to Helfer, who padded quickly to the door in search of lunch. "Thank you. Well, you made it all possible, you know. If you hadn't been outside that tower at just the right time to see Dereath..."

Archie looked down. "You know, sometimes you gotta make your own luck," he said indistinctly.

"What do you mean?"

The weasel looked around, then stepped a bit closer to Volle. Volle saw Forrin step forward alertly, and he waved the wolf back. "Well," Archie said, "I figured we knew he did it, and if I had been there a few minutes earlier I would've seen him. And I knew they wouldn't convict him without an eyewitness."

"You...you lied?"

"Shhh! In a manner of speaking. You know, got to do what you got to do to make sure the criminal is punished."

"Does Captain Nero know?"

"Not yet. I'll tell him."

"He'll be upset."

Archie tilted his muzzle challengingly. "I'm not afraid of him."

"I am." Volle barely heard his own words. Archie had reminded him of something.

You're not afraid, are you?

He heard his dream, and then he heard the large wolf's voice in his memory again.

There was no scent of fear on her body.

Nero's words. About the mouse, but Volle realized with a chill that Nero had wanted to examine the guard's body and hadn't. And he, Volle, had been right up next to the guard's body moments after death and there had been no residue of fear on it.

But the guards had been afraid of Dereath.

And Archie had lied.

Archie was saying something, but Volle's ears were filled with a rushing noise and he couldn't hear it.

You're not afraid, are you?

Dereath hadn't killed the guard. And there was only one other person who possibly could have, however he might have managed it, only one other person who had access to the knife and Volle's scent, who was so mild and weak-looking that no palace guard could possibly be afraid of him.

The person who was the last person he'd seen with Streak. Who was still not back.

He left Archie in mid-sentence and bolted for the door.

Forrin chased him; he heard the wolf behind him yelling for him to stop and wait. And he told himself that it didn't matter now, that if something had happened to Streak it was long over and there would be nothing he could do about it, but he couldn't slow his paws down. He took the stairs two at a time, dodging past surprised nobles and servants in the corridors until he stood outside Dereath's chambers.

He could smell Streak, faintly, a trace that had passed by here an hour or more ago. He paused to listen, and that pause allowed Forrin to turn the corner and spot him. "Lord Vinton," the guard bellowed. "What are you doing?"

Volle pointed at the door and then, because the guard's shouting had ruined whatever advantage of surprise he might have possessed, he opened it and stepped inside.

"Close the door, fox, if you would." The rabbit's high-pitched tone was considerably harsher now, more sinister. He stood easily beside a chair near the bedroom door, holding a knife to the throat of a securely bound Streak. The wolf's muzzle was tied shut, but his blue eyes widened at the sight of Volle. He made muffled noises and gestured with his muzzle for Volle to run.

"If you leave, I'll slit his throat. Just step in and close the door."

Forrin had stepped in behind Volle, and the rabbit's eyes flicked up to take him in. "Close the door *now*."

Volle jumped to comply. He heard other footsteps in the corridor as he closed the door.

"Lock it," the rabbit said.

The key was in the keyhole. Volle turned it and heard a loud click.

"That's good. Now we're all nice and comfortable—get back." Forrin had taken a step toward the rabbit. "Step off the edge of that rug and I kill him."

"You're still working for Dereath." Volle couldn't keep the growl out of his voice.

"In a manner of speaking." The rabbit laughed. "Killing you will establish that he wasn't the murderer, which will get him out of prison, and then he'll come find me—I'll have disappeared from here, of course."

"You could have killed me before this," Volle said. "Why wait?"

"He had other plans for you then. That didn't work out. So I figured I'd step in. I'm not much good at planning, but I am good at killing. I did that whore, and the over-muscled idiot, and you shouldn't be much more trouble. Don't worry," he added. "If you play nice, I'll leave your two friends alive. I only need to kill one of you."

"The corridor outside is full of people. Do you really think you'll get away?" The door handle was being pushed from the other side, but the lock held.

"There aren't that many people. But I will have to be quick. Here." With his free paw, he tossed Volle a length of rope that was on the side table. "Take your guard's sword and throw it behind you, then tie his paws behind his back."

Forrin growled, but Volle put a paw on his arm. "Forrin. It's okay. I don't want to risk Streak's life."

Streak protested loudly at that, trying to shake his head. He pushed forward against the knife, but the rabbit slid it easily away. "No, no," he said, "as long as you're alive, the fox will do just what I say."

Volle pulled Forrin's sword free and threw it behind them. "Kneel down. Please, Forrin."

With another growl, the guard knelt, and placed his paws behind his back. Volle tried to tie the rope lightly, but the rabbit noticed. "Tightly! That's better. Now, fox, come over here and lie down on your stomach. I'll make it quick, I promise."

Streak's protests grew louder. He tried to rock himself from side to side, but the chair was heavy and solid. Volle shook his head and mouthed, "I'm sorry," to him. He didn't know what he was going to do. He didn't want to die, but he couldn't stand here and watch Streak be killed. A low 'whuff' noise sounded near his waist, and he looked down at Forrin.

The wolf was gesturing very slightly with his muzzle to the wall. Volle couldn't see anything there. He looked back to make sure he was reading the sign right, and he was. He started to walk in that direction, hoping he would figure out what the wolf meant.

To his left, Streak was almost crying through his gag. The rabbit watched as Volle moved to his right, pretending to look for a large patch of floor on which to lie down. It came to him as he was right by the wall—Forrin wanted the rabbit to be distracted between himself and Streak, and to have to turn his back to the guard.

"Hurry up," the rabbit snapped as Volle took his time. "I won't kill him, but I can hurt him if you take too long."

"All right, all right." The knife gleamed in the light of the room. Volle moved back to the wall and got down on his paws and knees. He was sure the fear was coming off him in waves; he could smell it even more strongly than he could Streak's.

"All the way down!"

Trembling, he lowered himself to the ground. His ears remained pricked. If he stayed alert, he could hear the rabbit's movements and maybe block them or anticipate them.

There was a smooth ripple of air past his whiskers; the rabbit had turned away from Streak. Volle tensed himself, knowing he didn't have much chance against a trained killer, praying to Fox that Forrin had a better plan.

A cloth fell on his head, blocking his sight and filling his nostrils with the dusty smell of old linen. He moved instinctively to take it off, then stopped. He only had precious seconds, and any noise he made might cover the minute indications that could save his life, or at least prolong it.

He felt the rush of movement behind him, heard Forrin's roar and the rabbit's choked-off cry, and then both bodies landed heavily beside him and the rabbit's voice was raised in a shrill and horrible scream. It went on and on, and then it choked off in a crunch, gurgle and silence that was somehow worse than the scream itself. The smell of blood hit Volle full force, making him gag. Only then did he realize he was still lying down.

He tore the cloth from his head, scrambled to his feet and looked first at Streak. The wolf was staring wide-eyed at the floor, so Volle followed his gaze down. Forrin's jaws were bloody, his eyes were wide, and his chest was heaving. There was a tear in his uniform and blood on it, but Volle didn't think that was what was causing his distress. Beside him, the rabbit lay on his back, eyes glazed, blood still pumping out of the ruin of his neck and shoulder. Bits of cloth, fur, and bone dotted the gaping red wound that stretched from under his chin to his right upper arm.

Volle stared for only a moment, then sprang across the floor to Streak first, untying his muzzle and holding him tightly. Streak kissed him urgently, and as Volle pulled away, their eyes met and they both knew that Volle had to attend to Forrin.

He knelt behind the wolf, untying his paws as quickly as he could.

"Forrin," he said urgently, "are you all right? Forrin!"

Forrin turned his head finally, but it took his eyes several seconds to focus on Volle. When his paws were finally freed, he wiped frantically at his muzzle. "I…tasted…swallowed…" He panted harder, his eyes now unnaturally bright, and then he doubled over, panting and heaving until he vomited where Volle had been lying.

"Listen, Forrin, you did a noble thing. Canis will forgive you. You did the right thing. He was Darkness, and you got rid of him. You hear me? He was Darkness. Not you. You'll be all right." Volle kept talking, trying to soothe the wolf. When he looked up at Streak for suggestions, he saw to his surprise that Archie was untying the white wolf.

"Stay here," he said, getting to his feet, not even bothering to ask how the weasel had gotten in. "I'll get some water."

"All right. We're fine." Archie's voice had none of its usual irreverence.

Volle still hesitated, looking at Streak, until the white wolf said, "I'll be fine. Go!" And then he went.

A few servants had gathered in the corridor. "We heard a scream." "Is everything okay?"

Volle closed the door firmly. "Where's the nearest place to get water?"

One of the servants, an otter, pointed down the corridor. "Just there, there's a room with an open ceiling that we keep jugs in…"

"Take me there."

He returned a few minutes later with a jug of water. The otter followed him, carrying a basin. He nearly dropped it when he saw the carnage in the room, but kept his composure long enough to set it down. Forrin lurched toward the basin and plunged his muzzle into it, washing it frantically. He took water from the jug Volle set beside him and washed his mouth out, then drank deeply.

Streak was untied and standing with Archie, both looking helpless. Volle walked over and extended an arm, and Streak fell into his embrace, hugging him tightly. "Oh, fox," he said. "He brought me here and told me to sit down while he looked…hit me on the head, and when I woke up I was tied up."

"It's okay," Volle said, stroking his fur. "We're all right." But he wasn't sure that he was. He thought about how close it had been, and the shock and urgency that had overwhelmed him were subsiding. In their place was arising a cold, fierce anger.

Forrin was getting up. He looked around at them and rasped, "I have… to go…to the church…be cleansed…"

"I'll take you there," Volle said, but Streak nuzzled him and shook his head.

"I can go with him. I want to." The look he gave Volle said that he wanted to do it alone.

"I'll go too," Volle said anyway.

"You have things to do. Is the hearing over?"

"Yes. I won." That didn't seem nearly as important now.

Streak smiled. "I knew you would." He kissed Volle. "Stay here. I'll see you at the mansion tonight."

Volle caught his paw. "Promise?"

The wolf's muzzle tilted curiously, his ears canted. "Of course."

"All right." Volle let him go and smiled. "I don't want to lose you."

Streak didn't answer that, just gave him a sad smile and turned to escort Forrin from the room. Volle watched them leave, and he knew that Streak would not be going with him to the palace. He would have given his royal blood, his land, and even his freedom in that moment to keep the wolf by his side. When they disappeared out the door, he felt a pang in his heart like the cut of a knife. It was impossible not to associate that grief with the rat whose imprint was all over the room, from the furnishings to the scent that still hung in the air.

Archie had been giving instructions to the otter, and the servant left the room immediately after Streak and Forrin. Archie watched him go, and then looked almost fearfully at Volle.

Volle realized that his tail was lashing and his ears were down, fists clenched at his sides. He made an effort to relax. "I'm not mad at you, Archie," he said.

The weasel still looked glum. "Captain Nero and Lord Ikling will be here soon. I just sent for 'em. I guess I'll be turning in my resignation."

"You shouldn't have lied, but this wasn't your fault." He gestured to the rabbit's body, but couldn't bring himself to look at it.

"Cap'n would have figured it out if I hadn't lied about it. I could tell he thought it didn't add up."

"On the contrary, Archie, it added up just enough to keep me confused and unsure." Nero stood in the doorway. "You didn't see Dereath Talison kill the guard, did you?"

Archie shook his head. "No, Cap'n. I was so sure he had…"

"He might as well have. He certainly orchestrated the murder. The rabbit didn't get your scent, did he?"

He had asked this last of Volle, who shook his head. "I didn't think so," Nero continued. "It was very cunning, and if Archie hadn't lied, it was very probable that Dereath would never have been imprisoned." He glanced at the rabbit with more interest than revulsion. "I am curious about this one, though. How have I never heard of him before? I know most of the accomplished killers in the city."

Volle shook his head. "His name is Terril. I don't know where Dereath met him."

"I was merely thinking out loud," Nero said. "Of course nobody in this room would know. And it probably doesn't matter now, anyway. Simply an academic interest." He looked around at the room. "Your large guard did the damage, I suspect?"

"Yes," Volle said, and then remembered something. He walked across

"I think we can say that you've learned from this experience."

the room and picked up the sword, then looked at the rabbit. From this angle, the chair hid most of the worst of his neck. "He made me throw this away. Forrin forgot it when he went to the church. To be cleansed." The sword's blade was clean and bright, and it seemed to him that the sword itself had emerged through the ordeal unscathed, unlike the rest of them. It was hard and sharp, like the guard himself. He felt an obligation to keep it until Forrin could reclaim it.

Helfer arrived at that moment, bursting into the room and scanning it wildly. "Weasel and Gaia!" he exclaimed upon seeing the rabbit, and then turned to Volle. "Are you okay? Where's Streak?"

"He's all right. We all are, except for him. He took Forrin down to the church." Helfer approached him, but refrained from hugging him while he was holding the imposing sword.

"Lord Ikling," Archie said, "I have to tender my resignation."

Helfer spun to face the other weasel. "What? Why?"

Archie took a breath. "I lied about witnessing the murder of the guard, and in so doing prevented the apprehension of the real murderer. An' I put Lord Vinton here and his consort and guard in danger."

Helfer studied him and then turned to Captain Nero. "What's your recommendation, Captain? Should I accept his resignation?"

Nero studied the weasel, who was watching him resignedly. He stroked his whiskers and then said, "Yes, I believe you should."

Archie's shoulders sagged, but he kept his head up as Helfer said, "Very well. Archie, come see me later and we can discuss your replacement."

"Yes, my Lord." Archie started to trudge out of the room.

Nero stopped him with a paw on his shoulder. "Archie," he said, "I understand you've recently resigned your post."

Archie turned and stared at him. Nero went on. "Which is lucky for me. As it happens, I have been thinking about hiring an assistant to work with me in Divalia. Would you consider filling that position?"

Archie's stare turned to one of disbelief. He laid his ears back. "It's not nice to taunt me, Cap'n," he said.

"I would do no such thing," Nero protested. "Your passion and energy make you perfect for the job. True, we will have to work on your restraint and honesty, but I think we can say that you've learned from this experience. Have you not?"

Archie was standing straighter. "Yes, *sir!*"

"All right, then." Nero waved a paw. "Be ready to depart in the morning. And bring all your notes on this case. Your first duty will be to write a report to present to the King. How much of this scene did you see?"

"I heard him confess. I got in through the hole in the wall, but I was all the way on the other side of the room." He gestured to the door, which stood ajar. "I couldn't figure out a way to get across and help them without him killing the wolf. He had a knife at his throat, Cap'n."

"I understand." And Volle nodded too, because Archie was looking at him pleadingly.

"I would've run at him," Archie said. "If the guard hadn't…"

Volle smiled tightly. "I believe you would have," he said because he knew Archie was expecting it. He didn't know whether he believed it, but he knew there was nothing the weasel could have done. The anger was mounting in him again, and now that Nero was here to take charge of the scene, he didn't need to stay. What he needed to do was get out of here and be by himself for a while.

"I'll see you all later." He waved and headed for the door, ignoring the protests and calls from Helfer and Captain Nero. "I'll be okay," he assured them. "I just need to go." The tightness in his chest felt as though it would suffocate him if he didn't get out, so he slipped out the door and nearly ran down the hall.

He found the flight of stairs leading to the battlements, and ran up it, lifting his muzzle to the fresh, sweet air. Panting from the exertion and the tension in him, he leaned over the wall and breathed as deeply as he could. It was a relief to be away from the scent of the rat, but the anger stayed with him. He'd almost died, and Streak could have died as well. And Streak was going to leave him.

He wanted to talk to someone, but he didn't know whom. He knew what all his friends would say: Helfer would tell him that there would be others. He would be sympathetic, but he would shrug his shoulders and say it was all for the best. So would Tish. He had said all along that love was a vulnerability. Reese would make some comment about him finding another sex toy soon.

And what would he say to himself? Would he accept his fate and say there was nothing he could do? He remembered Xiller again, the long-dead cougar. He hadn't stopped him from leaving, hadn't even tried. And he'd never seen him again.

What would Xiller say to him now?

He hadn't been particularly wise, the cougar. But his heart had been strong, and his naivete had been endearing. If he were here, Volle thought, he would tell me to do whatever it took to be happy.

He raised his eyes to the sky. *What do you say, Fox?* But he knew the answer to that, too. Fox and Canis, kindred gods, set forth first and foremost duty to the pack.

Where is my pack? Is it my country? Or does your pack grow smaller as you grow older? It had been easy enough, six years ago, for him to assume the grandiose mantle of representative of his country, responsible for their welfare. The whole land had been his pack. But now, the world was more confusing. His obligations stretched from Caril to Divalia to the land of Vinton now, across nobles and kings, vixens and cubs, and to a white wolf at the edge of the pack, about to fall away from it.

But it was Canis who preached of loyalty to the pack. Fox was less ambitious. The pack, yes, but one's closest family first. Volle knew who his family were: Volyan, Ilyana, and her unborn cub. And Streak too, through every bond but marriage.

So what could he do? What had made him an effective agent was his tendency to lie low, to accept events as they came to him and craft his reaction to them. When he tried to act boldly, he had more often than not made a mess of things. His instincts told him that he should let Streak go, that the sadness would fade in time, that that was the best for everyone.

Sometimes, he thought, *instincts do not serve you well.*

He would not stand by and let the wolf leave his pack.

There was something he could do, something he had to do. As soon as he thought of it, it made perfect sense, and he hoped it would be enough. But before that, he had to do something about the tight spiral of rage he kept spinning into whenever he thought about what had just happened, how close he'd come to death. He'd thought that if he got away, breathed the fresh air, let his thoughts settle, that the knot in his chest would loosen, but that hadn't happened. *There's nothing you can do,* his instinct told him, *but calm yourself down.*

Wrong, he thought grimly. *There's nothing you* should *do.*

That might be more correct. But he knew as he set off down the tower stairs that whether he should or not, this was another thing he *had* to do.

The guard in front of the north tower was the stag Rogis. Volle took that as a sign from Fox—or Canis—that his decision was approved of on high. As he walked forward, he thought again of Xiller, and saw the spot where the cougar guard had stood, and a plan crystallized in his mind. He raised his unencumbered paw as he approached the stag.

Rogis greeted Volle warily, looking at the sword he was still carrying. "Afternoon, my Lord."

"Good afternoon, Rogis." Volle propped the sword against a wall and folded his arms. What he was about to do horrified him on one level, but he knew it was necessary, both for his profession and for his life. "I was wondering if you'd heard the news."

"News, my Lord?"

Volle told him briefly about the rabbit's attack and death, and explained why he was carrying Forrin's sword. He allowed himself to feel the events again as he told them, letting the anger simmer inside him. "So he was just a pawn of the rat you're guarding. Did his dirty work for him."

"He got what he deserved," the stag said.

"Indeed," Volle said. "I just came to have a word with the prisoner, to tell him that his servant has been killed."

He could see the doubt in Rogis's eyes as they flickered again to the sword. "I…"

"Naturally," Volle said smoothly, "I would remain in the doorway, and I think you should remain close by to make sure I don't do anything rash. But it would be best if you stayed out of sight."

Rogis nodded uncertainly. "Yes, my Lord." He hesitated another moment, and then climbed the stairs, glancing back frequently at Volle.

Volle waited halfway up the stairs until the door was unlocked. When Rogis stepped aside, he walked past the stag, set his paw to the door and pulled, thinking of the last time he'd opened it. There was no eagerness this time, just the hot wash of barely suppressed rage. He forced himself to breathe normally as Dereath came into view, seated at the bottom of the stair looking up, wearing the same clothes he'd been wearing at the hearing. Volle took pleasure in noting the rips and stains that were most uncharacteristic of the fastidious rat.

Dereath looked over at the door, and his narrow face split into a grin. "How sweet," he drawled. "You asked to share my cell. Well, I won't be here long, and all my toys are elsewhere, but I'm sure we can recapture the old magic." He patted the stone next to him.

"I'm not staying," Volle said. "I have a peerage to manage again." He enjoyed the flicker of disappointment that ran across Dereath's ears and whiskers.

The rat scowled, and then his expression lightened. "I didn't really think that Wallen would be up to the job, but there wasn't anyone else. I hoped his passion would sway the king."

"An Ursid?" Volle said.

"We make do with the materials at paw," Dereath said. "Don't get too comfortable. I'll be out of here soon enough and then you'll get what's coming to you."

"If you're waiting for your rabbit to help you, you'll be waiting a long time."

The rat tilted his head. "If he were arrested, I'd be already out of here. I guess that means he's dead." He shrugged. "Saves me the trouble of disposing of him later. I hope he put up a good fight, at least."

Volle saw Streak's panicked expression, Forrin's wide eyes and bloody muzzle. He squeezed his eyes shut and slid his ears backwards, listening for Rogis's breathing. The stag was listening.

"How many more cougar soldiers have to die, Dereath?" he said, not needing to fabricate the pain in his voice.

"Are you still on about him?" the rat said scornfully.

He'd taken the bait. "He didn't deserve to die."

"He was a soldier with a mission," Dereath said. "He deserved exactly what he got, and good riddance."

The same words he'd said earlier, designed to hurt. Volle heard the quick intake of breath behind him. His plan was working, but he felt no satisfaction, just an icy calm. "He was a pawn in your game. He deserved a better chance."

"You really need to break your habit of forming attachments to inbred, dimwitted gutter trash," Dereath sneered. "They make you easy to manipulate, because nobody cares what happens to them."

"I do," Volle said, refusing to rise to the rat's baiting. "And I'll continue to care."

Dereath shrugged. "Makes it easier for me. What happened to Terril, anyway?" He asked it deliberately, and Volle was sure he meant to underscore the fact that he had no attachment to the rabbit.

"He tried to hurt Streak, and Forrin tore his throat out." Volle said emotionlessly.

Dereath grinned. "Making up for letting you at the cinnamon, no doubt. He'll be hard to replace, I'll say that for him."

Volle felt his stomach churn, and took a step back outside the door. "I just wanted to tell you that your plans failed. And to get used to the feeling." He could see the stag now, and the flattened ears and dilated nostrils told him that Rogis would be very willing to carry out the second part of his plan.

"I'd be more worried if you ever learned from your mistakes." The rat examined his claws and looked back up lazily.

Volle felt a grim sense of satisfaction at being able to hear the rasping of the stag's breath behind those words. "I've learned more than you'll ever know," he said.

"Don't be so cocky," Dereath said. "Speaking of which, how's your little friend feeling?" He flexed his claws, rubbed his own sheath through his pants, and gave Volle a twisted smile.

Volle returned it in kind. "He's just fine," he said. "And so am I. Goodbye, Dereath."

He swung the door closed, cutting off the rat's retort.

Rogis didn't move as Volle slammed the door closed. The stag stared past him at the door, fingers clenched around the pommel of his sword. Volle put a paw on his arm, and the stag jerked to attention. "My Lord?"

Volle guided him down the stairs. "Might I have a word, Rogis?" he said quietly.

The stag looked towards the unlocked door, then reached for the keys at his belt. "My Lord, I should…"

"In a moment." Volle put a little more pressure on the arm, and the stag followed him. At the bottom of the stairs, Volle turned to face the stag. "I have a problem, and I wonder if I might share it with you."

"Of course, my Lord."

"You heard what he said just now, did you not?"

The stag growled deeply. "I did, my Lord."

"Is there any doubt in your mind of the prisoner's guilt?"

"None, my Lord."

"Nor in mine. Unfortunately, the prisoner has many friends, and a great deal of information accumulated about some high ranking Lords. And with the rabbit dead, it seems likely that he will go free. Nobody will be able to *prove* that he planned it all." He heard the stag's deep rumble, and nodded. "I feel the same. In fact, I feel that the prisoner poses a significant threat to the kingdom."

He paused, briefly, on the brink. Fox and Canis would approve of this, wouldn't they? He was defending his pack. Not avenging, but defending, because Dereath would get out of prison and he would never, ever stop hounding Volle and those dear to him. *Fox*, Volle prayed, *understand what I do and why, and let it succeed.*

"Rogis," he said, "do you believe that there can be heroes whose deeds are never acknowledged?"

"My Lord?"

He thought of Xiller, who'd been told he would be a hero for his terrible deed. "Do you believe that an individual might perform a great service to his country, but that because of…circumstances, that service might never be acknowledged?"

The stag looked confused. Volle didn't want him to lose his emotion, so when Rogis said, "I suppose so, my Lord," he was ready with his rejoinder.

"I believe Tephos is in need of such a hero now," Volle said. "I don't believe any of us will be safe if the prisoner there is released. Someone who would be willing to ensure that he never leaves that cell alive would indeed be doing a great service to his country. I wish I had the strength to do it myself."

"My Lord, you must not!" Rogis released his sword and reached out to Volle. "You have only just been restored…you would jeopardize your standing!"

Volle nodded. "I know." He looked up. "Then what am I to do, Rogis?"

He saw the determination he'd hoped to see. The stag's gripped his sword. "I will help you, my Lord."

Volle stepped closer to Rogis and spoke quietly, though he was sure that nobody was within earshot. "Rogis, I admire you. You have a strong heart, a great passion, and a wonderful sense of justice. I know you want more than anything for your friend to be avenged. What was his name?"

"Arnie…I mean, Arnut, my Lord. We called him Arnie."

"I'm certain that Arnut would not want you to sacrifice your reputation or your life, even to avenge him. Let me think a moment." Volle stepped back and looked down one of the corridors. "I was thinking of walking down that way. There's a lot of debris, there, though. I might easily slip and hurt myself."

Now Rogis looked confused again. "I suppose so."

"If you heard a crash in a few minutes, of course you would be expected to come see if I were all right."

"I would…?" The stag nodded doubtfully.

"And if you helped me up—clumsy fox that I am—and we returned to your post to find that you'd dropped your keys…why, anybody could have gotten into the cell in that time. You would only be guilty of a brief dereliction of duty, and I suspect you wouldn't even be punished." He paused. "*If* anything happened to him."

The stag's eyes lit up, and he drew himself up to his full height. "I see, my Lord."

Volle nodded. "Rogis, I believe you neglected to lock the door. When you go back up, you should make sure that the prisoner is safe. I'll wait here in case anyone else comes by, shall I?"

"That would be most kind of you, my Lord," Rogis said. "I won't be but a minute."

He clomped heavily up the stairs, and Volle leaned against the wall and waited, tensely. He could see now why he had had so much trouble putting to rest the notion of Streak's guilt. It returned to the question of whether Streak would kill someone if he thought they were a serious threat to Volle. The thought of the wolf killing someone had been troubling, yet impossible to dismiss. What Volle had not understood fully until now was that he'd believed that of Streak because the same capacity existed within himself.

He searched himself to see if there were any pleasure in him at what he had set in motion, but there was not, any more than there had been on a cold night many years ago when he'd given an assassin the location of Secretary Prewitt's chambers. The bear had masterminded the plan that, with Dereath's help, had taken Xiller away, tricked him into committing a horrible crime, and finally killed him. But Volle had felt no pleasure in his revenge, only, at best, grim satisfaction that it would finally be over, and at worst, sickness that it could not end any other way. Just as he felt now.

Behind him, he heard Dereath's voice cry out, and then he thought he heard a dull thud. After that, all was silent until the door opened and closed again. He heard the chunk of the key turning in the lock, and then the stag's footsteps on the stair. A moment later, Rogis stood beside him, keys dangling from his fingers.

"All well?"

"Indeed, my Lord," Rogis said. "The prisoner is...resting."

Volle nodded, feeling the tension drain out of him. The wall he was leaning against became much more necessary for support. "Door locked?"

"Yes, my Lord."

He examined Rogis's sword, but saw no sign of blood or fur on it. The stag was breathing heavily, but showed no signs of uneasiness or regret. Volle leaned back against the wall. "Did Arnut have a family?"

Rogis nodded. "A wife and a cub."

"Bring them to come see me when we return to Divalia," he said. "I'll make sure they're taken care of."

"Yes, my Lord. Thank you, my Lord."

"Since you're back, I think I'll go explore that corridor now," Volle said, picking up Forrin's sword.

"Be careful, my Lord," Rogis said. "There's a lot of debris down that way."

"I'll keep that in mind, Rogis," Volle said as he raised a paw and turned away from the cell in the tower. He saw the stag drop his keys to the ground, and smiled. "Thank you."

Chapter 15

Streak and Forrin were sitting in the parlor of their suite when Volle returned to Helfer's mansion, late in the day. Forrin sprang to his feet immediately. His uniform still bore the tear in its sleeve, though Volle could see a bandage underneath it, and there were still dark stains around the collar.

Volle held his sword out to him, but the wolf shook his head. "You may keep that, my Lord. I am disgraced. I violated the Word of Canis and ate of another's flesh, and I abandoned my charge. I must ask you to accept my resignation in disgrace from your service and from the royal guard."

He was deadly serious. His ears were down and his tail was curled tightly between his legs, but he looked Volle directly in the eye before turning his head to one side, exposing his throat.

"If you want to leave my service, Forrin, you are free to do so at any time. But I will not accept your resignation. You fought bravely in the only way you could to save my life and Streak's, and I would be proud and honored if you would continue to protect me and the ones I love." He held out the sword again.

"My Lord, I do not wish to leave your service. But I am unfit…"

Volle held out the sword, more insistently. "You are fit, Forrin. You are brave and capable, and I want you to continue to serve as my guard. Please, take your sword."

The wolf's ears came up slowly, and he stood more proudly. Carefully, he lifted the sword from Volle's paws and sheathed it at his side. "Yes, my Lord."

"Good. Now that's all settled. Are you okay? Did you see the Cantor?"

"Yes, my Lord. He cleansed me and blessed me and said that my actions did not have Darkness behind them."

"Good." Volle smiled and reached up to the wolf's shoulder. "I'm glad to have you back, Forrin. But if you'll excuse me…" his eyes slid around the wolf to where Streak was still sitting on the couch. The white wolf slowly got up.

Forrin nodded. "I understand, my Lord." His voice was soft, and Volle suspected he and Streak had been talking about Streak's decision.

Volle followed Streak into the bedroom and closed the door behind them. He crossed to the bed and sat down, patting the bed beside him. Streak stood by the door, holding his paws together close to his chest and rubbing his fingers slowly.

"I made my decision," he said quietly.

"I know. Come sit down. I just want to…"

"Talk me out of it?" Streak smiled sadly, but walked over and sat next to Volle anyway.

"If I can."

Streak shook his head. "I've thought about it a lot. I would just be a liability. You've got a wife who can give you cubs, you've got a guard," he gestured to the door, "who can protect you far better than I can. All I can be is a hostage, someone to get you raped, almost killed…" His eyes glistened, and he brought a paw to them. "I can't do that."

Volle put an arm around him. "Don't you know that I never wanted you to protect me or give me cubs? I wanted you with me because when we look at the world, we see the same things. We feel the same way. We make each other feel better. When I'm not being completely absorbed in other things," he admitted. "But I'll try to be better about that."

"It's okay," Streak said. "I like seeing you excited."

Volle resisted the obvious double entendre, for once. "I'm willing to take all those risks to have you with me."

Streak put a paw on his knee. "But I'm not."

"Don't you think I can decide what's best for me?"

"Please, Volle…"

Volle watched the white muzzle turn away from him. He said, very softly, "I quit."

Streak's ear flicked. "Good. It'll be easier if you just let me go."

"I'm not quitting trying to make you come with me." He kept his voice low. "I mean, I quit. I sent a message back to Ferrenis today. I'm not working for them anymore."

Slowly, Streak turned his head. "What?"

"I'm not a spy any more. I'm just Lord Vinton. Forrin told you I was reinstated, right?"

The wolf nodded. "But why? You loved that…"

"I love you more."

It was a pat thing to say, but he meant it, and Streak's eyes filled with tears as he said it. "I know you do, Volle, but it's so hard…"

"I know," Volle said, "but we can get through it together. And if you say no, I'm going back to the farm with you."

Streak's eyes widened. "Oh, you can't! You have obligations—a son, a family."

"I thought about that a lot. My family…my pack. You're a part of it too. I've spent most of my life accepting what Fox—or Canis—sends my way. But I can't accept you leaving. I could just tell you I love you and we would both part being miserable. I won't do that. I want you to come to the castle with me, Streak."

When Streak hesitated, Volle grinned. "I can make Forrin bring you."

The wolf was quiet for a long while. Tears started to roll down his muzzle, and Volle was starting to tear up himself when Streak's muzzle curved into a hesitant smile. "Well…Volyan will need a mommy."

Volle felt the relief wash through his body, the knot of tension in his chest loosening for the first time since that morning. He tried to laugh, but the laugh came out mingled with tears. "Didn't I already tell you you can't be Lady Vinton? You don't even have any dresses."

Streak pulled Volle to him, both laughing through their tears. "Me?" he said, and his tears turned the word into a squeak. "I was talking about you."

Volyan was delighted with the snow. He ran through the gardens and tried to gather up enough to throw, but it was still only a dusting, and he ended up just spraying a cloud of snow at Streak. The white wolf grinned at Volle and then took off after the cub, who squealed in delight and ran through the low hedges as fast as he could.

Volle paused by the statue of the lion warrior and dropped the flower he'd brought down. It was a Vellenland blossom, from the congratulatory arrangement Helfer had made for him upon regaining his peerage. He suspected that Laya had actually arranged the bouquet, because it was very much not a Helfer thing to do, but Helfer had been so proud of it, and Volle so touched, that he had accepted it at face value.

He stood looking at the statue and smiled. "I'm happy," he said softly. "Thanks for the advice."

Steps crunched in the snow behind him. He caught the scent of the black wolf before Tish spoke. "Reminiscing?"

Volle shook his head. "Looking forward."

Tish drew even with him. "A good practice, in general. Of course, when you reach my age, there will be so much more to look back on than to look forward to."

"You'll have plenty to do with Tika. We'll miss you here, though."

A paw settled on Volle's shoulder. "I'll miss you too. But it sounds as though you are filling my tracks admirably." He lowered his voice even though the gardens were empty. "I have received a letter from Avery."

"He's not happy, I suspect."

Tish shrugged. "He never is. At least he was pleased to hear that Lord Fardew is no longer an issue." Volle looked across the garden and nodded. Tish waited for a moment and then went on. "I'm not sure Nero is convinced he just fell down the stairs. Did he talk to you about that?"

"Of course," Volle said steadily. "Fortunately, during the short time he was unguarded, the guard was with me. So I couldn't have done it. I did tell Nero I regretted having pulled the guard from his post. I don't think he believed me."

"I understand he is still interviewing people, on the chance that it wasn't an accident. He seems to have no end of suspects."

"Mmm." Nero had uncovered a trunk full of damaging secrets about various Lords in Dereath's effects, and reportedly had been destroying it while interviewing the Lords involved. Volle didn't really want to discuss it any further. He had already received Nero's assurance that any documents concerning him had been burned. "You know, in a strange way, I almost miss him."

Tish barked a laugh. "Life too peaceful? Enjoy it while you can."

Volle grinned. "No, I mean…in a way, he knew me better than anyone. Better than I knew myself. He knew I would fall in love with Streak—he counted on it—and he never doubted that I would do anything for him. He knew it before I did." He looked up into Tish's smile, and shrugged. "It's easy to be more sympathetic now that he's gone. What else did Avery say?"

"He asked me to do my best to get you to change your mind, but if I read the subtext of his letter correctly, he is not as earnest about it as he could be. I have already composed my reply telling him that I was unable to, but pointing out the benefit of a friendly but inactive presence in the palace. Especially since I am leaving next week."

"So soon?" Volle turned.

Tish nodded. "We need to go before the snows get too thick. It is a long ride and will not be made shorter by inclement weather."

"I thought at least you'd stay through the winter."

Tish shook his head. "I'm sorry, m'boy. My son is ready. It is time for me to move on, and to stay longer would be foolish and pompous of me." He looked sternly down at the fox. "You will come visit us."

"Of course." Volle smiled.

They stood in silence, watching Streak and Volyan play in the snow. The wolf had grabbed the cub by his ankles and was swinging him around. Volyan's delighted shrieks echoed through the garden.

"You made the right decision," Tish said.

"I think I did." Volle turned. "Didn't you tell me that love was a liability?"

"Yes, as you will no doubt tell someone in the not-too-distant future, when Avery selects someone to send over here." The wolf smiled. "And like me, you will also tell him that you don't heed your own advice. Ilyana, however much she might wish to be in the palace, is an important and well-liked presence in Vinton, if the reports are correct. Streak is an important and loved presence here. And now that your title is officially granted and not acquired on some false pretext, I suspect you will treat it a bit more seriously than you have been, so you will need both: to keep your people happy, and to keep yourself happy."

"I'd been planning to be a better Lord," Volle said, and then squinted at Tish, his ears flicking. "You knew this would happen."

Tish grinned. "I know the King," he said. "He hates change. Having been forced to revoke your title, he only wanted an excuse to return it to you. A fox of noble blood, proven innocent of the charges of treason…how could he resist? I thought he would not be able to."

"Noble blood…" Volle pulled the pendant from under his winter robes and looked at it. "I've been meaning to ask you about that." He grinned at the wolf. "When did you have your duplicate of this made?"

Tish laughed, and shook his head ruefully. "I had thought I might put one over on you, at last. I should have known better. How did you know?"

"I didn't," Volle grinned, tucking the pendant back inside his robes. "But I do now."

"Ah ha ha!" Tish clapped him on the back and nearly doubled over laughing. "You precocious scamp of a fox!"

"It isn't real, then?"

"Oh, it's real," Tish said, "but it is not, as far as I know, a royal pendant. I first had the idea when I saw the quarters you were placed in, when you first arrived. You remember I told you it was an odd coincidence?"

"Yeees," Volle said, slowly. "I do remember that now. You never explained why."

"I thought it was interesting that your assigned quarters were the same ones once inhabited by King Bucher's son, the one he intended to become King after him."

"Really?"

Tish nodded. "The Prince was the only one of the family who did not live in the royal suite. Few people alive today remember that, but I remember visiting him there. He was kind to me." For a moment, his eyes drifted away. "I'm sorry. As I said, there is much more to look back on now than to look forward to. When I noted that, I had the idea that your unknown parentage could be used to our advantage with some more concrete evidence. I asked Seir if you had any jewelry you'd left behind, and she told me about the pendant. I had another made some years ago, and I kept it in a small wooden box I have, after asking the merchant to age it as best he could."

Volle shook his head. "You made up quite a convincing story about it."

There was a very long pause, so long that Volle thought at first that Tish was not going to respond. And then the black wolf spoke, very slowly. "The only part I made up," he said, "was about Archer getting away."

Volle swallowed. "Oh."

"I suppose I told it convincingly because I still, all these years later, wish with all my heart that it had been true. They found us…broke open the wardrobe…"

"It's okay," Volle said, shuddering. "I don't need to hear."

"No, you don't. You already know. And so you can understand why, for all these years, I have worked and worked to undo the damage done both by Bucher and by those who deposed him. I don't want any more killing. War between Ferrenis and Tephos will probably happen again, but we have staved it off for a good long time. This embassy will be a wonderful thing, and more good will come of it than anything else I have had a hand in, I think. And you are a Lord of Tephos—legitimately, I might add—and your children will be Lords in their own right." He looked at Volyan, and his muzzle stretched into a faraway smile. "I would not be surprised if, in a hundred years or so when the wheel turns to Canis again, the crown settles on the head of a fox who counts proudly among his ancestors the famous Lord Volle of Vinton."

Volle felt a swell of emotion and pride in his chest. "You really think so?" he whispered, looking at Volyan climbing over a kneeling Streak.

"I do."

"And you're saying you planned all this? The embassy, the nobility?"

"Planned is a curious word, Volle. If you had asked me when a bright-eyed fox arrived here over six years ago whether events would have unfolded exactly as they did, then I would not have been able to tell you. But I seized opportunities when they arose, and made slight adjustments where I was able, and always kept my goals in mind."

"You can't have known about the embassy, though. The King told me he was afraid of going to war, and that's why…" His voice trailed off, and he looked thoughtfully at the wolf.

"That's why what?" Tish leaned forward. "Volle?"

"I was just thinking of something the King said. Something funny."

Tish leaned back, folding his arms. "What was that?"

"When he told me about the embassy, he said he was about to tell me some things not even you had heard."

The wolf shrugged nonchalantly, but his ears were perked and his demeanor wary, and the humor was gone from his tone. "Believe it or not, I had not heard about it. I told you that."

"That's true." Volle rubbed his muzzle, watching Tish, not wanting to believe what he had just put together. "But the funny thing…the funny thing is, he said that *after* he told me about Dereath's trap."

He read the truth immediately in the wolf's eyes, and Tish knew he did. The wolf sighed. "Yes. I knew about that. Volle, listen. It was as much a trap for me as for you. They knew I was your friend. If I'd told you…"

Volle tried to keep the sense of betrayal from his posture and voice. "You said you didn't know. You let me…I could have been caught, or killed."

"I had shown you the hiding place, conveniently near the office of Defense. I knew nobody else knew about it because I made it myself, some years ago. I had confidence that you would not be caught. I had to seize the opportunity. I knew the King was hesitant because of the danger should the false plans leave the palace, and I thought there was a good chance that you would not only get away, but get away with them.

"As it happened, I was taken in by Dereath's story and I thought you'd gotten away. Seir assumed you'd fled the city as quickly as possible, without contacting her, and gone straight to Caril. We thought you might have gotten lost in the mountains, delayed by the winter. It wasn't until after three fruitless months of searching for you that we realized you had not gotten away. I visited the prisons, but they are large and it is not easy to arrange visits there. They tend to arouse suspicion. And then, Dereath returned with the news you had escaped."

"You just let me walk into that office."

"I had confidence in you. And you justified that confidence and then some. I cannot tell you the relief I felt when I heard you were safe." The paw on Volle's shoulder gripped him. "If you had been caught and lost, I would have accepted it as part of the life we lead. It is a hard world, and I know you know that. But it would have hurt."

Volle nodded. "So I was just a means to your goal," he said, trying not to sound as bitter as he felt. "You didn't even tell Seir that you just wanted to establish the embassy. That's all we meant to you."

"Haven't you been listening?" Tish removed his paw and folded his arms. "You are much more than that. I wasn't sure about you when you arrived, but I am now. If I put you through challenges, it's because I believed with my heart that you were strong enough to withstand them. If you had been caught and there were anything I could have done about it, I would have. I promise you that."

"It's just a little hard to hear."

"But you have to know it. There will be a day when Volyan, rebellious and young, will look to you for the support you've always given him, and you will have to cast him free. You have learned what it is to have a pack; you have not yet learned how to let your pack grow up with you. But you will. And when the time comes, you will know it, and even if he doesn't believe he can succeed without you, you will know he can, and you will let him prove it to himself."

Volle smiled then, looking at the cub. Volyan met his eyes and started running back toward him, with Streak following, both panting white breaths in the cold air. Perhaps it was not possible to hold both concepts of the Pack in one's life. Tish had chosen the larger Pack of country, while Volle had chosen the smaller Pack of family. He didn't feel like arguing with the wolf now, but he told himself in his heart that he would never betray Volyan, nor Streak either. "I'll look you up in twenty years and tell you if you were right. Until then, I'll have to take your word for it."

"I look forward to hearing about it." Tish smiled and stood aside as Volyan arrived and leapt up, grabbing Volle's robes.

"Daddy, Daddy, come play with me an' Daddy Streak!"

Volle knelt and smiled. "How about if we go inside instead? I bet we can get some warm milk from the kitchen."

Volyan pondered that. "Can we come back out after?"

"Of course we can." Volle smiled and nuzzled Streak as the wolf walked up.

"Hello, Tish," he said, and Tish bowed, smiling at the other wolf and at the cub.

"Daddy, carry me!" Volyan reached his arms up imploringly.

Volle bent down and hefted the cub into his arms. "Oof. You're getting too big for this."

"Daddy Streak carries me!"

Volle grinned at the wolf. "Of course he does. He's bigger than I am."

Volyan looked at the statue, now at his eye level, and creased his brow. "What's that?"

"Things aren't always what they seem."

"That's a lion."

The cub studied the statue for a second. "He looks scary."

"They can be." Volle smiled and turned toward the palace. Tish had already waved and was heading back down the path. "But things aren't always what they seem. Come on, let's get some warm milk."

Tails wagging behind them, the little pack walked back through the garden, into the palace, and home.

About the Author

Kyell Gold writes anthropomorphic erotica from an undisclosed location rumored to be in California. This is the second of two novels about Volle; the first, titled "Volle," is available from Sofawolf Press (www.sofawolf.com). His other works appear regularly in Sofawolf Press's "Heat," Osfer's Joint Publications' "FANG" (www.osfer.com), and his own LiveJournal (www.livejournal.com/users/kyellgold). He is currently working on an anthology of stories set in Volle's world, including the seminal story "The Prisoner's Release," initially published in "Heat." He lives with his very patient partner and their dog.

About the Artist

Sara "Caribou" Palmer spends most of her time in a 100+ year old house chasing her Egyptian Mau cats and her young daughter, and managing to find time to draw as well. She has been featured in several publications, and was the Guest of Honor at Anthrocon 2000. Her work can be found on the web at www.redpanda. com and in various Convention art shows around the country.

Also from Sofawolf Press

Volle by Kyell Gold – The highly acclaimed prequel to *Pendant of Fortune* tells the story of how Volle came to Tephos and his early days navigating the intrigue (and pleasures) of the royal city of Divalia. [ISBN 0-9712670-8-1]

Heat (Issues #1 - #3) – Sofawolf Press's yearly adult anthropomorphic magazine *Heat* presents illustrated stories, poems and sequential art of an erotic nature. A variety of quality contributors (including Kyell Gold's two part short story *Prisoner's Release*) and a high-quality artistic layout make *Heat* a cut above the usual erotic fiction magazine.

Black Iron by Ted MacKinnon – Sofawolf Press teams up with Sanguine Productions Ltd. to bring you this second novel based on their Ironclaw Fantasy Roleplaying System. Black Iron is a tale of good intentions and terrible consequences as an idealistic young Bisclavret noble tries to chart a course in life that puts him at odds with seemingly everyone around him. [ISBN 0-9769212-1-9]

Coming soon...

Black Dogs: The House of Diamond by Ursula Vernon – Best known for her stunning fantasy illustration work and award-winning online comic *Digger*, this first published novel displays the depth of her writing talent as well. Like her paintings, *Black Dogs* grows from solid roots in the epic fantasy tradition; but along the way gets twisted into a form that is as unique, irreverent, and often hilarious as the commentary that accompanies her art. [ISBN 0-9769212-4-3]

www.ingramcontent.com/pod-product-compliance
Lightning Source LLC
Chambersburg PA
CBHW071848020726
47502CB00003B/657